WOUNDED HEART
COLLEEN HALL

Best wishes to Cherie –
Colleen
I Sam. 12:24

WOUNDED HEART by Colleen Hall

ANAIAH FROM THE HEART
An imprint of ANAIAH PRESS, LLC.
7780 49th ST N. #129
Pinellas Park, FL 33781

First Anaiah From the Heart eBook edition November 2019

Edited by Eden Plantz and Kara Leigh Miller
Book Design by Anaiah Press
Cover Design by Laura Heritage

TO WARREN, WHO HOLDS MY HEART.

ACKNOWLEDGEMENTS

Special thanks to my children, Sean, Juanita, and Stephen, and to my daughters-in-law, Andrea and Laurilyn, for their moral support and help. They're also tech support for my website and my art department when I need invitations to a launch party or bookmarks designed.

Also, many thanks to all of my friends who encourage me, pray for me, and provide feedback as they walk the journey with me. I love you all!

Special thanks also to Eden, my editor, who made this book possible.

Kansas City, Missouri
Late May, 1870

CHAPTER 1

HE WAS THE MOST FASCINATING man she had ever seen, unlike the gentlemen she was accustomed to associating with in Boston. A fringed deerskin shirt molded to his wide shoulders and muscled chest. Deerskin trousers sheathed his legs. He sat on his long-legged gray grulla mustang as though man and horse were one.

Della Hughes gripped the top rail of the stockyard fence, not caring that the rail soiled her pristine white gloves. "Who is he?" she said, unable to wrench her attention from the man hazing the mares into a smaller paddock.

At her side, Lieutenant Emory Dyer also watched the horseman work the mares. "Hunter? That's Shane Hunter. He's the army scout your uncle hired."

"An army scout!"

Lieutenant Dyer shifted toward Della, propping an elbow on the top rail. His hazel eyes squinted as he studied her. "Don't get any romantical notions into your head. He doesn't mix much with females."

Della held her breath. She stared at Shane Hunter as he spun his mustang to cut off a group of mares who attempted to bolt away from the paddock gate. He seemed unaware of the people who lined the fence. His attention centered on the uncooperative mares. His gelding lunged, blocking the mares and sending them whirling in a blur of flashing manes and sleek hides back toward the gate. Dust from the horses' hooves hung in the air like an ocher mist.

"Hunter isn't what you'd call sociable." The weathered man on Della's left, wearing canvas trousers and battered boots, spoke up. "Lived some with the Cheyenne. People say he's more Cheyenne than white. Whatever he is, he's one tough hombre."

Della glanced at the man, then faced the paddock again. She focused once more on the horseman astride the grulla gelding. Shane Hunter had hazed the mares into the second paddock and now sidled his mount alongside the gate. He shoved the gate closed, leaned down, and secured the latch. The fringe on the front of his shirt danced with the motion. He straightened, then lifted his wide-brimmed horseman's hat and swiped an arm across his forehead. The slanting afternoon sun painted his tawny hair with brushstrokes of gold before he settled his hat once again on his head, tilting the brim low over his eyes.

As if he felt her scrutiny, Hunter swung his head toward her. Their gazes locked across the space of the paddock. Della felt his stare like a blow. She sucked in her breath, nearly stumbling back a pace at the impact. A bolt of heat sizzled through her, beginning in the pit of her stomach and flaring out through her chest and lower limbs. His eyes impaled her. She could neither move nor breathe, nor could she turn her gaze from his face. Then, without acknowledging her, he swung his mount about and jogged toward the opposite gate. Della's gaze followed his deerskin-clad back as he disappeared into the warren of fencing, loading chutes, and holding pens of the stockyards at the western edge of Kansas City.

Della sucked in a quivering breath. She trembled and ignored the urge to fan herself. No man had ever roused such a reaction within her. This gentleman had paralyzed her and captured her will with a single glance.

Beside her, Lieutenant Dyer stirred, turning away from the paddock. "I'd better get you back to the hotel, or your uncle will have my hide. He wants us all together for dinner tonight. We're meeting the men who will be helping with our venture."

After sending a final glance in the direction in which Shane Hunter had vanished, Della pivoted away from the fence. She tucked her hand into the crook of Lieutenant Dyer's proffered arm and strolled beside him. They walked into the shadows between two of the stockyard sheds. The plaintive bawling of cattle rolled out from the rough-planked walls.

Della shut out the sound, not wanting to dwell on the cattle or their plight. She hated to think of the poor beasts being loaded onto trains and shipped to eastern slaughterhouses. Trying not to breathe the bovine stench, she glanced up at Lieutenant Dyer. "We're having company for dinner?"

"Captain Asher, for one. He's the officer in charge of the cavalry detail your uncle has arranged to provide protection for us."

"Uncle Clint isn't taking any chances with those Morgans."

Lieutenant Dyer's unremarkable but pleasant face crinkled in a smile. "He has more valuable things to protect than horses. A wife and a chubby toddler who have stolen his heart are more important to him." He patted Della's gloved hand where it rested on his arm. "And, of course, he has the care of a beautiful niece who's too willful for her own good."

Della poked his shoulder with her free hand. "Willful! Me? Much you know about that."

"What would you call climbing out the window of the young ladies' academy and running away to see the circus? The headmistress was about to have the vapors when you didn't show up for dinner. I'd call that willful. And ill advised."

"Oh, pooh!" Della waggled her fingers as if to brush away his chiding. "I didn't run away, exactly. I wanted to see the dancing bear and the bearded lady. And when the trapeze artist offered to carry me across the wire to demonstrate his balancing skills, I couldn't resist. When would I ever have had another opportunity for an adventure like that?"

"When, indeed?" Lieutenant Dyer said. "The headmistress was convinced your uncle would seek to have her removed from her position because you risked your good name while under her care. You spoke to a member of the male sex to whom you hadn't been properly introduced. And you consorted with carnival people, all while being unchaperoned. The poor woman was distraught."

"I intended to return to my room before anyone missed me, but I forgot the time."

"I was present when your uncle received the telegram from the headmistress. You can be thankful you weren't close enough for him to get his hands on you."

Heat infused Della's cheeks. She lowered her gaze to the path before squaring her shoulders and tilting her chin. "I was just climbing back through the window into my room when the tree branch broke. How was I to know the branch would break?"

"You might have used the front door and the stairs and saved everyone's nerves when you broke your arm in the fall." Lieutenant Dyer shook his head. "You'll never know what it took for your uncle to smooth the incident over with the headmistress and the advisory board of the academy. The board members were determined to have you expelled. The men thought you weren't up to the genteel standards they required and your behavior would reflect on the school's good name."

"Well, that's in the past, and now that I'm twenty, I'm sure I'm a lady."

"Just you remember that, and no more escapades. Your uncle Clint has more important things on his mind right now than rescuing you from your own impulsive behavior."

They left the cattle yard and reached the street where their buggy waited. Lieutenant Dyer handed Della up into the equipage, loosened the reins from the hitching post, and climbed in beside her. The vehicle rocked with his weight. He settled himself on the black leather seat and turned the horse.

When they reached the hotel where Uncle Clint had reserved rooms for their group, Lieutenant Dyer deposited her at the front steps and continued around to the stables. Della paused, tipping back her head, and surveyed the hotel. Towering oaks on either side of the steps shaded the long veranda that fronted the building. Pink, orange, and yellow snapdragons flourished along the lawn's edge bordering the veranda and provided cheerful color to contrast with the building's whitewashed siding. Crimson tea roses added another bright splash of color. Wicker rockers boasting yellow cushions ranged along the porch, inviting guests to sit and relax. The whole scene evoked a sense of understated elegance.

She should enjoy the hotel's comfort these next few days. Once they left Kansas City for the West, no such luxuries would be found.

Aunt Coral, her uncle's Southern wife, waved to her from one of the rockers while a curly-headed sprite pattered about her chair.

Della gathered up her dimity skirts so as not to snag the hem while she mounted the stairs. She crossed the gray-painted veranda to her aunt's chair. Flossie, her two-year-old cousin, shrieked and scampered toward her, sorghum-colored curls bouncing, the skirts of her blue gingham pinafore swirling about her chubby calves. She babbled in a language only she understood, holding out a red tin top with stripes of yellow and blue circling its rounded body.

Della crouched and caught Flossie's warm, wriggling form. The toddler leaned into her, holding up the toy for Della's inspection.

"Play, Del. Play." Flossie shoved the top at Della.

"Do you think Cousin Della can make the top spin?"

Flossie nodded. "Spin top."

Della placed the toy's pointed bottom end on the porch floor and twirled the handle between her fingers to make the top rotate. Low humming came from the spinning toy. When the top reached the speed where it could balance, Della let go of the handle. The whirling top flashed in a blur of red, yellow, and blue, skipping across the boards.

Flossie giggled, clapping her hands, and darted to her mother. She flung herself at Aunt Coral's lap and pointed at the top, prattling.

Della rose, smiling. "She's easily amused."

A breeze wafted the scents of sun-warmed grass and roses across the veranda. The leaves of the oaks rustled.

Aunt Coral shook her head. "When she's getting her way. She can be a thundercloud if her wishes are thwarted." She stroked her daughter's curls, then lifted Flossie onto her lap and held her close.

Longing filled Della's heart when she glimpsed the maternal love evident on Aunt Coral's face, in the tenderness with which Aunt Coral held her daughter. Della's parents had been killed in a carriage accident when she was a child not much older than Flossie, so her memories of her mother were hazy and few. Her grandparents and her uncle Clint had reared her. Though she loved them dearly, she wished she'd known a mother's love like that of Aunt Coral's for Flossie.

Aunt Coral kissed the top of her daughter's head and gathered her against her bosom, rising. "It's time to turn this imp over to Silvie, and we need to dress for dinner."

Della scooped up the top from the veranda floor and accompanied her aunt through the wide front door and into the hotel's foyer. "I hear we're having company for dinner."

"Yes. Clint has invited Captain Asher to dine with us. You'll be pleased to meet him. He recently graduated from West Point. This is his first assignment to the West."

"And who besides Captain Asher?" With one hand trailing on the mahogany stair rail, Della climbed each step in rhythm with her aunt. Their skirts whispered against the patterned burgundy carpet runner.

"I believe he's also invited the army scout who'll be heading up our expedition, Shane Hunter."

"I saw him today when Uncle Emory and I were at the stockyards. He was putting the last of the Morgan mares into the paddock." Della paused and considered her impressions of the scout. "He's not like any man I've ever known."

Aunt Coral cut a sideways glance at Della. "I doubt you've ever met anyone like him. You wouldn't encounter him taking tea in a Boston drawing room."

Della hid a smile at the image of Shane Hunter—wearing his fringed buckskin shirt and trousers tucked into heeled leather boots—sitting in a Boston drawing room and holding a china cup in his large hands. Having Shane Hunter in a drawing room would be akin to setting a cougar loose among a flock of pigeons. "Boston matrons would swoon should Mr. Hunter cross their drawing room thresholds."

"From what I've heard of Mr. Hunter, I don't think anyone could entice him into a drawing room." Aunt Coral shifted Flossie to her other hip and reached for the crystal doorknob of the private suite her husband had reserved. "Captain Asher, on the other hand, would be very much at home in a drawing room. His father was in the diplomatic service, so he grew up in Europe and is much accustomed to society."

"He won't have a need for society where he's going." Della recalled the tales she'd heard about the West and wondered whether Captain Asher's background had prepared him for such an assignment. "I hope he knows enough to stay alive in Indian country."

"That's why we have Mr. Hunter. His experience and skills will guide us through the dangers."

They entered the elegant parlor separating Della's room from her aunt and uncle's bedchamber. Aunt Coral picked up the silver handbell resting on a lamp table beside a medallion-back sofa and rang for Silvie. Della headed toward her own room.

Inside, Bridgette, Della's maid, turned to her with an elegant evening dress in her hands.

"Your uncle Clint wants you turned out smart for dinner tonight. I think this gown will do." Bridgette held up the creation of ruched pink silk trimmed with lace and ribbon. Her round face glowed beneath her white mobcap.

Della peeled off her gloves and tossed them onto the bed. She sauntered toward Bridgette and stroked the frock's delicate fabric. "Yes, I think this gown will please Uncle Clint." And what would Shane Hunter think when he saw her wearing her fashionable finery? Or even the unknown Captain Asher?

When Della had been dressed and coiffed, she crossed the room to the mahogany-framed cheval glass and surveyed her reflection. Her curly dark hair had been swept up and back in a high knot, with a fringe of bangs dropping over her brow and ringlets curling over one shoulder. The gown boasted a fashionable off-the-shoulder square neckline and short, puffed sleeves. The skirt, tight at the waist, fell in a straight line to her feet in the front and was gathered about her hips in a bustle. A swath of foaming lace, silk tucks, and ruche formed an elaborate overskirt. A single dark pink ribbon had been tied about her neck. Diamond teardrops swung from her ears. In this gown, she could have graced any Boston drawing room.

Almond-shaped violet eyes fringed by smoky lashes gave Della's oval face an exotic look. The men of her acquaintance had never seemed to mind that she was taller than most women, and Della had never cared. Her height lent her a willowy appearance.

Bridgette hovered behind her, clasping her hands in her apron. "Will your uncle approve?"

Della swung about and studied her maid. Apparently, Uncle Clint's status as a general in the Union cavalry during the Civil War and his authoritarian air had impressed Bridgette, who seemed anxious to please her employer. Della patted Bridgette's shoulder. "Uncle Clint will be impressed with your handiwork, I'm sure. Even Boston's social matrons couldn't find fault with my appearance tonight."

Relief crossed Bridgette's face. "You're being ever so kind, mum."

Della heard footsteps crunch on the gravel walk beneath her open window and glanced outside. Shane Hunter approached from the direction of the stable, following the path around to the front of the hotel. He walked with a lithe, loose-jointed gait, shoulders squared. His low-crowned, broad-brimmed black horseman's hat hid his face from her view while his easy stride brought him closer to her window. Della remained motionless, watching him.

When he had almost reached her vantage point, he halted and turned his head, as though he felt her stare. Again, their gazes collided. His mouth firmed into an unsmiling line, and his lids hooded to half cover his eyes.

Della froze, holding her breath. The world outside seemed to have stopped. Once again, Shane Hunter had imprisoned her by his force of will. Silent moments ticked past while neither stirred. At last, the scout acknowledged her with a dip of his head and a finger to his hat brim before he continued along the footpath.

When he disappeared around the front of the hotel, Della stirred, drawing back from the window. There went the man whose knowledge of the West and whose experience with the Plains tribes would guide them across the vast Kansas prairie to the Colorado Territory. Captain Asher's cavalry detail might lend firepower to the group of men already assembled, but their lives rested in Shane Hunter's hands.

Turning away, Della breathed deeply and concentrated on slowing her racing heart. Now, she must go down to the private dining room and meet the man who twice in one day had captivated her completely.

CHAPTER 2

MOMENTS LATER, DELLA STEPPED OFF the last stair and turned down the hallway to the private dining room reserved this evening for their group. The murmur of voices drifted to her ears. Coming to a standstill in the open doorway, she swept the room with a quick glance. Several groups clustered about a Chippendale dining table draped with a snowy damask cloth and set with Staffordshire china and glittering silver.

She recognized most of the folk here. Off to the right, beside a mahogany Chippendale sideboard, Lieutenant Dyer chatted with one of her uncle's former cavalry officers who had signed on to their venture. To the left of the table, before a fireplace where a gilt-framed mirror rested above the marble mantel, presided Uncle Clint and Aunt Coral. Both wore evening finery. On their near side stood a handsome chestnut-haired officer dressed in a dark blue cavalry uniform. On their far side, looking out of place amid the green silk wallpaper, satin drapes, and glittering chandelier, towered Shane Hunter.

He removed his hat, and his sandy hair sprang free. It curled down the back of his neck in a style longer than fashion dictated. He'd obviously washed up before coming to dinner, for his face had a scrubbed look, and his hair was damp. He still wore his fringed deerskin shirt and trousers tucked into scuffed riding boots, though he'd brushed the dust from his clothes. He might not fit society's image of an ideal gentleman, but no one would dare belittle him.

At Della's appearance, Shane Hunter lifted his head. His nostrils flared.

The next moment, conversation dwindled as Uncle Clint strode toward her. He smiled down at her when he reached her side. He lifted her hand and placed it on his proffered forearm, then led her across the room to the fireplace.

They stopped before the cavalry officer, whom Della judged to be a few years older than herself. As he turned his attention to her, his sherry-brown eyes warmed.

"Captain Asher, may I present to you my niece, Miss Della Hughes? Della, Captain Quentin Asher." Her uncle patted her hand and released her, then stepped away a pace.

Quentin Asher took her fingers in a firm grip, bowing. He raised her hand to his mouth and placed a light kiss upon her knuckles, all polished sophistication and Continental charm. "Miss Hughes, the pleasure is mine."

Della performed a little curtsy, just to show him Americans could be as mannerly as Europeans. "I'm pleased to meet you, Captain Asher, and grateful to know we'll be traveling under your protection."

"Your uncle's contacts in the army made it possible for him to arrange for my posting in the Colorado Territory to coincide with your journey west. After all, since he has a contract with the army to provide remounts for the cavalry, it was in everyone's best interests for the army to provide a military escort." Captain Asher's perusal took in her stylish outfit. His lean face expressed appreciation for her allure. "I didn't expect my task to be brightened by such a beauty as yourself, Miss Hughes."

"I'm sure you'll be too busy to dance attendance on me. Besides, I want to do my part in riding herd on the mares. I certainly don't intend to spend the whole journey in a wagon."

"Then, perhaps, we can ride together sometimes."

"Perhaps I don't want to interfere with your duties."

Her uncle claimed Della's attention with a light touch on her shoulder. "Della, I have one more introduction for you."

They stepped away from Quentin Asher and drew near to Shane Hunter, whose height put him at eye level with her uncle. The scout watched her approach. Della couldn't guess what his thoughts might be. His expression gave away nothing.

Close up, Della noticed his eyes were blue. Hours in the sun had tanned his skin to a deep golden hue. Creases fanned out from the corners of his eyes. Chiseled features and a firm jaw hinted at character and strength. Though Shane Hunter stood unmoving, an air of leashed power emanated from him. Della shivered. Close proximity to the scout affected her as much as had their encounter at the stock pens.

"Shane, may I present my niece, Miss Della Hughes? She'll be traveling with us," Uncle Clint said. "Della, Mr. Hunter. He's been scouting for the army since the end of the war. I consider myself fortunate to have enticed him away from the military."

For a moment, Shane Hunter didn't respond. Just when Della wondered whether he'd acknowledge her, he dipped his head in a slight nod.

"Miss Hughes." Slow and easy, he uttered the words in a velvet baritone.

"Mr. Hunter. I'm pleased to make your acquaintance. Uncle Clint must trust your skills, or he never would turn the leadership of his venture over to you."

"Your uncle still maintains the leadership of his venture. I'll merely use my knowledge of the land and of the tribes to lead you to the Colorado Territory and to minimize the risks."

"I hope to have the adventure of my life."

Shane Hunter's lips firmed. "This isn't an adventure, Miss Hughes."

"Perhaps *adventure* wasn't exactly what I meant. Perhaps what I meant was *liberated*. I've been liberated from the stuffy strictures of Boston society. I hope I left all that behind when I came out here."

Wearing a violet gown of a style similar to Della's, Aunt Coral rustled forward. "If everyone will take their seats, the waitress will serve us."

With Uncle Clint at the head of the table and Aunt Coral seated at the opposite end in her role as hostess, Della took a chair on her uncle's left. Captain Asher snagged the place next to her, with Shane Hunter at Uncle Clint's right hand.

When the waitress had served them and departed, Aunt Coral addressed her husband's former officers. "I must express my appreciation for your willingness to help my husband move his horses to the Colorado Territory."

Both men glanced at Uncle Clint, who'd been their commanding officer during the Civil War, and then back at Aunt Coral.

"Five years of Southern occupation was enough for us, ma'am," the older of the two replied. "When your husband mustered out, we had no reason to stay, so we couldn't turn him down when he asked us to join him in supplying remounts for the army's Indian war."

"He appreciates having all you men who are so loyal to him staying on in his employ." Aunt Coral directed a loving look down the table at Uncle Clint.

Quentin Asher laid down his fork. "I didn't realize the men your uncle hired had served with him during the war."

"Most of them served under him. Since we came to Kansas City, he's hired two or three new men who've had experience trailing cattle, but the rest were part of Logan's Cavalry."

"I heard of your uncle's reputation at West Point. Even five years after the war, General Logan's name commands respect among the instructors."

When Della glanced at her uncle, he was conversing in low tones with Shane Hunter, who listened with grave attention and nodded.

Conversation flowed around the table as the meal progressed. Unless addressed directly, Shane Hunter remained quiet.

Captain Asher leaned around Della. "How soon are you planning to leave?"

"If we can finish laying in supplies this week," Uncle Clint said, "we should be able to leave on Monday."

"I haven't been given many details. Exactly what will my troops be guarding?"

"I have one hundred Morgan horses that will be moved from Kansas City to my property in the Colorado Territory. I'll have four wagons loaded with supplies and twelve head of oxen. We'll be a tempting target for rustlers and Indians. The men whom I've hired as wranglers have all had fighting experience, so you can count on them for support if we run into trouble."

"How long before we reach Colorado Territory?"

Uncle Clint turned to the scout. "What's your estimate, Shane?"

"On a good day, we should be able to make twenty miles, but most days, we'll probably average about fifteen. It will take us six to eight weeks to reach your property, dependin' on what we run into along the way."

"I have every confidence that my detail of trained army soldiers will handily dispatch any savages who would be so foolish as to attack us."

Della caught her breath. Wasn't Captain Asher aware of Shane Hunter's history with the Cheyenne? Surely, he must be ignorant of the fact, or he wouldn't have spoken with such indiscretion.

Uncle Clint leaned back in his chair, one hand resting on the carved armrest. "Well, Shane, what have you to say to that? I have my own thoughts, but you know the tribes much better than I do."

With her attention fixed on the scout, Della waited for his response. Everyone at the table had fallen silent. Shane Hunter laid his fork on his plate and frowned across the table at the captain, spinning out the moment. "You must have heard the story of Captain William Fetterman."

"We studied the details of the massacre at West Point."

"Then, you should know that he was drawn into an ambush by a large coalition of Cheyenne, Arapaho, and Lakota Indians." Hunter paused. "General Logan's horses will be a temptation to maraudin' tribesmen. You'd be wise not to underestimate the tribes or expect them to fight by white man's rules."

Captain Asher's face flushed. "Surely, the savages are incapable of executing an organized attack."

"Tribesmen may not fight the way we do, but if Captain Fetterman were alive today, he'd tell you they can be skilled tacticians when necessary."

"I still find it difficult to believe that Indians could defeat trained army soldiers," Captain Asher said.

"If you intend to stay alive, you'd better believe it," Hunter said. "I've kept my ear to the ground, and I haven't heard anything to indicate the tribes are massin' for any kind of large-scale attack. Still, we'll have to be on the lookout for small groups of warriors. Stealin' a few horses out from under the noses of white men can be a challenge they might not be able to resist."

Uncle Clint leaned forward, his serious gaze sweeping the men around the table. "I've purchased enough of the new Winchester repeating rifles to arm our whole company. That will give us a distinct advantage."

"Winchesters!" Captain Asher leaned around Della again, staring at the general. "How did you manage that?"

"I have my ways."

Conversation buzzed.

Aunt Coral turned to her husband. "You're full of surprises tonight."

He shrugged. "I don't intend to lose a single horse to a rustler or a tribesman, and I intend to keep my family and the men in my employ safe, with the help of almighty God. I'll do whatever it takes to accomplish that."

When the meal concluded, Aunt Coral rose. "Why don't we retire to the drawing room? We can continue any discussion there, and perhaps Della would favor us with a song or two. She's quite an accomplished pianist." She smiled at Della. "I hope you don't mind me volunteering you, Della."

"If everyone can tolerate me banging out a few pieces, I don't mind."

"I'm sure Miss Hughes will exceed our expectations with her proficiency." Quentin Asher grinned down at her with gallant coquetry.

"You may regret your words after I've played a song or two. You most likely will be searching for an excuse to entice me from the piano." Della smiled back at the captain. She glanced across the table at Shane Hunter. The scout watched her with a brooding expression, but once again, she couldn't interpret his thoughts.

With one arm about his wife's shoulders, Uncle Clint shepherded his guests into the hotel's drawing room. When Shane Hunter hung back, Aunt Coral halted in the doorway. She turned. "Please, join us, Mr. Hunter. You will do my husband and me a great honor if you would stay."

Hunter took a deep breath, as if steeling himself for an unpleasant task. "Certainly, Mrs. Logan," he said with unexpected charm. "How can I refuse such a gracious invitation?"

Della strolled to the carved mahogany grand piano in one corner of the parlor while the others settled themselves on couches or chairs. Quentin Asher accompanied her and leaned against the piano's casing while she perused the available sheet music. Beethoven's "Moonlight Sonata" caught her attention. After she spread the pages on the rack, she lowered herself to the piano stool and shifted her skirt to give her freedom to use the pedal. She paused, head bent, fingers poised above the keyboard. Closing her eyes, she shut out the murmuring voices behind her and listened to the music in her head. The notes swelled within her.

After several drawn-out moments, Della opened her eyes. She leaned forward, and her hands came down on the keys. The melody poured forth. The rolling, measured notes of the sonata filled the parlor. Della forgot everyone in the room, forgot Captain Asher reclining against the piano, forgot everything except the music swelling within her.

When she finished, she sat unmoving for a brief moment, hands suspended above the keyboard. When a smattering of applause broke out, she dropped her hands to her lap and spun about on the stool. Everyone except Shane Hunter smiled and clapped.

Isolated from the others, Hunter stood across the room beside the drapery of the tall windows lining the hotel's front. His presence compelled her attention. Della couldn't help but look his way.

He loomed, his booted feet planted wide on the Aubusson carpet. His gaze captured hers. He neither smiled nor clapped but stood alone, wrapped in the stillness she was beginning to associate with him. He finally acknowledged her performance with a nod, and his simple nod meant more to Della than the accolades of all the others.

Quentin Asher broke the spell when he stepped toward her. With boldness, he gripped her hand and lifted her to her feet, then raised their clasped hands in a victorious gesture. "Miss Hughes has just delivered one of the best renditions of the 'Moonlight Sonata' I've ever heard."

Della shook her head and pulled her fingers from his grasp. "I'm sure you're being kind. I merely play for pleasure."

"Don't be so modest, Miss Hughes. I've attended performances in Vienna, Paris, and Rome. I don't believe I've heard that piece done as well even in Europe."

Della shook her head again, relieved when Lieutenant Dyer rose and approached her. He bussed her on the cheek in an avuncular fashion. "I never tire of listening to you weave your magic on the piano."

"Thank you, Uncle Emory." The courtesy title slipped off her tongue with ease. Emory Dyer had been an officer in Uncle Clint's cavalry unit all during the war and had served with him during Reconstruction. In the years since the war, he'd become part of their family unit. "I'm glad you enjoy my efforts."

Conversation broke out. Emory Dyer steered Della across the room, where she received the compliments of the others. All the while, a visceral awareness of Shane Hunter overshadowed her. She noted when he left his place by the windows and strolled to where her aunt and uncle stood in conversation with one of the other officers. After a brief consultation, he pivoted and strode toward the door.

He was leaving without a word to her. Della disentangled herself from the conversation as quickly as she could and hurried from the parlor. In the empty foyer, she paused, glancing about. She rushed toward the door, swung it wide, and spied Shane Hunter's tall form at the bottom of the veranda steps.

"Mr. Hunter!"

He halted and swung toward her, though he didn't move closer.

Della sped to the edge of the veranda. "Mr. Hunter, you didn't say good night."

His face remained expressionless. After a moment, he moved on silent feet up three steps so only two treads separated them. Dusk had settled over the city, making his face a pale blur beneath the brim of his hat.

She was too aware of him for her own comfort. His nearness set her pulse to racing, and her breath snagged in her throat. Her palms grew moist. The power she sensed in this man should have frightened her. Instead, his strength wrapped about her like a protective cocoon and called to her feminine heart.

"Good night, Miss Hughes." His voice, smooth and with a hint of a Western drawl, stroked her nerves.

"Why are you leaving so early? You needn't hurry off."

"I don't socialize much. My mustang is all the company I need."

"Surely, you can't spend your time alone." The thought appalled Della. "Don't you get lonely?"

"Bein' alone and bein' lonely aren't necessarily the same thing. I don't mind my own company."

"But . . ."

"If you get lonely, perhaps the West isn't the place for you."

"I'll be with Uncle Clint and Aunt Coral. And Uncle Emory."

"A word of advice, Miss Hughes. Think very carefully before you leave Kansas City. Once we're on the trail, there's no turnin' back. If you find the going too difficult, no one can leave the wagon train to escort you back."

Della stared down at him. He stood with one hand on the stair rail and one foot propped on the next step. A hard expression set his face in stern lines. That he should question her resolve or her abilities rankled.

"I'm not a quitter, Mr. Hunter."

"Perhaps not, at least up to this point in your life. But the journey we're about to undertake isn't a stroll across the Boston Common. The West is an unforgivin' land. It takes no pity on a tenderfoot. The days are hot, and the nights are cold. Any number of things could kill you before we reach the Colorado Territory. A fall from a horse, an accident while crossin' a river, snakebite, fallin' off a wagon in front of a wheel. Your uncle can't spare a man to play nursemaid to you."

"I don't expect him to."

"You'll have to get along on your own and not depend on anyone to help you."

In the thickening darkness, the crickets sawed. Leaves rustled in the breeze. The scent of dew-wet roses filled her nostrils. Della laid a hand on the veranda balustrade, clenching the wood until her knuckles whitened. She stared at the enigmatic man below her. "I won't expect anyone to help me."

Hunter didn't reply. He gave her fashionable gown, her elaborate coiffure, and her jewelry a slow perusal. "Miss Hughes, did you dress yourself tonight?"

Confused at his apparent change of subject, she shook her head.

"Did you style your own hair?"

Thinking of Bridgette, Della shook her head again.

"Who will do that on the trail?"

"I . . . I'm not sure. I guess I will."

"And how will you do that? Have you ever dressed yourself, Miss Hughes?"

Della hesitated, resenting how useless his words made her feel. "No, I've always had a maid to help me."

"You'll have to dress yourself and comb your own hair on the trail. You'll have no maid to help you. And have you ever ridden astride?"

"No. At home, all of the ladies ride sidesaddle."

"There's no place for a woman ridin' sidesaddle on the trail."

Della fell silent.

Shane Hunter drove his point home with relentless precision. "Your uncle has invested every penny of his inheritance and his fortune in this venture. He must be able to give all of his attention to overseein' the wagon train. You'll be a liability. I don't mean to be unkind, Miss Hughes, but go back to Boston. Don't be the cause of your uncle's failure."

Della lifted her chin and stared down her nose at him. "I can learn. I can learn to ride astride and to dress myself. I won't be a liability to Uncle Clint. Besides, Aunt Coral is going with him."

"As she should. She's his wife. Her care is his responsibility, but I wager she can dress herself and comb her own hair."

The truth of his words landed a blow to Della's optimism, but she resolved to meet his challenge. "I can learn to take care of myself. Besides, women have been traveling west for at least two decades. I'm sure I'm not the first unmarried lady to venture west."

"Of course not, but if you had opportunity to mingle with other emigrants, you'd find those women are used to doin' for themselves. They do their own cookin'; they sew their families' clothes; they do the laundry and help on the farm. They're better suited to hard work and life in the West."

"You don't know me at all. I promise I can learn whatever I need to and not be a burden to Uncle Clint."

Hunter studied her for a moment. "I may not know you, but I've known plenty of other society women like you. They're useless for anything except decoratin' a man's arm. I hope you're up to the challenge of this journey. And another thing—you're a distraction to the captain. Quentin Asher should never forget why he's with this wagon train."

Leaving Della seething, the scout pivoted and jogged down the steps. Once on the path, he paused to glance up at her. "Let me compliment you on your performance tonight. I don't know when I've heard anythin' so beautiful. You play the piano like an angel." With those words, he vanished into the darkness.

His compliment mollified her, leaving her bemused. Behind her, the hotel door opened and closed. She turned to see

Captain Asher standing on the veranda, silhouetted against the lamplight shining through the door's etched-glass window.

"Is he gone?" he asked.

"Yes. He said he doesn't socialize."

"You were out here so long, I wanted to be sure you were all right."

All right? Was she all right? She might never be quite the same after meeting the scout.

"He's an odd man," Captain Asher said. "He probably can't even manage a turn around the ballroom floor."

"I imagine, in Indian territory, he doesn't need to manage a turn around a ballroom floor. Dancing isn't a skill that keeps one alive out here."

"He's not our kind of person."

The captain's superior tone rankled, though Della said nothing. An unfamiliar sense of displacement filled her, making her feel as though a stranger had taken up residence inside her body. When Quentin Asher cupped his palm about her elbow and urged her into the hotel, she accompanied him without resisting.

"We'd like you to play another song before we break up for the night. I'll turn the pages for you."

CHAPTER 3

DELLA ENTERED THE SUITE'S PARLOR and shut the door behind her. Captain Asher had detained her with a question as the group broke up, so her uncle and aunt had gone upstairs before her. When she slipped inside, they were still in the parlor, standing close together, with Uncle Clint's hands linked behind the small of Aunt Coral's back. Her arms curled about his lean waist. His head was lowered so their foreheads touched, and they murmured in low tones.

Della halted, reluctant to interrupt them. A pang stabbed her heart at the tenderness of the scene. Uncle Clint loved his wife so dearly, so completely, that seeing them in such an embrace caught her by the throat. Her eyes welled. Someday, she hoped, when she found a man she could spend her life with, she'd enjoy an all-consuming love such as her aunt and uncle shared.

Uncle Clint lifted his head and glanced toward her, but he didn't release his wife. "Come join us, Della. We were just discussing our plans."

"What plans?"

"Shane has recommended that you ladies dispense with your normal wardrobe and wear a split riding skirt and blouse while we're on the trail. It will be safer for you and much more practical."

Della crossed the room with slow steps until she reached her uncle and aunt. "A split riding skirt! What a scandal we'd cause in Boston."

Aunt Coral chuckled with rich, throaty humor. "Or in Columbia. We'd set the society tabbies on their ears."

Uncle Clint smiled. "Fortunately, we're not in either Boston or Columbia, so we needn't concern ourselves with offending anyone." He placed a gentle kiss on his wife's forehead. "I've made arrangements for a seamstress to come to our suite tomorrow afternoon for your fittings. She's been paid well to guarantee your clothes will be ready before the end of the week. That should give you time to learn to ride astride before we actually set out."

Della watched her uncle as he spoke. A few strands of silver threaded the dark hair at his temples, but otherwise, he looked much the same as he had when he married Aunt Coral. He still retained a cavalryman's lithe fitness and the austere good looks that made Della think him the handsomest man she knew.

Aunt Coral gripped her husband's biceps, tipping back her head to scrutinize his face. "You have so much depending on you now; I don't know how you have time to think of us." Her petite stature, molasses-colored hair, and delicate features lent her a quiet beauty.

"You ladies and our little Flossie are the most important things in my life. Your safety is paramount to me, so no detail concerning you is too small for my attention."

Della hugged her uncle. "Thank you, Uncle Clint." She stifled a sudden yawn. "It's been a long day. I think I'll head off to bed now."

Bridgette had waited for her in her bedroom. She'd laid Della's night rail across the bed and folded down the covers.

Della noticed the preparations Bridgette had made for her bedtime ritual and recalled Shane Hunter's words. Every night of her life, a maid had turned down the blankets on her bed and helped her remove her clothes. Each night, a maid had taken the pins from her hair and brushed her tresses before braiding her long curls into a twisted rope.

On the trip to the Colorado Territory, Della would have to manage on her own since Bridgette wouldn't be going with them. Uncle Clint had already purchased her train fare back to Boston.

"Did you have a good time at dinner, mum?" Bridgette asked.

23

Della moved away from the door. "Yes. Yes, I did. We had good discussions about our journey."

Bridgette slipped behind Della and unhooked her gown, her fingers traveling from the nape of Della's neck to her waist. The pink gossamer fabric loosened about her shoulders and drooped down her arms.

"And was Captain Asher ever so handsome?"

Quentin Asher's refined features swam in Della's mind. She smiled. "Yes, I think you'd consider him handsome."

Bridgette sighed with theatrical drama while she lifted the gown over Della's head. "I do so favor a man in a uniform."

When Della donned her linen night rail, she seated herself at the bench that stood before the dressing table. Watching in the mirror while Bridgette plucked the pins from her upswept tresses, Della thought again about the army scout. She imagined Hunter's disapproval should he see Bridgette's attendance on her now. He'd think her a helpless, useless creature who couldn't manage without someone to assist her. She straightened her spine. She wasn't useless or helpless. She could learn how to manage by herself. She would!

With all the pins removed, her hair tumbled in a chocolate cloud of spiraling curls over her shoulders and back. Seeing the riotous mass in the looking glass, Della sighed. Her hair had always been a trial. There was so much of it, and it refused to be tamed. Despite the best efforts of her hairdresser, some strands always escaped the pins and curled about her face.

Bridgette picked up her silver-backed brush and applied it with even strokes to Della's tresses. After several strokes, Della twisted on the bench and looked into Bridgette's round, plain face.

"Bridgette, will you teach me how to style my own hair? Something simple. I'll have to do it myself when we're on the trail, so it must be something I can fashion quickly. I can't hold everyone up while I fix my hair."

Bridgette stepped back and tilted her head. "A single braid, I think. That would be the easiest for you."

"Can you show me in the morning? I only have a few days to learn."

"A French braid. That will still have some style, but it will be practical, too."

"Yes. I can learn to do a French braid. I'll watch you in the mirror tonight." Della turned around to face the glass, observing Bridgette beginning to braid.

"You may not look like you're styled for society," Bridgette said, "but with a French braid, you'll still catch the eye of that handsome Captain Asher."

"I'm not sure I want to catch Captain Asher's eye."

"Whyever not?" Bridgette paused, her hands poised over Della's back and her expression puzzled.

"He's very charming and sophisticated, and he comes from a good family, but I'm not sure he's what I'm looking for in a husband."

"He seems like just the kind of man you should marry."

Della shrugged, thinking instead of a tall, quiet man with sandy-blond hair who spoke no honeyed words nor attempted to impress her. "Why are we discussing husbands? I should be concerned with staying alive on the journey."

Bridgette giggled, her fingers once again plaiting Della's dark hair. "Aw, mum, what else should we talk about?"

Smiling, Della shrugged again. "What else, indeed?"

CHAPTER 4

DELLA STEPPED INTO THE STABLE just after breakfast the next morning. The pleasant scents of hay and horses rushed to greet her. She squinted while her eyes adjusted to the semidarkness after the bright sunlight outside. Pausing just inside the door, she viewed the activity in the barn.

The horses had already been hayed and watered. Their contented munching and the occasional stamp of a hoof were familiar sounds. Two stable hands moved down the rows of stalls on either side of a central aisle, grooming each horse with a soft-bristled brush.

At the far end, she spied Scipio, her uncle's personal horseman. Peeking at the long skirt of her emerald-green riding habit, she caught up the train and strolled down the center aisle. She halted when she reached the horseman. "Good morning, Scipio."

Scipio slid the bolt on the stall door he'd just closed and turned to Della. "Mornin', Miss Della." He stared down at her from his titan height, his dark face curious. "What can I do for you?"

Knowing her errand would be frowned upon by both Uncle Clint and Aunt Coral should they learn of it, Della didn't answer. Instead, she turned toward the stall Scipio had just exited.

Behind iron bars running from the top of the stall's half wall to the ceiling paced a glossy Thoroughbred stallion. His ebony hide gleamed in the stable's dim light. Lifting his beautiful head, he looked at Della with his wide-spaced eyes before he resumed his pacing. As he passed the corner feeder, he snatched a mouthful of hay and turned about, strands of timothy trailing from his muzzle.

"Uncle Clint told me you're taking Zeus by railroad out to the Colorado Territory instead of taking him on the trail with us." No gentleman would mention such a thing in the presence of a lady, but Della had overheard enough conversation between her uncle and aunt to understand Uncle Clint intended to use Zeus as a stud for the Morgan mares to develop a horse with a bit more size for the army's use.

Scipio nodded. "Best to ship Zeus by train."

"I've been hearing about the dangers we'll encounter. I know Zeus is far too valuable for Uncle Clint to risk riding him overland." Della swung back to face Scipio.

Scipio had been one of two servants to stay with Aunt Coral at Elmwood Plantation in South Carolina after the Civil War. When Aunt Coral moved from Elmwood to Columbia to work for Uncle Clint, she'd taken Scipio and Silvie to the city with her. Uncle Clint had entrusted the care of his horses to Scipio, and now, no one else had the responsibility. "Scipio, would you please tack up Captain for me?"

Suspicion crossed Scipio's broad face. He frowned down at her. "Miss Della, I know your uncle doesn't want you to be ridin' out alone."

Employing her most cajoling manner, Della smiled at the groom. "He's busy at the stock pens and won't even know I'm gone."

"Don't matter. Can't you wait until your uncle Emory can go with you?"

"No. This is something I must do now."

Scipio shook his head. "I don't like it, Miss Della. Your uncle will skin my hide if he finds out I've let you ride off alone."

"I'm just going to where the emigrant wagon trains are camped. I'll be perfectly safe."

Scipio crossed his muscular arms across his broad chest. "I can't go against your uncle. I know he don't want you to be riding about the city by yourself."

Della tipped up her chin and narrowed her eyes. Where cajolery wouldn't work, determination might. "If you don't tack up Captain for me, I'll find someone who will."

Scipio stared down at her, his brown eyes flinty. At last, he sighed, letting his arms drop to his sides. "You're one headstrong young lady, Miss Della."

"So I've been told. Thank you for tacking up Captain, Scipio."

He grunted a response, turning toward Captain's stall.

Della trailed behind Scipio to Captain's loose-box stall. The gelding had been one of Uncle Clint's remounts who'd survived the war and had been gifted to Aunt Coral when she married.

Scipio lifted the halter and lead rope from their peg beside the stall half door. He paused with one hand on the latch, slanting a glance at Della. "Does your aunt Coral know you're takin' her horse?"

"She told me I can ride Captain whenever I want. Now that she has Flossie, she doesn't ride much."

Scipio didn't comment. He opened the stall door and slid inside. Captain swung about toward him, ears pricked. Scipio stroked the gelding's neck before fitting the halter over his head and clipping the snap to the ring above the throatlatch. With the lead rope held in both large hands, he led the dapple gray out of the stall.

Della stepped back. Uncle Clint had an eye for horseflesh, she admitted. Captain was a fine Thoroughbred gelding, long legged and powerful. His dappled coat had faded with the years, so now, he gleamed with a silvery sheen.

Scipio tacked up Captain and had the horse ready for Della in a matter of minutes. He led the gelding outside and gave Della a hand up into the sidesaddle. With one knee hooked around the horn and the other foot securely in the stirrup, she took the reins.

"I'll be back before the noon meal."

"And your uncle will have skinned me alive and hung my carcass out to dry."

Della chuckled. "There's no one else he trusts to care for his horses, so I think you're safe."

She signaled Captain, and the gelding danced out of the stable yard. Once on the street, Della turned the horse toward the outskirts of Kansas City where the emigrant wagon trains camped. While most of her attention centered on navigating the traffic on the city streets, part of her mind pondered her errand. Even she couldn't understand why she felt the necessity of meeting the emigrant women. Ever since Shane Hunter had compared her with the women of the wagon trains and found her lacking, a consuming desire to meet those women filled her. What were the qualities they possessed that Hunter admired? How was she so different from them?

The last wagon train of the season was camped in a large flat area west of the city. Whatever grass had grown there earlier in the spring either had been trampled beneath the wheels of Conestoga wagons or had been eaten down by the mules and oxen of the settlers. Now, packed earth stretched in a terra-cotta carpet beneath the wagons, which had been arranged in a loose circle on the plain. A bustle of activity surrounded the camp. Horses, mules, and oxen were tethered haphazardly outside the circle of wagons. Barefoot children ran about. Women bent over iron pots that hung from tripods above cooking fires. An ear-shattering clanging rang out as a blacksmith pounded a red-hot horseshoe on his anvil. Other men loaded barrels, wooden boxes, and trunks into the backs of the canvas-covered wagons.

When Della drew near the camp, men stopped to stare. Women straightened from their fires, clutching long-handled stirring spoons. Children stopped their play and huddled in groups to watch her approach. Conversation ceased.

For the first time in her life, Della felt out of place. Her tailored emerald-green riding habit and the stylish straw hat perched atop her braid and tied with a green satin ribbon beneath her chin were in stark contrast with the men's full cotton shirts, loose dark trousers, and heavy boots and with the women's drab butternut linsey-woolsey dresses. Sunbonnets shielded their faces, faces now turned toward Della with closed expressions.

She halted Captain a few yards from the settlers. Why had she come? Their hostile features betrayed the fact that they resented her presence. Did they think she'd come to gloat over her elevated station?

One of the men stepped forward. He snatched his battered felt derby from his head and crushed it against his chest. "What can we do for you, miss? Are you lost?"

How should she reply? Now that the moment was upon her, she couldn't think of what to say. The urge that had driven her to seek out the emigrants drained away, leaving her floundering. She shook her head, grasping for a truthful answer. "I . . . I'd like to know where you're going and why you're going there."

The men exchanged puzzled looks, while some of the women left their cook fires to move closer.

"We're heading to California over the Mormon Trail, then turning south on the California Trail at Fort Hall," the spokesman said.

Della nodded, though she had no idea where Fort Hall was or where the two trails parted.

One of the women sidled closer. Hard work and childbearing had taken their toll, for her hands were roughened, her face weathered, and her figure thickened. "Why are we going? We want a better life for our children."

The emigrants murmured and nodded.

"I'm traveling as far as Wyoming," a burly man said from the back of the group. "Going to try my luck on the goldfields."

Della scanned the group again. "You must be convinced things will be better in California to risk your families on such a trip."

The settlers looked at one another and nodded, then returned their attention to Della. "We didn't have anything to keep us in Indiana," one of the men said. "We heard stories about California, so we decided to try our luck there."

Silence descended while the group studied Della, as if she were a strange species they'd just discovered. A breeze eddied about them, stirring dust and bringing the scent of livestock. The sun beat down, casting their shadows across the flattened earth. "And why are you asking, miss?" the man asked.

Della hesitated, reluctant to confess her deficiencies. The others waited, stoic. She breathed deeply and confessed the failings Shane Hunter had enumerated. "I'm about to embark on a journey with a wagon train, and I've been advised to go back to Boston. The trail boss doesn't think I have what it takes to make the trip."

At first, no one commented, though Della felt them assessing her fashionable riding ensemble, her hair, even the quality of the horse she rode. To them, it was apparent she'd never done manual labor and had the means to employ domestics to do for her.

"Don't mean to be unkind, miss, but I think the trail boss has a point," the woman who'd spoken earlier said. "Might be better for you to go back east, where you came from. You don't appear suited to the trail."

Della's heart sank. Beneath her, Captain stamped at a fly, raising a spurt of dust, and shook his head. The bit jingled. Other than that, there was no sound. Della looked again at the group, picking out individuals. They might not have had the advantages she'd had, but she saw something in all of them that inspired her. Courage and determination shone on their faces. These were brave people, willing to give up the security of their homes to launch into the dangerous unknown in order to better themselves.

Could she do less? Their courage bolstered her own. She'd learn to take care of herself and not be a liability to Uncle Clint or to Shane Hunter. Remembering the scout's opinion of society women who had no value beyond decorating a man's arm, she determined to prove she could be more than that.

Della urged Captain around the men, riding closer to the women. They watched her approach, their expressions wary. She felt set apart from these hardy souls, yet she yearned to belong to the sisterhood who left safety and security behind to set out into the unknown with their husbands and children. Reining in her mount, she looked down upon the cluster of women. She gripped the leathers, unsure of how to express herself.

She drew a deep breath. "Please, how will you do it? How will you get through each day when there's so much danger?"

The matrons exchanged glances, then turned their attention once more to Della.

"We just do what has to be done. We don't think about the danger; we just do what we have to."

"And what is that?" Della couldn't begin to relate to what the ladies meant.

A frail wisp of a woman with faded blond hair tipped her bonneted head to look up at Della. "Why, we light the cook fires, fix meals for our menfolk, wash the dishes, and see to the children. We mend our clothes and anything else that needs doin'."

"But most of all, we have hope," the first matron said. "The dangers are nothin' compared to the hope of a better life for our children. We want more for them than what we can give them back home."

The women nodded.

Enlightenment shone like sunshine in Della's heart. "I see. I, too, have hope for a better life."

Silence fell while the emigrants studied her with open curiosity. "Beggin' your pardon, miss," one of the women said, her voice timid, "but what more could you want to make your life better?"

Della lifted her chin. "Freedom. I want freedom."

The ladies had no response to her declaration, so Della swung Captain around and urged him back toward the men.

"When are you leaving?" she asked as she signaled her gelding to halt.

"Tomorrow morning," the man who seemed to be in charge said. "We're already late. It will be tight for us to get over the pass before the snow flies."

"I wish you good success."

Hooves pounded as a horse approached at a canter. Captain Asher, resplendent in his cavalryman's blue uniform, galloped up on a sorrel gelding. When he was within a stride of her, he pulled his mount to a halt. The gelding braced and squatted on his haunches, plunging to a stop beside her, his hooves digging into

32

the soil with a swirl of dust and bouncing pebbles. Captain sidled and snorted at the other horse's precipitous stop.

"Captain Asher. What brings you here?" Della asked when she'd quieted her mount.

"Your uncle sent me to fetch you. He couldn't come himself. He and Hunter are deep in a serious discussion." Quentin Asher touched the brim of his cavalryman's hat in acknowledgment of her presence. He glanced at the emigrants, now standing silent several yards away. "Miss Hughes, I don't know why you're here with these people, but it's time to return to the hotel. General Logan is worried about you."

Guilt niggled at Della. "Is he very angry? I'd hoped to be back before he returned."

"When we got back, Scipio told us where you'd gone. He was profusely apologetic for letting you take Captain out alone, but apparently, your uncle is used to your behavior. He didn't blame Scipio."

"I know I should have waited for someone to accompany me, but this is something I had to do myself."

They turned their horses toward Kansas City and kept them at a sedate walk. Captain Asher turned a charming smile on Della.

"I'm beginning to see that you're a young lady who knows her own mind."

She grimaced. "You're being kind. Uncle Clint will tell you I'm impulsive and headstrong."

"Don't be too hard on yourself. I like a lady with some spirit. I've been around too many society misses who are like lukewarm dishwater."

"That's something I've never been accused of being."

"I imagine that's the truth. Tell me—what are your plans once we reach Colorado Territory?"

Della shrugged. "I intend to stay with Uncle Clint and Aunt Coral for a while. After that, who knows? Perhaps Uncle Clint will have something for me to do helping him with his horse business. I want to be useful."

Quentin Asher's eyes gleamed, his handsome face alight. "A beautiful young lady like yourself should have no trouble finding a husband. Perhaps a military officer or a businessman in Denver."

"Perhaps, but that's one of the reasons I left Boston. A young lady of my years was expected to find a husband and marry well. I want an adventure first."

The captain cocked his head. "I expect you'll have enough adventure by the time we reach your uncle's ranch to last you a lifetime."

"And what are your plans, after you leave the army?"

Asher stared ahead between his horse's ears. "Colorado Territory is growing. In a few more years, it will be admitted to statehood. There's opportunity out here for an ambitious man of good fortune to rise to the top. I have my eye on becoming a state senator, perhaps one day even the governor. And I'll need a woman of beauty and refinement at my side to help me accomplish those goals." He flicked a glance at her.

She pretended not to notice. Leaning down, she patted Captain's neck before she looked at her companion. "Very lofty ambitions. I hope you reach them."

When they arrived at the hotel stable, they halted their horses outside the wide, open double doors. Captain Asher dismounted and hurried around to assist Della. He reached up and gripped her by the waist. She leaned down to place her hands on his shoulders, and he lifted her to the ground.

"Thank you," she said.

His brown eyes were warm as he looked down at her. "The pleasure is mine."

Uncle Clint appeared in the stable doors with Shane Hunter at his side. "Della, I see you're up to your old tricks." He strode toward her. When he reached her side, her drew her apart a little way. "It was inexcusable of you to put Scipio in a position that you knew would pit him against my wishes."

Della hung her head. "I'm sorry, Uncle Clint, but I just had to visit the emigrant camp. I needed to talk to the women there."

"You couldn't wait until someone could accompany you?" He fisted his hands on his hips, displeasure clear on his lean Yankee features.

Della looked into her uncle's face, aware of Captain Asher standing behind her, holding the reins of their mounts, and of Shane Hunter looming several paces beyond Uncle Clint's shoulder. Their silence exacerbated her uneasiness. She bit her lip. "I'm truly sorry. I know I should have waited, but Aunt Coral and I have fittings with the seamstress this afternoon, and you men are so busy getting everything organized for our trip, I was afraid I'd miss the emigrants if I waited. They're leaving in the morning." She laid an imploring hand on his chest. "Am I so terribly wicked?"

Her uncle sighed and covered her hand with his own. "You're a shameless minx, but I forgive you. Go on back to the hotel. We'll be up shortly for lunch."

Standing on tiptoe, she kissed her uncle on the cheek. With a pat on her hand, he released her. Looking past his shoulder, she encountered Shane Hunter's gaze. Once again, she couldn't read his thoughts, for his expression remained shuttered. He must have learned the skill of inscrutability while living with the Cheyenne.

Della stepped around her uncle and approached the scout. The hem of her riding skirt dragged in the dust. Absently, she lifted the train out of the dirt while she tipped her head back to look into his face. "I've been thinking about what you said last night."

Several beats ticked past. "And what did I say last night?"

"You told me I can't care for myself and that I should go back to Boston."

"I assume that's why you felt the necessity of visiting the emigrant camp this morning." The brim of his black felt hat cast a shadow across his face.

Della nodded. "I had to find out for myself what those women have, what makes them an asset instead of a liability."

"And what did you learn?"

"I saw they work hard; they care for their families and husbands. They're willing to give up everything they have in order to better their situations for their children."

"And did you decide I was right, that you should get on the train and go back east?"

Della's cheeks burned, but she lifted her chin and glared at him. "No, I resolved to stand on my own. Bridgette has taught me how to fix my hair."

Hunter's attention flicked to her hair, absorbing the spiraling tendrils that escaped from her plait and coiled about her face, then trailed down the length of her French braid.

His slow, intent perusal affected Della as a physical touch, though he hadn't moved. Heat flooded her. She forgot to breathe.

"Did you do that yourself?"

"Yes." She struggled to pull her thoughts from the impression of Hunter's fingers in her tresses. "I braided my hair without Bridgette's help."

A tiny smile lifted one corner of his mouth. "A wonderful accomplishment. On the trail, you'll have to do your hair in the dark. The rising bell sounds at four o'clock in the morning."

Della wasn't sure she'd heard him correctly. "Four o'clock?"

"Yes. We need to get an early start. Do you still want to go?"

She hesitated, thinking ahead to all the early mornings that awaited her should she travel with the wagon train. Back east, she'd avoided early mornings whenever possible, and she'd never risen at four o'clock in her life. Squaring her shoulders and straightening her spine, she looked Hunter in the eye. "Yes, you can't discourage me or make me change my mind."

Silence fell while the scout shifted his weight to one hip and looked her up and down. Della remained motionless beneath his scrutiny, only half-aware of the leaves of the oak tree beside the stable whispering in the breeze.

"When the seamstress gets your split skirt finished," he said at last, "I'll teach you how to ride astride."

"You'll teach me?"

"If you're set on going with us, you'll need to be proficient in the saddle. I'll teach you."

Della bristled. His offer—when nearly every word he'd spoken to her made her feel like a useless ornament—rankled. She straightened and glared at him. "*You'll* teach me? Suppose I'd prefer to have Captain Asher teach me? He's been ever so agreeable to me."

If her challenge dented Hunter's self-assurance, he didn't show it. His composure remained unruffled. He shrugged. "I'm sure the captain would enjoy the privilege. By all means, if you prefer for the captain to teach you, ask him. I'm sure you won't have to ask twice." He touched the brim of his hat and nodded a respectful adieu, then stepped around her.

Chagrined, Della bit her lip. She didn't really want Captain Asher to teach her to ride astride. She much preferred to have Shane Hunter's company, though, until this moment, he hadn't shown any desire for her companionship. Men like Captain Asher had been easy conquests ever since she'd attended her first soiree. In contrast, Shane Hunter was a man such as she'd never before encountered, one who could walk away from her without a backward glance. A feminine desire to breach his defenses filled her, overriding her irritation. "Mr. Hunter!"

Hunter pivoted to face her, though he didn't speak. His blue gaze roved over her.

"I'd rather have you teach me to ride astride, if the offer is still open."

He didn't gloat or show any triumph. Instead, he nodded, then chuckled, surprising Della. "And I'll teach you how to tack up your own mount. No one will have time to saddle your horse for you."

CHAPTER 5

THAT NIGHT AFTER DINNER, DELLA and Aunt Coral sat on upended wooden buckets in the central aisle of the stable. Behind them, the men whom Uncle Clint had hired to help him drive the horses to his property stood about in a loose group, waiting for the general and Shane Hunter to begin the meeting. Captain Asher stood beside Della, engaging in light flirtation.

The evening sun slanted into the stable through the open double doors at the far end, casting long shadows and illuminating the interior with gold. Horses poked their heads over the half doors of their stalls, watching the humans with equine curiosity.

"Do you know what Uncle Clint is going to say?" Della asked, leaning toward her aunt.

Aunt Coral smiled. "He discussed this meeting with me, but you'll have to hear it from him."

Quentin Asher bent toward Della. "I hope you'll be able to ride with me as we trail the horses. We can discover the West together."

Cocking her head, Della peered over her shoulder at the captain's earnest face. "Perhaps. I'm sure that would be most pleasant, but I don't want to keep you from your duties."

"My duties with this wagon train will be light. It should be no hardship to mix pleasure with responsibility."

Della recalled Shane Hunter's warning about distracting the captain, so she made no response. At that moment, her uncle stepped to the front, and she turned to face him. Conversation died amid shuffling of feet and shifting of bodies.

"Thank you for coming tonight. I want to discuss business with everyone so we'll all be aware of how the wagon train will function. Mr. Hunter will share some of his knowledge of the West so we'll understand a bit better what we're facing." Impressive with his military bearing yet at ease before his audience, Uncle Clint's gaze swept the group.

"First of all, I want to thank each of you for signing on. The task before us won't be easy, and I can't promise you a comfortable journey, but I know each one of you is equal to the challenge. Most of you have ridden under my command, and I know your mettle. You won't let me down." He swept them again with a piercing gaze.

Della looked about her at the men. Those who had ridden with Logan's Cavalry during the war still wore their military trousers paired with flannel shirts. All the men sported colorful bandanas knotted about their necks and heeled leather riding boots. The resolve on their faces exhibited the respect with which they regarded the general.

"My wife and child and my niece will be traveling with us. Their safety will be of utmost importance." Uncle Clint paused again.

"We'll be trailing a hundred prime Morgan horses, a mixed herd of mares and geldings. I don't need to tell you that we'll be a target for rustlers and tribesmen. We can never let down our guard."

Della glanced at the men again. They manifested the manner of battle-hardened veterans, toughened in the crucible of the Civil War. Their eyes reflected the horrors they'd seen in the conflict. Not a man of them would falter or shirk his duty if blood needed to be shed to protect the women or the horses. The newcomers her uncle had hired here in Kansas City also appeared to be capable men.

"Our train will travel six days a week, and we'll rest the stock on Sunday. On Sunday morning, anyone is welcome to join my family and me in a time of Bible study and prayer."

Uncle Clint motioned toward Captain Asher. "The army has kindly provided us with a military escort for extra protection. Captain Asher's detail will ride along with us and engage any threats should that be necessary."

COLLEEN HALL

Quentin Asher acknowledged the introduction with a nod and a wave.

"The day-by-day routine will be handled by the trail boss, Shane Hunter. Everyone will defer to him in matters of procedure. Now, I'll turn the meeting over to him."

Hunter looked over the group in his silent manner. His gaze rested for a moment on Della. The glance he spared her sizzled between them, sending a *frisson* of awareness shivering along her spine. With the exception of the rustling of horses, silence descended on the stable. Curiosity about the army scout who had been hired to boss the wagon train held everyone in thrall.

Tonight, Hunter wore his fringed buckskin shirt and trousers. The tails of a faded blue silk bandana tied about his neck draped over the front of his shirt. Beneath his low-crowned black cowboy hat, his chiseled face was resolute. A wide gun belt rode low on his hips. A Colt revolver, its walnut handle worn smooth, rested in a tooled leather holster tied down about Hunter's thigh. He looked tough and capable. Della shivered.

"We'll be livin' and workin' together for the next six weeks. I expect everyone to pull his own freight. No one shirks his chores, and I won't tolerate fights. At night when we camp, we'll have guards posted around the herd in two-hour shifts."

He paused, raking the group with a penetrating stare. "The risin' gong will sound at four o'clock. We'll be on the trail by six. We'll pause at noon for an hour to eat and rest the livestock, then be on our way again. By five o'clock, we'll start lookin' for a place to camp for the night. The first week, we'll travel slow and take shorter days to break in the oxen."

Hunter stepped closer. "Within a few days after we leave Kansas City, we'll be in Indian territory. We all need to be alert for anythin' that seems out of the ordinary." His perusal touched each face, commanding attention. "If you have silver on your guns, bridles, or saddles, remove it. Silver reflects the sun and can give away your position to the hostiles. If anyone is ridin' a white horse, find another mount. A white horse in the West can get you killed."

40

Della shot a quick sideways look at Aunt Coral. Her aunt's lips firmed, then relaxed. Aunt Coral would have to find another horse to replace Captain.

"Many of the rivers in this part of the country have quicksand beds. When we encounter such a river, keep the horses moving. You can navigate quicksand if you don't stop. When the wagons cross, you must keep the oxen moving, or you'll lose the ox team, the wagon, and everything in it."

Hunter's regard paused once again on Della. The heart-stopping sensation when their gazes connected snatched at her breath. The air between them crackled and fizzed. Attraction snared her in its coils, tangling her in an invisible skein. At last, he began speaking as though the moment between them had never occurred.

"We'll bypass the Overland Trail that other wagon trains have used and travel a more southerly route through Kansas instead. That should give us plenty of grass for the horses, and we also should avoid other travelers."

When Hunter finished speaking, murmurs of conversation broke out. Captain Asher pivoted. After shoving through the group of horsemen standing in the aisle, he strode from the stable without a word to Della. She had little time to puzzle over his abrupt manner before one of the men her uncle had hired in Kansas City worked his way through the crowd and stepped over to her. Della rose at his approach. Beside her, Aunt Coral also rose and drifted across the aisle to her husband's side.

"May I be so bold as to introduce myself?" the cowboy asked. "I know you're General Logan's niece, Miss Della Hughes."

"I am. And who might you be?" Della studied the young man before her. Of average height, he topped her by merely a few inches. Freckles dotted his pleasant face. His brown eyes twinkled.

"Just call me Rusty."

"Rusty." She glanced at his auburn hair shining beneath his hat. "I see that you're well named."

Rusty grinned. "Yup. My momma saw right away I was going to be a redheaded young'un."

Della couldn't help but return Rusty's infectious grin. "And how did Uncle Clint find you?"

"He didn't. I found him. There was talk about the Yankee general who was taking a herd of horses to the Colorado Territory. Heard he was hiring a few more men, so I found him and got myself hired."

"And where do you hail from, Rusty?"

"I was born in Tennessee but drifted west as soon as I was old enough to leave home. Been trailing cattle for the past ten years, from Texas to Dodge City. I figure moving cayuses has to be a heap better than eating dust when I'm punching dogies."

"I can imagine, and I'm sure your cattle experience will help us with the horses."

"It can't hurt. Do you intend to ride along with us or pass the time in a wagon?"

"I'll ride much of the time. Mr. Hunter has recommended that I learn to ride astride, so before we leave, I'll have to master that skill. I intend to do my part trailing the horses."

Rusty's grin widened, creasing his cheeks and crinkling his eyes. "I'd be happy to help you learn to ride astride, Miss Della."

Surprised at his overture, Della studied his face and wondered whether he was serious. "Thank you for your offer, but Mr. Hunter has promised to teach me."

The grin vanished from Rusty's face. He glanced at Shane Hunter, who was absorbed in conversation with Uncle Clint. "The scout is teaching you to ride? The lucky dog."

As if sensing he was the topic of conversation, Shane Hunter lifted his head and stared across the width of the stable at Della and Rusty. Della's face heated, as if she'd been caught gossiping.

"Well, I reckon I'd better mosey," Rusty said. "If you change your mind and want some fun while you're learning, just holler. I'll come runnin' to show you how to fork a cayuse." He nodded to her, then wheeled and sauntered from the stable, whistling a lively tune.

Della watched him leave, then looked over at Hunter. The scout still stared at her, his eyes narrowed and intent, his mouth hard. Though his expression remained inscrutable, Della had the uncomfortable feeling he disapproved. Was he going to blame her every time one of the men talked to her? She lifted her chin and stared back.

She could socialize with whomever she chose. Since the wagon train was composed mostly of men, she'd be talking to a lot of males in the next several weeks. She'd try not to be a distraction, but she wouldn't avoid the company of the drovers, either. If Shane Hunter didn't like it, he'd just have to deal with it.

CHAPTER 6

AFTER BREAKFAST THE NEXT MORNING, Della hurried
to the stable, hoping to catch her uncle before he left. The wide
double doors on the end closest to the hotel had been rolled
partially open, and Della slid through. She'd taken only a couple of
steps down the aisle when male voices, engaged in a heated
conversation in the tack room, caught her attention. She paused.
Should she leave and return later?

When she recognized one of the voices as belonging to
Uncle Clint, she tiptoed closer. The second speaker made an
impassioned reply. Captain Asher. The other person in the
conversation was none other than Captain Asher.

Why should Captain Asher and her uncle be having a
disagreement? Her curiosity overcame her, and she crept closer to
the tack room. Just outside the door, she halted.

"I most emphatically object, sir," Captain Asher insisted. "I
cannot take orders from a civilian."

Della held her breath, waiting for her uncle's reply. He'd
been a general too long to let a mere captain question his
judgment.

"Cannot? Or will not?" His voice was quiet, although his
tone brooked no opposition.

Quentin Asher sputtered.

"Shane Hunter knows this land. He knows the dangers, and
he knows more about the tribes than any man in the west. I trust
my family to him. Consider any order he gives as coming from
me."

"But the man has never been an officer."

"He fought with distinction during the Civil War. When, I believe, you were moving in diplomatic circles in Europe with your father."

"General Logan, sir, I implore you to reconsider. Under my leadership, my military detail will provide adequate protection. Mr. Hunter should do nothing more than serve as guide to us while we cross the plains to your homestead."

Standing motionless to one side of the tack-room door, Della marveled at her uncle's restraint. That Captain Asher should continue to question orders given by a retired officer of much superior rank showed either a high degree of arrogance or a lack of discretion. The following silence quivered with tension.

"Captain Asher"—Uncle Clint's harsh voice was edged with irritation—"I'm entrusting the safety of my family, my horses, and my wagons to the experience and knowledge of a man who has been in this territory for most of his life and who actually lived with the Cheyenne for several years. You have no experience of the West or of fighting the tribes. Why should I entrust that which I count most dear in this life to you?"

"I am an officer."

"Let me make myself clear. I have no intention of removing Shane Hunter from his position of leadership. If you cannot place yourself under his authority for the duration of our trip, then I'll have your orders rescinded and will find another officer to escort the army detail."

Della leaned forward, waiting to hear the captain's response. Several beats of silence ensued.

"Very well, sir," he said, his voice tight. "I'll consider myself under his command but with strong objections."

"Noted. Just be sure those objections don't keep you from doing whatever Hunter tells you in any situation requiring armed intervention."

"I'll do my best."

"See that you do. You're dismissed."

Swift footsteps thudded across the floor. Della barely had time to whisk away from the door before Quentin Asher erupted from the tack room, his pale face set in furious lines. He brushed past her without acknowledging her and flung himself out of the stable.

Della waited several moments before she moved to the tack-room door and peeked inside. Her uncle stood in the middle of the room, the blue flannel shirt he wore molding to the muscular lines of his rigid shoulders. He held Zeus's bridle in one hand, down along his side. The reins dangled on the floor.

She took a step inside. Uncle Clint lifted his head.

"May I come in, or will I disturb you?"

He gave a gusty sigh. "You won't disturb me. I suspect you heard that conversation."

"I was looking for you when I heard the two of you talking."

"I hope that young man won't be a problem. We'll need to pray for grace—and for the Lord's hand to be on all of us as we embark on our journey."

Della crossed to her uncle's side. "Yes. We'll need wisdom and the Lord's protection." She indicated the bridle he held. "I see you're planning to ride Zeus."

"I want to get in a last ride or two before I ship him out by train. After riding him all through the war and these years past, it will be hard for me to accustom myself to another mount. Zeus and I are a team."

Della glanced about the room, noting the neat rows of saddles mounted on racks attached to the wall. Bridles hung from large pegs above the saddles. Brushes and currycombs rested on shelves along another wall. Beneath the shelves, large wooden boxes held odds and ends of tack and rope, all the accoutrements of equine care. Organization reigned. Not an item was out of place.

"I wanted to ask you if I could choose a horse to ride. Sitting all day on a wagon seat holds no appeal for me. I'd rather ride herd."

"Shane can help you choose a mount. Coral will need a horse, as well, since Captain won't be suitable for her to ride here in the West. I've decided to ship him to Denver with Zeus."

"Aunt Coral will miss him."

The corners of Uncle Clint's mouth tugged up in a little smile. "I remember the first time she rode Captain. She nearly made my heart stop when he almost went down with her. He and Zeus collided, but she managed to stay aboard."

Della smiled. She never tired the hearing stories of Uncle Clint and Aunt Coral's stormy courtship. "I suspect the horses helped bring the two of you together."

Uncle Clint grinned. "Riding gave us a good excuse to spend time together."

"Mr. Hunter has promised to teach me to ride astride."

"You couldn't have a better teacher. The man rides like a centaur."

"I noticed," Della said. "Uncle Emory and I saw him at the cattle pens."

"I'll let you in on a secret. My wife already knows how to ride astride. Her brother taught her when they were children."

Della propped both hands on her hips. "That's a very well-kept secret. I didn't know Aunt Coral could ride like a man."

"She never talks about it because she doesn't want to cause a scandal, but it's a skill that will be useful in the West." Uncle Clint reached for a saddle and blanket on one of the racks. "I'll tack up Zeus and head out to the cattle pens."

A short time later, her uncle led Zeus outside while Della watched from the stable yard. The stallion walked with arrogant grace, his eyes alert and his ears pricked. Uncle Clint lifted a foot to the stirrup.

"Papa! Ride, Papa!"

He dropped his foot to the ground and turned just as Flossie scrambled from her mother's arms and launched herself toward her father, curls bobbing. He stepped forward to meet her, scooped her up, and held her high over his head. Flossie squealed and giggled, grabbing her father by the hair and knocking his cavalryman's hat from his head so it hung by its strap between his shoulders.

"Imp! What are you doing here?" Uncle Clint cradled his daughter against his chest, while she patted his face with tiny hands.

Aunt Coral, dressed in an apple-green day dress of ruched organdy, approached her husband. "She begged to come down to the stable to see her papa and his horse." Aunt Coral smiled. "I'm not sure which one she most wanted to see."

"I'm sure she must have come to see Zeus. Now that she's here, I have time to give her a ride before I leave." Uncle Clint handed Flossie back to her mother.

Aunt Coral took her daughter and clutched her tightly enough to make Flossie squirm. "Clint, should you?" Aunt Coral's forehead puckered. "You know Zeus can be unpredictable."

"Zeus will be a perfect gentleman." Uncle Clint gave the stallion an affectionate slap on the shoulder before he swung into the saddle. He reached down, plucked his daughter from her mother's arms, and settled her in front of him. With one arm hooked about her tummy, he held her securely against his stomach while his other hand grasped the reins. He heeled the great black horse into a walk. Flossie shrieked with excitement.

Della glanced at her aunt. Aunt Coral's hands clenched at her waist. Her face was pale while her gaze followed the stallion and his riders. She attempted to reassure her aunt. "Flossie will come to no harm. Zeus will behave himself."

Without removing her attention from her husband and child, Aunt Coral shook her head. "I hope so."

"If Uncle Clint thought Flossie was in any danger, he wouldn't let her ride Zeus."

"Zeus isn't always so calm."

After a short circuit of the stable yard, Uncle Clint rode back to the women. He gave his daughter a one-armed hug, then leaned down and returned her to her mother. "I should be back for the noon meal." He wheeled Zeus, signaled the stallion into a canter, and left the yard.

Walking back to the hotel, Della fell into step beside her aunt. The morning sun warmed their faces, and the oaks that flanked the path cast dappled shadows across the ground. Flossie scampered ahead, chattering about her ride.

Aunt Coral sent Della a mischievous glance. "I noticed that you had not one but two men dancing attendance on you last night."

Della thought back to the meeting in the stable, frowning. "Captain Asher and who else?"

"A certain redheaded cowboy, who has too much brass for his own good."

"Oh! You mean Rusty. He introduced himself and offered to teach me to ride astride."

"Did he, now?"

"He seemed very pleasant. I feel as though I've made a new friend. I suppose we'll all be friends before we reach Colorado Territory."

"I hope so. I fear there may be some discord between Captain Asher and Mr. Hunter."

Recalling the argument she'd overheard in the tack room, Della agreed. "I think you may be right. I hope they'll be able to work together."

"There will be enough danger on the trip without the two of them quarreling."

"Somehow, I can't imagine Mr. Hunter quarreling with anyone. I do think he'll have his way, however. Captain Asher is no match for a man of Mr. Hunter's experience."

CHAPTER 7

TWO MORNINGS LATER, AFTER THE seamstress completed one of the riding outfits, Della leaned against the paddock's railing and appraised the horses inside, considering which one to choose for her personal riding mount. Beside her, Shane Hunter propped himself on the fence, his forearms resting on the top rail, his black western hat pushed to the back of his head. One booted foot was hooked over the bottom bar.

"Do any of them catch your eye?" He tilted his head to catch her reply.

Della tried to quiet the butterflies in her stomach. He still affected her as no other man ever had. She looked at the mares again, forcing her attention back to the reason they were at the stockyard.

The mares displayed the strong, sturdy lines of their breed. Uncle Clint had paid good money to purchase horses whose lineage could be traced to Black Hawk, grandson of Justin Morgan. Her uncle wanted horses with the stamina and agility of the foundation sire, qualities that were critical for mounts used in the army's Indian War.

She considered Hunter's question, aware of his scrutiny. She cut another glance at him. His head bent close to hers, his blue eyes intent and crinkled at the corners. A serious expression graced his features, though grooves bracketed his mouth in a slight smile. With the sun behind them, the brim of his hat shadowed his face.

Della shifted and crossed her arms on the fence rail. Her elbow bumped his. A jolt sizzled through her, and she eased her arm away. Taking a deep breath, she once again forced her thoughts from the distracting man beside her. She pointed to a blaze-faced mare standing off to one side. "I like the looks of that chestnut."

Hunter straightened and dropped his foot to the ground. "Good choice. Let's catch her up."

When he'd dropped his lasso about the mare's neck, he led her outside the paddock. He haltered her and tied the lead rope to the fence rail with a slip knot. Della stepped close to the horse, stroked the mare's golden-red neck, and fingered her flaxen mane.

"She'll make you a fine mount. Always trust her instincts." Hunter spoke across the Morgan's back, one hand hooked over the chestnut's withers. "My mustang has saved my life more than once."

Della nodded. "I'll remember that." She took a breath and looked at him, a touch of uncharacteristic uncertainty making her swallow hard. "I want to learn as much as I can about the West. Will you teach me?"

"You, a city girl? What exactly do you want to learn?" Hunter's attentive blue gaze roved over her face, as if trying to gauge the sincerity of her request.

"Everything! The West is so different from Boston. I want to learn how to get along with the land and the people."

"You intend to stay out here? I figured you'd hightail it back east once you made it to the Colorado Territory."

Della looked about her at the wooden stockyard fences, the cattle milling in the pens, the sheds, and the open spaces beyond. A train whistle blasted nearby, drowning out the other urban sounds. Energy pulsed in the air. The city's raw vigor embraced her. Glancing back at Hunter, she shrugged. "I may find the West suits me very well."

Hunter held her gaze for several drawn-out moments until Della forgot to breathe. The city's clamor faded away. The air crackled between them. Neither spoke while, beneath the thrumming silence, an unspoken dialogue weighted the atmosphere. Just when Della thought she'd burst from the tension, Hunter turned away.

"Let's tack up this mare. Come around here where I can show you how. The next time, you'll have to do it yourself."

Della ducked beneath the mare's neck to reach the chestnut's left side. Hunter hefted a western saddle in one hand and a saddle blanket in the other. With patient precision, he demonstrated the steps of tacking up a horse. Della stood beside him, watching, yet all the while aware of his appeal. Tall though she was for a woman, the scout topped her by several muscled inches. His height and strength made her feel pleasantly feminine.

When Hunter had slipped the halter from the mare's head and replaced it with the bridle, he turned to Della. His blue gaze took in her form. "I see you're wearin' more sensible riding clothes than that green habit you wore the other day."

Della glanced at the fawn-colored split riding skirt that brushed the tops of her leather riding boots. A long-sleeved russet blouse with ivory buttons marching down the front completed her outfit. The simple clothes gave her an unaccustomed sense of freedom. No corset constricted her waist. No layers of petticoats hampered her walk. "Uncle Clint had the seamstress make up these riding clothes for Aunt Coral and me. I feel wonderfully free. This outfit is much more suitable for riding than my green habit."

Hunter shook his head. "That getup you were wearing the other day was entirely unfit for hard riding. It would have been hazardous to your safety."

Della grinned at him. "I'd cause quite a scandal back in Boston should I appear riding astride in this outfit."

"Definitely avoid Boston while you're wearing that." His gaze darted to her hair. "The new hairstyle is very fetching. Are you still fixing it yourself?"

Della fingered the French braid that hung down her back. Flyaway tendrils had escaped her plait and coiled about her face. "Yes. I need a lot of practice." She brushed at a wisp of dark hair the breeze had draped across her cheek.

He flicked the brim of her stylish straw bonnet with a long finger. "That little geegaw won't last a day on the trail. I'll get you a real hat."

"One like yours?"

He nodded. "A hat like mine serves a more useful purpose than mere fashion. Now, let's get you on this horse." With both of his hands resting on her shoulders, he maneuvered her close to the mare's side. Where his fingers cupped the points of her shoulders, she felt the warm, sinewy strength of him through her blouse. "Grab the saddle horn with your left hand and the cantle with your right."

Della complied.

"Can you get your foot into the stirrup?"

She lifted her left foot, toeing for the stirrup. Having ridden sidesaddle, she'd always used a mounting block or appealed to a groom for help. She'd never appreciated how tall a horse could be or how she'd have to stretch to reach the stirrup. When she'd managed to fit her toe into the stirrup, she glanced at him over her shoulder.

"Up you go. Swing your right leg over her rump."

Della pushed upward and the next moment was astride the mare's back. Hunter stood at the chestnut's left shoulder, looking up at her.

"Now, isn't that more comfortable than sidesaddle?"

She shifted her weight, getting used to the unfamiliar feel of a horse between her legs. "It will be, once I get used to it."

"Riding astride is safer for you because your balance is centered."

"I see what you mean."

"Keep your heels down. If you should get thrown, you want your feet to clear the stirrups. If your heels aren't down, your feet can get caught, and you could be dragged."

She shivered at the mental image. "Heels down. I won't forget."

Hunter flipped the reins over the mare's head and passed them to Della. "I'll get my mustang, and we'll take a ride out of the city."

He stepped toward his long-legged gelding, who stood patiently in a head-down, three-legged stance at the rail, and a cheerful voice hailed them.

"Miss Hughes! I see you've forked a cayuse. You cut a fine figure."

Della reined her mare around and caught sight of Rusty. He leaned on a pitchfork beside a pile of hay. She waved at him.

"Thank you. I have a good teacher."

"Anytime you want to practice your riding skills, give me a holler. I'll take you out."

"I'll keep that in mind."

Hunter had mounted and brought his grulla close to Della's mare. "Are you ready, Miss Hughes?"

After bidding goodbye to Rusty, Della fell in beside Hunter. They navigated the stockyard pens until they left the warren of fencing, sheds, and rail lines behind. Avoiding the Kansas River, which coiled about the stockyards in a lazy loop on the Kansas side of the city, they headed toward a grassy, open region.

The freedom the split skirt gave Della opened a whole new riding experience for her. She turned to her companion. "This is wondrous! Society has deprived women of a truly extraordinary experience by dictating we must ride sidesaddle."

"If you stay in the West, you need never concern yourself with that."

"I don't think I can ever ride sidesaddle again."

Hunter smiled at her. Startled to see such a lighthearted expression on his face, Della forgot what she'd been about to say.

"Are you ready for a trot?"

In answer, Della squeezed the mare's sides. The chestnut responded by breaking into an easy, ground-devouring jog. Hunter's mustang kept pace with her. Glancing over at the scout, Della signaled her mount into a gallop. The mare leaped forward. Hunter's grulla lunged into a run, and the two horses thundered over the grasslands.

Della thrilled at the feel of the powerful animal beneath her. The mare's breath rasped as she sucked in great gulps of air. Her golden mane flashed with the speed of her passage. As she rode astride, at one with her mount, the flowing, bunching muscles of the galloping horse beneath her made her feel as if she straddled the wind. She gloried in the sensation and in the companionship of the buckskin-clad man riding at her side. The restraints of her upbringing fell away, setting her free. She laughed, and the wind snatched the sound away.

They brought their mounts to a walk. "I can't thank you enough!" she said. "I don't know when I've enjoyed anything as much."

"This was an easy enough pleasure to arrange." Once more, he flashed her an unexpected grin.

"And the mare is a joy to ride."

"You can thank your uncle for that. He's the one who purchased her."

"Uncle Clint is a good judge of horses. And he's convinced Morgan horses will make excellent mounts for the western army."

Hunter nodded. "During the Civil War, Morgans were prized by Union cavalrymen. Anyone mounted on a Morgan horse was the envy of the other men."

Leaning down, Della ran her hand down her mare's satiny red-gold neck. "I can see why."

They rode over the wide, sunny grassland, letting their mounts set the pace. A companionable silence fell, one Della didn't feel compelled to break. She watched Hunter out of the corner of her eye. Though a big man, he rode with natural grace, his body moving as one with his horse. She wondered about his life with the Cheyenne—why he'd lived with them and for how long. When her curiosity could be contained no longer, she broached the topic.

"Mr. Hunter, I've heard it said that you lived with the Indians for a time. How long was that?"

The scout didn't acknowledge her question at first. Della began to wonder whether he intended to reply. After several moments had ticked by, he turned his head and looked at her. She caught her breath at the shuttered expression on his face. His mouth was a grim slash.

"Nine years."

"Nine years! Such a long time. Why did you live with them?"

Hunter narrowed his eyes. "Miss Hughes, hasn't anyone ever told you that you ask too many questions? Didn't you learn in that fancy finishing school where your uncle sent you that it's rude to pry?"

Chastened, Della looked down at the reins she held.

"Come. It's time to go back." Hunter reined his gelding about. Touching his heels to the mustang's sides, he signaled his mount into a gallop without looking to see whether Della accompanied him.

After a heartbeat of confusion, she let her mare follow. With the chestnut running, Della kept her gaze on Hunter's wide shoulders. The rawhide fringe on the back of his deerskin shirt fluttered with the wind rushing past. Except for his sandy hair, he looked more Indian than white, she admitted.

What was his secret? Why had he lived for nine years with the Cheyenne? And why had he left? From his reaction to her questions, the circumstances that had brought him into the tribe and the years he'd spent there had had a profound effect upon him. The experience wasn't something he talked about freely. She guessed a tragedy must be tied up in his tale.

Della determined that she'd learn his secret. Somehow, she'd coax him into telling her about his life with the tribe and what had taken him there. There was a story to be told, and she'd convince Hunter to share the tale with her.

Great Plains, Kansas
June 1870

CHAPTER 8

THE CRACK OF A RIFLE shot woke Della. Groaning, she rolled over onto her back. One arm flopped across her eyes. She snuggled beneath the wool blankets on the floor of the wagon, cocooned in the warmth of her bedroll, wishing she could stay there until the sun thrust its golden edge over the rim of the prairie.

How could it be four o'clock already? It seemed she'd barely laid her head on her pillow. It couldn't be time to begin another day. Outside her wagon, sounds of the camp stirring to life assured her the rifle shot indicated it was indeed time to rise. She opened her eyes to an inky darkness. The murkiness in the wagon's interior resembled a thick, suffocating shroud. To a city-bred woman, a prairie night away from the gaslights of civilization swallowed the earth with a stygian blackness.

With a sigh, Della sat up. Every muscle in her body ached, and she stifled another groan. She'd been so thrilled at the prospect of riding astride that she'd overdone. Her shoulders, her lower limbs, and her back all screamed when she moved. How could she face another day in the saddle? Yet the prospect of spending the day on the wagon's hard seat held no appeal.

Aunt Coral had ridden at her husband's side every day of the three they'd been on the trail. Della resolved not to quit while her aunt showed no signs of flagging.

Voices outside her wagon reminded her she couldn't linger in her warm blankets another moment. Pushing the covers down to her waist, she sat up. A frigid blast of air ran its icy fingers over her skin. Shivering, she staggered to her feet and fumbled in the darkness for her clothes. Tossing her flannel night rail aside, she pulled on her riding clothes as quickly as she could. When she'd dressed, she felt for her brush on the sack of rice where she'd set it the night before, close at hand so she could find it in the dark. She dragged the brush through her tangled mass of curls, trying to bring a measure of order to her hair. Giving up, she tossed the brush aside and plaited her tresses in the darkness without the aid of a mirror.

That task done, she located the black felt cowboy hat Hunter had procured for her and jammed it on her head. Next, she folded her blankets and laid them across a stack of bean sacks. Finally, she snatched up the waist-length sheepskin jacket she'd wear until the sun warmed the plains. She shrugged into the coat.

Half a dozen one-hundred-pound muslin sacks of beans had been piled next to the bags of rice along one side of Della's wagon. A space on the opposite side had been left clear for sleeping. Della had wedged a small trunk filled with her clothing and personal items between the wagon's wooden side and muslin bags of dried apples. She placed her hairbrush in the trunk and shut the lid. Then, feeling her way along the sacks of supplies that filled most of the wagon bed, she crept to the rear of the Conestoga. She pushed aside the privacy cover that hung over the oval opening of the canvas top and crawled outside.

Della stood for a moment at the wagon's end. Dew clinging to the prairie grass soaked her riding boots. She shivered in the chill. Aching all over, she hesitated to move, but the smell of bacon and coffee made her stomach growl. Her stiff muscles protested when she walked around to the front of the chuck wagon, where a fire provided some warmth.

The tail of the chuck wagon had been let down. A stack of tin plates, cups, and forks had been arranged on the makeshift table. Della picked up her utensils and turned to the cooking fire.

Silvie, who had first been Aunt Coral's nanny at Elmwood Plantation and later her companion, stood by the fire. When Della approached the group who had already assembled for breakfast, Silvie stepped toward her, wiping her hands on the apron she wore over her gingham dress.

"Miz Della, you look fit to drop. Just you sit yourself down, and I'll fill your plate." Silvie snatched up Della's tin plate and turned away to pile bacon, beans, and a biscuit on the dish.

While she waited for her breakfast, Della glanced at the people gathered about the cooking fire. Men either coming in off the last watch of the night shift or preparing to start the horses on the day's trek convened around the fire. The flames cast a flickering orange glow on their faces and clothes. Some of the men stood while they ate, shoveling food into their mouths. Others squatted on the grass.

Behind them, the darkness loomed as an impenetrable wall. Uncle Clint and Aunt Coral sat on a blanket opposite her. Flossie snuggled on her father's lap, a biscuit in her tiny hand.

Della stepped closer to the fire's warmth. Aunt Coral, as she had the other mornings, handed Della a second blanket. "Thank you." Della dropped to the ground, and curled her legs beneath her. Silvie drew near with a full plate. Bending down, she handed Della her breakfast.

"Thank you, Silvie. You're very kind."

"You look worn to the bone." Silvie shook her dark head. "You need a good rest in the wagon today. I tried to tell Miz Coral she needs a rest, too, but she wants to stay with her man. Flossie and me, we'll just ride along with Toby in the chuck wagon."

"To tell the truth, I don't think I could sit on a wagon seat. I'm too sore."

Silvie chuckled. "Your saddle won't be much better." She motioned to the tin cup Della had set on the ground. "Let me have your cup, and I'll fetch you some coffee."

While Silvie poured coffee from a battered tin pot by the fire, Della dug into her breakfast. Since leaving Kansas City, she'd acquired a ravenous appetite. She decided the prairie air, combined with the hard work of riding herd on the horses, had triggered her hunger. For the first time in her life, she didn't care that the rations on her plate weren't ladylike portions. She wolfed down the simple fare, cooked over a fire built from buffalo chips, as though the food were the daintiest of delicacies prepared in a Parisian kitchen.

Silvie approached with the coffee.

"Thank you, Silvie." Della took a cautious sip of the steaming liquid. The coffee, strong and bitter, scalded her tongue, but it warmed her insides.

Movement off to her left caught her attention. Shane Hunter, leading his grulla mustang, materialized out of the darkness. At the edge of the firelight, he dropped the reins, ground-tying his mount, and picked his way through the men toward the chuck wagon. He paused next to Della.

The fire danced behind him, transforming him into a tall silhouette looming before her. Della felt rather than saw his stare. She froze with her fork halfway to her mouth.

Neither spoke for a long moment. Then, Hunter nodded. "Mornin', Miss Hughes."

"Good morning, Mr. Hunter."

"The early hour seems to agree with you."

"Really?" Della grimaced. "Silvie just informed me that I look worn to the bone."

Another moment passed while Hunter seemed to consider his reply. "Perhaps Silvie doesn't see you the way I do." Without giving Della an opportunity to respond, he moved toward the tail of the chuck wagon and picked up a dish and utensils.

Della gaped at him, watching while he strolled to the fire and filled his plate with an economy of motion. What had he meant by that? With most men of her acquaintance, she'd have taken the comment as a compliment, but with Hunter, she couldn't quite tell.

The scout moved around the fire and squatted beside her uncle, not glancing at her again. The two men conversed in low tones while Della finished her breakfast.

Dawn had chased away the darkness and spread a gray luster across the land by the time the men had eaten and dispersed to catch up their mounts. Toby, the cook, had heated water drawn from a nearby creek and washed the dishes in a wooden bucket. The men hired to drive the oxen had yoked the cattle to the wagons, two teams per wagon.

Shane Hunter left to scout without looking in her direction.

Trying not to limp as she walked to her wagon, Della glanced at the cavalcade. Four wagons made up their train—a wagon for herself, one for Uncle Clint's family, one for Silvie, and the chuck wagon. Each Conestoga carried supplies for their journey, allowing just enough room for the occupants to bed down on the floor. The men employed by her uncle to ride herd on the Morgans slept in their bedrolls about the fire.

Della reached the back of her wagon. She'd stowed her saddle, blanket, and bridle inside the night before. Since she planned to ride with the drovers today, she must climb into the wagon and haul out her tack, catch up her mare, and toss the saddle over the chestnut's back. She'd never realized how heavy a western saddle could be until she tried to lift one. Now, because of her aching shoulders, she wondered whether she could even lift her rig. She sighed, tempted to spend the day snuggled in her bedroll. Pushing away the enticing thought, she squared her shoulders and lifted her chin. Somehow, despite sore muscles, she'd manage.

She placed one foot on the wooden lip running along the bottom edge of the Conestoga and gripped the top rim of the wagon's frame, intending to hoist herself inside. A male voice hailed her. She stepped down and turned. Captain Asher approached, leading both her mare and his sorrel gelding. He looked eye catching in his pristine cavalryman's uniform.

"Miss Hughes, I took the liberty of catching up your mare for you. I thought you might need a hand tacking her up."

Grateful for the captain's thoughtfulness, Della smiled at him. "That would be most kind. The saddle is dreadfully heavy."

"And doubtless, you'd never saddled a horse yourself until this week."

"Never."

Quentin Asher passed her the mare's lead rope and his gelding's reins. "If you'll hold the horses, I'll get your saddle for you."

In much less time than it would have taken Della, the captain tacked up her mare and handed her the reins. "May I request the pleasure of your company today as we ride?" The corners of his eyes crinkled while he cajoled her with a grin.

Mindful of Shane Hunter's warning regarding the captain, Della hesitated a moment. "If you're certain you shouldn't be protecting our company instead, I'd be delighted to ride with you."

"We haven't yet seen any sign of hostiles or any other threat. I'm certain today will be uneventful."

Della hoped he was right. "Well, then. Let's mount up."

Another rifle shot gave the signal to begin. With plodding steps, the oxen strained against their yokes. The wagons rumbled through the prairie grass, one after the other. A Jersey milk cow, tied to the back of the chuck wagon, ambled along.

Della and the captain urged their mounts to the right flank of the horse herd. The herd, with its accompanying riders, topped a slight rise and left the wagons behind.

The sun broke over the distant expanse of the horizon and turned the sky eggshell blue. A luminous light gilded the cavalcade. The Morgans settled into a steady walk.

"I'd be ungallant if I didn't compliment you on your riding outfit," Captain Asher said. "That split skirt becomes you, and you wear it with flair. I applaud your courage by daring to appear in public dressed as you are."

"Mr. Hunter recommended it. I've found these riding clothes to be extremely comfortable and practical."

"Ah, the scout." Asher's mouth turned down. "I might have known. As fetching as it is, I hope that once we reach your uncle's ranch, you'll again wear conventional dress."

Something in his tone caused Della to look at him. "Why should I? These riding clothes suit me very well."

The captain met Della's gaze, his amber eyes intense. "You're a refined lady who belongs in a drawing room, attending teas, or gracing a ballroom floor. This rough-and-tumble life you're living now is all well and good for the horse drive, but surely, you don't intend to remain sequestered out in the territory permanently. You're much more suited to life in Denver, where you should dress as befitting your station."

Looking away, Della stared ahead through her mare's twitching ears at the open prairie rolling ahead of them. "I'm sure we'll visit Denver occasionally. Uncle Clint will have business dealings with the bankers there, and I know he'll want to enter society. Of course, he'll take us with him when he goes."

"Miss Hughes, I hope you don't think my interest in your future unseemly. I don't want to be premature, but you'd make an admirable wife for someone with political and social ambitions. Someone such as myself."

Della swiveled her head in her companion's direction, regarding him with surprise. She'd sensed his interest in her, but she hadn't thought he'd bring his intentions out into the open so soon. His reference to marriage made her uncomfortable. A life such as he described would return her to the social strictures she'd left behind in Boston.

Asher's handsome countenance appeared set beneath his wide-brimmed cavalryman's hat. "Don't be coy, Miss Hughes," he said when she didn't reply. "You must have sensed my regard for you."

"I'm not being coy. I'm just not sure what to say, and I do think you're being premature."

The squeak of the saddle leather, the swish of their mounts' hoofbeats through the grass, and the motion of their horses beneath them smoothed over a moment that had turned awkward. The captain shrugged.

"Very well. I'll say no more for now, but you can be sure we'll discuss this at a later date."

"Perhaps. Now, why don't you tell me about your life in diplomatic circles? You certainly must have tales to share."

"My parents and I were attending a dinner in Paris given in honor of Queen Victoria and Prince Albert, who were guests of the French government at the time," he said, allowing her to change the subject. "It was shortly before Prince Albert's death . . ."

By midmorning, the sun had arced into the sky, beating down with fierce intensity. Della wiggled out of her jacket. After rolling it up into a bundle, she tied it behind her saddle seat. The breeze that blew every day on the plains buffeted her. The tails of the red bandana tied about her neck fluttered.

They stopped for their nooning beside a shallow stream. Tall, broad-leaved cottonwoods cast welcome shade along the water's edge. The riders dismounted, watered their mounts, stripped the tack from them, and hobbled them close by. When the wagons caught up with them, they ate a cold meal left over from breakfast.

Della could scarcely walk to the chuck wagon. The muscles in her limbs and between her shoulders burned, as well as muscles in unmentionable places. When the call came to mount up after their nooning, she gritted her teeth and caught up her mare. Again, Captain Asher performed the service of tacking up the Morgan for her.

Della stood at her horse's shoulder, wondering how she could lift her foot into the stirrup. She grasped the saddle horn, then dropped her hand to her side. Drooping against her chestnut mare, she pressed her forehead into her mount's neck and closed her eyes. Exhaustion pulled at her, dragging her down into lethargy.

"Do you need assistance?" Quentin Asher asked behind her.

She whirled and eyed the captain, who was holding his gelding on a loose rein. "As much as I hate to admit it, I'm not sure I can mount by myself. My limbs refuse to work."

"Let me help."

Without waiting for Della to respond, the cavalryman tossed her into the saddle. They'd just gathered their reins when Lieutenant Dyer trotted up.

"Captain Asher, you won't mind if I ride with Della this afternoon, I'm sure. I crave some time with my favorite young lady."

The younger man glanced at Della, then acquiesced with barely concealed ill grace. When Asher departed, Della turned to the lieutenant. "Uncle Emory, what's all this about?"

Emory Dyer winked at her and grinned. "That young man needs to get his mind off courting you and onto the reason he's been assigned to accompany us. I thought some time away from you might help him remember why he's here."

Della smiled back. "You're a conniving man, but I thank you. I'll enjoy riding with my adopted uncle."

They reached the horse herd, which the other riders had already bunched and started on the afternoon's journey. Falling into place at the flank of the herd, they let their mounts set their pace.

"Uncle Emory, Mr. Hunter didn't return for lunch. Do you know where he is?"

Dyer squinted against the sun, staring into the vast distance. "Since we're not following a defined trail, he ranges ahead of us, scouting the best way to take the wagons and the herd. While he's out there, he cuts back and forth, looking for Indian sign or any other threat. We may ride fifteen or twenty miles a day, but he and that mustang of his travel two or three times the distance."

"He must be very tough."

Dyer eyed her. "*Tough* doesn't begin to describe him."

When they stopped for the night, Della crawled out of the saddle. Her legs shook. She removed her tack and turned the mare loose. After staggering to the cooking fire beside the chuck wagon, she dropped onto the grass.

Aunt Coral joined her, her hazel eyes filled with sympathy. "I never knew I could hurt in so many places."

"I don't think I can move." Della groaned.

"I keep telling myself it will get better. By this time next week, I'm sure we'll be as saddle hardened as any of the men."

Shane Hunter rode into the camp just as everyone else finished supper. After caring for his horse, he strode to the chuck wagon and fixed himself a plate.

Della watched him eat, wishing to engage him in conversation but too weary to make the effort. When she'd rested enough to move, she forced herself to her feet and made her way to her wagon. Climbing into the wagon bed required every ounce of determination she could muster, but she managed. Her blankets beckoned her with a siren's allure. She couldn't wait to curl up in her bedroll and fall into the welcome oblivion of sleep.

She removed her boots; then, a firm rap sounded on the back of the wagon. She scrambled to the Conestoga's end, lifted aside the privacy flap, and peered out. Shane Hunter stood in the gathering dusk at the back of her wagon, distinctive in his fringed buckskin shirt and trousers, his gun belt riding low.

"I don't mean to disturb you, Miss Hughes, but I have something that might help you."

Della raised her eyebrows. "What makes you think I need help?"

His teeth flashed white in the dusk when he smiled. "Perhaps, it's the obvious fact that you can hardly walk."

She stared at him with haughty disdain. "I'm sure you're mistaken. I'm merely a trifle weary from my ride."

Hunter shifted his weight to one leg and hooked a thumb in his belt. "The fact that you hobbled to your wagon has nothing to do with you being more than 'a trifle weary'?"

"Of course not."

"Very well. Apparently, you don't need my help." He wheeled and began striding away.

Della's burning muscles reminded her she did indeed need help. Pride wouldn't give her relief from her pain. "Mr. Hunter!"

Hunter halted and swung about. He waited for her to speak, not offering any words to make her sheepish admission of need easier.

She abandoned her haughty pose and slumped against the wagon's wooden end. "If you have anything that can provide relief for my aching limbs, I'd be most grateful."

He moved closer and pulled a small drawstring pouch from his trouser pocket. He thrust the bag through the opening in the wagon's top. "Rub some of this salve into your muscles. You'll feel better in the morning."

Della took the bag from him. "I don't think this is enough for my whole body."

Hunter grinned. "I admire your pluck, Miss Hughes, but ride in the wagon tomorrow. No one will think less of you if you rest for a day."

"I don't want to hinder Uncle Clint's endeavor."

"You're more likely to hinder his endeavor if you fall out of the saddle and hurt yourself because you're too sore to ride. Or if you can't toss a saddle over your horse and need someone to do it for you."

Recalling Captain Asher's welcome assistance that day, Della wondered whether the scout knew who had tacked up her mare. She didn't press the issue. "I do appreciate your help. Thank you."

He dipped his head. "Good night, Miss Hughes. Sleep well."

"Good night, Mr. Hunter."

When the scout had gone, Della dropped the privacy flap over the opening and sank onto the floor of the wagon. In the dimness of the Conestoga's interior, she examined the pouch he'd given her, turning the bag over. The sack was made of butter-soft deerskin. A curious starburst pattern of blue, red, and white beadwork decorated one side. The tote resembled nothing she'd ever seen. The pouch must have had its origin in the Cheyenne village where Hunter had lived. Once again, curiosity about that segment of his life consumed her. Her imagination conjured images of painted warriors dancing about a fire and women with braided dark hair standing beside their tepees, yet she had nothing on which to base her speculations. Hunter had shut the door on her questions, so all she had was his admission he'd lived with the tribe for nine years. Her determination to wrest his secret from him intensified.

Della lifted the sack to her nose, sniffing. A musky scent wafted from the deerskin. The smell of the bag, combined with other unfamiliar features of the West—the buffeting breeze, the far-flung spaces, the wide bowl of the sky, the acrid scent of the alkali water in the streams—called to a primitive side of her nature she had suspected existed yet had been afraid to acknowledge. A storm of emotions assailed her, tearing her from the mooring of her strict Victorian upbringing.

Now, she embraced the unsettled region through which they traveled—the wildness of it, the danger, and the hardship. She didn't know what the future held or whether she'd even live to reach the Colorado Territory, but of one thing, she was certain.

The drawing rooms of Boston held no more appeal for her. She could never go back.

CHAPTER 9

ALL TRAVEL STOPPED THEIR FIRST Sunday on the trail. After breakfast, Della perched on a wooden stool near the cooking fire. Flossie snuggled on her lap. To one side sat Aunt Coral, with Silvie on her other side and Emory Dyer standing behind them. Those drovers who elected to attend the service stood or squatted in a semicircle about their group. Uncle Clint stood beside the fire, his Bible in his hands.

Toby, their cook, had produced a violin from the chuck wagon. He accompanied their hymn singing with surprising flair.

Now, Della listened to her uncle preach, though her attention wandered. She had never before attended church in the outdoors but always sat in the cushioned pew that had belonged to the Logan family ever since the church was built. The swelling notes of an organ had accompanied the congregational singing. Stained-glass windows depicting biblical scenes turned the sunshine streaming into the nave into a rainbow pattern on the floor. The clergyman's voice proclaiming a lengthy sermon in solemn tones sounded from the high, carved pulpit. An atmosphere of reverence overlaid the service.

Yet here, in this informal gathering, with neither a roof above them nor a pulpit before them, Della felt the Lord's presence. They didn't need a church for God to bestow His blessing on them. She took comfort in the knowledge.

Shortly after Uncle Clint began to speak, Della sensed movement to her left. On silent feet, Shane Hunter joined their group, coming to a halt at the edge of the row of men. In his hands, he held a small, battered Bible. His face was expressionless beneath the brim of his western hat. As if he felt her stare, he swiveled his head in her direction. Their gazes connected. Heat flared in Della's stomach. Her breath caught. When she twisted back around, she couldn't pick up the thread of the sermon. The brief connection with the scout had scattered her concentration to the four winds.

After lunch, the women gathered their laundry and made their way to the shallow stream near their camp. Della carried her soiled clothes wrapped in a sheet. Aunt Coral and Silvie carried theirs in similar bundles. When they reached the lazy creek, they dropped their burdens onto the sandy bank.

"Silvie, you'll have to show me what to do," Della said. "At home, a laundress always washed my clothes. I never gave a thought to the process."

Silvie held up a scrubbing board and a bar of laundry soap. "It's not hard. Watch me." Kneeling on the stream's bank, she pulled a petticoat from her bundle and dipped it into the sluggish brown water. She demonstrated how to wash the garment and spread it out on the grass to dry in the sun.

Aunt Coral had already cleaned a pile of Flossie's clothes and her own with a scrubbing board by the time Della finished washing two of her split riding skirts and one blouse.

Pushing a wayward strand of curly hair out of her eyes, Della leaned into the stream and applied herself once more to her task. The water splashed on her skirt, and she tore a fingernail on the scrubbing board's metal ridges.

Silvie eyed her with sympathy. "Miz Della, why don't you rest? I'll finish your laundry for you."

Della shook her head. "Thank you, Silvie, but I must wash my own clothes. I can't let you do my work."

"You ought to take Silvie up on her offer," Captain Asher said from behind them. He watched them, a picture of military elegance in his uniform. "Washing clothes isn't a task for a young lady such as yourself."

Della rolled back on her heels, twisting to better see him. She tipped her head back to look up at him. "I won't be a slackard. I need to be responsible for my own laundry."

WOUNDED HEART

The captain shrugged, disapproval pulling down the corners of his mouth. "I applaud your determination to be independent, but I'm sure Silvie is used to doing laundry. Let her do yours. You shouldn't soil your hands with such drudgery."

His words, hinting at Silvie's servant status, rankled. Della scrambled to her feet, water dripping from her hands and skirt. She stalked toward him, halting only when she stood a handsbreadth away. Lifting her chin, she narrowed her eyes. "What a dreadful thing to say! Silvie's not a laundress. She's part of our family."

"I only intended . . ."

"How do you think Silvie feels, hearing you talk like that?"

"I didn't think it mattered. She's not one of us."

Della poked him in the chest. "Don't you have to ride herd on the horses? Or perhaps oil your saddle? I'm sure there are tasks waiting for you to do. Please, leave us."

Quentin Asher captured her hand and held it against his uniform tunic. "My apologies. I intended no harm. I merely had your best interests in mind." He paused, perusing her face with his sherry-brown eyes. "My wife will never do her own laundry. I'll provide every comfort and luxury possible, as befitting her station."

"May I remind you that I'm not your wife?" She pulled her hand from his.

"Not yet, but I hope to one day make that a reality."

"Your hopes are premature."

"Perhaps, but I'll keep pleading my case. My intent is that soon, you'll look fondly on my suit." The captain backed away with his hands raised, palms out. "You're overwrought. I'll take my leave, and by the next time we meet, you'll have forgiven me."

He pivoted and sauntered toward the wagons, which had been parked in a rough circle. Della watched him for a moment, then spun about and returned to the stream's bank. She dropped once more to her knees and touched Silvie's shoulder.

"I'm sorry, Silvie, for the captain's thoughtlessness."

Silvie shrugged. "Never you mind, Miz Della. I've heard worse."

Aunt Coral resumed scrubbing the night rail she'd been cleaning when Quentin Asher interrupted them. She glanced at Della. "That young man has lived too long in the exclusive atmosphere of Europe's diplomatic service. I hope his experiences in the West will temper his ideals somewhat."

"I certainly hope so. His snobbishness doesn't set well with me."

By the time they finished the laundry, their damp clothes littered the grass. The sun beat down on their apparel. The afternoon breeze eddied over the garments, evaporating the moisture. Della cast one last look at their clothing and turned away, stretching her spine.

Shane Hunter approached, a stack of tin plates in one hand.

Della straightened, forgetting her aching back. She took two steps toward the scout, nodding toward the tinware. "I see you've raided Toby's chuck wagon."

Hunter glanced down at the platters. "I needed them for target practice."

"You're going to shoot? May I come with you?"

Hunter halted beside her, looking down into her face. "You want to watch me shoot?"

She nodded.

Hunter shrugged. "I must maintain my edge, so I continue to practice. I hope you won't be bored."

Falling into step beside him, Della shook her head. "Certainly not. Can you teach me to shoot?"

He cast her a sideways glance. "You're serious about this?"

"Yes. I may need to know how to use a gun someday."

"If you're set on learning, I can give you a lesson this afternoon."

They walked away from the camp and up a knoll, their feet swishing through the rich prairie grass.

"Thank you for loaning me your salve. I was amazed at how much better I felt after I'd used it." Della peered up into his face.

"And spendin' the next day resting in the wagon helped, I'm sure."

"How did you know? You're usually gone before the rest of us eat breakfast, and you return late in the evening. I rarely see you."

"It's my job to know everything that happens in this outfit."

Della didn't reply. She wondered whether he knew Captain Asher had been seeking out her company and perhaps being a little negligent of his duties. But she didn't want to pursue that topic and changed the subject. "I've never seen anything like your pouch. And I suspect the salve wasn't something a doctor would prescribe."

He maintained a few moments of silence. "The pouch is Cheyenne. And the salve is a combination of herbs and bear grease made by the tribe's women."

Excitement bubbled through her at his admission. That he'd shared this snippet of his life gratified her. "Well, it worked, and I'm grateful."

When they crested the rise, Della looked about her. The plains stretched before them, rumpled grasslands rising in imperceptible degrees to the unseen Colorado mountains. Apricot-colored evening primrose; daisy-like yellow ragleaf, and orange globeflower grew in scattered profusion. Their petals added color to the prairie. Wild roses lifted their pink faces to the sky. Above them, a red-tailed hawk hung suspended, riding the air currents on motionless wings. Not far away, the horses and oxen spread out, heads down, muzzles buried in the buffalo grass. Back east, she'd never seen anything like this boundless splendor.

Della lifted her face to the limitless sky and closed her eyes. The restless wind plucked tendrils from her braid and tossed them about her head. Spreading her arms, she spun in exuberant abandon. When she stopped, Shane Hunter was eyeing her.

"You haven't been eatin' locoweed, have you?"

Della laughed. "No locoweed. It's just that I feel so free here! No Boston matrons are frowning at me because I broke one of society's rules. Uncle Clint despaired of making a lady out of me." She pivoted again.

The tin plates held down along his side, Hunter looked her up and down. "You're like a bird who's been kept in a golden cage and has just been freed."

Tucking a loose curl behind her ear, Della nodded. "I didn't even know I was in a cage, but now that I've tasted freedom, I know that it's true."

"The Cheyenne would give you a name that embodies your spirit. You're *Aenohe.*"

Intrigued, Della smiled at him and tried to repeat the word. "Aah-no. What does it mean?"

"'Hawk.' You have the freedom-loving spirit of the hawk. Your name should be *Anovaoo'o Aenohe.*"

"And what does that mean?"

"'Beautiful Hawk.'"

His words silenced Della. She stared up into his face. He returned her stare, his blue eyes intent, his chiseled features expressionless. What had he meant? Had any of her Boston beaux uttered the words, she would have thanked him for the pretty compliment and forgotten about it. With Hunter, the tribute must have a deeper meaning. She suspected he rarely paid compliments to women.

"Thank you. That was lovely."

The wind buffeted her, slapping her riding skirt against her legs. She lifted a hand to her hair, attempting to tuck loose chocolate-colored strands back into her plait. Hunter's stare captivated her.

Without replying, he reached out and caught a curling tendril that had fluttered across her cheek. It snagged in the calluses on the pads of his fingers. With tender awkwardness, he brushed the hair from her face, smoothing the strand back against her head. For one moment, his fingers clenched in her hair before he dropped his hand to his side.

Della's breath caught in her throat. She couldn't speak. Hunter's action had paralyzed her.

He dispelled the moment by putting the plates into her hand. "When I'm ready, toss one plate at a time into the air, one after the other. Flick them with your wrist to give them a good spin."

She swallowed, trying to gather her scattered thoughts. "How will I know when you're ready?"

"I'll tell you."

Fascinated, Della watched while he loosened the leather thong over the handle of his Colt and pulled the six-shooter from its holster. He checked the chamber and spun the cylinder before he dropped the weapon back into the gun belt. Then, he plucked a few short blades of grass and held them high. Opening his fingers, he watched while the wind snatched the grass and blew the blades back toward them.

"Why did you do that?" Della asked.

"I have to know the direction of the wind and how strong it is to factor that into my aim."

The scout stepped away, facing into the breeze, standing with his legs spread and his weight evenly balanced. He dropped his hands to his sides, one palm hovering over the walnut handle of his Colt.

"Now," he muttered.

She tossed the first plate high overhead, spinning it away from them in a shining arc. The wind caught it and flipped it end over end. She sent a second plate sailing after the first, followed by a third.

Hunter's gun hand flashed downward. In a blur of motion too fast for Della to follow, the Colt leaped into his palm. The muzzle lifted. The six-shooter roared. Three bullets, one after the other, hit the plates as they reached the zenith of their arcs. The bullets pegged the plates, pinging as the shots pierced the center of each dish. The targets tumbled over and over to the ground and lay mangled and bent in the grass.

Hunter dropped his Colt into its holster.

"Three more!"

Della hurled three more plates skyward. Once again, the weapon flashed and spit bullets. Each one found its target, making the dishes ring. The ruined tinware plummeted earthward.

77

The scout holstered his six-shooter. In rapid succession, he snatched the weapon from its case and fired the empty gun, then dropped it back into its sheath. He repeated the action over and over. The gun fit smoothly into his palm to become an extension of his hand.

At last, Hunter ceased his practice firing. He slid the empty casings from the revolver's chamber and plucked six bullets from the gun belt about his waist. While he fed the new rounds into the cylinder, frowning a little as he concentrated, Della stepped close.

"That was wondrous! I've never seen anything like it."

He glanced up, sliding the six-shooter into its holster. "That was nothin'. I usually don't have the opportunity to test the wind or control circumstances as I did just now. Usually, I have to fire off the back of a gallopin' horse."

"And do you normally hit your target?"

He lifted his hat, swiped a sleeve across his forehead, and returned the hat. He tilted the brim down over his eyes. He shrugged, then fisted his hands on his hips and looked across the range. "Boys who grow up in the West learn to shoot when they're young."

"I don't know much about the West, but if I were to guess, I'd say you have an exceptional gift with firearms."

Hunter glanced at her, shrugging again. "It's both a gift and a curse."

They stood in silence for several heartbeats, their gazes snared.

"Will you teach me?" Della finally asked.

He nodded. "One day, you may need that skill to save your life."

His words sent a shiver down her spine. Peril filled the journey ahead. Hardship and danger would be commonplace when they reached the Colorado Territory. Unless she elected to return to Boston, a six-shooter might be all that stood between her and death.

CHAPTER 10

DELLA SETTLED HERSELF ON THE curving rock and sighed with pure bliss. The boulder's surface still felt warm from the sun's rays, giving her the sensation of being wrapped in a wool blanket. She peeked back at the camp. No one had missed her. Toby bustled about the chuck wagon, cleaning up after the evening meal. The drovers who weren't guarding the herd lounged about the cook fire. Aunt Coral and Silvie busied themselves with Flossie's nighttime routine.

She had at least half an hour of solitude before dusk settled over the prairie. Bracing herself on her arms, she leaned back and lifted her face to the sky. She closed her eyes and luxuriated in this brief interlude of privacy.

They'd been on the trail for a week and a half, and quiet moments alone were elusive. Della congratulated herself for managing to escape this evening unnoticed.

She opened her eyes and straightened. The water beckoned. The stream purled along the edge of the rock with a soothing murmur. She imagined the cool current bathing her feet. It would be a rare treat to dangle her bare toes in the stream. Cutting another glance at the camp, she saw no one had yet missed her. She could do as she pleased.

Before she had second thoughts, Della pulled off her riding boots and her socks. She eased down the boulder's surface and edged closer to the creek. Here, the rock broke away in a steeper decline, pitching toward the water. A crevice scored the side. Scooting along like an inchworm, she eased toward the water, her toes scrabbling for purchase.

She lost her balance. Plummeting headlong, she tumbled over the ridges of rock into the water. Her right foot caught in the crevice and twisted painfully before jerking loose.

Flinging out both hands to break her fall, she plunged headfirst beneath the water. Her palms slapped against the streambed. The water closed over her, tugging her down into its icy depths. Darkness engulfed her. Her lungs burned while the current rolled her over and over. She banged into the sand and rocks that littered the creek's floor. Panic lanced her as she struggled to halt her wild tumbling. An overwhelming urge to scream made her swallow water. She choked.

When she thumped into a small boulder, she grabbed at an outcropping of rock and hung on. Sputtering and flailing, she flipped upright. Her feet scrabbled for purchase. When she could stand, she fought to keep her head and shoulders above the surface. She coughed and spit out mouthfuls of muddy water, then dragged in deep breaths of air as she staggered toward the bank. The muck sucked at her feet, as if to drag her down.

Della reached the creek's edge and toppled onto the sand. Her breath rasped in the silence. Panting, she lay without moving for several moments before she rolled onto her back and sat up. Water plastered her hair to her scalp and cascaded down her clothing. She shivered, then took stock of her limbs. Her wrist throbbed, and her right foot ached. She peeked at it. Scratches where the rock had abraded her skin oozed blood. Her ankle had begun to swell, and sharp pain seared the injury. She grimaced.

She glanced again toward the camp. She'd have to hobble or crawl until she got close enough to call for help. Gritting her teeth, she grabbed the boulder and levered herself upright. Agony in her wrist and ankle sliced through her. She caught her breath and stood motionless, waiting for the pain to ease.

Muffled hoofbeats caught her attention. Della turned her head toward the sound.

Shane Hunter, sitting relaxed in the saddle, rode along the water's edge on his way to the camp. When he drew abreast of her, he halted his mustang and leaned down to rest an elbow on his saddle horn. With his other hand, he thumbed back his cowboy hat, then squinted at her. "If I were a gamblin' man, I'd wager you took a tumble into the creek."

Mortified that he should see her in such condition, Della tried for a haughty air. "I merely thought to cool my feet in the stream."

His skeptical expression told her she hadn't fooled him. His gaze traveled from the top of her dripping hair down to her bare toes. "Uh-huh. And I suppose the water just happened to splash all over you when you put your feet in. And from the looks of your ankle, it beat you up in the meantime."

Della's shoulders slumped, and she leaned against the boulder to ease her weight from her injured foot. "If you must know, I fell off this rock. I truly did want to soak my feet."

Hunter swung down from the saddle, dropped the reins, and sauntered toward her with his easy stride. He drew near, all muscled grace. Her heart hitched. The air shifted with his approach.

He pulled up a handspan from her and looked down. Their gazes locked. His expression tightened, betraying the yearning neither could deny or admit. He reached out, curled his fingers about her injured hand, and lifted it without his scrutiny leaving her face. "Miss Hughes." His voice rasped, ragged and tight.

Della couldn't reply, not sure what he wanted from her.

At last, he broke the connection smoldering between them and turned his attention to her wrist. Cradling the injured member in his large hand, he examined the bruised and swollen area. "Looks like a sprain. Let's sit you down and take a look at that ankle." With chivalrous solicitude, he released her hand. Gripping her by the shoulders, he eased her down onto the grass and propped her against the boulder. He crouched beside her, twisted toward her foot, and prodded the purpling bruise with gentle fingers.

Della winced.

Hunter glanced over his shoulder at her. "You've sprained your ankle as well as your wrist. You'll be spending the next few days riding in the chuck wagon with Toby."

She stared at the wrist she cradled in her lap. "I'll be bored to tears before the first day is over."

"I have something that might help you to heal faster." He rose and strode to his horse. After rummaging in his saddlebags, he returned with his canteen, a folded white cloth, a metal bowl, and a leather pouch. He squatted beside her, laid the articles on the grass, and unfolded the cloth.

"Do you always carry a medicine chest with you?"

"If I need medical attention when I'm riding the plains, I won't find a doctor within a hundred miles. I have to treat myself."

Della hesitated before she posed her next query. "Did you learn those skills when you lived with the Cheyenne?"

Hunter paused and glanced at her. Finally, he nodded. "Healing skills are passed down from one generation to another."

"Well, I'm certainly benefiting from your knowledge." Della watched while he cleansed the scratches on her foot with a section of the cloth dampened with water from his canteen. Next, he made a poultice by mixing herbs from the pouch with water and applied the dressing to her sprains. Finally, he bound her wrist and ankle with strips torn from the cloth.

When he finished, she wiggled her foot. A dull ache had replaced the sharp pain that had shot through the injury before Hunter's ministrations. "It feels better already. I don't think a doctor could have done as well."

Hunter shrugged. "Out here, we don't depend on doctors." He gathered the materials he'd used and returned them to his saddlebag.

While they'd been occupied with her injuries, the sun had fallen over the horizon. Twilight cloaked the earth, and shadows pooled beneath the cottonwood trees lining the stream. Della shivered again. Her damp clothing clung to her with icy fingers.

Hunter untied his black duster from the roll behind his saddle and shook it out. He strode toward her. "You're cold. Let me wrap you in my coat, and we'll get you to your wagon." He stooped and curved an arm about her shoulders, then lifted her to her feet and propped her against the rock. "Keep your weight off that foot."

Della shifted her weight to her good foot and put one hand against the boulder for balance. Hunter wrapped his duster around her like a cocoon and buttoned her in. When he'd slipped the last button through its hole, he rested both hands on her shoulders, framing her neck with long fingers. His thumbs stroked the soft skin beneath her chin.

The planes of his face grew taut. The air between them heated until Della felt certain they'd be scorched from the emotion simmering beneath the surface. She thought he might kiss her, but instead, his hands slid from her shoulders and down her arms. The tight look left his face. When he spoke, the moment might never have happened.

"I'll take you directly to your wagon so you won't be a spectacle in the camp and will send your aunt to help you get settled." With that comment, Hunter scooped her up in his arms and tucked her head beneath his chin. Leading his gelding on a loose rein and cradling her against his chest, he carried her toward the camp.

Della closed her eyes and leaned against him. She wished she could stay in his arms, close to his heart, forever.

CHAPTER 11

"MISS HUGHES, YOU SHOULDN'T BE up. You'll damage your ankle," Captain Asher said. He hurried toward Della.

She waited for him to reach her. She rested her weight on her good leg and clutched the outside of her wagon bed for support. Late-afternoon breezes eddied about her, carrying the sweet scents of sun-warmed grass, wildflowers, and fresh air. Sunshine the color of champagne tinted the rolling landscape.

After several days spent lounging inside her wagon with her foot propped up, Della reveled in being outside.

The captain came to a standstill beside her. Though Della knew he'd spent the day in the saddle, his blue army uniform appeared as pristine as though he'd just donned it. He shoved his cavalry hat off his forehead. "Here. Lean on me." He curved an arm about her waist and drew her close against his side. "Let me take your weight."

Della leaned against him. Her arm stole about his back, and she gripped him to help her balance.

He tilted his head to peer into her face. His brown eyes gleamed with solicitation. "If you're ready, we'll head to the chuck wagon. I presume you were on your way to the campfire?"

"Yes. I couldn't abide another moment in my wagon. I thought I could make it to the fire on my own."

"Why didn't you call out to Toby? He could have helped you."

"He's busy preparing supper. I didn't want to bother him."

Captain Asher shook his head at her. "Hang on, now. Here we go."

When he'd tightened his grip on her, they stepped forward. Their uneven pace through the grass resembled the three-legged races Della had participated in as a child, and she couldn't prevent a giggle.

Captain Asher cocked an eyebrow at her. "What?"

"This takes me back to my childhood. During many a July Fourth celebration, I ran in three-legged races. I was always determined to win." She sighed. "I don't think we'd win any races tonight."

The captain looked at her in mock disbelief. "You don't think we could win a race? I'd say we make a splendid team." He halted their progress, then whirled her up against his chest, one arm beneath her knees and the other about her shoulders.

Della squeaked, gripping him around the neck. "What are you doing?"

"We're going to win this race." He dashed the remaining distance to the chuck wagon. When he reached the campfire, he stopped and let Della's feet slide down his length to the ground. With tender care, he lowered her to the grass and knelt beside her while she stretched out her injured leg.

"All right. I admit we can win a race." Leaning back and bracing herself on her outstretched arms, being careful not to put too much weight on her injured wrist, Della smiled at him.

The captain grinned, his eyes dancing. "I usually win at whatever I set my mind to."

Though he spoke in a light tone, Della guessed he was warning her he intended to win her hand.

"Miss Hughes, I hope this accident has shown you the folly of frontier life. For women such as those in the wagon train back in Kansas City, frontier life might be something to aspire to, but for you, a gently bred young lady accustomed to genteel society, this life is far too rough and dangerous. To say nothing of being primitive."

Della glanced at his earnest countenance, then dropped her gaze to her feet. She pretended to be absorbed in a study of her injured, shoeless foot. With her ankle still swollen, she couldn't fit a shoe onto her foot, so she wore only socks and slippers.

"Miss Hughes, I must press my suit. A marriage to me would give you the life to which you're accustomed."

Della abandoned her inspection of her slippers and brought her attention back to his face. His handsome face, she admitted. Why couldn't she feel moved by his declaration? Any young lady of her acquaintance in Boston would swoon at the prospect of marriage to the wealthy, well-connected cavalryman. She drew breath. "I'm honored that you desire to make me your wife, but I cannot commit to a relationship with you. I'm not at all sure that I want to return to society life."

"How could you prefer this"—his arm swept out to encompass the prairie's expanse—"to life in polite society?" The lowering sun gilded his puzzled features.

At that moment, Toby, a wiry grizzle-haired man with an enormous black handlebar mustache, rattled the dishes to remind them they weren't alone. He stomped over to the fire and stirred the stew bubbling in the cast-iron pot hanging from a tripod over the flames. Muttering to himself, he turned his back on them and returned to the chuck wagon and the biscuits he was making.

His interruption silenced their conversation. Captain Asher plucked a blade of buffalo grass and rolled it between his thumb and forefinger, eyes downcast.

Sensing he had more to say, Della waited.

An uneasy expression crossed his face when he lifted his gaze to her once again. "Since we're at an impasse regarding our courtship, I must speak to you about a different topic. I haven't had an opportunity for private conversation with you since that Sunday you were washing clothes in the river."

Della waited, not commenting.

"Looking back, I see that my attitude toward Silvie was inconsistent with the spirit of equality that characterizes the West. Reflection has shown me that the division of social class that's normal in Europe isn't as distinct out here. I know I appeared at a disadvantage to you."

Della looked at him. His expression seemed earnest. "Silvie may have been born a slave, but she's been a free woman for most of her life. She's like a mother to Aunt Coral, and we've taken her into our family as one of us."

"I see that now. I'm truly sorry for my comments."

"You might want to tell Silvie."

The captain hesitated. "I've never apologized to a freed slave before. I've never apologized to anyone beneath me socially before. You expect too much."

"If you're truly sorry, Silvie should hear it from you."

"A man has his pride."

Della kept silent, letting him wage his own battle. Only he could make this right. When she thought he'd turn away without promising to settle his wrong with Silvie, he glanced at her again.

"It won't be easy, but I'll apologize to Silvie."

"Thank you. She'll be most appreciative of your kindness."

Relief crossed his face. "I'm grateful to be back in your good graces."

Della smiled at him. "You're a rascal, Captain Asher. A very charming rascal."

He grinned. "A charming rascal is an improvement over what you must have been thinking of me these days past."

"I'm sure it is."

"I'll be content with that for now, but I'm hoping for more in the future."

"You're a persistent, charming rascal."

"Persistent and hoping to win your hand and heart."

Della shook her head, smiling at his audacity in spite of herself.

Toby rang the gong to call those men who weren't riding guard on the horse herd. A general rush toward the tail of the chuck wagon ensued.

Aunt Coral, with Flossie perched in her arms, strolled toward her niece. "It's good to see you here with the rest of us. I'm glad you felt well enough to join us for dinner."

Della cut a glance at her companion. "Captain Asher was kind enough to help me."

The captain had risen at Aunt Coral's approach. Now, he executed a bow as courtly as though they graced a ballroom floor.

"Your niece was determined to get some fresh air, so what kind of gentleman would I be if I'd let her hobble here on her own? And I'll fill her dinner plate, if she'll be so kind as to allow me the privilege."

"Of course. How can I refuse such an offer?" Della smiled at him.

Several evenings later, Della sat on the ground, leaning against the front wheel of her wagon, her legs stretched out. Shane Hunter knelt beside her, examining her injured foot. He'd checked her sprained appendage each night after he returned to camp, administering a fresh poultice and putting on a clean wrapping.

Della studied his profile while the examination absorbed his attention. Her gaze moved from his face, down his strong neck, and over his muscled shoulders. She thought back to her beaux in Boston. Shane Hunter might not be able to take a turn about a dance floor, but he made the men of her acquaintance appear insipid by comparison. Not one of them could administer the aid Hunter had given her or manage the rigorous schedule the scout maintained. Nor could any of her beaux ramrod the wagon train and guide them across the plains to the Colorado Territory.

His callused fingers probed her ankle with gentle expertise. He tipped back his head to look into her face. "The swellin' is almost gone, though your foot is an interestin' shade of yellow. In a couple more days, you might be able to wear your ridin' boots." A smile deepened the creases about his mouth and crinkled the corners of his eyes.

His smile did odd things to Della's insides. Her heart flopped in her chest, and her pulse quickened. She swallowed. "Thanks to you."

He shrugged. "You have a healthy constitution and a strong spirit. That helped."

"And your remedies." Hunter had been teaching her something of the herbs and roots used by the Cheyenne for healing. "I hope to someday know enough about your kind of medicine to help me once we reach Uncle Clint's ranch."

Stillness settled over him while he pinned her with a penetrating stare. A heartbeat of silence pressed between them. "You're thinkin' of stayin' in the West, then?"

His intensity scattered Della's thoughts, leaving her feeling like a green schoolgirl. She grabbed at her composure and tried not to stammer. "I-I'm considering it. I'm not sure a life in Boston would suit me anymore."

"You're determined—I'll give you credit for that. And you're learnin'."

"You're a most capable teacher."

Hunter held her gaze for a moment longer before he turned his attention once more to her foot without acknowledging her compliment. "You don't need a poultice anymore. I'll just wrap your ankle."

Della concealed a sigh of frustration. Her intuition told her that Hunter returned her interest, but for reasons she couldn't imagine, he refused to acknowledge their mutual attraction or pursue her. His resistance made her determined to win him over. Somehow, she'd find a way.

CHAPTER 12

DELLA DISMOUNTED WITH EASY GRACE and loosened the saddle girth. Now that her ankle had healed, she'd begun riding again with the cowboys.

After unsaddling her mare, she rubbed the horse down with a handful of grass and turned her loose. The chestnut ambled away toward the herd, shaking her head and switching her tail.

Della hefted her tack, then carried her saddle, blanket, and bridle to the back of her wagon and lowered them to the ground. In the weeks since they'd left Kansas City, she'd toughened up, and now, dismounting from a position astride seemed as natural as if she'd never needed a mounting block. She could lift her own saddle without depending on the kindness of one of the drovers to do it for her. Those simple accomplishments filled her with immense satisfaction.

After stowing her rig in her wagon, Della continued to the chuck wagon. Weary drovers had begun to gather about the cook fire, waiting for Toby to give them the signal to begin the meal. She joined Aunt Coral and Silvie, standing close to the chuck wagon. Flossie squatted by the wheel, poking at something in the grass.

"Cousin Del, look!"

Della stooped beside the toddler, looking at the object that had captured Flossie's attention. A reddish ladybug clung to a blade of grass. "That's a ladybug, Flossie." Della tore the stalk off at the base and held it out. "Here you go."

Flossie took the blade and held it close. The insect crawled along the stalk, then took flight. Astonishment crossed Flossie's face. "Gone, Del." She waved the blade of grass.

"The ladybug flew away." Della patted Flossie's head and straightened.

At that moment, Toby gave the signal for supper to commence, and the cowboys lined up at the tail of the chuck wagon to get their tin plates and eating utensils.

After supper, the men relaxed, reclining on the grass while Toby cleaned the dishes and put away the remains of the meal. Some of the drovers pulled pipes from their pockets and lit them. Others cleaned their weapons. Some conducted murmured conversations.

Dusk settled over the prairie. In the fading light, the sky curved over the land in a dome of palest eggshell blue. Wild creatures settled down for the night. Mockingbirds called from the cottonwood trees lining the bank of the nearby stream.

Quentin Asher squatted beside Della, who sat on a wooden stool. He entertained her and Aunt Coral with tales from his life in Europe.

Toby appeared from the front of the chuck wagon, carrying his violin. "Are you gentlemen and ladies ready for some music?"

Captain Asher rose and stepped forward. "I, for one, would like to dance with this beautiful lady." He gripped Della's hand and pulled her to her feet. "Toby, can you play a waltz?"

In response, Toby lifted the violin, placed it beneath his chin, and ran the bow across the strings. After adjusting the tuning pegs, he launched into a Schubert waltz.

"Will you dance with me?" The captain turned Della toward him.

"It seems I have no choice," she said, though she smiled up at him.

Curving an arm about her waist and holding their clasped hands high, he swept her into the steps of the waltz. A moment later, Uncle Clint and Aunt Coral joined them. The drovers scooted to one side of the fire to make room for the dancing couples.

Quentin Asher was an accomplished dancer, but with his European diplomatic background, Della would have been surprised to find otherwise. Closing her eyes, she gave herself up to the pleasure of the dance, only half-aware of her uncle and aunt waltzing close by. When the music trailed away and the dance stopped, she opened her eyes to see her partner gazing down at her.

"You waltz divinely," he said.

"I could say the same about you." She stepped out of his arms and turned to the cook. "Toby, you're a master violin player. Why are you wasting your talents out here feeding hungry horse drovers instead of using your musical abilities?"

As if embarrassed by her compliment, he looked down and scuffed the toe of one boot in the grass. Finally, he shrugged and glanced up at her. "Being a musician is a risky business. I like to get paid regular."

"Well, we're certainly benefiting from your talents."

At that moment, Flossie, who had been standing beside Silvie, launched herself at her father's knees. "Me, too, Papa."

Uncle Clint scooped up his daughter and whirled her about. "Toby, how about another tune? One more appropriate for a two-year-old."

Once again setting the violin beneath his chin, Toby drew the lively notes of "Oh! Susanna" from his instrument while Uncle Clint lifted Flossie high and cavorted about the fire. She giggled and shrieked, her fingers gripping her father's hair. At the end of the song, the general returned his daughter to her mother. "Off you go, imp. It's bedtime for two-year-olds."

Aunt Coral bore their daughter away to the wagon while Flossie wailed. "More, Papa."

While they'd danced, darkness had crept across the land, stealing the light from the sky. The drovers appeared as shadowed shapes circling the cooking pit. The fire painted the wagons' white canvas tops a flickering copper.

Rusty shouldered his way closer to the cook fire. "I think it's time for a song from my trusty harmonica." After fishing the instrument from his shirt pocket, he drew it across his lips. A warbling scale sounded. Slouching on one leg with both hands cupping the harmonica, he took a breath and began to play. The tune of "Sweet Betsy from Pike" poured forth in sweet harmony, followed by "Bury Me Not on the Lone Prairie."

Entranced, Della watched, unable to believe the music Rusty drew from the simple instrument. "Rusty, that was beautiful," she said when he finished. "I didn't know a harmonica could sound like that."

"My daddy taught me. In the evenings, we'd all sit on the porch, and my daddy would play." He stuffed the harmonica back into his shirt pocket and turned to Della. In two strides, he reached her side and caught up her hand. "Toby, how about a reel? I have a hankering to kick up my heels."

Toby fiddled with furious abandon while Rusty whirled Della about, dipping and stomping. The other drovers clapped and whistled. At the end of the dance, Rusty tipped Della backward, bending her toward the ground. She gripped his arms and laughed up into his grinning face. When Rusty straightened and stood her upright, she laid one hand on her racing heart. Her breath rasped in shallow gasps.

"I think one dance with you is all I can manage."

Rusty chuckled. "Not every girl can keep up with me."

"I can see why."

"Thank you, Miss Della. You're a good sport."

Della turned away. Quentin Asher stood near the chuck wagon beside her uncle Clint and Emory Dyer, glowering at Rusty. Rusty ignored him and joined the other drovers. Not wanting to face the captain's misplaced displeasure over her dance with Rusty, she took refuge beside Silvie while her breathing returned to normal.

A movement in the darkness off to her left caught her attention. She squinted. A tall form took shape as a man approached the fire. Della's heartbeat sped up when she recognized Shane Hunter.

He moved into the circle of light cast by the flames and approached the chuck wagon. After snagging a tin mug off the makeshift table at the wagon's tail, he strolled to the cook fire and poured himself a cup of coffee from the battered pot resting on a flat rock beside the fire. He lifted the cup to his lips and drank, his back to her. As if he sensed her watching him, he pivoted. His gaze met hers through the firelight.

Toby had struck up another tune, and the drovers sang along, a bittersweet ballad about star-crossed lovers. The music faded away while Hunter and Della stared at each other. He sipped again, his gaze never leaving hers, his face framed by the black hat he'd thumbed back on his head. She forgot to breathe.

At last, he looked away.

Would he come over and talk to her? She'd scarcely seen him since the last time he'd changed the dressing on her ankle. She waited. Beside her, Silvie stirred.

"I'd best be heading to bed, Miz Della. Don't let these men keep you up too late."

"I won't."

Silvie turned toward the wagon where she slept. Captain Asher stepped to Della's side as soon as Silvie disappeared into the darkness.

"I must leave now for my shift riding herd. Otherwise, I'd ask for another dance."

"There'll be other nights for dancing. We still have a long way to go before we reach Uncle Clint's property."

"I'll claim every dance you'll give me."

When he'd vanished into the darkness, Della returned her attention to Shane Hunter. The scout had moved to stand beside her uncle and Lieutenant Dyer. The men appeared engrossed in a low-toned conversation. She wished Hunter would ask her to dance, but she supposed he didn't waltz. Perhaps he could do a country dance with her instead, though he seemed to have forgotten her. After a few moments of indecision, Della ambled toward the men. They broke off their conversation when she halted beside them.

"What bit of news has you men involved in such serious conversation?"

When the men exchanged somber looks but didn't reply, anxiety niggled at her. Della eyed the three of them. "What is it? What aren't you telling me?"

"You may as well tell her, Shane," her uncle said. "By tomorrow, the whole camp will know, since I'll have to alert the men."

Della turned to the scout. "Tell me what?"

"We're being trailed."

"Someone is following us? Who?"

Hunter shrugged. "I'm not sure, but I suspect they're rustlers, hoping to cut some of the horses out of the herd."

"Or just follow along behind and wait until we've reached the Colorado Territory," Uncle Clint said. "They'd be wise to let us do all the work and then haze out a few horses to sell once we get to my property."

"It appears that may be their plan, since they haven't made any attempt to overtake us."

"How long have they been following us?" Della asked.

"Almost from the time we left Kansas City. They're staying about half a day behind. I've spotted their campsites while I was scouting around. Today, I shadowed them while they followed us."

"How many are there?" She didn't bother to ask whether the riders had known Hunter was tracking them. They'd have seen him only if he permitted it.

"Three. They look like saddle bums."

"What I was doing was common knowledge around the stockyards in Kansas City," Uncle Clint said. "Anyone could have planned to rustle some of my horses."

Hunter nodded.

"I'll send Captain Asher's patrol after them tomorrow morning. It will be good experience for them, and a show of military force might deter whatever plans those saddle bums have."

"Whoever is trailing us knows they're outnumbered, so anything they try will be by stealth," Hunter said. "In their place, I'd let us do the work of moving the horses to the Colorado Territory. Once we reach your ranch, it will be easier for them to cut out a few mares and trail them over the Rockies to sell in California. There's a lucrative business moving stolen horses over the mountains and selling them further west, where they can't be traced."

"That sounds likely. Still, I'll warn the men and will double the night guard. As we get further west, the likelihood of encountering hostiles increases, as well."

CHAPTER 13

DELLA GLANCED AT EACH MAN standing around her. Their expressions appeared resolute yet unintimidated. "Between the cavalry detail and the men of Logan's Cavalry, the horses should be well protected," she said.

Uncle Clint nodded. "My men will protect you women and the herd with their own lives, if necessary."

"Mr. Hunter is teaching me to shoot." Della gestured toward Shane Hunter, who stood beside her.

"I appreciate that. It's wise for a woman to know how to handle a firearm here in the West," her uncle said. "Coral's brother taught her to use firearms, but she should brush up on her shooting. I'll supply both of you with a Colt in case you should need it."

Lieutenant Dyer grinned. "Just be sure you don't shoot one of the horses by mistake."

Della wrinkled her nose at him. "Mr. Hunter will turn me into a crack shot—just you wait." She turned to the scout. "Do you dance, Mr. Hunter?"

"If you mean, do I waltz or dance a reel, the answer is no."

"But surely, you must dance something."

"I don't think a Cheyenne sun dance is exactly what you have in mind."

"Oh, I see what you mean." Della eyed him with resolve. "I can teach you to dance. Toby will accompany us."

"I think not, Miss Hughes."

"Well, then, if you won't dance with me, will you at least take a stroll?"

Hunter met her gaze with a hard stare. At last, he nodded. "I'll accompany you on a stroll."

"Let me get my jacket. It will be cold away from the fire."

Hunter ambled beside her to her wagon and waited while she climbed in. She snatched up the sheepskin jacket and shrugged it on, then clambered over the wagon's tail and dropped to the ground.

"I must say, you've quite mortified me, Mr. Hunter," Della said when they'd left the wagons behind.

Hunter glanced down at her through the darkness. "And how is that, Miss Hughes?"

"I've never before had to beg a man to dance with me. Or even to stroll with me."

They took several strides in silence. "I'm not much used to keepin' company with beautiful young women. Scoutin' for the army doesn't give one much opportunity to polish one's social skills."

Della took note of the indirect compliment, though she didn't comment. Instead, she yearned to learn about the part of his life he kept secret. They didn't have the kind of intimacy that would allow her to pry, so she set about trying to discover the parts of his life he might be willing to share. "Uncle Clint said you'd served in the War Between the States."

"I was servin' as an army scout when the war broke out. Most of the regular army was sent back east to fight, so I went along. I knew how to fight, and I knew how to move about undetected. I spent most of the war collectin' information behind enemy lines and relayin' it back to my commanding officer."

"So, you were a spy!"

"I didn't consider it anything so dramatic. I simply collected information that would be valuable to the Union forces."

Della's admiration for Shane Hunter increased. He might downplay his role in the war, but she knew what would have happened to him had he been captured. He would have been executed for spying.

They crested a slight rise. The plains spread before them, indistinguishable in the blackness. The sky blazed with stars, millions of diamond chips glittering on a black velvet blanket. They seemed so close Della thought she could reach up and touch them. She tipped her head to look at the heavens. "I never knew there were so many stars."

Hunter followed her gaze. "The night sky is one of the things I love most about the West. And when there's a full moon, it seems like daylight."

Della peered at him. His features were a pale blur in the darkness. "When we first left Kansas City, I thought the dark would smother me. I think I'm adjusting to it now."

"Some people never get used to it. Not everyone is cut out for life in the West."

The steady tearing sound of horses cropping grass nearby brought a comforting normalcy to the moment. Then, the yips, barks, and ululating wails of a coyote pack over the rise shredded the tranquility of the night. Della shivered.

"That's something I'm not sure I'll get used to."

"Usually, coyotes give humans a wide berth."

"They sound wild and feral to me."

"They are wild and feral. Be thankful they're not wolves. Wolves are somethin' to be concerned about."

They listened while the coyotes' baying died. The night was silent once again.

"Were you born in the West?" Della wondered.

He shook his head. "My family hails from Philadelphia. I was born there."

He seemed willing to talk, so Della pressed on with another question, hoping he wouldn't rebuff her. "How did you end up out here?"

Hunter glanced away, pausing. "My father was a career officer in the army. He was sent west when the Indian troubles started after gold was discovered in California in '49. The tribesmen resented the horde of settlers that traveled through their territory on their way to the goldfields, so the army constructed and manned forts along the trails to keep the peace."

"An impossible task."

"A definite clash of cultures. The white man is invading territory the Indians have used for huntin' for decades. We continually break the treaties we've signed with them. It's bound to cause conflict."

"But aren't the Indians cruel and dangerous?"

Again, Hunter paused and looked away. He hesitated so long Della thought he wouldn't answer. "They can be but not always. In some cases, women and children have been adopted into the tribes. White women have married native men."

An air of impenetrability settled over him. He appeared to have reached the limits of what he'd allow her to question. Still, Della's curiosity prompted her to push with one more inquiry. "Mr. Hunter, I can't help but wonder . . . why haven't you married?" She turned to face him fully.

He swung his head toward her. "I'm not a marryin' sort of man," he said, his tone gentle.

"Surely, you must want a wife and family."

"Not all of us are so fortunate as to have such a blessin'. My life isn't the kind I can ask a woman to share."

"You do us women an injustice. Not every woman would shirk a life with you."

Hunter smiled, a regretful smile that pulled at the corners of his mouth and tugged at Della's heart. "You're very kind to say so, Miss Hughes, but you have no idea of what a life with me would entail. I can't ask a woman to endure that sort of hardship."

Della shook her head and started to protest, but Hunter reached out and covered her lips with gentle fingers.

"Shh . . . There are things you don't know or understand that make it impossible for me to marry." His hand dropped to his side.

"But . . ."

"No more questions. Just accept the fact that I can't marry. I came to terms with my lot in life a long time ago."

They'd reached an impasse. The attraction that thrummed between them every time they were together vibrated the air around them. Della stepped closer. Surprising even herself, she laid one hand against his cheek. Beneath her hand, she felt the warmth of his skin and the slight stubble of the day's growth of beard. His long fingers wrapped about her wrist. They stood unmoving for several moments, locked in a tableau they were powerless to break.

"May I ride with you tomorrow?" Della said at last.

"I leave before the wagon train stirs, and I get back after everyone else has eaten. Are you sure you're up to it?"

She nodded. "I won't slow you down."

"Very well." An unexpected grin flashed across Hunter's face. "And if you slow me down, I promise I'll leave you beside the trail for the wagons to pick up."

CHAPTER 14

A SERIES OF SHARP RAPS against the side of her wagon woke Della. She came to consciousness with a rush and sat up. Last night, Hunter had promised to wake her by tapping on the wagon's side.

Della thrust the covers down and scrambled from her bedroll. The icy air bit at exposed skin. Shivering, she dressed as quickly as possible and braided her hair. Fumbling in the darkness, she located her hat and jammed it on her head.

A thrill of anticipation shivered through her at the prospect of spending the day in Shane Hunter's company. The more time she spent with him, the more she longed to be with him and know him better. His life's secrets challenged her. His admission that he could never marry piqued her curiosity and made her determined to find out why he thought he should remain unwed. Perhaps that was why he never sought out her company nor tried to develop a relationship with her, though her feminine instincts told her that he was as attracted to her as she was to him. Neither of them could deny the mutual interest that pulled them together.

Della drew on her jacket and left the wagon. When she reached the cooking fire, Shane Hunter waited beside the coffeepot. He bent down, lifted a tin mug full of the brownish liquid from the rock on which it had rested, and handed the cup to her. Their gazes met through the flickering firelight.

"I wasn't sure you'd actually get up," he drawled.

"I said I wanted to ride with you today. I meant it. By the way, thank you for the coffee."

He toasted her with his mug and lifted it to his lips, watching her over the rim while he sipped.

She grimaced when the liquid's strong flavor hit her mouth. Swallowing, she shook her head. "This isn't exactly what I'd call coffee."

Hunter grinned. "Any cowboy will tell you that coffee isn't worth drinkin' unless you can float a horseshoe in it."

"If I had a horseshoe to put in this coffee, I'm sure it would float."

Toby appeared from one side of the chuck wagon and stirred the contents of the iron pot hanging from a tripod over the fire. A skillet of fried bacon sat to one side of the fire. "Breakfast is ready if you want to eat."

Della smiled at him. "Don't you ever sleep?"

"Don't need much sleep, Miss Della."

"It's a good thing, since you're up before any of us to fix our breakfast."

Just as Della reached the tail of the chuck wagon to get her plate, her uncle, Lieutenant Dyer, and several other drovers materialized out of the darkness, having just finished their shift riding guard over the horse herd. With her plate and fork in hand, she turned to face the men.

"Della! I'm surprised to see you up this early," Uncle Clint said when he stopped beside her. "Whatever could induce you to get out of bed before it was absolutely necessary?"

"I'm riding with Mr. Hunter today."

With a raised eyebrow, her uncle glanced at the other man. Hunter nodded. "Are you sure you won't be an impediment to Shane's scouting?"

"I can keep up with him."

Another glance at Hunter confirmed what Della said. "Well, then, as long as Shane is willing, I won't object." Her uncle leaned down and placed a quick kiss on her forehead. "Just be careful. Now, I'm off to get a bit of shut-eye before rising time."

They'd finished eating and Hunter had gone to catch up their horses when Quentin Asher and his patrol appeared. The captain hurried to Della's side while his cavalrymen prepared to eat.

"Miss Hughes, how fortunate that I should have the opportunity to see you before we leave. You can wish me Godspeed."

"I understand Uncle Clint wants you to find the men who are following us."

"Yes. I hope my patrol and I can rout out the rustlers."

"That would make us all feel much safer, and Uncle Clint will be relieved not to have outlaws trailing us."

"I'm sure I can deal with them."

Shane Hunter, leading both his horse and Della's, walked into the circle of firelight. He halted beside Della and handed her the reins of both mounts. "I'll fill up our canteens, and then, we'll be off."

A look of puzzled disapproval crossed Quentin Asher's face. "Miss Hughes, you're going out with this scout?"

She nodded. "I'm riding with Mr. Hunter today."

"I must object. It's neither safe nor proper for you to be alone with him all day."

"I'll be perfectly safe with Mr. Hunter, and Uncle Clint has given his permission."

"Still, I'm surprised you'd risk your reputation in such a manner."

Della tamped down a spurt of irritation at the captain's unwelcome interference. She'd given him no reason to believe he could dictate her actions. "My reputation will survive. Mr. Hunter is completely trustworthy."

"I implore you to refrain from riding with him."

Hunter had maintained his silence, letting Della deal with Quentin Asher, until the officer maligned his honor. "I reckon Miss Hughes is a woman grown and knows her own mind. I'll treat her with the respect a lady deserves."

Asher wheeled toward Hunter. "If you were a gentleman, you wouldn't allow her to sully her good name by spending the day alone with you."

Grim coldness settled over Hunter's features. "This isn't Paris, Captain. Out here, we don't quibble over such niceties."

"I refuse to withdraw my objection."

Hunter narrowed his eyes. "I didn't realize you were in a position to offer your objections over whom Miss Hughes spends her time with."

The captain drew himself up and lifted his chin. "Then, let me put you on notice that I hope to make Miss Hughes my wife. That gives me certain rights where she's concerned."

Della caught her breath. Quentin Asher presumed too much. She'd never promised to accept his proposal, and unless she did agree to plight her troth to him, she was free to do as she pleased. Protestations over his presumption filled her mind.

"Has Miss Hughes agreed to become your wife?" Hunter asked before she could voice her objections.

Asher hesitated. "No."

"Then, I fail to see how you have rights dictatin' to Miss Hughes what she can or can't do." Hunter cocked his head at Della. "Miss Hughes, do you wish to change your mind about our plans for today?"

"No. I want to ride with you."

"The lady has spoken. Our plans will remain unchanged."

Captain Asher clamped his mouth into a tight line, eyes flashing. He pivoted on his heel and stalked away.

Della trembled a little at the confrontation. The volatile tension between the two men hung as a palpable haze in the air. Although some of the friction between Hunter and Captain Asher might be because of her, there were other issues involved. Resentment over the scout's authority factored into Asher's hostility. Della couldn't do anything about that, but she could help by being honest with her suitor. She must make the captain understand he had no claim over her.

A gentle touch at her elbow recalled her to the present. She turned her head to see Hunter eyeing her with concern. "Are you all right?"

She nodded. "Yes. I'm sorry about that. Captain Asher has proposed marriage to me, but I haven't accepted his suit. He had no right to confront you."

Hunter shrugged. "I've faced down worse than him." He strode around to his mustang's side, rummaged in his saddlebags, and removed two canteens, then did the same with Della's mare. He filled their canteens with water from the wooden barrels lashed to the side of the chuck wagon and stowed them once again in their saddlebags.

Toby walked over to them with a cheesecloth-wrapped parcel. "Here are some biscuits and bacon for your lunch. I don't think Miss Hughes is ready for that venison jerky you eat when you're on the trail."

Grinning, Hunter accepted the packet. "If I wish to eat well, I should take Miss Hughes with me every day."

"Thank you, Toby," Della said. "I don't know what venison jerky is, but I'm sure your biscuits will be more palatable."

Toby bobbed his head. "Just you make sure that big galoot you're riding with remembers you're a lady. He may forget altogether. When you're saddle sore and need a rest, don't let him tell you he doesn't have time to stop."

Della smiled, cutting a glance at Hunter. "I'll remember."

"I've already warned Miss Hughes that if she slows me down, I'll leave her beside the trail for the wagons to pick up," Hunter said.

Toby waggled a bony finger beneath the taller man's nose. "You know better than that. If I find you've treated her rough, I'll take a horsewhip to your hide."

Hunter lifted both hands, palms out. "You've made your point. Now, unless you have more fatherly instructions for me, we'd best be on our way."

While Hunter stashed the packet of food in his saddlebags, Della mounted her mare. Hunter toed for his stirrup and swung a long leg over the back of his gelding. They left the camp and skirted the horse herd, heading west.

Hunter's grulla mustang set the pace at a fast walk. They rode without speaking until the sky lightened to a silvery sheen. Landmarks began to show as distinct shapes in dawn's pearly light. At the base of a sloping bluff, Hunter halted his mount.

"We'll take a breather here." He swung down from the saddle.

Della dismounted and stretched, grateful to have her feet on the ground. They'd been riding for three hours, and she was ready for a break.

"Are you thirsty?"

"A little."

"Just take a few swallows."

She stepped to the back of her saddle, rummaged in the saddlebag, and found the canteen. She unscrewed the lid and lifted the flask to her lips. Though the water was tepid, the liquid refreshed her parched throat. She replaced the lid and returned the canteen to the pouch attached to the back of her saddle. When she turned around, Hunter was just putting away his own flask.

"What now?"

"We wait. When the sky has brightened some more, I'll reconnoiter a bit before we move out." Hunter dropped his reins, ground-tying his mount, and stepped around his horse's head.

Della joined him. "You do this sort of thing every day?"

"Yes. I scout ahead to find the best route to take the horses, find waterin' places, and look for Indian sign. When I get back to the wagon train at night, I let your uncle know the best way to go the next day. And if I've seen Indian sign in the area, I let him know that so he can warn the men."

"And have you seen any Indian sign?"

"Nothin' less than two days old."

When the sun had crested the distant edge of the earth and lightened the sky, Hunter indicated the ridge before them. "I'll ride to the top of that bluff and see what's up ahead." He gathered his reins.

"I'll come, too."

They mounted and turned their horses up the ridge. With their hooves digging into the earth, the horses scrambled up the incline. Before they reached the top, Hunter reined in his gelding and gestured for Della to do the same.

"Never show yourself against the skyline." He dismounted and let loose his reins.

Della slid from her mare and joined the scout. He dropped to his belly and inched along on his elbows, squirming through the grass to the top of the bluff with Della at his side. When they reached the top, he put a finger to his lips and shook his head, motioning for silence. She nodded. Mouthing "Stay here," he removed his hat and laid it in the grass beside her.

She watched while he crawled to the crest and peered over, just enough so his eyes cleared the ridge. He lay there unmoving until she thought her limbs would go numb. Finally, he turned to her and motioned her up beside him. Della scrambled the last few feet to the summit, halted beside Hunter, and peered over.

The vast, treeless vista of the plains spread before them, stretching away until the land met the sky. At first glimpse, the grassy range appeared flat, but after studying the panorama below, Della saw bluffs, coulees, and washes rumpling the surface of the earth. Cottony clouds cast their shadows across the land. The hot wind, sliding down from the mountains to the west, kissed her face and tugged at the brim of her horseman's hat. It brought with it the scents of summer and sun-warmed grass.

"This country constantly amazes me," she whispered. "It seems so lonely yet so beautiful."

"It has its own kind of beauty, but it's a harsh and unforgivin' land. Never forget that."

"Do you see anything that looks suspicious?" she asked.

"No. I'll watch for a few more minutes, and if everything looks clear, we'll go. The disadvantage is that an army could hide in any of those coulees down there."

When Hunter was satisfied it was safe to proceed, they backed down the slope to their waiting horses. He retrieved his hat, and they mounted. Squatting on their haunches, their horses slid down the steep incline to the bottom of the bluff. Della let her mare pick her own way down the grade, trusting her mount to find the best way.

They reached level ground. Hunter reined his gelding to the left. "I don't want to take the horse herd and the wagons over that bluff, so we'll have to find a way around."

Trotting her mare beside his mustang, Della realized there was no place she'd rather be at that moment than exploring this untamed land in the company of the strong, capable man at her side. The day stretched before her, offering limitless opportunity and adventure.

CHAPTER 15

ABOUT MIDMORNING, DELLA SHED HER jacket. She rolled up the sheepskin coat and tied it behind her saddle. From a brassy sky, the sun beat down with relentless intensity, making her glad her hat protected her face from sunburn. A trickle of sweat ran from her hairline down her cheek, and the back of her neck was damp. She'd never before felt such heat.

"Does it ever rain out here?" She swiped at the offending moisture on her face with the tails of the bandana tied about her neck.

Hunter gave her a sideways look, then stared ahead over his mustang's ears. "Just wait until you experience a plains summer storm. One can blow up in a matter of minutes and leave havoc behind. It will be an experience you won't forget."

"Do you think we'll have a storm before we reach the Colorado Territory?"

He sent her another glance. "If we have only one, we'll be fortunate."

Just then, several prairie chickens exploded with a whoosh and thunder of wings from the buffalo grass ahead of them. Della's mare shied and leaped sideways. Della rode out the shy and remained in the saddle. When she'd quieted her mare, they swung back alongside Hunter's gelding.

"Well done, Miss Hughes."

"I'm glad I wasn't riding sidesaddle." She hesitated, wondering what Hunter's reaction would be to her next request. "Mr. Hunter, would it be terribly presumptuous of me if I asked you to call me by my first name? 'Miss Hughes' sounds much too formal."

Their horses took several strides before Hunter replied. He favored her with a long look. "I'll call you Della if you'll do the same."

Della giggled. She couldn't resist teasing him. "Very well. If you insist, I shall also call you Della. It seems an odd request, and I do hope we won't confuse the rest of our party." She tossed him a cheeky grin.

For a moment, Hunter maintained his impassive expression before his lips twitched; then, he cast her a sideways glance and broke into a full-throated chuckle. "Well played, Miss Hughes."

He paused, and the smile they shared set Della's heart pounding.

"I'd be pleased if you'd use my given name. Not too many people call me Mr. Hunter. Every time you address me as Mr. Hunter, I want to look around, wondering who you're talking to." The twinkle in his eyes told her he jested.

She grinned back at him. "Very well. I'll call you Shane, and you can address me as Della."

They took their nooning in the shade of cottonwoods growing along a wide stream. After letting their mounts drink their fill, Shane hobbled both horses and loosened their girths before he removed their bridles. While the horses grazed, he and Della sat on the riverbank and ate the lunch Toby had packed for them.

"If we eat all of this now, what will we have for supper?" Della asked.

"Well, now, I could feed you some of that venison jerky Toby mentioned. Or I can shoot a rabbit and roast it. Have you ever tasted rabbit, Della?"

"Rabbit? No, I can't say that I have."

"Tonight, I'll introduce you to one of the delicacies of the West. We'll have roasted jackrabbit."

Della wrinkled her nose. "Will it taste better than venison jerky?"

She distrusted the grin Hunter gave her. "Much better."

"Why do I get the feeling you're about to have a jest at my expense?"

"You'll see that I've told the truth after you've tasted roast jackrabbit."

Della shook her head at him, though she couldn't hide her smile.

After he finished his lunch, Hunter rose and paced along the stream's bank. Della swallowed the last bite of bacon and took a swig of water from the canteen before she joined him.

"What are you looking for?"

"This stream has quicksand. I'm looking for the safest place to take the horses and the wagons through."

"Quicksand! Will we be able to get safely across?"

"As long as we keep moving, we'll manage, but we can't let the horses or oxen stop in midstream." He squatted, studying the sluggish current. When he rose, he cast a glance at the sloping riverbank. "I think there will be the best place to cross." He gestured to a spot near where they stood.

After they mounted, Hunter led the way down the bank to the place he'd chosen for the herd and the wagons to cross. His mustang waded into the stream without hesitation. The water rose around the gelding's belly.

Her mare followed with only a moment of unwillingness and splashed into the river. Looking down, Della watched the water climb higher with each step her mount took until the liquid lapped at her boots. She raised her legs to avoid wetting her footwear. Halfway across, her mare panicked at the quicksand sucking on her hooves. She flailed, her thrashing legs sending geysers of silver drops shooting upward. Floundering, the horse fought to maintain her footing. Della struggled to stay aboard and keep the chestnut moving.

Shane's grulla scrambled up the opposite bank, and the scout wheeled his mustang. When he saw Della's mare wallowing in the current, Shane heeled his mount. The horse plunged into the stream, spraying water with each leaping stride. In moments, they reached Della's side. Shane leaned down and grabbed her mare's reins. He turned his gelding and led them to the bank.

They reached safety. Of their own accord, the horses halted and stood with heads lowered, blowing, while water streamed from their sides and legs. Shane loosened his grip on Della's reins and looked at her.

She glanced at him, intending to thank him, but the tormented expression in his eyes made what she'd been about to say fly out of her head. Della forgot she'd been drenched in their mad plunge through the stream.

Neither spoke.

The rustling leaves from the cottonwood trees growing along the bank and a magpie scolding from the branches were the only sounds to intrude upon the moment.

Shane stretched out a hand and touched her cheek with gentle fingers, as if to convince himself she was unharmed. "I thought you'd go under. Once the quicksand gets you, it doesn't take long to suck you down."

"You would have pulled me out."

He nodded, wearing a grim expression. "Or died trying."

"Thank you. I think you may have saved my life."

"You might have gotten your mare across, but I've seen horses and oxen panic while crossing a stream such as that one and balk. When they stop, the quicksand traps them and sucks them under. Once, a wagon and a whole team of oxen disappeared beneath the sand that way."

About the middle of the afternoon, they rounded the side of a sloping bluff. The plains unrolled before them, level for several miles. Della caught her breath at the sight of shaggy bison spread over the plains, grazing on the rich grasses. The great, shaggy beasts darkened the prairie, their heads down, their humped backs draped in curly hair.

"There must be hundreds of them," she breathed.

"Right now, there are. In fifteen years, they'll be nothing but a memory."

Della shifted in her saddle, glancing at Shane. "Why do you say that?"

"Hide hunters and sport hunters slaughter thousands of buffalo each year. The army understands that as long as there are buffalo, the tribes will remain strong, so our military encourages the killing of buffalo. Indians use every part of a buffalo and only kill as many as they need, but we white men slaughter them and leave them to rot, taking only the hide."

Della surveyed the prairie again, trying to imagine the land empty of the beasts. "What a tragedy." She looked over at Shane. His eyes had a far-away expression, and his face was grim. She wondered at his thoughts. She guessed the sight of the bison evoked powerful memories of his life with the Cheyenne.

At that moment, both horses lifted their heads and pointed their ears toward something to their right. Shane scanned the landscape for whatever had caught the horses' attention. A cavalcade of a dozen mounted Indian warriors filed down a low hill about a quarter of a mile distant.

"Ease your mare back behind this bluff."

Della caught the urgency in Shane's low voice. Without questioning him, she backed her mount until the bluff they'd just rounded hid them from view.

Shane stepped from the saddle and rummaged in his bags, then pulled out a small pair of field glasses. "Come with me."

Della got down and followed when he scrambled up the low bluff. Near the top, he dropped onto his stomach and wormed his way to the summit. After removing his hat, he peered over. Using the field glasses, he swept the landscape below.

Della crept up beside him and whisked off her own hat. Below, the warriors galloped among the fleeing buffalo, who thundered across the plains, tails up. Shots rang out, and a buffalo cow near the back of the herd dropped. Another cow nearby stumbled and fell. A third cow collapsed onto the grass, legs flailing. Della watched as each warrior ran his pony alongside a cow and fired down upon the beast. The herd vanished over a distant rise with the hunters still among them. A pang for the slaughtered buffalo filled her.

Shane lowered the field glasses.

"Who were they?" Della asked.

"That was a Lakota hunting party."

"How can you tell they're Lakota?"

"They're shorter and darker than Cheyenne. And the beadwork on their clothing is Sioux."

"I have so much to learn."

"You'll have to learn it another time. We need to leave before they come back to dress out those cows."

Shane rode with caution while backtracking along the path the hunting party took toward the buffalo, his rifle across his knee and the thong over his six-shooter's handle loosened. Not wanting to disturb him, Della didn't try to talk. They covered several miles before he was satisfied they wouldn't stumble upon a Lakota encampment when the wagon train came this way.

"Tell me what you see," Della finally begged. "How do you trail them?"

Shane halted his gelding and slid his Winchester into the rifle scabbard. He stacked both hands on the pommel. Then, leaning down, he pointed to where the grass had been flattened. "That's where their horses walked. They rode in single file, so there's only one trail, and if we hadn't seen them, we wouldn't know how many were in their party. They came from the north. I don't have time to track them all the way to their camp."

"Would you have kept tracking if I wasn't with you?"

Shane looked at her and shrugged. "Perhaps. It would depend on how far I had to trail them. I wouldn't go so far that I couldn't get back to the wagon train to warn your uncle."

"Tell me what else you see when you track them. If we hadn't seen them, how would you know this trail was made by horses?"

He sent her a piercing look as if trying to gauge the sincerity of her interest. "The direction of the grass will tell you if a man walked there or a horse. A man will flatten the grass forward. A horse will kick it back behind him in the direction he came from."

"I'll remember. And I'll remember whatever else you teach me." She settled back in her saddle, her hands resting on the horn, and scanned the range. The vast, treeless, rumpled plain stretched as far as she could see. The limitless blue sky arced overhead. The immensity diminished her, leaving her feeling insignificant. She could love the land, but she feared it, as well. She had so much to learn if she wanted to survive on this frontier.

They ate their supper beside a shallow stream. When they pulled up, Shane said, "I'm afraid supper will be venison jerky after all. The sound of a rifle shot carries a long way out here."

Della settled herself beside Shane and stretched out her legs, leaning against the bole of a cottonwood tree. Their shoulders brushed. The warm contact sent a delicious thrill down her side.

Shane cut a hunk of the dried meat with his knife and offered it to her. She took the jerky gingerly and turned it about in her fingers, studying it.

"Will I like it?"

"Try it and see."

Della took a small bite. The meat tasted salty but surprisingly good. She chewed, and the tough meat swelled in her mouth. She kept chewing. Shane grinned at her.

"A little of that goes a long way."

Della nodded, unable to speak. When her jaws ached, she swallowed. "I think one bite is enough for me."

"Suit yourself, but you'll be hungry before we get back to the camp."

"If I get hungry, you can cut me another piece."

They sat in companionable silence for a time while the sun dropped closer to the horizon and the shadows lengthened. After a bit, Shane roused and looked at her.

"Your uncle seems very fond of you."

"Yes. He's really more of a father to me than an uncle."

"And why is that?"

"My mother was Uncle Clint's older sister. She and my father were killed in a carriage accident when I was a little older than Flossie. I hardly remember them. Uncle Clint took me in and raised me, with help from my grandparents and boarding school."

"I'm sorry you never really knew your parents, but your uncle Clint is a fine man. He's done well by you."

"I know. I couldn't ask for more love even if he was my real father. And Aunt Coral has become like a mother since she married Uncle Clint." Della drew up her legs and wrapped her arms around her knees, canting her head to look into Shane's face. Curiosity burned within her. In this moment of sharing, she wondered whether he'd answer her questions. "Shane." His given name felt comfortable on her tongue, as if they'd been friends for a long time.

He glanced at her, a wary expression warning her he might shut her out again.

"Can't you tell me what happened?"

She didn't need to explain. They both knew what she meant.

For a long moment, he resisted. Della held her breath, not looking away from his face. He held her gaze without blinking.

"Why do you want to know?"

"I want to know you, to understand you. To know what made you the man you are."

He sighed and turned his head to stare at the chuckling stream. "It's not a pretty story."

"Tell me. I can bear it."

CHAPTER 16

"I WAS SEVEN YEARS OLD." Shane spoke in a low, ragged tone, as though the words were torn from him. "My father was a colonel and a career army man. Due to the Indian troubles, my mother and I stayed behind in Philadelphia when he was sent west. After a time, conditions seemed quiet enough for us to visit him at Fort Bridger, where he was stationed in southern Wyoming Territory."

Shane paused, and Della waited.

"We'd been at the fort for several weeks when the Indian trouble took a turn for the worse. My father and his troops were sent out to settle the trouble. Fearing for our safety, he put my mother and me on a stagecoach that was headed for Denver."

He eyed her again, his expression somber, one eyebrow lifted. "Are you sure you want me to continue?"

"Yes. Don't spare me. I can't understand the man you are now if you withhold anything."

"In my experience, most young ladies would rather swoon than sully their ears with my tale."

"I'm not 'most young ladies.'"

"I'm beginning to see that." The corners of his mouth quirked in a brief smile. Hunter took a breath. "A detail of twelve troopers rode out with the stagecoach to provide protection. Traveling with us were the wives and children of some of the other officers, a journalist, and a doctor. The journalist was planning to write a series of stories on the wild West for the eager public back east."

From Shane's tone, Della gathered the journalist had never written his stories.

"We were three hours from the fort when we were ambushed by a Cheyenne war party twice the size of our army detail. In those days, there were no repeating rifles, so the cavalrymen were at a disadvantage."

Shane paused again, his features tight. "It was over in a matter of minutes. The men put up a good fight, but they were no match for the Cheyenne. Everyone was brutally slaughtered. My mother shielded me with her body, but I saw enough to give me nightmares for months."

Della sucked in a breath, her imagination filling in the details he'd omitted. The attack had been more violence than any seven-year-old boy should have experienced. She laid a sympathetic hand on his arm. "And your mother? What happened to her?"

"My mother was fortunate, if you can call being taken captive fortunate. My mother is a lovely blond woman, and the chief took a fancy to her. She refused to be parted from me, so the chief indulged her. He allowed me to live. We were thrown across the back of one of the stagecoach horses and taken to the Cheyenne village."

"The Lord protected you and kept you alive."

Shane nodded. "If it hadn't been for God's mercy, my mother and I could easily have been slaughtered. Instead, the women and children were spared, and we were all taken to the chieftain's encampment."

While they'd talked, dusk had settled across the plains. A salmon-colored wash streaked the sky. The calls of mockingbirds roosting in the cottonwoods filled the air with music. The evening's peace mocked Shane's tale. Della still clutched his arm, but she didn't loosen her hold.

"The life of a captive white woman isn't easy. A captive is treated as a slave. My mother suffered, but the Lord protected us in the village." Shane paused. "I'm not sure how to put this to a sheltered young lady, but you've no doubt heard about what society politely terms 'a fate worse than death.'"

Della's face heated. "Yes."

119

"Any white woman captured by the tribes can expect such a fate, multiple times, with many of the braves. Which is why men out here warn their women to save one bullet so they can take their own lives in order to prevent such a fate."

"Your mother?"

"My mother had no weapon, so it wasn't possible for her to shoot herself. She could have used a sharp tool to end her life, as she was put to work skinning the hair from the buffalo hides. But my mother is a God-fearing woman. She believed it was wrong to take her own life. And she feared what would have happened to me had she killed herself. So, she lived. In the Lord's sovereignty, the chief who had taken a fancy to her offered to marry her. He protected her from the other men, so she never experienced the fate most other white women endure."

"Did she marry him?"

"She did what she had to do to survive. She married him, and she adapted to tribal life. By Cheyenne standards, her husband was kind to her. She had an exalted position in the tribe, since she'd married the head chief. As for me, he loved my mother so much he adopted me. I became his own son. If I'd stayed with the tribe, I would have been the chief one day."

"Shane. What an honor!"

"It could have turned out much worse. After a while, I became completely immersed in Cheyenne culture. I forgot my American way of life. If it hadn't been for my mother, I would have forgotten how to speak English. She made me speak English to her so I didn't forget. She helped me memorize Bible verses and taught me Bible stories to counter the animism of the Cheyenne religion."

"She must be a very wise woman."

"She is. The verse she took to heart during her captivity and that gave her courage was 'I will never leave thee, nor forsake thee.' God's promise to always be with her got her through all those years when we lived with the tribe. She never felt abandoned by the Lord."

He paused again, and Della sensed the next part of his tale wouldn't be easy. She squeezed his arm.

"My mother had three children by her Cheyenne husband. I have a half brother and a half sister. One child died in infancy. My brother is eight years younger than me, and my sister is a young woman."

"It must seem odd to you."

"Not really." Shane shrugged. "I'd forgotten I was white. All the other Cheyenne families had brothers and sisters." He took a swallow from his canteen. "When I was sixteen, we were rescued by soldiers who happened upon our village when the warriors were away on a hunting expedition. My mother refused to leave her children behind, so all of us were taken back to the fort. Since our bodies hadn't been among those discovered in the stagecoach after the attack, my father had never given up hope that one day we'd be found." He shook his head. "You can imagine his shock when my mother returned to the fort with two half-Cheyenne children."

"It must have been very difficult for him."

"It was. My father is a godly man, so he didn't blame my mother for what had happened to her, but they struggled with their marriage. It took a while, but they finally worked through all that. I'm sorry to say I was a trial. Perhaps it was the violence of the stagecoach attack, but most memories of my real father had been wiped clean. I felt no connection to him, and I resented his taking the place of my Cheyenne father. I wanted to go back to the village. My Cheyenne father had been teaching me everything a warrior should know and preparing me to lead his people, when suddenly, I was ripped loose from all that was familiar and thrust into a way of life completely foreign to me."

As if unable to remain still, Shane surged to his feet and stood with his back to Della. She scrambled up and moved close. Her hand hovered over his back for a moment before she laid her palm against the tense muscles beneath his deerskin shirt. She felt him take a shuddering breath.

"I watched the white men and women shun my mother for what happened to her. They blamed her for marrying a tribesman. Those self-righteous people looked down on her for even being alive. According to white society, she should have done the decent thing and killed herself. A white woman who has lived with an

Indian man is considered no better than a woman of the streets. They were especially unkind to my brother and sister. So, I caused trouble. I was rebellious. I defied my father and spat in the faces of the people at the fort for how they treated my mother. Finally, my father sent me back to his family in Philadelphia, hopin' that would straighten me out."

"Did it?"

Shane turned slowly to face her. Her hand slid from his back to her side.

"I suppose, but I was a troublemaker in school. The other boys taunted me and called me 'Indian lover.' I bloodied a few noses for that. The girls pretended to be afraid of me. The teachers despaired of what to do with me."

"What happened to your brother and sister?"

"My brother never adapted to living in white society. After a couple of years, he ran away from the fort and found his way back to the tribe, which was quite a feat. The Plains tribes are nomadic. They follow the buffalo, so they move around. I can't imagine how he found the tribe, but he did. He still lives with them and is quite a warrior." He paused and sighed. "My real father resigned his military commission and moved with my mother and sister to California, wantin' to make a new start there."

"And you?"

"When I finished school, I left Philadelphia and returned to the West. I joined the army as a scout until the Civil War broke out. After the war, I resumed scouting for the army. By that time, I'd settled down and gotten over my bitterness. I learned to forgive, so the Lord could forgive me."

Shane fell silent while Della thought over all he'd told her. His tale overwhelmed her, being so much more than she'd imagined.

"Della."

She glanced at him. "Yes?"

"Now, you see why I can't marry. I'm neither white nor Cheyenne. Out here, most people don't think much about a white man living with the tribes, but a man who has lived with them should never marry a white woman. I can't ask a decent woman to share that taint."

"If you loved a woman, shouldn't she have a say in the matter? Not all women are such timid creatures."

"Society is too cruel. I couldn't ask any woman I loved to endure that hardship."

"I'd be willing to face anything for the man I loved."

Shane smiled at her, a sad smile that barely lifted the corners of his mouth. "You're very brave, but your life of privilege hasn't prepared you for a society that will turn its back on you for marryin' a man like me."

Della lifted her chin and narrowed her eyes. "If I loved such a man, I hope he'd consider me brave enough to stand by his side and face down society. I've had society matrons twit at me before because I couldn't seem to follow every single social rule. It wouldn't be the first time society has frowned on me."

"A life with me would take you beyond anythin' you experienced in Boston."

"Shouldn't that be my choice?"

Somehow, they'd gone from discussing marriage in general terms to referring to the two of them. Neither denied the yearning that drew them together.

Shane leaned forward and cupped her face in his big hands, stroking her cheeks with his thumbs. His fingers speared into her hair. He perused her features, as if memorizing them. "I suppose it's time we addressed what's between us, what we both know we've been feelin' almost from the first moment we met. You're everything I could ever hope to have in a wife. You're brave and courageous and beautiful. Havin' you as my wife would give me great pleasure, but I could never be so selfish."

"I should never be so cowardly as to quail from being your wife."

"You don't know what you say. Before long, you'd resent bein' married to me."

"Never. I think you're afraid to risk loving."

He shook his head. "I may love, but I'll never be so foolish as to act on that love and ruin the life of a good woman by marryin' her."

"Please, don't deprive us both of a life together." She curled her fingers around the back of his neck. His skin felt warm and smooth beneath her palm. She traced his tanned features with a tender gaze. Squint lines fanned out from his eyes, and grooves bracketed his mouth. The life he'd lived etched his face.

"I would never put a woman I loved through what my mother experienced."

"You don't know me if you think I'll give up so easily."

"You don't know me if you think you can sway me."

Della smiled into his eyes. "I think you may have met your match."

"You're settin' yourself up for heartbreak."

"We'll see." Della vowed she'd meet his challenge. Somehow, she'd wear down his resolve to never marry.

CHAPTER 17

THEY REACHED CAMP WELL AFTER the others had eaten. The campfire gleamed like a beacon, beckoning them toward its blaze and warmth. After caring for their horses and turning them loose to join the herd, they strolled without speaking toward the chuck wagon.

Before they reached the circle of firelight, Hunter grasped Della's arm and swung her to face him. They stood nose to nose, close enough to touch.

"I can't marry you, Della," he said, his voice rough. "You'd best consider Captain Asher's suit."

"I can't marry where my heart doesn't lead me."

"All the issues we discussed aside, bein' married to an army scout is no life for a lady. That rough kind of life would destroy you. And I'd be gone much of the time, leavin' you alone. I can't do that to you. Asher can offer you luxuries and the kind of life that should be yours. Marry him."

"Do you think I can't live without luxuries? That I need silk and satin—and domestics to work for me?"

Shane sighed. He whisked off his hat with his free hand, bent his head, and touched his forehead to hers. "Ah, Della, you're such an innocent. You've never seen the rough life of an army fort. You don't belong there. You're so fine, with your Beacon Hill accent and your genteel ways. Army life would break you, and I'd have to watch, knowin' I was the cause. I can't do it."

"You're making this decision for both of us, without considering my wishes." Della looked into his eyes, so close to hers. She placed her hand on his buckskin-clad shoulder, aware of his firm muscles and the strength beneath her palm. "What about your mother? She lived with your father at Fort Bridger."

"Yes, but he had officer's quarters and family money to cushion the hardship. I have nothin' to offer a wife but myself and a scout's salary."

"Your love would be enough."

"Your uncle would never allow you to marry me. He wants better for you than what I can offer."

"Uncle Clint wouldn't stand in my way. He knows you're an honorable, God-fearing man. And he understands love. I'm sure you've seen how much he loves Aunt Coral."

"I have. He's a fortunate man to have found such a love, but he's in a position to provide well for his family. I'm not."

"But—"

Shane placed a finger on her lips. "Hush. No more talk of marriage. We'll put this behind us and carry on as before. You must consider Asher's suit."

Della shook her head. "I can't."

"You must. Promise me."

"You ask too much."

"One day, you'll thank me. Now, promise me."

They remained locked in a silent battle of wills, their foreheads still touching, with Della's hand on Hunter's shoulder and his fingers wrapped about her arm.

"All I can promise is that I'll try," she said at last. "I promise no more than that."

"I can be strong enough for both of us." He stepped away, loosening his hold on her, and settled his hat once more on his head, tilting the brim low.

Her hand slid from his shoulder and down his arm. She felt every muscle, every sinew beneath her fingers. His body heat warmed the smooth buckskin sleeve of his shirt. The loss of contact with him pierced her heart.

They turned toward the campfire, and together, they walked into the circle of light. The inches that separated them seemed to Della an unbridgeable chasm.

Every man lounging about the fire watched their entrance. Della moved to the blaze and spread cold hands to its warmth, though her chill had nothing to do with the night's temperature. She might never be warm again. Her heart felt like a frozen lump in her chest.

Toby bustled toward her, holding a mug of coffee in his outstretched hand. "Miss Della, how did you fare? Did that big galoot treat you fine, or should I horsewhip him?"

Della couldn't look at Shane. "You needn't horsewhip him. He took excellent care of me." She reached for the tin mug and sipped, grateful for something to do with her hands.

"Did you have enough to eat?" Toby hovered, concern etched on his homely features. "I can warm up some beans."

"Yes, we ate supper, and I'm not hungry. But thank you for asking." The thought of food made her nauseated.

Quentin Asher appeared at her side, solicitous concern written on his face. Della preferred to avoid talking to him just at that moment, with Shane standing not three feet away. The promise she'd made to the scout hung in the air between them.

"Miss Hughes, you look weary. The miles you've ridden today have been too much for you."

She lifted her head and looked at the captain, wishing she could appreciate his concern for her. All she wanted at that moment was to escape to her wagon and crawl into her bedroll. She had no desire for conversation, but the training she'd received from childhood caused her to straighten her spine and smile at him. "I am weary. I think I'll retire now." She stooped to lay the tin mug on the ground near the coffeepot.

She'd taken several steps in the direction of her wagon before she remembered the cavalry's mission that day. She turned back toward Captain Asher and caught him watching her. "Did you find the rustlers?"

He shook his head. "All we found was the ashes of their campfire."

"Perhaps you'll catch them soon."

He nodded. "Good night, Miss Hughes."

"Good night, Captain."

Shane Hunter stood just beyond the captain. She couldn't look at him. She wouldn't look at him. Della couldn't help herself. She glanced over Quentin Asher's left shoulder to the man who had just turned her life upside down. The firelight painted one side of his face with its flickering glow. Shadows masked the other half, though Della saw his heartache in the taut lines of his face. How had she ever thought him inscrutable? His stark expression betrayed his feelings for her and an awareness of the impossibility of their situation. Their gazes met. The emotions they both felt simmered between them.

Aware of Quentin Asher still watching her, Della swept her lashes down, breaking the contact with Hunter. She wheeled, stepped into the darkness, and made her way to her wagon, careful to keep her head high and her back straight.

The Conestoga reserved for Uncle Clint and his family was parked near her own. When she passed their wagon, she heard her uncle's low voice through the canvas cover. She checked her stride, straining to listen. Prayer. Her uncle was praying, invoking the Lord's blessing and protection on their venture. He prayed for each person in their group, and when he finished, Aunt Coral added her own prayers.

Della crept away, not wanting to intrude upon their private family moment. How she yearned for a marriage such as theirs!

She crawled into her own wagon and undressed. After slipping her flannel night rail over her head, she made up her bedroll and slid beneath the covers. Lying on her back, the blankets tucked around her chin, she stared at the canvas cover arching over her head, a vague gray expanse in the darkness.

When she'd set out that morning, she'd had no notion she and Hunter would become entwined in a tumultuous, doomed relationship. Now that she knew his history and understood the events that had shaped him, she realized why he'd never attempted to develop a romance with her. Until she pushed, however innocently, and forced him to reveal his past, he'd been content to love her in secret.

And love her, he did, though he hadn't uttered the words. What he felt had been plain on his face in the firelight. A man who normally kept his thoughts and feelings private, she could only guess what allowing such a personal emotion to show in public had cost him. Yet her fledgling love turned bittersweet at his stubborn refusal to consider a marriage between them.

She recalled the Bible verse Shane's mother had claimed during her captivity. What had been true for his mother was true for her. The Lord was with her. Her Heavenly Father knew of her situation. She comforted herself with the thought and sent a prayer for grace and wisdom heavenward.

CHAPTER 18

AFTER THEY FINISHED BREAKFAST THE next morning, Uncle Clint called the entire company together for a meeting around the campfire.

"Today, we'll face our first serious challenge. A stream with quicksand lies ahead, and we'll cross it this afternoon. The distance we cover will be shortened due to the time it may take us to cross the stream, but it can't be helped." The general then turned the meeting over to Shane Hunter.

Della hadn't seen the scout since their parting the night before. She wasn't sure how to behave toward him or how he'd treat her. Should she speak to him, or should she avoid him?

Shane stepped forward. His gaze swept the group, then rested on Della, and the message in his eyes told her he'd been seeking her. Unspoken communication vibrated between them, making her heart leap into her throat and lodge there. The air quivered with their mutual yearning. After a moment, he wrenched apart the connection and began to speak.

Beside her, Aunt Coral stirred and cast her niece a questioning look. Aunt Coral had noticed the exchange, but at that moment, Della couldn't bring herself to discuss her situation. She shrugged, and Aunt Coral turned her attention back to Shane without pressing for details.

"When we reach the stream, we'll put the horses into the water at a lope. The faster they cross it, the less time they'll have to panic. Those of you who are driving the oxen, keep them moving."

He paused and glanced at the group again. "Yesterday, I saw a Lakota huntin' party in the area where we'll be today. Keep a sharp lookout. If you see anythin', get me."

The meeting broke up. The men left the camp to go about their duties in preparation for the day's journey. Shane didn't glance at Della again, instead engaging Uncle Clint in conversation. She turned away to catch up her mare. Shane had told her they'd return to the way things were before their conversation, despite the feelings between them. Still, an arrow of disappointment pierced her when he didn't seek her out.

Della promised herself she wouldn't let him leave things as they'd been. She wouldn't make it easy for him to write off a future for them. She'd fight for him.

"Miss Della!"

A cheerful voice interrupted her musings. Rusty planted himself in her path. "Miss Della, I've come to ask if you'd ride with me today."

In spite of her unsettled mood, she smiled at the irrepressible cowboy. His unfailing good humor lifted her spirits. "I'd be pleased to ride with you."

Rusty whipped his cowboy hat off his head and slapped it against his knee. He executed an Irish jig and laughed. "Whoo-ee! I'll have the prettiest gal in all of Kansas at my side today!"

Della laughed with him. "I'm sure you're being kind, but I thank you for the compliment."

"No, ma'am. Your beauty puts the sun to shame." With an elaborate flourish of his hat, he executed an exaggerated bow. "Let me saddle my cayuse, and we'll be off."

With the exception of Rusty, a somber atmosphere infected the drovers and the women alike when they broke camp that morning. Even the Morgans seemed to catch the mood of the humans and behaved with unusual cooperation. The horses bunched together, not trying to scatter. Shane ranged ahead but always remained within rifle shot of the group.

They reached the stream midway through the afternoon. Whistling shrilly and swinging their coiled lariats at the herd, the drovers spooked the Morgans into a lope. The horses hit the water at a run, plunging and leaping, geysers of water shooting upward.

Della's mare hesitated, then jumped into the river in a spray of liquid. Della clung to her mount, riding out the frenzied lunging of her horse battling through the stream.

Shane materialized beside her on his big grulla. She glanced at him. Concern tightened his eyes and firmed his mouth. Her heart warmed. He had been watching for her and positioned himself near her to offer his aid should her mare panic. He had the responsibility of the whole horse herd and the wagons, yet he'd been so conscious of her safety he'd situated himself to protect her.

Their mounts scrambled up the far bank, water streaming down their legs. Hunter swung his gelding close to Della's mare. Their knees bumped as the horses jostled. The contact burned through her riding skirt. Shane's nostrils flared, and Della had the satisfaction of knowing he'd been as affected as she.

He reined his mustang around and heeled the gelding into a gallop, away from her, away from the shared feelings that lurked just beneath the surface. He ran from her and the lure of their mutual regard.

Rusty came up behind her, whooping and waving his hat. His brown eyes sparkled. "Come on, Miss Della! Let's get these cayuses bedded down." His dun cow pony shot past her, mud clods spraying from his hooves.

They camped that night near the stream. The atmosphere about the campfire was festive, for they'd navigated the quicksand without losing a single horse or wagon. After supper, Toby produced his violin.

Captain Asher planted himself before Della. "I believe you promised me another dance." He thrust out a hand toward her.

Della smiled up at him and placed her hand in his, though her heart couldn't delight in the opportunity to dance with the suave captain. She'd rather pass the time in the company of a certain scout, whom she spied hanging back at the edge of the firelight. "I believe I did," she said, remembering her promise to consider Quentin Asher's offer of marriage.

"A waltz, Toby, if you please. Miss Hughes will dance with me, and I want a waltz."

132

Toby ran the bow of his violin across the strings, warming up. A moment of silence hung about the campfire before the stately strains of a waltz filled the air. The captain pulled Della close, a trifle too close for her comfort, and the next moment, they were sweeping about in the steps of the dance. The buffalo grass made a carpet beneath their feet.

When they made a turn that put Della in view of where Shane Hunter had been standing at the edge of the firelight, she looked over Captain Asher's shoulder, hoping to see the scout. The spot where Shane had stood was empty. He'd vanished into the darkness. The anticipation of seeing him and perhaps passing some time in conversation with him evaporated. Emptiness filled her chest, choking her. All the bright gaiety of the night dissolved.

Della looked up into Quentin Asher's face. His attention focused on her, his gaze roaming over her features. Tenderness filled his handsome countenance. She forced her lips into a smile. Her future might rest with this man. She'd best get to know him.

CHAPTER 19

ON THE SIXTH SUNDAY THEY'D been on the trail, Della sat on an overturned wooden bucket beside Coral, with Silvie beyond, during the morning church service. While she listened to Uncle Clint preach, she discreetly cast about the group of men ranged around her. Quentin Asher stood close behind her, but the one man she longed to see wasn't present. Shane Hunter had attended every Sunday service since they'd left Kansas City, so now, she wondered at his absence.

Her mind turned to her dilemma with the scout. In the three weeks since he'd revealed his past to her and all but admitted he loved her, she'd not had a moment alone with him. He left the camp well before dawn and returned after she crawled into her blankets at day's end. In the company of the drovers or her family, he spoke to her, but their conversations were brief and impersonal. He kept his emotions guarded, never giving her a glimpse into his heart. Della grieved over the loss of the familiarity they'd briefly shared and wondered how to reclaim the intimacy.

Quentin Asher, on the other hand, seemed to have decided to press his suit. He kept her company in the evenings whenever he wasn't taking his shift guarding the horses. When his duties allowed, he rode at her side during the day, unless Emory Dyer or Rusty had already claimed the privilege.

After her uncle closed the service in prayer, Captain Asher leaned down. "I look forward to watching you shoot this afternoon."

Della rose from her makeshift seat and turned to face him. She wrinkled her nose at him. "Aunt Coral and I have been collecting quite a crowd whenever we practice our shooting. One would think the men have never seen women handle firearms before."

"Perhaps it's the proficiency with which you ladies have learned to hit your target that has impressed the men."

"Both of us have had excellent instructors. Most of the credit must go to them."

A dark cloud crossed the captain's face at her reference to Shane Hunter's firearms skills. "I'm known as a crack shot myself. You could have asked me to give you shooting lessons."

Della shrugged. "I didn't know you wanted to teach me."

"I would have been honored and delighted to instruct you. As I suspect I shall be doing on any number of topics for the rest of our lives once we're married."

"I haven't yet agreed to your suit." He seemed about to protest, so she raised a peremptory hand. "Please, don't mention marriage again. We have plenty of time to discuss whether or not we're suited."

Behind her, Toby bustled about the campfire, preparing the noonday meal, clanging the spoon against the iron skillet.

Asher glanced past her shoulder. His eyes narrowed, and his lips twisted. His shoulders stiffened; his hands balled into fists. Wondering at her companion's abrupt change of mood, Della spun.

A man sitting tall in the saddle, riding his grulla gelding with easy grace, trotted into the camp. A black cowboy hat rode low over his brow and shaded his eyes, but Della knew he'd seen her. She felt his glance as a touch.

A doe antelope was draped across the front of his saddle. The horseman halted his mustang and let the deer slide to the ground. "Here's supper, Toby. I thought we could do with a change from beans and bacon."

Toby stepped closer and stooped to examine the kill. He glanced up. "Thank you kindly, Hunter. Everyone will appreciate some fresh meat tonight."

Without looking in Della's direction again, Shane turned his mount and loped out of the camp. She watched his buckskin-clad back until he disappeared over the next rise toward the horse herd. Would he be gone for the rest of the day, or would he return to eat and help her with her target practice?

She didn't really need his oversight now. Uncle Clint had helped Aunt Coral brush up on her firearms skills. He could include her in the lessons, as well, and spare Hunter the task of tutoring her. Somehow, the luster went out of the day at the possibility she wouldn't see Shane again. Having him oversee her target practice had added piquancy to the exercise. She'd basked in the unspoken dialogue smoldering beneath the surface of every encounter with the scout.

Later that afternoon, Della joined her uncle and aunt for their shooting session. To her annoyance, Quentin Asher attached himself to her and strolled through the buffalo grass at her side. She'd rather not have the captain about just when she might have an opportunity to engage Shane in conversation.

"Can we better our shots from the last practice?" Della asked Aunt Coral as she halted beside her.

Aunt Coral chuckled. "I'm sure we can." She glanced around at the men who had gathered to watch. "I could do better if I didn't have such a large audience," she whispered.

"The extra practice we've been doing in the evenings has helped."

"You ladies have surpassed all of our expectations," Asher said with suave gallantry. "You put us mere men to shame."

Tingling at the back of her neck told Della that Shane Hunter had joined their group. She spun. The scout stood mere yards from her, between Lieutenant Dyer and Rusty. He slouched on one leg, his thumbs tucked into his belt. Their gazes tangled, and Della's pulse kicked into a faster rhythm. Her heart thumped against her ribs. He stood so close, yet the situation between them created an unbridgeable crevasse.

He wore his black cowboy hat tilted low over his brow. Hunter tipped his head down a fraction, and his hat brim shielded his eyes from Della's stare. What she could see of his face was expressionless, his mouth tight. She wanted to run to him, to grasp his arms and shake him until he showed some emotion. Even anger would be preferable to his present impassivity. She would do anything to rouse him, though it meant risking his displeasure. Without thinking of the possible consequences, she sauntered toward him, her riding boots swishing through the grass. She halted mere inches from him. "Are you here to help me, Mr. Hunter?" Calling him Shane under the present circumstances seemed inappropriate.

Shane lifted his head and stared at her. Something she couldn't define flickered in his eyes. "I think you've progressed beyond needin' my help."

"Certainly not. There is much more I can learn from you." Della raised her chin a notch and challenged him with her eyes. "I'm still a mere novice."

The hot wind stirred the air around them. The buffalo grass rippled while the Kansas sun blazed down upon the prairie. All that faded from Della's awareness in her confrontation with Shane.

He remained silent and motionless. His gaze burned through her. Della's heart jerked, though she didn't flinch. She returned stare for stare.

Quentin Asher stalked up to Della and grasped her elbow. "The scout doesn't want to help you. Leave him be. I can teach you what you need to know."

Not by so much as the flicker of a glance did Shane acknowledge the captain. Instead, his attention bored into Della's face. The air hummed between them, making her marvel that the others could remain unaware of the tumult raging between herself and Shane.

Asher shook her elbow. "Come on, Miss Hughes. Let's shoot."

Della pulled her arm from the captain's hold. "Mr. Hunter began my shooting lessons. I want him to finish them."

"Miss Hughes, let it go. Never mind that scout." Asher's rough, urgent voice rasped over her nerves with irritating insistence.

Della continued to ignore him. "Mr. Hunter, are you going to quit on me?" She flung the challenge at him.

Lieutenant Dyer cast a sharp glance at her and shifted his weight. For once, even Rusty didn't have a comment. Beside her, Captain Asher snorted.

The moment the words left Della's mouth, her audacity startled herself. In the genteel circles in which she'd been reared, a lady never publicly confronted a gentleman. She might ply her wiles on him in private to get her way, but in public, she remained biddable. Had she pushed Shane beyond his limits by her unladylike behavior?

Hunter and Della remained locked in their private duel. Tension stretched between them, until Della thought the very air must crackle like lightning. Shane's stare sizzled over her face, hard and bold, until she quailed inwardly. Still, she refused to back down. At last, when she thought she might collapse from the strain, he relented.

He shrugged. "Who am I to deny a lady? Never let it be said I don't finish what I begin." He stared down at her, the brim of his hat casting a shadow across his face. They both knew the real issue wasn't his reluctance to continue her shooting lessons. "Shall we begin?"

Without glancing at Quentin Asher, who still stood at her side, Della pivoted and paced beside Shane to where her uncle and aunt waited.

The captain was furious with her, Della knew. His displeasure rolled toward her in waves. She'd have a difficult time smoothing his ruffled male pride later, though at the moment, she didn't care.

They stopped beside her uncle and aunt. Aunt Coral looked at her curiously, and Uncle Clint shook his head. The box with the Colt revolvers lay at his feet. The general bent, scooped the weapons from their container, and handed one to each woman.

Aunt Coral checked the cylinder of her handgun. After finding it empty, she levered in six bullets and snapped the cylinder closed. Uncle Clint had set up several empty peach and tomato cans, scavenged from Toby after meals, as targets. The women sighted and began to shoot.

Every nerve in Della's body seemed attuned to Shane's presence beside her, throwing her into a fit of jitters. Her first two shots missed their targets. Aware of him watching her, she took a deep breath and forced her shoulders to relax. She glanced at him, but his expression told her nothing.

After her fourth shot, he stepped closer, positioning himself behind her. He placed his hands on her shoulders. The toe of his boot tapped the inside of her left heel.

"Bring your foot out and forward. You want your shootin' foot to be at the instep of your support foot. Flex your knees just a bit."

He'd told her all this at her first shooting lesson, but that was before they'd spent a day alone together and discussed marriage. Before he'd set forth his case for why he could never marry. Before she'd begun to love him. Now, she couldn't focus on her aim. She could only feel him close behind her, his warm strength at her back. His arms enfolded her, and his hands wrapped about hers on the six-shooter's grip. He curled his long, callused fingers about her smaller ones, and she stopped breathing. She was achingly aware of his closeness, his low voice in her ear.

"Your arms should be like this." He demonstrated, moving her hands. "Pull back on the hammer. Now, squeeze. Don't jerk."

Della fired, and the can leaped, tumbling end over end into the grass.

"Try the next one."

She shot again, and once more, the can bounced. Beside her, Aunt Coral fired off several shots, hitting her cans with each bullet.

Shane dropped his hands from hers and moved away. "Practice that stance even when you're not actually shootin' so you won't have to think about it if you ever need to use that Colt. Of course, most likely, you'll be shootin' from behind a wagon wheel or a boulder, so you should practice from those positions, too."

Della nodded, unable to speak. Without Shane's nearness, her pulse slowed. Her heartbeat stopped thundering in her ears.

She emptied the chamber and reloaded. "Now, let's see what you can do with a movin' target," Shane said.

He strode to where the cans lay scattered in the grass. After gathering them up, he glanced at her to see whether she was ready. She nodded, trying to ignore the fact that several men had fanned out behind her to watch. She focused instead on Shane, waiting for him to toss the cans high. Recalling the skill with which he pierced the tin plates the first time she'd seen him shoot, she tried to imitate what he'd done.

When he tossed the cans skyward, one after the other, Della lifted her six-shooter and aimed. She fired, though she hit only half her cans. When the last one fell into the grass, she glanced at Shane. The veiled expression in his eyes told her nothing, although he nodded.

After the shooting session, he halted beside her. His chest brushed her shoulder. He stared down at her for a long, silent moment. Then, he bent close to her ear. "I know what you're up to. These games of yours will get you nowhere. I haven't changed my mind." He bit off each word.

She stared into his set face. "You're wrong to think I can't be happy with you wherever you are."

"I told you before"—his voice hissed in her ear—"life on an army fort in the conditions in which I live would break you. I won't be the cause of all the joy and beauty bein' crushed out of you. That's if society didn't crush you first."

Before she could reply, he spun on a booted heel and stalked away. She watched his long strides take him down the gentle slope toward the camp, the fringe on his buckskin shirt dancing, his broad shoulders squared.

"Whatever is going on between you two?" Aunt Coral had been watching the exchange, and now, she stepped close to Della. Della glanced at her aunt and saw curiosity in her hazel eyes, as well as a generous dollop of sympathy.

Her sympathy nearly undid Della. Tears welled in her eyes and clung in salty droplets to her lower lashes. She dashed them away. "Aunt Coral, he's the most stubborn man."

"This isn't the place to discuss your problem, but perhaps tonight, after Flossie is in bed, we can talk."

Della nodded, missing the counsel of a mother more than at any other time in her life. "I'll come to your wagon."

Aunt Coral nodded. The arrival of Captain Asher precluded further conversation on the topic.

"Miss Hughes, a private word with you, if you please."

Aunt Coral and Della shared a glance before Della turned away to face her irate suitor. She attempted without much success to conceal her impatience. "Yes?"

"Miss Hughes, I must protest your deportment. A lady should never engage in such forward behavior as you displayed this afternoon. And to let a man to whom you're not betrothed touch you in that manner is most scandalous. You must be more careful of your good name."

The captain's censure revived Della's flagging spirits. She lifted her chin. "My good name is my own affair."

"I recently approached your uncle to ask his permission to make you my wife. You are nearly affianced to me. That makes your behavior my affair."

The captain's stiff posture and pale countenance warned Della she pushed him too far, yet she couldn't hold her tongue. "May I remind you again that I'm not affianced to you? I haven't yet agreed to your marriage proposal, so your concern about my behavior is unacceptable."

"But as my wife—"

"I told you once I'm no dishwater miss. If you disapprove of my behavior, perhaps you should look elsewhere for a wife."

He clamped his mouth shut, displeasure plain on his face. Della swept past him. She marched toward Lieutenant Dyer, who had begun the trek back to the camp.

"Uncle Emory!"

He halted and turned to face her. Della increased her stride to catch up. "Uncle Emory, may I accompany you back to camp?"

When she reached his side, she took his arm. Emory Dyer regarded her with suspicion. "What mischief are you up to now, missy?"

Della shrugged and made a little moue. "I think I'll remain a spinster. I'm not sure I want a man ordering my life about."

He hooted. "I might have known. Your captain is displeased with you over your boldness toward Shane Hunter."

"I wasn't bold."

"You challenged him before a group of men. Men never appreciate appearing petticoat ridden in public, so you've no doubt displeased him. And now, your captain is jealous, as well." He shook his head. "Your behavior has done nothing but alienate you from both men."

Della sighed. "You never take my side. I don't know why I talk to you."

They began strolling toward camp. She felt Quentin Asher's glower stabbing her spine all the way to the bottom of the knoll.

CHAPTER 20

SHANE HUNTER HAD DISAPPEARED BY the time Della and Emory Dyer reached the camp. Della attempted to put their encounter from her mind. She tried to convince herself she didn't care if Hunter avoided her or if she'd made him angry with her insistence that he continue her shooting lessons, yet deep inside her heart, she knew that wasn't true. His displeasure made her miserable.

Toby outdid himself that evening. Everyone enjoyed antelope steaks and biscuits made from the fresh milk of the Jersey cow, with dried-apple pie as a treat.

Quentin Asher stalked into the camp and brushed past Della on his way to the chuck wagon to get his plate and utensils. A disgruntled expression pulled his mouth down at the corners. He piled his trencher with food and joined the men on the other side of the fire without looking in her direction.

Della sät in the grass beside Aunt Coral and her uncle. The antelope steak on her plate might as well have been sawdust. The juicy meat was tasteless, though not because of Captain Asher's peevishness. She attributed her wretchedness to Hunter's vexation with her.

"Toby, if you feed us like this every night, I hope we never reach Colorado Territory," Rusty said. He popped half a biscuit into his mouth.

"We can't get to Colorado soon enough for me," a former officer from Logan's Calvary said. "I wish those men who are trailing us would give us an excuse to deal with them, but they stay half a day behind us. They never get any closer, but they dog our trail."

"They're like a burr under a saddle blanket," another drover said. "You know they're there, but you can't see them."

"Maybe they just want to follow us to Colorado instead of traveling by the usual overland route." Rusty licked honey from his fingers. "There's more grass for their horses the way we're going."

"Nope. They're up to something," one of the drovers commented. "I wish I knew what it was."

"We'll find out one of these days, and we won't like it when we do." The officer poured the last of his coffee onto the ground and stood up.

Without speaking, Shane joined the men and lifted a tin plate from the tail of the chuck wagon. He walked to the fire and forked a steak from the skillet before adding a couple of biscuits. He moved away from the blaze, squatted on the edge of the circle of men, and began to eat.

Della kept her head lowered over her plate, eating her dried-apple pie without enjoyment. Shane never acknowledged her presence on the other side of the fire.

A sudden chill gust made the brim of her hat flap. Della lifted her head when another squall of cool air beat at her face. What she saw beyond the camp, along the rim of the horizon, made her breath catch in her throat. A black smudge of cloud churning toward them blurred the line where earth and sky met.

Shane rose and twisted toward the western plains. When he saw the cloud, he tossed his plate onto the grass and spun back toward the camp. "We've got a prairie thunderstorm comin', and we've only got minutes to prepare." He glanced at the women. "You ladies get into your wagons and hunker down. Close all the flaps of the wagon covers. Make sure the canvas is tied down securely."

The men leaped into motion at the words *prairie thunderstorm*. They'd all heard of the violent storms that could sweep across the plains without warning.

"Keep the horses and the oxen bunched. Try to keep them from stampedin'." The words had barely left his mouth before he was running toward the herd.

Uncle Clint thrust Flossie, who had been sitting on his lap, into Aunt Coral's arms and leaped to his feet. He disappeared into the wagon he shared with his wife and reappeared a moment later carrying his rig.

Della, Aunt Coral, and Silvie stood in consternation as confusion resounded around them. Aunt Coral clutched Flossie against her bosom so tightly the child squirmed. The wind beat at them while the obsidian cloud bank spread across the sky. The scent of rain filled the air.

Uncle Clint came to a brief standstill beside the women. "Get into your wagons and pray for safety." Then, he was running, his long strides devouring the distance to the herd.

With her precious bundle clasped to her, Aunt Coral struggled to her wagon. Silvie gathered her skirts and followed. Della hesitated, while Toby scurried about, gathering up plates, mugs, and the skillets of food and stowing them in the chuck wagon. When he began pulling up the stakes that held up the canvas flap over the wagon's tail, she jerked up the stake nearest her.

Toby pried the stake from her hand. "Get in your wagon. A prairie thunderstorm is no place for a young lady."

Della turned and hurried to her wagon. A blast buffeted her back, tugged at her braid, and plastered her split riding skirt against her legs. When she reached her wagon, she climbed in and closed the flap. The Conestoga rocked with the tempest, and the canvas top rippled against the curved oak ribs holding up the fabric.

She chewed on her lip. She could stay safely ensconced in her shelter, waiting out the storm, or she could catch up her mare and help the men with the horses. Both Uncle Clint and Shane Hunter had told the women to stay in their wagons, though the thought of waiting inside while the storm raged held no appeal. She could ride as well as any of the men and could help keep the Morgans from stampeding. An extra rider might make a difference.

After a moment's debate, she shrugged into her jacket. Her fingers, made clumsy by haste, fumbled with the fastenings. When the last button was secure, she snatched up her bridle from atop the flour sack where she'd laid it. Looping the leathers over her shoulder, she slipped from the wagon.

She reached the Morgan herd without being noticed. The horses milled about, snorting, their heads up and eyes rolling. The drovers were already mounted and riding in a circle about the herd, keeping the horses and the oxen bunched in a tight group. Della stopped, searching for her mare.

Astride his dun cow pony, Rusty halted beside her and grinned down at her. "What are you doing here?" he shouted over the moan of the gusting air.

"I want to help with the horses!"

"You should be in your wagon, but it's too late now for you to go back. I'll catch up your mare for you."

He wheeled his gelding, loosened his lariat from the saddle, and plunged into the herd. Della watched the Morgans part before his cow pony, letting horse and rider through. With an easy twist of his wrist, Rusty tossed the rope. The loop settled about her mare's neck. With her mount in tow, he returned.

The chestnut, wild eyed with fear, refused to stand still. She danced about, her ears flicking.

Rusty stepped down from his mount. "Give me the bridle."

Della handed the leathers to the cowboy, and within moments, he'd worked the headstall over the chestnut's ears and slipped the bit into her mouth. Holding the reins high up by the bit, he turned to Della. "Let me give you a hand up."

She hurried to her mare's side. Rusty tossed her onto the Morgan's back and gave her the reins.

He stood at her horse's shoulder, one hand fisted in the mare's mane, and looked up at her. "If your uncle ever finds out I helped you, he'll have my hide."

"I won't tell."

He nodded, wheeled, and leaped into the saddle. He turned his cow pony and jogged away.

Beneath her, the mare trembled. Della felt her mount's tremors, and a thrill of fear mingled with excitement shot through her. She reined her skittish Morgan about and began a circuit of the herd.

While Rusty had been dealing with her horse, the ebony storm cloud had consumed the heavens. A stygian blackness cloaked the plains, obscuring horses and riders. The grass bowed before the onslaught of wind. Della thought she saw Shane Hunter riding toward her around the edge of the herd, but a rattle of hail concealed the rider from view.

The pellets beat against Della's face and hands. She tipped her head down so her hat brim shielded her face. Her mare quivered and shook her head.

A moment later, a deluge of rain descended, soaking Della within an instant. A sheet of lightning ripped the sky, illuminating every horse, every rider, and every blade of grass with an alabaster gleam. An instantaneous crash of thunder shook the earth, as if a heavenly cannon had exploded.

The horses screamed. Driven by panic, they bolted across the plain in a wild frenzy. The riders wheeled and gave chase.

Della's mare, caught up in the herd's terror, nearly leaped out from beneath her. Della clamped her legs about the chestnut's ribs and hung on. Remaining astride her mare's slippery back took every ounce of horsemanship she possessed. Her mount had the bit between her teeth and ran with unchecked abandon. Nothing Della did could control her.

Another bolt of lightning lit up the range. Thunder blasted, shaking the ground once more. The keening wind snatched Della's cowboy hat from her head so it hung by its strap and bounced against her shoulder blades with each stride her horse took. Water sluiced down her face. She blinked to clear her eyes.

Before the thunder's rumbling died away, lighting tore the heavens again, nearly blinding in its brightness. Thunder deafened them. The land shook. Even as Della clung to her mount, she exulted in nature's wildness. The elements reached into her core and ignited a tumult deep within her. All her life, she'd suppressed something elemental and primitive in her being, and now, here on the untamed frontier in the midst of a furious storm, her spirit flew free. She let loose a wild, unladylike yell. The scream of the wind and the volley of rain swallowed the sound.

Della didn't know how far they ran. Her world shrank to the horse plunging beneath her, the other Morgans galloping beside her, the gale tearing at her hair, and the pummeling rain. Everything else had disappeared in the darkness.

Lightning exploded again, one flare followed by another. Thunder bellowed.

The ground rose in a shallow hillock. Her mare flew up the incline and plunged down the slope. Halfway down, her mount dodged around a growth of prairie roses. Without a saddle to provide stability, Della tipped sideways. Her chestnut's lunging stride unseated her, and she slid from her horse's back. She skidded into the ground while her mare galloped on with the other horses.

The thick buffalo grass cushioned Della's fall. She scrambled to her feet and watched the horses bolt past, leaving her alone on the prairie in the blackness and rain.

CHAPTER 21

THE LAST OF THE HORSES vanished in the deluge. The reality that she was completely alone on the plains crashed over her. She'd heard tales around the campfire of men unhorsed on the range, only to die of thirst, Indian attack, snakebite, or wolves. Men or women without a horse were at the whim of this merciless land. Their bones might be discovered months or years later. Often, they were never found.

Panic washed over her, almost paralyzing her. She had no idea where she was or how far from the camp she'd come. No one except Rusty knew she'd ridden out with the horses. How long would it be before she was missed?

She recalled Shane Hunter's tale of his mother's captivity, of how she never felt abandoned by the Lord. The verse his mother claimed filled her mind, and Della recited the words out loud. "I will never leave thee, nor forsake thee."

The Lord was here, with her in this storm. She might be alone on the prairie, but the Lord knew where she was and would never leave her. That reality calmed her anxiety. Her pulse settled to its normal rhythm as peace filled her. She sent a prayer for wisdom and safety heavenward.

Would Shane Hunter track her and find her? Should she stay here or try to make her way back to the camp?

Della dropped to the grass, grabbed for her hat, and settled it on her head, tipping the brim down so it protected her face from the lashing elements. She hunched her shoulders and rested her forehead on her drawn-up knees, circling her legs with her arms. The rain slashed down. She huddled into her jacket against the onslaught. Without the adrenaline pumping through her body, the chill breath of the storm smote her.

She lost track of time. Wind buffeted her. Her soaked clothing clung to her skin, and she shivered. Her teeth chattered.

Another flash of lightning stabbed the sky, bringing a light brighter than day to the earth. Thunder shook the ground once more. Just before darkness swallowed the light, a horse and rider came into view, slogging up the slope. The rider sat tall in the saddle, his black hat tipped down as he studied the trail left by the stampeding herd.

Shane Hunter. He was searching for her. Relief such as she'd never experienced washed over her. Della jumped up. She cupped her hands around her mouth. "Shane! I'm here!"

The wind snatched the words from her lips and whirled them away. She stumbled toward him through the darkness, tripping over the bunched grass. She fell to her knees. She pushed to her feet and struggled on to where she'd seen him in the lightning's flash.

Lightning illumined the world once again, revealing Hunter. As if he felt her presence, he glanced up. She had a glimpse of his face before darkness enveloped the world. Even during that brief instant, the force of his presence smashed into her, driving the breath from her body. She halted and stood swaying, waiting for him.

Thunder crashed. Rain pelted earthward.

Shane reined in his horse a scant yard from where she stood. The gelding braced and sank to his haunches, hooves digging into the grass as he ploughed to a stop. Shane kicked his feet from the stirrups and leaped from the saddle before his mount plunged to a standstill.

An unruly tumult of emotions exploded in Della's chest. Hunter reached her in one long stride. She tipped back her head to look into the pale blur of his face when he loomed over her.

His hands flashed out and gripped her shoulders, squeezing hard. "Don't you ever do what you're told?" His voice was ragged and rough.

Della struggled to absorb his words, his anger. She laid her hands on his chest, curling her fingers into the dripping oilskin of his yellow rain slicker.

"Why didn't you stay in the wagon? Don't you realize you could have been killed out here?"

"I only wanted to help."

Shane didn't reply. His glare bored into her. Della refused to wilt. She glared right back.

"Do you know what I felt when I saw your mare gallop past without you? I died a thousand deaths." Shane stepped closer, so close his slicker brushed the front of her fleece jacket and the toes of his riding boots grazed the outside of her boots. "I wasn't sure if I'd find you at all or if you were badly injured. I thought you might have been trampled when you were thrown."

Della's breath caught in her throat. She couldn't speak. Her heart slammed against her ribs. Her fingers clenched his slicker. She stared up into his face, a face that could have been carved from New England granite. White lines bracketed his tight-lipped mouth.

Without warning, Hunter's hands dropped from her shoulders to her arms, and he jerked her against his chest. His arms looped about her back, drawing her against him. The brim of his black cowboy hat knocked her hat from her head. His mouth swooped down on hers. In his kiss, Della sensed a frantic mixture of anger, desperation, relief, and love. She responded with equal ardor. She loosened her hold on his slicker. Her arms stole up to clutch him about the neck.

After a time, his mouth gentled, and she gloried in his tenderness. At last, he broke off the kiss. His lips roamed her face, dropping sweet kisses on her cheeks, her nose, and her closed eyelids. He brought up one large hand to cup the back of her head and tucked her face into the curve of his neck. His other hand splayed over her back. When he pressed her tight against his hard chest, Della felt his heart pounding beneath her cheek.

For a moment, neither spoke. They stood clasped together, savoring the joy of being alive and of being in love and delighting in their embrace.

Almost without their noticing, the storm blew out. The rain slackened to a drizzle before ceasing altogether. A final mutter of thunder in the distance heralded the death of the tempest. While the storm raged, the sun had curved down to the horizon. Now, twilight fell, leaving the sky a pale, washed blue.

"I was so frightened when I saw you'd been thrown," Hunter said into the silence of the evening. "I thought I might have lost you forever."

"I hoped you'd find me. If anyone could, I knew it would be you. I just didn't know how long it would be before anyone realized I wasn't at the camp."

Shane dropped his chin to look at her. Della lifted her face from his neck. Their noses were mere inches apart.

"I saw you when Rusty caught up your mare." She watched his mouth as he spoke. "I was on my way over to tell you to go back to the camp when the horses stampeded. After that, I lost sight of you."

"I'm sorry I caused you to worry, but I thought one more rider would be helpful."

"Riding in the Boston Common was nothin' like what you did tonight—and bareback, as well. I was more worried about you than the horses, when I should have been focusing on the herd."

Della ignored the twinge of guilt his words evoked. After all, she'd had the best of motives when she joined the riders. Instead, she laid one hand against his cheek, rough with a day's growth of stubble. She made no reply, instead tacking off on another topic. "Why have you been avoiding me?"

Gripping her shoulders again, he put her away from him and stared into her eyes. "I haven't been avoidin' you, exactly."

"What would you call it, then? You scarcely speak to me, and you stay gone from the camp. I hardly see you."

"I told you to accept Captain Asher's suit. I didn't say I'd stay around to watch the courtship."

She grabbed his arms. "Is that why you avoid the camp? You don't want to see Captain Asher with me?"

Shane nodded. He glanced away before swinging his gaze back to her. "When I see him with you, talkin' to you and smilin' at you, it puts a black hole in my heart. I have to stay away."

Della stepped closer. She raised one hand to trace his lips. "You stubborn man. Don't you know I can never love Captain Asher? He may court me until we're both bent with age, but I'll never love him. Another man holds my heart."

Shane covered her hand with his and wrapped his fingers about hers. Beneath the pads of her fingers, his mouth puckered in a kiss. She smiled up at him.

"Ah, Della, darlin', what are we going to do? Nothing has changed. I still can't marry you."

"You could, if you weren't so stubborn."

He shook his head. "You know why I can't."

"We can. You deprive us both of a life together if you doubt me."

"I don't doubt you, but I know what life in the West is like for a woman. Captain Asher can take you away from here and give you the kind of life you were born to enjoy."

"You would have me give myself in marriage to a man I don't love, when my heart belongs to you?"

With his free hand, Shane swiped his hat from his head and blew out a breath. Della reached up and thrust her fingers into his shaggy, rumpled hair, reveling in its soft texture.

Shane stood unmoving, not breathing. His eyes glittered. "Della..."

Beneath his perusal, Della remembered she was soaking wet. In her wild ride, her hair had sprung free from its braid, and now, damp tendrils coiled in unruly abandon about her head. Groaning, she pulled her hands from his neck and tried to restore order to her mane.

Shane settled his hat on his head and watched her struggle for several moments before he brushed her hands away. He gathered hanks of her hair in both fists and brought the strands around the front of her jacket, then smoothed his fingers through the chocolate tresses with tender reverence. "Leave it. Your hair is beautiful."

153

"But it's so curly."

"What's wrong with curly hair? It fits you. Like your spirit, it runs free."

Della shivered, as much from his words as from the cold. With Shane, she had the freedom to be herself, not bound by convention's dictums. She needn't concern herself with keeping her hair under strict control and behaving with meek decorum, so opposed to her nature.

"You're cold. Let me get my coat." Shane stepped to his mustang and rummaged in his saddlebag, then pulled out his black canvas duster. He returned to her side and wrapped the coat about her.

The duster enveloped her, heavy and warm. While its weight settled about her shoulders, Della slid her arms into the sleeves. She pushed back the cuffs, which hung well over her fingertips, and secured the coat by its metal buttons.

Standing close before her, Shane reached around her to pull her hair out from beneath the fabric. With careful attention to her curls, he arranged the mass over her shoulders, tangling his fingers in its strands. With both hands in her hair, he pulled her closer with inexorable resolve. His face reflected both awe and a man's appreciation for her beauty.

Sensing his intent, Della's breath caught. When the front of the duster bumped his chest, he bent his head. His fingers slid through her curls. His palms framed her face while his mouth found hers. Della's arms reached up to encircle his neck, and her eyes drifted closed.

All thought fled in the sweet passion of his kiss. All the love he hadn't yet confessed poured from him, all the yearnings he couldn't deny. Della received his unspoken avowals with joyful assent, returning his passion with fervor. When he broke away, she lifted a dreamy gaze to his face, so close to hers.

"Darlin', you make it hard to remember why I can't marry," he muttered.

"Can't you consider it, even a little bit?"

His fingers tightened against the side of her head. "I knew I couldn't marry the moment I returned to white society. I've never considered it. To ask me to ponder marriage now is like askin' the river to change course and flow uphill."

Standing on her tiptoes, Della cajoled him with a shy kiss. She squeezed the hard ridge of muscle along the line of his shoulders. "We can pray about it. The Lord will guide us."

"I know. But how can I pray for somethin' that would be the most selfish act of my life? How can it be right for me to ask God for somethin' I know isn't good for you?"

"Oh, Shane, I love you for your thoughtfulness toward me and your concern for my well-being, but we don't know the future. We don't know what's best. Would the Lord give us this love, only to deny us?"

"Perhaps He has a higher purpose for us, a lesson for us to learn through denial."

"We won't know unless we move forward, with prayer."

Shane compressed his lips and glanced over her shoulder. Della gave him a little shake.

"Please, Shane."

He swung his gaze back to her face, a frown crinkling his forehead. "It goes against my good sense to pray for something which is so wrong for you. Marryin' me will only bring you heartache and regret."

"Never. I could never regret marrying you. Everything that's your life, I'd share with you and be happy in the doing of it."

"So you say now." A corner of his mouth twitched in what might be a smile. His fingers traced a gentle path along her jaw and down her throat before he clasped her shoulders again. "You almost make me believe I wouldn't ruin your life."

"For so long you've believed you shouldn't marry that you can't see the possibilities."

"And you're so young you can't see the realities."

Della huffed. "I'm not that young." A rosy blush stained her cheeks, and she looked away. A lady never admitted her age. Once again, her unruly tongue had tripped her up.

A genuine smile that gleamed in his eyes quirked his lips. "What are you—the ripe old age of twenty?"

She cast a demure glance at him. "A lady never admits her age."

"Still, in terms of experience, you're a mere babe."

"If you mean I'm not soured by cynicism, then perhaps, I am young. But that means I can still see the possibilities."

With a sigh, Shane enfolded her in a close embrace, laying his cheek on her hair. "If I agree to pray about a marriage between us, will you promise to continue considering Captain Asher's suit?"

"I can't promise anything more than that I'll try. Anyway, he's displeased with me. I'm not sure he still wants me for his wife."

Shane straightened, looking down into her face. "Why is he displeased with you?"

"He took exception to the way you stood so close to me during our shooting session."

"I made him jealous?"

"Very, and he reproached me for being careless of my good name."

"Apparently, he thinks I'm careless of your good name."

"He didn't say that."

"He reproached you instead." Shane's mouth tightened. "If he has something to say, he should say it to me, not you."

"He asked Uncle Clint for permission to court me, so to him, that means he has a say in my behavior."

"I don't like it."

"I don't like it much, either. I'm only allowing him to continue his suit because of my promise to you."

"And I can't promise to watch him with you."

"I'll put a stop to it anytime you say the word. Anytime you're ready to admit we should marry."

Shane cupped her cheek. "I promised to pray about it. That's as far as I'm willing to go right now."

Della turned her face and kissed his palm, the rough palm of a man who daily used his hands. She laid her smaller hand over his, and for a moment, they stood together. Their long shadows blended on the grass in the last glimmer of light before the horizon swallowed the sun.

"I should take you back to camp before I head out to help round up the herd."

Della sighed. "I'm sure Aunt Coral is frantic with wondering where I am."

"Rightfully so." With an arm about her shoulders, Shane steered her toward his mustang.

The hem of his duster dragged on the ground. Della held up the coat so she wouldn't trip.

They reached his gelding. He looped the reins about the grulla's head and toed for the stirrup. After swinging his leg over his mount's rump and settling his weight in the saddle, he kicked his left foot free of the stirrup and reached down for her hand.

"Put your foot in the stirrup, and I'll pull you aboard."

Della grasped his hand and lifted her foot to the stirrup. With Shane tugging her up, she swung on behind him and straddled his horse. The high cantle of his saddle poked her in the stomach, but she endured the discomfort in order to be close to him. She gripped him about the waist while he reclaimed his stirrup and heeled his mount into motion. When the mustang settled into a walk, she rested her head between Shane's shoulders and closed her eyes. The strong muscles of his back made a pillow for her cheek while the miles disappeared beneath his grulla's hooves.

CHAPTER 22

WHEN THE CAMPFIRE CAME INTO sight at the bottom of the slope, Shane reined in his gelding and twisted toward her. Della straightened, pushing her hair out of her eyes. She looked into his face. Though darkness veiled his features, she felt his regard like a touch.

"Della, darlin', I'm askin' for one more kiss before we join the others."

"You needn't ask. I'll give you all the kisses you want."

He lifted his free hand, speared his fingers into her tangled locks, and clenched the curling strands. "Your hair is so soft." He sifted the tendrils before he wrapped his hand about the back of her head and tugged her closer. "Rememberin' this will ease my heartsoreness."

Their mouths met with urgency. Della gripped his shoulder. Her whole world consisted of the man astride the grulla mustang. She forgot the camp waiting below, Uncle Clint, who would undoubtedly be furious when he learned what she'd done, and the scattered Morgan horses. Shane Hunter filled her senses and her heart. Nothing else existed at that moment except the two of them.

When their lips parted, Della stared at him, shaken by the emotions she felt. Shane's thumb stroked her cheek. "We must ride into the camp now. What we've shared today doesn't change anything."

Della peered into his eyes, searching for the love she knew he harbored for her. "You promised to think about marriage and to pray about it."

"I will. And you mustn't forget your promise to me." His hand slid along her jawline and dropped to his side.

"It's not a promise I can easily keep."

"You must try." He turned, nudging his mount into a walk. Della clung to his waist, her chin resting on his shoulder. "Shane?" she said after a moment.

He turned his head toward her. "Yes?"

"Will you tell Uncle Clint what I did?"

When he paused, her heart clenched.

"I won't mention it unless someone figures it out, but then, I won't conceal it. Unless Rusty or I find your mare first and get her bridle off before anyone else sees it, the fat will be in the fire for sure."

"Uncle Clint will be so angry with me."

Shane didn't reply, but he squeezed her hand.

When they reached the camp, Toby was stirring a pot of beans. The scents of fried bacon and coffee made Della's stomach rumble. Her aunt Coral and Silvie were eating, sitting close to the fire. Several cavalrymen had been sent back to guard the camp, and they sat about with the women.

Della and Shane rode into the circle of firelight. Shane halted his gelding. His muscled arm gripped Della about the waist and swung her to the ground before he dismounted. Together, they faced the anxious people waiting for them.

Aunt Coral and Silvie, along with the soldiers, had risen. Flossie skipped toward her and hugged her about the knees, tipping her little head back to look at Della.

"Cousin Della, were you lost?"

Della knelt beside the toddler. "Yes, Flossie. I was lost, but this kind man found me." She glanced toward Aunt Coral.

Worry, relief, and disapproval flashed across Aunt Coral's face. "We didn't know what happened to you. You disappeared without telling any of us where you were going."

Della rose, clutching the hand Flossie thrust at her. Beside her, Shane remained silent, letting her make her own explanations. "I was wicked to go away without telling you, but I knew you'd try to stop me. And I wanted to help with the horses." She hung her head, while Flossie scampered back to her mother.

Aunt Coral sighed. "I hope you realize what would have happened to you alone on the prairie if Shane hadn't found you."

"I had plenty of time to think about it."

Shane stirred. "Toby, a plate of those beans and some bacon sure would fill the hole in my stomach." Dropping the reins to ground-tie his mustang, he stepped toward the fire.

Toby bustled toward him, offering him a plate and fork, then procured the same for Della. "Miss Della, you shore are a sight. Sit yourself down right here and eat before you swoon dead away."

When they finished eating, Shane removed his mustang's tack, then turned the gelding loose to graze. Exhaustion pulled at Della, but she waited until he attended to his horse before she left the campfire. He stepped back into the circle of light, carrying his saddle over his shoulder and his bedroll beneath his arm. He came to a standstill beside her, studying her with a knowing gaze.

"Go to bed, Della. You're dead on your feet."

She shared a glance with him, her heart tripping at his nearness. "I will, but first, I must thank you for saving my life."

His stare burned over her face, and he nodded. "I would have searched every ridge, every coulee, and every blade of grass until I'd found you."

"I know." Mindful of the others who watched them, Della refrained from saying what was in her heart. "What are you going to do now?" she asked instead.

He lowered his saddle to the ground and dropped his bedroll beside it. When he straightened, he cocked one hip and thumbed his hat back. "I'll get a few hours of shut-eye and rest my horse before I head on back to help find the herd."

"But where will you sleep?"

"Where I usually do. On the ground. I have my blankets and my saddle for a pillow. I reckon that's all I need."

Della was about to protest when she recalled his past life with the Cheyenne. He hadn't slept in a bed for all those years, so perhaps a bedroll on the ground suited him. She clamped her lips shut and nodded. "Well, good night, then."

"Night, Della."

She pivoted and trudged toward Aunt Coral and Silvie.
"I'm sorry I caused you to worry."

Aunt Coral touched her shoulder. "I'm grateful you weren't hurt and that Shane found you."

Della nodded. "Will you tell Uncle Clint what I did?"

"If he doesn't know, I won't tell him, but if he figures it out, then you must confess everything to him."

Della's shoulders slumped. Uncle Clint always knew everything she did. "He'll be angry."

"Undoubtedly. Now, off to bed with you. We'll talk in the morning."

Della dragged herself to her wagon and tumbled into her blankets. Even the dread of her uncle's displeasure couldn't keep her awake. She plummeted into sleep and didn't rouse until the sun warmed her wagon the next morning.

* * * * *

Shane and his mustang were gone when Della stumbled to the chuck wagon midway through the morning. Toby saw her glance about the camp, searching for sight of the scout.

"He left before daylight. We won't see him again until he brings the horses back."

The camp seemed empty without Shane's presence. Della kept busy, though her thoughts kept returning to the agreement she and Shane had made. Surely, after praying about a future that included marriage, he couldn't deny that they belonged together.

While they waited for the return of the men and horses, the women spread their garments out on the grass for the sunshine to freshen. Toby reorganized the cooking supplies in the chuck wagon.

During Flossie's afternoon nap, Aunt Coral settled herself beside Della on the grass near their wagons. With her split riding skirt tucked about her knees, Aunt Coral reached for a blade of prairie grass and plucked it off at the root. She twirled it between her fingers while she contemplated her husband's niece, her head tipped to one side. "So, tell me. Whatever is going on between you and Mr. Hunter?"

Della glanced at her aunt. She tore off a handful of grass and shredded it between her fingers. "We love each other."

For a long moment, Aunt Coral didn't reply. She continued her perusal of Della's face until Della squirmed. "Has he told you?"

Della sighed and looked down at her hands. The mangled grass gave off the pungent smell of sun-warmed vegetation. "He hasn't used the word, exactly, but he does."

"And the problem is?"

"He refuses to consider marriage."

"So, the two of you have discussed marriage."

Della nodded.

"There must be a powerful reason to prevent him from marrying."

"There are two, precisely. One is his own secret that I'm not at liberty to share. The other is his position as army scout. He believes life at a fort is too harsh for me and he won't be able to provide well enough for a family."

"I see." Aunt Coral twirled the blade of grass again, staring off over the undulating prairie. "And where does Captain Asher fit into this?"

"Shane made me promise to consider the captain's suit because he can provide well for me."

Aunt Coral glanced at Della again. "The captain requested permission from my husband to court you officially."

"I know. He told me."

"Does Captain Asher have the qualities you're looking for in a husband?"

Della considered the question. "I'm used to men like him, men who come from the same social circles as we do. But I've gotten a taste of the freedom of the West, where I don't have to be concerned if my reputation is in shreds because I spoke to a man to whom I hadn't yet been properly introduced."

"Captain Asher certainly is a stickler for etiquette."

"He is." Della sighed. "Captain Asher has political aspirations. I'm not sure I can tolerate a lifetime of trying to abide by every social rule, something that would be expected of the wife of a man in public service. Society's rules are so confining. I would no doubt ruin his career by committing a faux pas."

Aunt Coral smiled. "I think it unlikely you could ruin his career."

"He keeps reminding me that his wife must be above reproach. What I really want is a marriage like yours. Anyone can see how much you and Uncle Clint love and respect each other."

Aunt Coral's expression softened at the mention of her husband, and her hazel eyes smiled. "I consider myself extremely fortunate to have won the love of such a man as your uncle. He has been God's gift to me when I thought I would never love again."

Pouring her troubles into Aunt Coral's sympathetic ear gave Della relief, though she still hadn't resolved her problem.

That night, tucked into her blankets in her prairie schooner, the plaintive howl of a wolf rolled across the prairie. A tremor shivered down her spine. If Shane hadn't rescued her, she'd be alone on the plains, lost, and without a means of defending herself. Wolves would have found her easy prey.

CHAPTER 23

ON THE THIRD DAY AFTER the storm, the thunder of hooves and the shrill whistles and yips of the riders heralded the approach of the herd. Della, accompanied by Aunt Coral and Silvie, hurried out to watch the men bring the horses in and turn them in a milling circle to halt their mad gallop. Shading her eyes with a hand, Della scanned the group. She searched for a tall, sandy-haired rider dressed in buckskin. Her gaze roved over each drover, accounting for her uncle, Emory Dyer, Rusty, and Captain Asher. Among the other men at the back of the herd, she finally found the figure she sought. She feasted her eyes upon him, anticipating the moment when they could meet again.

When the men had settled the Morgans and turned their own mounts loose with the herd, they descended upon the camp. Their vociferous voices demanded food. Toby had a stew simmering in a pot over the cook fire in anticipation of their return.

"If I ever straddle a cayuse again, it will be too soon for me." Rusty hobbled into the circle around the fire, rubbing his back with dramatic flair. He limped to where Della stood beside the wheel of the chuck wagon. "Miss Della, I'm pleased to see you made it back to camp safely."

"Uncle Clint knows what happened, doesn't he?" Della searched Rusty's freckled face for a clue about what to expect from her uncle.

The cowboy nodded. "Captain Asher found your mare running loose with several other horses. Your uncle figured out what you did when he saw the bridle."

Della's heart sank. Not only would she be reprimanded by Uncle Clint; Quentin Asher would also be sure to acquaint her with his displeasure. "Did they find out you helped me?"

"Yep. I had to fess up to what I'd done. Your uncle was madder than a wet catamount when I told him I'd helped you. He took a strip off my hide without saying a single cuss word, though."

"I'm so sorry I got you into trouble." Della glanced across the camp at her uncle. He stood with one arm about Aunt Coral's waist, Flossie in his free arm. Flossie patted her father's face, while Aunt Coral clung to her husband. Uncle Clint would have words for her before the evening was finished, Della knew. She dreaded the confrontation. Once again, her behavior had disappointed her uncle.

She encountered Shane Hunter only once that evening, though she tracked him while he ate standing at the back of the group around the fire. When he strolled to the cook fire to refill his tin coffee mug, she cornered him.

"Avoiding me won't work, you know," she whispered, reaching for the coffeepot after he returned it to its place on a stone beside the fire.

Shane sipped his coffee, regarding her over the rim of his mug. He swallowed and lowered the cup. "Did you think I'd single you out for special attention here in the camp and jeopardize your chances for marriage with Captain Asher?"

"Stop being so noble. I can handle Captain Asher. What I can't handle is the pain you bring me every time you avoid me."

For a brief moment, Della glimpsed Hunter's own pain, a flash in his eyes so brief she almost thought she'd imagined it, before he shuttered his expression. "I'm trying to do what's best for you. And for us."

"Who gave you the right to decide what's best for me?" Goaded beyond discretion, she thumped her chest with a knuckle. "Or for us?"

Shane's mouth firmed. He tilted the brim of his hat lower over his eyes. "I won't discuss our personal affairs here, in full view of the whole camp." His low tones had a bite. "Good night,

Miss Hughes." With a flick of his wrist, he tossed the remainder of his coffee into the fire. He brushed past her without a glance, then stalked to the chuck wagon and flipped his empty mug into the battered metal dishpan resting on the wagon's tail.

With her heart shredding from the pain of his dismissal, Della watched him disappear into the twilight, his long strides taking him toward the horse herd. Swinging her attention back to her uncle and his wife, she caught Aunt Coral's knowing and compassionate gaze. That Aunt Coral knew of her situation with Shane Hunter and could sympathize brought a measure of comfort to Della's battered spirit. She tried to smile at her aunt, though her lips wobbled. She turned away and hurried to her wagon before Captain Asher could accost her. At that moment, she felt too heartsore to deal with him.

In all fairness to Shane Hunter, he had justification for brushing her off. What had she been thinking to goad him in public?

When darkness shrouded the range and the camp had settled down for the night, a series of imperative raps sounded on the wooden bed of her Conestoga. Della recognized her uncle's summons. Dreading the imminent confrontation, she tossed a shawl over her night rail and crawled to the back of the wagon. She brushed aside the privacy flap and peered out.

Uncle Clint's tall form loomed not three feet from the end of her wagon, her bridle looped over one shoulder. With her heart thumping, she clambered through the canvas cover's opening and scrambled to the ground. The dew-wet grass engulfed her bare feet and soaked the hem of her night rail, though both discomforts faded when she looked up at her uncle's stern face.

He let her squirm for several moments. "Didn't I expressly tell you to go to your wagon during the storm?"

Della hung her head. "Yes."

"Did you think it was a suggestion?"

She hesitated, then lifted her face. His forbidding expression wasn't encouraging. She swallowed and shook her head.

"Why didn't you do what you were told?"

Della reflected that her uncle's years as a general during the Civil War certainly had refined his leadership qualities. She felt like a raw recruit being hauled before his superior officer for dereliction of duty. "I wanted to help with the horses." Her voice sounded small in the prairie's silence.

Uncle Clint's stare bored through her. "Didn't you think for a moment there was a good reason I wanted you to stay in your wagon?"

Della couldn't meet her uncle's eyes. She looked away over the dark grasslands.

Her uncle sighed. When she looked at him, his expression of disappointment compounded her guilt. "Della, I appreciate your desire to help us, but sometimes, there are more ways of helping than taking action. None of us questions your riding skills or your courage or your determination. But your very presence out there in the storm was a factor that increased the risks for the men. You caused one of my riders to disobey my orders in order to help you, and because of you, Shane Hunter, the lynchpin upon which this whole enterprise rests, was forced to divide his attention between his duties and the very real necessity of taking time away from looking for the horses to search for you."

"I realize that now," Della confessed. "I didn't think about those things when I rode out."

"I hope you understand the danger you were in, especially after you were thrown. You could have died out there, and if Shane hadn't found you, I would have had to take several men off their search for the horses to look for you."

Della bit her lip. "I'm very sorry, Uncle Clint. I never meant to cause you any trouble."

"I'm sure you didn't intend to."

She bridged the gap between them and hugged him. "I'm sorry to be such a trial to you. You must wish I'd stayed in Boston."

His arms stole around her, and he returned her hug before he curled his hands about her shoulders and put her away from him. He looked down into her face. "I don't wish you'd stayed in

Boston, but I do wish you'd obey me. I can't be always wondering if you're safe or if you're getting into trouble."

"I promise to behave. You won't have to worry about me for the rest of our journey."

He shook his head. "I'm sure you have the best of intentions." He shrugged the bridle from his shoulder and held it out to her. "Here's your bridle. It will need new reins. Your mare broke them when she stepped on them after you fell. And the headstall will need to be oiled."

Della took her bridle and examined the leather straps.

"You must oil the headstall yourself. Don't ask one of your admirers to do it for you."

She glanced at him. "I understand." His point about her taking responsibility for the consequences of her actions was clear.

"I'll see that your reins are replaced."

"Thank you."

He hugged her again. "Good night, Della. We all can use a good night's sleep."

"Uncle Clint? Did you find all of the horses? And the oxen?"

A shadow crossed his face, and he shook his head. "Six horses were never found after the storm, but we managed to locate all of the cattle."

"I'm sorry about the horses."

He nodded.

"Good night, Uncle Clint."

He turned away and took a step before he swung back toward her. "In all of the confusion of the storm, I forgot to tell you that Captain Asher has requested your hand in marriage. I wanted to let you know."

"I already know. He told me."

"I wish I'd had the opportunity to speak to you about it before he mentioned it to you. I wasn't sure what you felt for him."

"I'm fond of him, but I don't love him. I want to love my husband the way Aunt Coral loves you."

A smile creased her uncle's lean face. "If you love your husband the way Coral loves me, he'll be a most fortunate man."

He placed a peck on her forehead. "Don't feel that you must accept the captain's suit. You're welcome to stay with Coral and me as long as you want."

* * * * *

Uncle Clint decreed they remain camped for one more day. The horses and the stock could use an extra day of rest, and the men would spend the time repairing their equipment. That afternoon, a familiar voice hailed Della while she sat on an upturned bucket, mending a tear in the sleeve of one of her blouses.

"Miss Hughes, may I have a word with you?"

Della glanced up. Quentin Asher stood before her, erect in his cavalryman's pristine uniform, with his hat adjusted to the correct angle. Despite the heat, the travel dirt, and the sweat, he presented the suave appearance of a spit-and-polish soldier. His handsome image should make any girl swoon. Della's heart remained unmoved.

"Shall we take a stroll?"

She nodded. She laid aside her mending and fell into step beside him. They left the camp and rambled toward the nearby stream and the cottonwoods growing along its banks. When they reached the edge of the brownish water, they halted. The captain turned to face Della, an earnest expression on his handsome face.

The leaves of the cottonwoods rustled and twisted in the breeze. The shade provided welcome relief from the sun and cast flickering shadows over the cavalryman's features.

"Miss Hughes, I fear I must apologize for my hasty words last Sunday afternoon. In my eagerness to declare you my affianced wife, I perhaps assumed too much." He reached out and claimed both of her hands in his. "I love you, and seeing that scout take liberties with you proved more than I could bear."

His fervent tone melted Della's reserve. He seemed genuinely contrite. She squeezed his hands and smiled. "No woman is immune to such a moving tribute. I accept your apology."

"Can you find it in your heart to return at least a measure of the love I feel for you?"

The prairie wind buffeted her while she glanced away over the rolling grasslands. Thinking of Shane and her consuming emotions for him, Della hesitated. There were many kinds of love, but could the fondness she felt for Quentin Asher ever be enough to sustain a marriage? "I'm very fond of you, Captain, but I'm not sure I can ever love you the way you wish I could."

Disappointment flashed across his face. "It's not what I'd hoped for, but it will do for now. I'll keep trying to win your heart." In a courtly gesture, he dropped tender kisses on the knuckles of each hand.

"Perhaps, I'm not right for you. You told me once you like a lady with spirit. You have political aspirations. I fear I may have too much spirit for the wife of a man in public office. I foresee myself as a liability to your career."

He pressed her hands against his chest, drawing her close. "And I told you I prefer a woman of spirit over a dishwater miss. I have no doubt that once we're married, you'll settle into your role as an officer's wife and, eventually, the wife of a political figure. You've been prepared for just such a position."

He spoke the truth. She'd been groomed all her growing-up years to take her place in society at the side of a man of her own class. She could more readily fill that role than she could the wife of an army scout who slept in a bedroll with the stars for a roof. Still, her spirit rebelled at the vision of living out her life in society. She relished her newfound freedom. Because of her love for Shane Hunter, she'd be willing to stand beside him wherever his duties as a scout took him.

Quentin Asher stroked a finger along her jaw. His touch recalled her to the present and their conversation. Shaking her thoughts from a life with Hunter, she looked into the captain's sherry-brown eyes.

"Della—may I call you Della?"

She nodded.

"Della, will you consent to be my wife? If I could call you mine, you'd make me a happy man."

Most young ladies would be over the moon at such a declaration. Della felt only dismay. She wasn't ready to make such a decision—and certainly not to consent to be his wife. A sensation of suffocating entrapment overcame her.

"People marry for reasons of practicality all the time," the captain said when she didn't speak. "I love you, so a marriage between us won't be for such a pragmatic motive on my part. My love for you will be enough for us both, and I'm confident you'll make me a fine wife. I can foresee our future. One day, after I've spent some years in political office, perhaps I could take up a diplomatic post in Europe. You would enjoy Europe and would grace the capital cities of any country with your charm and beauty."

His determination tumbled Della along willy-nilly in the enthusiasm of his ardor, and his persistence overwhelmed her. She clutched at the slipping edges of her will, seeing the control of her life being wrenched from her grasp by his resolve. She gasped for breath as a drowning man would gasp for air. "Captain—"

"Quentin. Call me Quentin."

"Very well. Quentin, I can't agree to marry you. Please, give me more time. Perhaps, after we've reached Uncle Clint's ranch and you've moved on to your normal duties, we can discuss marriage again. Time apart for reflection upon the matter would be beneficial."

"I need no further reflection, but if you feel the necessity, I can be generous. As long as you come to me as my wife in the end."

"I can't promise that."

He lifted a hand and cupped her cheek. "I appreciate the proper modesty you're displaying by demurring at my offer of marriage. Of course, you can't accept me the first time I ask you. No genteel young lady accepts a gentleman's first proposal. You're a credit to your upbringing."

Della nearly laughed. No one had ever told her she was a credit to her upbringing, and she suspected the captain might change his mind if he knew her better. Before she could comment, he bent his head and placed a chaste kiss on the corner of her mouth. She felt nothing, none of the stirrings of warmth Shane's kisses had roused.

"I'll give you a proper kiss when you agree to be my wife. Until then, this will have to do."

Della stood without moving, feeling no urge to snuggle closer to the captain or to wrap her arms about him. Her doubts about a marriage between them grew. She could think only of Shane and how he moved her.

A shout interrupted the moment. One of the cavalrymen jogged toward them.

Quentin released her hands and turned to face the soldier. "Yes? What is it, Private Bates?"

The private's glance flicked to Della before returning to the captain. "You're needed back at the camp right away. Bring Miss Hughes with you."

"Why? What's wrong?"

"Indians."

CHAPTER 24

QUENTIN GRABBED DELLA'S HAND AND hauled her along with him as he sprinted toward the camp. She tried to keep pace with him, but her boots weren't made for running, and she stumbled over the thick buffalo grass. When they reached the camp, he dropped her hand.

"Stay back here by the wagons." He thrust his way through the men gathered at the edge of the camp.

Della saw her aunt Coral and Silvie standing beside the chuck wagon's tail. She noted Flossie was nowhere to be seen, so she guessed the toddler was in the wagon for her afternoon nap. She hoped the child would sleep through the tribesmen's visit.

She halted beside her aunt. "What do they want?" she whispered.

Aunt Coral was pale. "I'm not sure." Her voice remained steady. "They just appeared suddenly."

Della scanned the scene before her. A group of perhaps twenty mounted warriors faced Shane and her uncle, both of whom had managed to mount up to meet the visitors. The former members of Logan's Cavalry created an armed phalanx behind them, resolute in their commitment to protecting the women and horses. The men held their rifles barrel down, yet no one doubted their ability to bring those rifles to bear on the warriors in a moment should it become necessary.

Captain Asher's cavalry detail spread out at one side. He had worked his way to the front and now stood at Uncle Clint's right side.

Della glanced toward the horse herd. The rest of the cowboys had bunched the Morgans into a tight huddle and were riding in lazy circles about them. Their Winchesters lay across their laps, where the men could swing their barrels up and discharge them if they needed to protect the herd.

The wind rustled the grass with its hot breath. Tense silence hummed through the air. Della strained to hear Shane speaking, but his back was toward her, and she couldn't decipher his words.

Fringed leather pants similar to Hunter's encased the warriors' legs. Sleeveless beaded deerskin vests covered their chests. Their sinewy arms sported metal bands above their elbows. Tall moccasins came to just above their ankles. Eagle feathers had been woven into their long dark hair. Each man gripped a metal-tipped lance in one hand and a rifle in the other.

Della scrutinized their faces—hard, fierce faces that showed no expression. A *frisson* of excitement mingled with apprehension shivered down her spine. These tribesmen were everything that easterners imagined them to be and more. Every penny postcard boasting a photo of western Indians couldn't compare to these mounted warriors. Grateful that Uncle Clint had provided such strong protection for them, Della waited to see what would happen next.

The leader of the band, whose spotted mount stood a pace ahead of the others, gestured with his lance. His eagle-feather headdress trailed down his back. He spoke in rapid, guttural tones. When he lapsed into silence, Shane replied in the same language. He made a chopping motion with one hand and shook his head.

For a moment, the chief didn't reply. Dignity cloaked his proud carriage. When he spoke again, harshness colored his voice.

Again, Shane responded in the same language and shook his head. The chief stared at him with unblinking intensity while the silence stretched out. Tension twanged along taut nerve ends.

Shane stared back. He sat his gelding with relaxed ease, showing not a hint of apprehension, both hands lax on his saddle horn. His mustang switched its tail and stamped at a fly while the two men engaged in a silent duel.

At last, the chief stabbed his lance at the sky and gave a high-pitched yip. He wheeled his spotted pony and kneed it into a gallop. His warriors, mimicking his cry, reined their mounts about and followed their leader in a wild plunge of flashing manes and bunching muscles. The thunder of their horses' hooves sounded in the afternoon's stillness until they topped a rise and vanished over the other side. The grassy plains spread, empty and hot, where an instant before, the tribesmen had been.

For a moment, no one moved. They remained in the frozen tableau they'd maintained while the warriors faced off with them. Then, in the silence, relief spread from one person to another. Low-pitched conversations broke out. Della sidled closer to her uncle and Shane Hunter, who conferred.

She had taken a dozen steps when Quentin Asher strode around to the front of Hunter's mount.

The captain glared at the scout, his posture stiff. "Why didn't you let us shoot the hostiles? We outnumbered them and could have scored a decisive victory."

Astride his tall mustang, Shane's hard profile cut a silhouette against the blue Kansas sky. He thumbed back his hat and shifted in his saddle before he addressed the captain. Stacking his hands on his saddle horn, he leaned forward and stared down at the man who stood in the grass below him. "A victory? I didn't know we were engaged in a battle."

"They were a threat to the women's safety and to all of us."

"They didn't come to make war. They came askin' for food and whiskey. Would you have preferred we murder them in cold blood?"

"We could have made an example of them and sent a message to other hostiles in the area that we aren't to be trifled with."

"We would have brought the Cheyenne nation down upon us. They would have respected us had we killed their men in battle, but to gun them down when they're here to parley with us would be seen as an act of treachery."

Asher's mouth set in mulish lines. He fisted his hands on his belt, arm akimbo. "I say we should have made an example of them."

"Well, Pilgrim," Shane drawled. "It's a good thing you're not makin' the decisions here."

Picking up his reins in one hand, he signaled his grulla into motion. The gelding stepped straight toward the captain. Captain Asher stood in stubborn resistance, his chin jutted, while Shane rode him down. At the last moment, the captain jerked aside, and Shane's stirrup grazed his uniform tunic as the scout rode past.

Uncle Clint fixed a stern expression on Captain Asher when the scout vanished in the direction of the herd. "May I remind you that Shane Hunter makes the decisions while we're on the trail?"

The younger man didn't reply, but obstinate displeasure colored his expression. Disagreement radiated from his rigid stance.

Della let out a shaky breath she didn't realize she'd been holding. For Captain Asher to challenge Shane in such a public manner showed the extent of the resentment he harbored against the other man. And from the little she'd learned of the western code, she understood that Shane had no choice but to openly assert his authority over the captain. For him to let a provocation go uncontested would make him appear weak before the men.

Uncle Clint turned his bay gelding and rode toward the chuck wagon. When he reached Della, he reined in.

"Uncle Clint, what did they really want?" She looked up into her uncle's face.

"Just as Shane said, they wanted food and whiskey."

"Of course, we don't have any whiskey, but why didn't we give them food?"

"Shane told me to never give tribesmen anything. Only trade with them, or they consider it a sign of weakness. I think they were testing us."

That evening, Shane called the men together around the campfire. The women huddled on the group's fringe.

"We'll double up the shifts tonight. For those of you who aren't sleeping, some will ride herd on the horses and the rest will guard the camp. Dawn will be the critical time. Don't expect a frontal assault. We're too well armed, and we outnumber them. They'll doubtless try to infiltrate the camp and the herd. Distrust every shadow and every clump of grass. Every shadow could be a

Cheyenne brave. Guard your backs and keep your sidearms handy."

Della exchanged glances with Aunt Coral, who held Flossie close to her heart. Shane's words shattered the peace of the evening.

After giving instructions to the men, Shane paced toward the women with his loose-jointed stride. Della watched him approach, her heart kicking against her ribs. In addition to his six-shooter, tonight, he'd strapped a Bowie knife in its sheath about his waist and tied it down.

He halted before them. "You ladies should bed down together in one wagon. I'll make sure you have firearms, but I hope you won't have to use them."

"I know you'll do your best for us," Aunt Coral said in a calm voice, though Della knew she concealed anxiety over Flossie's safety. "We're indebted to you."

"Mr. Hunter," Silvie said, "we trust you to keep us safe."

"I'll do my best." He swung his head toward Della. Beneath the brim of his hat, his gaze burned over her. "You do exactly as you're told. Don't leave the wagon until I tell you it's safe to come out. I need you and Coral in the wagon to protect Flossie and Sylvie."

Knowing his concern was warranted, she nodded.

All that long night, the women huddled beneath their blankets in the Logans' wagon. Since they'd been on the trail for several weeks, many of the supplies that had filled the wagon's bed had been used, so the women had room to stretch out their legs while they leaned against the Conestoga's side. Silvie prayed aloud, her simple prayer for protection exhibiting childlike faith. Flossie, sensing the women's anxiety, didn't settle down to sleep. She crawled over the laps of the women, going from one to the other, until exhaustion overcame her. She collapsed in her mother's lap, her head pillowed on Aunt Coral's bosom.

Della reached down and rested her hand on the Colt revolver lying on the wagon's floor beside her. The cold metal reassured her. Should it become necessary, she had the means to protect Flossie and Silvie. If they all must die tonight, she'd die defending them.

The verse Shane Hunter's mother had chosen for her encouragement—"I will never leave thee, nor forsake thee"—filled Della's mind. The same Lord who had protected Mrs. Hunter during her years with the Cheyenne would protect her tonight in her time of danger.

As the night waned, the women napped fitfully. Weariness overrode their fear.

A wild yell and loud gunshots jerked Della from her doze. She leaned forward, reaching for her six-shooter. Aunt Coral and Silvie stirred, and Flossie wailed.

The pounding of hooves followed, punctuated by men's shouts.

Della thrust the blanket off her lap and came to her knees. She stared at the back of the wagon through the grayness of early morning, waiting to see whether the privacy flap would move. She thumbed back the hammer of the revolver and held the gun steady, aimed at the wagon's tail. Behind her, Aunt Coral cocked her own weapon. "Shh . . . hush, little one," Silvie whispered. "You're safe with me."

Flossie's wails subsided to a whimper, while silence descended over the camp. The women waited, their breathing ragged in the wagon's stillness. After some moments, men's voices sounded, approaching the camp. Della lowered the hammer on her six-shooter and laid the weapon on the floor. She slumped against the Conestoga's oak side and rested her head against the planks. Aunt Coral laid her own revolver down and snatched Flossie from Silvie's arms. Whatever danger had lurked outside had been routed.

Sharp raps sounded at the back of the wagon. "Ladies, it's safe to come out," Uncle Clint said.

Aunt Coral set Flossie on the floor and scrambled on hands and knees toward her husband. She thrust aside the privacy flap and tumbled through the oval opening into Uncle Clint's embrace. His arms closed about his wife, crushing her against his chest. He laid his cheek on the top of her head and rocked her with loving fervor. "You're safe now. You're safe."

"Papa!" Flossie ran toward her father and reached for him through the opening. "Papa!"

Uncle Clint plucked his daughter from the wagon, then held his wife in a one-armed embrace and his daughter against his side.

Della crawled out and stood beside her uncle, followed by Silvie. "What happened, Uncle Clint?"

"A few of the Cheyenne sneaked close to the herd. They tried to pull some of our men off their horses and steal their mounts. If they'd been successful, they could have run off many of our Morgans."

"Was anyone hurt?" Aunt Coral asked from the shelter of her husband's arm.

"We lost one man, and another one was injured." Uncle Clint's grim tone reflected the burden he carried over a death at the hands of marauding tribesmen.

An image of Shane Hunter prostrate and silent in death flashed before Della's eyes. "Who?" she asked in a sharp tone.

"Major Green. He'd been with me since the First Battle of Bull Run. I hate to lose him here, in the West, when he survived the war."

Relief so acute she nearly swayed filled Della's chest to the bursting point. Fearful her face should betray her, she turned away. Although she regretted Major Green's death, she couldn't help but be thankful the man she loved hadn't been among the casualties.

"I think we could all use a cup of coffee." Uncle Clint steered Aunt Coral to the front of the wagon and urged her toward the chuck wagon and the fire. Della and Silvie trudged behind.

Dawn painted a band of light along the horizon, hinting at the coming day.

When they reached the chuck wagon, a group of drovers circled the cook fire. Toby bent over one of the men who sat on the ground with his back toward them. Della couldn't see the man's injury since Toby blocked her view.

"This is going to sting some." Toby swabbed the wound with a rag.

The wounded man hissed. "Are you trying to kill me? What have you got there?"

"Just something to keep sepsis from setting in. Now, hold still. I've got to stitch you up."

The man twisted and glared at Toby. "Stitch me up? You're not coming near me with a needle and thread. Just slap a poultice on me, and I'll be right as rain tomorrow."

Toby shook his head. "Nope. You need stitching." He handed the drover a short leather strap. "Put this between your teeth while I stitch. Bite down when the pain gets too bad."

Della shuddered and averted her gaze. Her stomach rolled at the thought of the agony the wounded man would endure while Toby stitched the knife gash on his back.

In the next moment, she felt Shane's gaze upon her. Even without seeing him, she sensed his closeness. She lifted her chin and encountered his blue stare from across the cook fire.

His nostrils flared. He stood with his booted feet planted wide, his shoulders squared, his head thrown back so the brim of his hat didn't shield his face. The flickering flames washed his features in amber. They stood motionless, a silent island amid the bustle of the camp, yearning for each other. Time hung suspended while a force stronger than themselves smoldered between them. Only when Quentin Asher took her arm and turned her toward him did Della recall the present.

"Della, you shouldn't be here. This is a situation best left to us men. You ladies should return to your wagons until we're through."

Della glanced at him. He seemed distressed to see her in the camp. Craning her neck to peer around him, she spied the blanketed body lying on one side of the fire. Major Green had been laid out in preparation for burial. She looked back into her suitor's face, wishing she could better appreciate his old-world chivalry. "Thank you for wanting to shield me, but I won't be sheltered from life's hardships. If I can't endure what the West thrusts upon us, I should return to Boston."

"But Major Green was killed in a violent way. Violence should have no part in a lady's life."

"I appreciate your desire to protect me, but I'm no shrinking violet. When we bury Major Green, I'll be there at the graveside to show my respect for his bravery."

"I'm beginning to see the frontier is no place for a genteel lady. When we marry, you'll stay in Denver until I can muster out of the army and join you in civilization."

Della refrained from reminding him she hadn't yet consented to wed him. At that moment, debating the issue seemed a waste of breath. On one topic, Shane and Quentin Asher agreed, she mused. Both men insisted the frontier was no place for a lady.

She glanced over her shoulder to where Shane had been standing. The spot was empty.

CHAPTER 25

A WEEK LATER, DELLA SHIVERED a little in her sheepskin jacket when she stretched out her hands to the cook fire's blaze. The predawn chill penetrated the layers of clothing to her very bones.

"Here, Miss Della," Toby said. "This coffee will warm you."

Della took the proffered tin mug and sipped, enjoying the hot liquid sliding down her throat. "Thank you, Toby. This is just what I needed." She inhaled the coffee's strong scent. She'd gotten so used to campfire coffee she'd forgotten the mild, sweetened blends she'd drunk in the elegant breakfast room at home in Boston.

Crickets sawed a monotonous tune. Over a distant swell of ground, the yips and barks of a coyote band filled the night with their music.

Movement off to one side and the sound of footsteps crunching through the grass caught Della's attention. A full moon riding the crest of the sky silvered the prairie. The horses and the riders guarding them were visible in the moonglow drenching the plains. Its luster limned Shane Hunter, leading his saddled mustang, in alabaster.

Shane dropped the reins to ground-tie his gelding at the edge of the firelight and strolled toward her, his attention fixed on her face. She met his stare with one of her own.

He came to a standstill a mere handspan from her. Tipping back her head, she looked into his eyes, which at that moment were narrowed.

"And what are you doin' up at this early hour?"

"I hoped I could accompany you today. You haven't seen any Indian sign for several days, so I thought it would be safe for me to ride with you."

He hesitated for long moments. His gaze roved over her face. His perusal touched her with tenderness. Della felt as though he'd caressed her. She caught her breath. His scrutiny dropped to her mouth, lingered there, then swung back to her face. In his eyes, she saw the love that he hadn't yet admitted to her aloud. She saw the love—and the pain.

Over at the chuck wagon's tail, Toby rattled plates and mugs. The sound jarred them from their preoccupation with each other.

"There's plenty of Indian sign out there, but none of it is less than a day old."

Della gave him her most winsome smile. She curved the fingers of her free hand about his upper arm. The muscle beneath his buckskin sleeve felt warm and rock hard. "Please. We've scarcely had time to talk, and we're already in the Colorado Territory. Soon, we'll be at Uncle Clint's ranch. Let me come with you."

As if of its own volition, his hand crept up to cover hers. Shane's warm, calloused fingers squeezed her smaller ones. "I think you've addled my wits. I know I should refuse you, but I can't seem to find the strength to say the words."

"I'll do whatever you tell me."

"See that you do. We'll be ridin' with great caution and little talkin'."

She nodded.

When they'd eaten and Shane had filled their canteens from the water barrels, he caught up her chestnut and tacked up the mare. They rode out of camp and passed the horse herd.

Emory Dyer, riding on the near side of the herd, loped his mount toward them. When he'd reined his gelding to a halt, he slouched in the saddle seat. "Does your uncle know where you're going today?"

She hung her head. "I completely forgot to tell him. Would you let him know I'm riding with Shane?"

Sighing, the lieutenant shook his head. "It's a good thing I saw you. Your uncle would have sent the army out looking for you when you turned up missing."

Shane cast Della a sharp glance. "You didn't mention that General Logan didn't know you were goin' with me."

His censure filled her with remorse. "I'm sorry. I should have thought of it." She brightened. "Toby saw us ride off. He knows I'm with you."

"Still, you should have told your uncle."

Emory Dyer gathered his reins. "Hunter, I don't envy you. That gal sure is a handful." Having said his piece, he turned his mount and cantered back to the herd.

Della looked at Shane, her failings once again overtaking her. His disappointment in her and his rebuke hurt her more than she could have imagined. "I truly am sorry."

Shane shrugged. "You're a tenderfoot."

"I still have so much to learn about surviving in the West."

"Out here, forgettin' one detail can be fatal. You have to remember even the little things. If you intend to stay here, you'll have to do better."

His face was faint but clear in the moonlight. Their gazes locked, love's flame overriding the reproach of a moment earlier.

"I'd stay in the West if you gave me a reason."

The air once again vibrated with the longing between them, snaring them with skeins of yearning, hope, and despair. "I'm still prayin' about that," Hunter said at last.

"And that will do, for now."

They signaled their mounts to move, caution reflected in every move. Shane rode with two Colts strapped to his gun belt and his Bowie knife sheathed in one boot. His Winchester lay across his lap. His gaze swept the plains, looking for anything that might signal danger. They frequently stopped while he listened for any hint of peril.

Della was content to ride at his side, watching him and feeling no compulsion to talk. She marveled at his knowledge of the land. He seemed more comfortable here on the range than he had in Kansas City among the buildings and bustle of civilization.

The sun chased the moon from the sky, and with the sun, the prairie exploded into color. Columbine added splashes of blue amid the grasses. A meadowlark called before bursting from its perch on a blade of grass and streaking toward the sky with a whir of wings. Its vivid yellow breast flashed in the clear morning light. Ahead of them, a band of antelope bounded away at their approach.

On one of their frequent stops, Della shed her jacket. While Shane dug his field glasses from his saddlebags, she rolled up her jacket and tied it behind her saddle. Shane lifted the glasses and surveyed the prairie in a slow sweep. Della glanced about, wiping the perspiration from her face with the bandanna tied about her neck.

The land here seemed mostly flat, broken only by billowing, grassy swells. It had been imperceptibly lifting toward the mountains for most of their trek from Kansas City, and now, Della could see a blue smudge on the far horizon where the Rockies met the sky. The vastness of the land, with its lonely emptiness, dwarfed and terrified her. Yet, even while the majesty of the frontier intimidated her, its splendor tugged at her heart. She could love this country as well as fear it, if she stayed.

Shane touched her shoulder. She glanced at him without speaking when he passed the field glasses to her. "Look over there, in that little dip." He pointed to their left.

She put the glasses to her face. The distant prairie jumped into view. At first, she saw only grass and tufts of foliage, but then, motion caught her attention. She shifted the glasses a trifle, and a herd of wild horses filled the lens. The lead stallion stood a bit apart from his band of mares, his head lifted. His nostrils flared as he tested the wind. Della caught her breath and lowered the glasses.

"They're magnificent! So wild and free." She glanced at Shane. His attention was not on the mustangs but on her. His intent gaze roamed over her face, warm and loving. Her heart hitched, and her pulse skittered. Without even realizing what she did, she leaned toward him.

Under leg pressure from Shane, the grulla sidled closer to Della's mare until the scout's tooled leather riding boot bumped her foot. Shane reached out and curled his fingers about her neck beneath the brim of her hat. With gentle pressure, he tugged her closer to him.

With one hand on her saddle horn and the other on Hunter's shoulder for balance, Della leaned into him. Shane bent and tipped his head so their hat brims wouldn't bump. His mouth found hers. Della's eyes drifted closed. He put all the love he couldn't vocalize into his kiss, and she responded, sharing with him the love that filled her heart.

Her hand lifted from his shoulder to his neck. His shaggy hair curled over his collar, and her fingers clenched in the sandy-colored strands. His fingers speared into her braid and cupped the back of her head, holding her still for his kiss. At last, he lifted his mouth from hers and dropped light pecks all over her face.

She opened dreamy eyes and looked into his. His eyes were bluer than the Colorado sky. Squint lines fanned out on either side of his face, a face she'd learned to love. She studied his features, realizing how dear he'd become during their weeks on the trail. For the first time, she considered the possibility that he wouldn't come around to agreeing to marriage. What would she do should he refuse? Her life would be an empty wasteland without him.

"Della, darlin'." His ragged voice drew her from her dismal thoughts. "What are you doin' to me? I was content with my life until you came into it. Now, you've set my heart on fire, and my life will never be the same. You've made me hunger for things I never thought would be mine, a life with a woman at my side."

"Shane, why does our love have to be so difficult? Together, we'll be strong enough to face whatever life deals us. Together—and with the Lord—we'll be strong."

"You make it sound possible."

"It is possible. I know it's possible."

His hand dropped from the back of her head. He curled his arm around her shoulders, tipped her out of her saddle, and pulled her across his lap, shifting her so she faced him. The cold metal of the rifle's barrel pressed into the back of her legs. He jerked the

Winchester from between them and slid it into the scabbard hanging beneath the stirrup leather on the horse's off side. With the rifle out of the way, he turned his attention to her. He gathered her close, both his arms wrapping about her back and pressing her against his muscled chest. She clutched him about the neck while he kissed her again, hungry kisses that stole the breath from her body and betrayed the depth of his feelings. At last, he broke off the kiss and tucked her face into the curve of his neck.

She breathed in the scents of sun-warmed air, leather, and horse, sighed, and snuggled closer. For long moments, they didn't move. Insects hummed in the grass, the horses stamped at bothersome flies, and above them, a red-tailed hawk screeched. At last, Shane stirred. With his hands on her arms, he pushed her upright.

"We've dallied too long, and you've distracted me enough. I've been careless."

Della laid her palm against his cheek. "I love you."

His eyes darkened. "Don't say that. As much as I enjoy hearin' you say you love me, it makes everything so much more difficult to sort out."

"But I do love you. Whatever happens between us, always remember that."

He didn't reply. Instead, he looked deep into her eyes while the mustang shifted beneath them and shook its head. After one final, swift kiss, he lifted her back into her own saddle.

They headed toward a shallow stream to make their nooning. When they pulled up their mounts at the edge of the grass, Hunter raised a hand. "Stay where you are," he muttered. "Don't get down."

He swung off his mount and moved to the water's sandy bank, where dirt met prairie grass. Crouching, his gelding's reins held loosely in one hand, Shane examined the ground. Hoof marks made by unshod horses pocked the sand.

"What is it? Who's been here?"

He continued to study the stream bank. "These hoof marks were made by Indian ponies. Recently, less than two hours ago." He scanned the opposite verge. Hoof marks scarred the smooth soil on the other side of the creek. "They stopped to water their horses and crossed the stream here."

"How many?"

"About a dozen." Hunter rose and moved to Della's side. He reached up, grasped her about the waist, and hauled her from the mare's back. "I'm goin' to reconnoiter."

"What about me?"

"You'll stay here. I'll come back for you." The moment her feet touched the ground, he dropped his hands from her waist and turned away.

"You're going to leave me alone?"

He nodded in abstracted affirmation while he studied the terrain along the stream's edge. Della stepped closer to him, looking up at his profile. Gone was the romantic companion who'd held her so tenderly earlier in the morning. In his place, a warrior had emerged, intent on protecting the one under his care. He'd see her safely through this threat.

Shane grasped her hand and led her through a dense thicket of brush and trees growing along the stream. When the foliage screened her from sight, he left her to gather the horses' reins and led them into the underbrush. He tied them to a shrub, then returned to the riverbank. Walking backward, he brushed out their tracks with a leafy branch and then sprinkled dirt over the brush marks to obliterate any sign of their presence.

He joined her in the copse, moved to his mustang's flank, and rummaged in the saddlebags.

"I reckon I won't be gone long, but I need to get a bead on which direction they've gone and if they kept movin'." He pulled out a pair of moccasins and sat long enough to remove his boots and slip on the soft footwear. He shoved to his feet and pulled his spare Colt from its holster. Spinning the cylinder, he checked the chambers, then snapped it shut. He held it out to her, butt first. "Take my six-shooter. Use it only if anyone actually gets into this clearin'."

The weapon felt heavy, though reassuring. "Thank you."

"Watch the horses. If anyone comes around, they'll let you know. And if the birds and insects suddenly go silent, that means someone is approachin'."

She nodded.

"When I come back, I'll hoot like an owl three times. Like this." He demonstrated.

"You sound exactly like the real thing," Della said.

"I learned to do that as a boy." The glimmer of a smile lifted the corners of his lips. "When you hear the owl call three times, that will be me. Don't shoot me."

He lifted one hand to her face and cupped her cheek. His thumb stroked her bottom lip. "Wait here for me."

He dropped his hand and turned away. Like a wraith of smoke, without a sound and without disturbing a leaf, he vanished.

CHAPTER 26

DELLA STARED AT THE EMPTY air where Shane Hunter had stood a moment before. Only his promise to return for her kept the panic at bay. She was alone on the prairie with nothing but a six-shooter to protect her. No one except Shane knew where to find her. What if something should happen to him? What if he didn't return for her? She'd never find her way back to the wagon train on her own.

The thought of tribesmen roaming close by filled her with anxiety. She recalled a verse from the Psalms that she'd memorized as a child. She whispered the words to herself. "Be of good courage, and he shall strengthen your heart, all ye that hope in the LORD." The promise of the Scriptures brought her a measure of peace. Her breathing steadied, and her pulse slowed.

The prairie sun beat down upon the land. The wind sighed through the branches, rattling the foliage. Della waited in the shade of the brush, listening to the insects sawing in the bushes and trying to be patient. Salty drops of perspiration ran from her hairline down the side of her cheek. After loosening the bandana from about her neck, she dabbed at her face with the blue cotton. She dropped to the ground and leaned against the bole of a tree.

Nearby, the horses swished their tails and chewed leaves from the limbs. Their presence steadied her and gave her companionship. She didn't feel quite so alone.

Eying the sun's position, Della tried to judge the passage of time. She estimated Shane had been gone more than an hour when an owl hooted from some bushes a few yards away. The sound was repeated twice. Shane! He'd returned. Relief flooded her, and she scrambled to her feet.

A moment later, he ghosted into the glade as silently as he'd gone. Della launched herself at him. His arms closed about her. Her cheek rested against his buckskin shirt.

"I thought you wouldn't come back."

"I told you I would."

"I was afraid something had happened to you."

"Nothin' would happen that would keep me from comin' back for you."

With her fingers wrapped about his biceps, she leaned against his encircling arms to look into his face. "What did you find?"

"They kept movin' west. They seemed to be a huntin' party, but there's a lot of other Indian sign out there." He kissed her lightly, then put her away from him and turned toward the horses. "Let's mount up."

"Here's your six-shooter." Della scooped the revolver from the ground where she'd left it beside the tree and passed it to Shane.

He dropped the weapon into his spare holster and tied the leather thong about the wooden butt, then removed his moccasins and put on his boots. With the moccasins stashed in his saddlebags, he led the horses out of the glade.

They mounted and rode for an hour before Shane allowed them to halt in the lee of a shallow ridge amid a tumble of large rocks. He swung down from his mustang's back and came around to Della's side. He reached up for her, and his large hands closed about her waist. She leaned down to him, and he pulled her from the saddle.

They stood in a loose embrace for several moments. Della studied his face, lovingly caressing his features with her gaze. "Wouldn't it be something if we were the only people here and we could keep riding? Just the two of us."

"A nice dream but not practical."

She wrinkled her nose at him. "Where's your sense of romance?"

He trailed a long forefinger along her jaw, then linked his hands behind the small of her back and pulled her closer. "The

Dakota tribe tells the legend of a brave, though shy, warrior who loved a beautiful Indian maiden. He wanted to make her his wife, but he was so shy he couldn't speak to her. He watched the other young warriors bring their courtin' blankets to her family's tepee and throw their blankets around her and talk to her."

Shane paused.

"Well, what happened?" Della asked. "How did he get the girl?"

"The young man was sure the beautiful maiden hadn't noticed him, so he left the village in despair. He walked for four days and stopped to sleep at the edge of the forest. In a dream, the Elk Men came to him and told him they would help him win the love of his maiden. They gave him a flute made of cedarwood and told him to play it. The music would be so beautiful the maiden would fall in love with him." Shane paused again. His eyes smiled down at her.

Della gripped his shoulders and shook him. "Tell me the rest. I'm sure the maiden learned to love her brave suitor."

"In the mornin', the warrior woke. A cedarwood flute was laying on the ground beside him. He took the instrument and ran back to his village. When he reached the hill above the village, he began to play. The music was so beautiful that every unmarried woman in the tribe fell in love with him, but the beautiful maiden knew he played only for her. She joined him on the hill and knew that the flute said the words he was too shy to speak. The flute told her the warrior loved her."

Della sighed. "That's a beautiful story."

"Because of that legend, cedarwood flutes are played only durin' courtship and have been adopted by other tribes." Shane placed a kiss on her mouth. "If I had a cedarwood flute, I'd play it for you."

"That's the most beautiful love declaration any man has ever given me."

He cocked an eyebrow at her. "And have you had many declarations of love?"

Her lashes swept down while she fingered the colored beading on the front of his buckskin shirt. "A lady never tells."

"I'll take that to mean you've had men fallin' at your feet since you grew out of your pinafore."

Della giggled.

Shane let her go and turned away to rummage in his saddlebags.

Della wandered to the oversize rocks jumbled along the base of the ridge. She lowered herself to a smooth stone about the size of a love seat. Leaning back on her outstretched arms, she lifted her face to the sky. The ridge above cast a wide slice of shade over the rocks, and she enjoyed the respite from the sun. She closed her eyes.

A sudden angry buzzing roused her. Puzzled, she glanced to her left. Partially shielded by an overhanging rock, a thick brown snake marked by darker patterns on its back coiled mere inches from her hand. Before she could react, the reptile struck, sinking its fangs into the muscle just above her elbow. Burning pain shot through her arm.

In a blink, the rattlesnake retracted its fangs. Its hideous triangular head rose as if the reptile prepared to strike again.

Shane spun. His Colt flashed into his palm and roared. Smoke spiraled in lazy coils from the six-shooter's muzzle.

Horror gripped Della. She leaped from the rock, whirled, and stared at the creature. Shane's bullet had shot off the reptile's head, and now, the snake writhed in death.

Shane leaped to her side. "Darlin', where did it get you?"

Della lifted her arm and looked at the wound. Two puncture holes in the sleeve of her blouse marked the spot where the rattlesnake had struck. Crimson droplets stained the fabric. "Here." Faintness washed over her, adding to the searing agony of the bite. She swayed.

Shane caught her about the shoulders and eased her down onto the buffalo grass, propping her against the rocks. He reached into his boot, pulled out his Bowie knife, and slit her sleeve from shoulder to wrist, then bunched the fabric beneath her arm. With aching gentleness, he wrapped his fingers about her bicep and examined the bite. Della risked another glance. Swelling and angry redness marred her skin at the wound site.

Shane lowered her arm. "Keep your arm down. It will slow the venom." He cast her a reassuring look. "Don't move. I'll be right back."

Della closed her eyes. His hurried footsteps faded as he crossed the grass to his mustang. Nausea roiled in her stomach. Her face and limbs felt numb, and her throat tightened. She struggled to draw air into her lungs.

Moments later, Shane knelt at her side. Cracking open her eyes, she watched him arrange dried grass into a pile and extract the makings of a fire from his tinderbox. With an economy of motion, he scratched a match against the sole of his boot, lit the fire, and poured water from his canteen into the tin pan he carried in his saddlebags. From a deerskin pouch, he shook a measure of dried herbs into the water and set the pan in the flames. Next, he shoved the blade of his Bowie knife deep into the fire.

Della closed her eyes again, not wanting to know what he intended to do with the knife. She clamped her lips against the nausea churning in her belly. She wouldn't humiliate herself in Shane's presence by being sick. She wouldn't. The pain in her arm and the numbness of her hands and feet terrified her.

Shane roused her by a touch on her shoulder. "Darlin', drink this." Squatting by her side, he held his tin cup to her lips.

She opened her eyes and stared at his face hovering close above her. Now, his features—and everything she looked at— seemed blurred. Her panic kicked up a notch when she couldn't quite focus. "What is it?"

"Tea made with dried plantain leaves and black cohosh. Drink it all. I've made a poultice from the herbs to draw out the venom."

He held the mug for her while Della drank. The tea tasted bitter, but she drained the liquid to the dregs. When she'd swallowed the last drop, she leaned her head back against the rock and closed her eyes again.

Still crouching beside her, Shane squeezed her shoulder in a tender caress. "Darlin', look at me."

Della lifted her lids and stared into his eyes, squinting to focus. Concern darkened his eyes and deepened the grooves in his cheeks.

"Della, I'm goin' to hurt you."

"Hmm?" She struggled to make sense of his words.

"I'm goin' to take my knife and cut across the bite marks. You need to bleed. Some of the venom will come out with your blood. Then, I'll pack the wounds with the poultice to draw out as much of the venom as possible." He squeezed her shoulder again. "I won't hurt you more than I have to, but I must work fast, and the blade will be hot."

She nodded. His words made her heart thump against her ribs. Breathing as deeply as she could, she forced herself to calmness.

She vowed the West wouldn't conquer her. Even in this extremity, she'd fight and survive.

Shane bent and placed a swift kiss on her lips, then twisted toward the fire. When he pivoted back to her, his Bowie knife in one hand, a jolt of panic shot through her. With his other hand, he grasped her arm about the wound, making it impossible for her to move. The blade of the knife glowed red.

Their gazes met for a single instant before Shane placed the tip of the blade against her skin and pressed the edge into the muscle. The acrid scent of burning flesh filled her nostrils as the blade bit into her arm. Agony greater than anything she'd ever known sliced through her. Della turned her head away, gritting her teeth, determined not to scream. He made another slash across the second bite mark and then tossed down the knife. Della's head fell back against the rock, and she swallowed a whimper of pain.

Shane loosened his hold on her and pressed against the incisions to force blood from the wounds. Warm liquid ran down her arm and dripped into the grass. The misty blackness that had hovered about her enveloped her, dragging her into its depths.

When she woke, she lay on the ground with Shane's bedroll beneath her, her jacket bunched beneath her head. Her arm throbbed. She glanced down. A white cloth had been wrapped about the bite. Shane sat beside her, leaning against the rock, his Winchester cradled in his arms.

As if sensing she was awake, he looked over at her. He reached out and stroked her hair, running his hand down her braid. "How are you feelin'?"

She took stock of her body. She could see clearly now, and the numbness had left. "A little better, I think."

"You gave me a scare."

Nodding, she ran her tongue over dry lips. "Could I have some water?"

Shane reached for his canteen and slid an arm beneath her shoulders. After lifting her into a sitting position, he held the canteen to her mouth and tipped it. Lukewarm, brackish water slid down her throat, but the liquid tasted like nectar. After a few swallows, he laid her down and capped the container.

"We have to conserve our water. You won't be able to travel tonight, so we'll stay here an extra day."

"Uncle Clint will be worried."

Shane shrugged. "He knows you're with me. I hope he trusts me to keep you safe." He reached out and curled his hand about hers, his long fingers dwarfing her smaller ones. "Darlin', you were very brave. You make me proud."

"I told you I was tough. I just didn't know I'd have to prove it like this."

He squeezed her hand. "I misjudged you. I thought you were a useless society miss."

Exhaustion pulled at her, and darkness swirled about her again. She closed her eyes. Relaxing into the blankets and breathing evenly, she listened to the horses cropping grass nearby and the insects whirring. "Shane, I love you."

A beat or two of silence followed. "I love you, too, Della, my darlin'."

CHAPTER 27

DELLA WOKE BY DEGREES, WONDERING why she wasn't tucked snugly into her Conestoga at the camp. Instead of Toby rattling pans in preparation for breakfast, a meadowlark called close by, and a breeze rustled the grass near her. A horse cleared its nostrils and stamped. Sunlight shimmered against her closed lids. She opened her eyes to see pale blue sky above her instead of the gray canvas of her wagon's top. Her arm throbbed, and yesterday's encounter with the rattlesnake rushed back.

She and Shane had spent the night on the plains because she'd been unable to travel. Shane, with his knowledge of Cheyenne remedies, had saved her life.

She lifted her head and saw him crouching beside a tiny, smokeless fire. The tin pan he carried in his saddlebags rested over the flames.

He swung his head in her direction. A slow smile creased his cheeks, and he rose with the fluid grace that marked all his movements. Three long strides brought him to her side. He knelt and laid his work-roughened palm against her cheek. "Mornin'. I hope you're feelin' better than you were last night."

Della took stock of her condition. Except for the throbbing of her arm and a sensation of weakness overlaid by a general malaise, all the other symptoms of the venom had vanished. She swallowed to moisten her mouth. "I am, mostly." Her voice croaked.

"I'm brewing you some herbal tea. Unless you want more jerky, I have no food to offer you. I've rigged a snare to catch a rabbit, but so far, I haven't caught one." Shane stroked her hair as if he couldn't bear not to touch her. His fingers clenched in her braid. He leaned down and buried his face in the crook of her neck. His other arm stole about her shoulder and lifted her against his chest, turning her so her cheek pressed against his deerskin shirt, yet careful not to jostle her injury. "Della, darlin', I spent the night wonderin' what I'd do if you died." His voice sounded ragged. "I can't imagine the world without you."

His heart beat with a steady rhythm beneath her ear. The sound reassured her, letting her know Shane's strength and knowledge would see them through this difficulty. She raised her head and looked into his beloved face, mere inches above her own. "I have you to thank that I'm still alive."

He squeezed her, then laid her back down on the bedroll. "That tea should be ready now."

He stood and returned to the fire. After folding his neckerchief into a pad, he used the fabric to guard his fingers from the hot metal. He lifted the pan from the fire and poured the tea into the tin cup he used the night before.

Shane crossed to Della's side. He knelt again and swirled the tea in the mug. "This is too hot to drink. It will have to cool some."

Della nodded. "What will we do now?"

Shane rocked back on his heels. "You won't be able to ride. I'll chop down a couple of saplings to rig a travois for you. We'll get back to the wagon train with my gelding towin' the sled."

"Do you think the wagon train moved on without us?"

He shook his head. "When we didn't show up last night, your uncle probably decided to stay put until we return. He may have sent out riders to try to locate us, but I doubt he moved on."

After Della drank the tea, Shane tacked up his grulla and led the gelding toward her. He loosened the leather thong over the butt of his spare six-shooter, pulled the weapon from its holster, and laid it in the grass at her side. "If you need me, fire two shots. That will leave you four if you must defend yourself. I'll try to stay within hearin' distance and will come runnin' if you signal."

They both knew that here on the plains, trees grew only along the water. He must locate a stream in order to find saplings to fashion the travois.

"I'll be fine." She smiled at him, trying not to betray how uneasy she felt at his leave-taking.

Shane went down on one knee and curved an arm beneath her shoulders. Lifting her up a trifle, he bent and kissed her, a kiss that held all his love, his frustration at their circumstances, and his relief that she lived. When their lips parted, his stare burned over her face before he laid her down.

"I'll be back as soon as I can."

The sun was inching toward its zenith, and the shade from the boulder next to Della had almost vanished when Shane returned, dragging two long saplings stripped of their branches.

He rigged a travois by thrusting the poles through the sleeves of his canvas duster and lashing the poles to his saddle with lengths of rope from his saddlebags. Once he secured the sleeves of his duster to the saplings in the same manner, he broke camp.

Before he carried her to the travois, he crouched beside Della and held out his canteen. "Are you thirsty? I refilled our canteens at the stream, so you can drink all you want."

She glanced at him. "Thank you. I'm parched."

He lifted her and propped her back against his shoulder. She took the canteen and drank with thirsty abandon. When she finished, she passed the canteen back to him.

After capping the bottle and stowing it in his saddlebags, Shane crossed to Della's side. In minutes, he had her settled on the travois and his bedroll tied behind her saddle. He mounted his grulla. Ponying Della's mare beside his mustang, with the travois dragging behind his mount, they left the camp and made their slow way back to the wagon train.

By the time they reached the caravan, night had stolen the daylight from the sky and draped a black canopy over the prairie. Stars glittered as they crested a shallow rise and looked down on the camp. A bonfire lit the night with its flickering rays and painted the wagons' canvas tops amber.

"We're here," Shane said as Della faced backward on the sled. "The camp is in the hollow."

They bumped their way down the slope. When they approached the circle of firelight, a shout went up from the camp.

Uncle Clint, with Aunt Coral at his side, was the first to reach them. Emory Dyer and several drovers swarmed about the little cavalcade.

Shane halted his weary grulla at the edge of the light cast by the campfire. Before he could dismount, Uncle Clint leaned over Della, grasping her hand in his large one. Aunt Coral peered over his shoulder, concern puckering her brow.

"Della, are you all right?" Her uncle squeezed her hand.

"We were so worried," Aunt Coral said.

"I'm fine." Della ignored the exhaustion that drained her. She tried to smile. "I was bitten by a rattler, but Shane killed the snake and then fixed me up with his Cheyenne remedies. He saved my life."

Shane had dismounted and stood by.

When she lapsed into silence, Uncle Clint straightened and turned to the scout. He thrust out a hand. "Thank you for saving my niece's life. We can never repay you."

Shane shrugged, then took the proffered hand and shook it. "Miss Hughes was under my protection. I could let nothing harm her. You don't owe me anything."

While she made a bedroll beside the fire, Aunt Coral fussed over Della. Uncle Clint laid his niece on the cocoon of blankets.

"Would you rather go to your wagon?" Aunt Coral asked.

"No. I just want to lie here and enjoy everyone's company," Della said. "But we're both hungry. Is there anything left from supper?"

Toby bustled over and handed Della a plate of beans and bacon with a fluffy biscuit on the side. "I knew that hombre would bring you back, so I saved some food for you."

Della took the plate, smiling at him. "Thank you, Toby. This smells delicious." The plain fare seemed to be the most delicious cuisine she'd ever eaten. Before she dug in, she glanced across the fire at Shane, who was unhitching the poles from his saddle. "Come eat with me, Shane."

Without pausing, Shane cocked his head to look at Della. "I must tend to the horses first. I'll eat later."

"Yes, of course. I wasn't thinking." Disappointed though she was that Shane wouldn't join her, she realized he was right to put the horses first. A true horseman always cared for his mount before seeing to his own needs.

Aunt Coral settled herself on the grass beside Della and linked her arms about her drawn-up knees. "Tell us in more detail what happened. We knew it had to be something serious to keep you away from the camp."

Uncle Clint knelt on Della's other side, and Emory Dyer stood at her feet, looking down at her. Della's gaze roved over each one. Balancing her plate in one hand, she stretched out her other hand toward her uncle. "I'm so sorry I caused you to worry, but this time, it wasn't my fault. Truly."

Uncle Clint took her hand and held it against his chest. "I'm not blaming you, Della. Why don't you tell us what happened?"

After drawing a breath, Della launched into her tale. "Shane told me you'd stay here until we came back," she said when she finished.

"Of course. This morning, I sent out a couple of men to try to find you."

"Shane said that's what you'd do." If her family thought her use of the scout's given name odd, no one mentioned it.

"And I sent out Captain Asher and his men." Uncle Clint shook his head. "He vexed me with his importuning to let him search for you. I sent him off to get him out from underfoot. I only hope he can find his way back in the dark."

"Della, we'll stop talking so you can eat," Aunt Coral said. "I know you're famished."

The drovers drifted away to take up their duties guarding the horse herd while Della cleaned her plate. Uncle Clint and Aunt Coral sat by her side without speaking.

Della had just finished her biscuit and laid her plate on the grass when Captain Asher's cavalry detail rode into the firelight with the thud of hooves and the jingle of tack. The captain spied Della sitting beside the fire, flung himself from his mount, and rushed to her side.

"Miss Hughes, you've returned safely!" He went down on one knee and took possession of her hand. "I was beside myself with worry. What happened that would keep you out all night and a day with that scout?"

Captain Asher's disdainful tone in reference to Shane Hunter set Della's teeth on edge. She pulled her hand free. "Mr. Hunter saved my life when I was bitten by a rattler."

"A rattlesnake!" Anger lent an edge to the captain's tone and sharpened his features. The flames played over his face, taut with vexation. "How could he be so careless as to allow you to be bitten?"

"It wasn't his fault!" Della exclaimed, thankful that Shane had taken the horses to join the herd and wasn't present to hear the insult. "I'll not allow you to malign him. He saved my life."

"He shouldn't have—"

"Captain Asher, now is not the time to cast blame. My niece has just had a very harrowing experience, and she doesn't need to be reprimanded by you." Uncle Clint's sharp voice cut across the cavalryman's diatribe. "I suggest that you see to your mount immediately."

After taking one look at the general's forbidding expression, Captain Asher snapped his mouth shut and rose with a jerky motion. "Certainly, sir." Not glancing at Della again, he spun and stalked to his gelding. He gathered the horse's reins and led the sorrel into the darkness toward the herd.

Before too many days passed, Della felt recovered enough to begin riding again. At first, she managed only an hour or two at a time, but as her strength and health returned, she spent more time in the saddle.

The plains climbed toward the distant Rockies by almost imperceptible degrees. Each day took them closer to their destination, while July slipped into August.

When they halted for their final encampment, the western mountains that had once been a blue smudge against the sky now appeared as a ragged and forbidding bulwark above the plains.

A festive atmosphere filled the company that evening. After the men had eaten, Toby tuned his violin for dancing. Aunt

Coral and even Silvie danced. Della whirled from one partner to another, being careful not to let Captain Asher monopolize her. She danced with Rusty, Emory Dyer, her uncle, and several of the cowboys. Even as she laughed and twirled, the one man she ached to be with remained on the edge of the firelight, watching, the brim of his black hat pulled low. His unwavering stare burned into her. Della sizzled with longing to speak to him, to lay her hand against the side of his face, and to share a kiss, but his unapproachable air deterred her.

When Quentin Asher attempted to maneuver her away from the others, Della pretended ignorance of his designs. She had no desire to be alone with him on this last evening of their journey.

"I'm sure Aunt Coral needs me to help her put Flossie to bed," she hedged when he pressed her to stroll with him.

"Your aunt doesn't need you. She's got Silvie to help her."

"Silvie is enjoying herself too much. Let her dance. I'll help Aunt Coral." Della stepped toward her uncle's wife, who at that moment gathered a drooping Flossie in her arms and headed toward the wagons. "See—Aunt Coral let Flossie stay up past her bedtime and is now taking her back to the wagon."

Della escaped with Aunt Coral and the toddler. She read a story to Flossie by lantern light after the child was tucked into her bedroll in the wagon. "Aunt Coral, go on back to the campfire and enjoy another dance or two," Della said when she finished the story. "I'll stay here with Flossie until you and Uncle Clint are ready to retire."

Kneeling in the wagon's bed, Aunt Coral glanced across her daughter to Della, who was leaning against the side of the Conestoga with her arms around her drawn-up knees. "Are you sure?" Doubt tinged her voice.

"Yes. I don't mind staying with Flossie, and I'm avoiding a certain cavalry captain." Della grinned. "Go on and dance some more with that handsome husband of yours."

"How can I refuse such an offer? Thank you." Aunt Coral cast one more look at her daughter before she scrambled to the back of the wagon and clambered over the tail.

When they finished breakfast the next morning and broke camp, Captain Asher approached Della, leading his sorrel on a loose rein. "Miss Hughes, may I speak privately with you?"

She concealed a sigh. She looped her mare's halter and lead rope over her shoulder. Catching up her mount for the day's ride would have to wait. "Very well."

Captain Asher dropped his gelding's reins to ground-tie him, took her elbow in a loose grip, and guided her away from the caravan. The wagons formed a line with the oxen hitched to their yokes, waiting for the signal to begin the final leg of their trek. The browning swells of the prairie spread out on either side of the vehicles.

He halted them at a distance where they could speak privately.

"Miss Hughes . . . Della, I regret that we couldn't have come to an understanding before we parted. I would have liked to have our betrothal settled before I took my detail to Fort Bridger."

Della looked back at the wagon train, at the Conestogas and the chuck wagon with their rounded canvas tops. Her wagon had become her home during the journey. Before the sun set this day, they'd reach Uncle Clint's ranch, where a new home awaited her should she decide to stay.

Bringing her thoughts back to the captain, she swung her gaze to his face, shaded from the sun by his cavalryman's hat. "I'm not at all sure a betrothal between us is possible."

He touched her face with gentle fingers. A tender expression softened his eyes. "You say you don't love me, but I'm convinced that one day, you will. My love for you will carry us both until then."

Della submitted to his caress, though she couldn't help but compare Shane's touch with the captain's. "It's more than the fact that I don't love you. I don't think I'm suited to be your wife."

"Of course, you'll make a most suitable wife for me. If you have doubts, I can guide you through the challenges of adjusting to the state of wedlock."

Resenting his notion that he must guide her, Della opened her mouth to protest. Captain Asher forestalled her by placing a forefinger across her lips.

"Shhh . . . Say nothing now. Next month, I'll accompany the quartermaster of Fort Bridger when he comes to purchase Morgans from your uncle. Will you consider my proposal while we're apart?"

Recalling her promise to Shane, Della nodded a reluctant acquiescence.

The captain beamed and reached for her hand. Bowing with Continental suavity, he feathered tender kisses across her knuckles. He straightened and smiled down at her. "Until we meet again, then. I hope you'll make me a happy man when I come to the ranch."

They returned to the caravan. With a final farewell, he mounted and rode out of the camp with his cavalry detail, headed for Fort Bridger. The wagon train would continue to the Logan ranch without an escort.

As soon as the detail vanished over the nearest rise, Della put Quentin Asher from her mind. Adjusting her mare's halter over her shoulder, she went in search of Shane. Perhaps they could spend the last day on the trail riding together.

Colorado Territory
Late Summer 1870

CHAPTER 28

DELLA LIFTED HER HANDS FROM the keyboard and whirled on the velvet-covered piano stool. Captain Asher leaned against the piano, having turned the pages for her while she played. Uncle Clint and Aunt Coral sat on a medallion-back sofa between two windows in the parlor. A bluff, hearty man with a full chestnut beard, wearing the uniform of a cavalry major, stood before the empty fireplace grate.

"Well done, young lady. Well done." The major waved his hand toward her. He held a cup of tea in one large paw. "Captain Asher has been singing your praises ever since he arrived at Fort Bridger. I can see he hasn't exaggerated."

Della cut a glance at the captain, who smiled at her with proprietary pride. She wasn't sure she appreciated the possessive gleam in his eyes. He seemed altogether too sure she would agree to his marriage proposal.

"Thank you, Major Sloan. I do enjoy playing the piano."

"Well, now"—the major stepped toward the middle of the room, making a shooing motion—"suppose you young people run along outside. General Logan and I have business to discuss."

Cupping his hand beneath her elbow, Quentin Asher assisted Della as she rose. With Aunt Coral trailing behind them, they left the room.

"Shall we take a stroll outside?" Captain Asher asked.

"That would be most pleasant."

They halted when they reached the foyer. "Mrs. Logan, would you care to join us?" the captain said.

She came to a standstill beside them, her inquisitive hazel gaze resting on her niece's face. "Thank you, but I must ensure that the men have enough tea and cake to see them through this business transaction. Della, would you prefer to help me serve the tea?"

"If you don't need me, I'll take a stroll with Captain Asher."

Aunt Coral shook her head. "I can get along without you. Silvie will help me serve. You enjoy yourself tonight, since the captain will be leaving in the morning."

Quentin Asher turned them toward the door. Stained-glass insets on either side of the wide mahogany portal cast rainbows across the hardwood floor. He opened the door. They passed outside onto a wide porch with white spooled railing. Pausing on the top step, he looked about the ranch yard.

"The general has made a nice place for you here."

"Uncle Clint promised Aunt Coral that when they came West, he'd provide for her in the manner to which she was accustomed. She lived on a plantation before the war."

"He certainly has provided a luxurious place." He glanced back at the house. "I never expected to see a two-story house in the wilds of the Colorado Territory."

Della turned to survey the home her uncle had provided for his wife. Whitewashed clapboards shone in the afternoon sun. Tall windows flanked by black shutters lent an air of elegance. "One would never guess the structure of the house is adobe."

The captain sent her a curious glance. "Adobe?"

"Living on the plains as we do, wood is very scarce. Most buildings are made of adobe or sod. Uncle Clint refused to put his family in a sod or adobe house, but wood was too expensive to use on the whole structure. So, he compromised by having the house constructed of adobe. He had the wood and clapboards brought in from Denver by wagon. The outside of the house is covered with clapboards, and the inside is plastered and wallpapered. All the doorways are framed in, just like a regular house."

"I never would have guessed. Your uncle is a clever man."

Della smiled. "He loves Aunt Coral very much, and he didn't want her to be without the things she would have had in Boston if they'd stayed there. He had all of their furniture shipped by rail from their home in the East. Everything was waiting for us when we arrived."

"I wish I could have come all the way to the ranch with you."

Della didn't comment. The pressure of Captain Asher's daily presence and his expectation that they'd marry had been taxing. She'd been relieved when the cavalry had separated from their wagon train.

Captain Asher and the quartermaster had arrived yesterday from Fort Bridger to look over the horses that were available for immediate sale and to come to an agreement with Uncle Clint about their purchase.

Quentin Asher looked Della up and down. "I'm pleased to see you're dressed as a proper young lady once again. You're a vision of loveliness."

Della glanced at her slim afternoon gown of primrose yellow. An insert of tiny pleats along the bottom of the skirt gave it a Parisian flair. The overskirt of ruched white lace had been drawn up in the back to drape the bustle, and a swath of flounced fabric trailed behind. A gold chain with a large topaz in an elaborate frame nestled against her neck and lent elegance to the dress's square décolletage. Narrow sleeves flared at the wrists.

In truth, she much preferred the freedom the split riding skirt and simple blouse had given her. The afternoon dress's yards of fabric felt confining, but she refrained from mentioning that to the captain. "Thank you."

His glance traveled upward to rest on her tresses. "You haven't quite achieved the style you wore in Kansas City, but at least, your hair isn't hanging down your back for all the men to ogle."

His proprietary attitude rankled. Della bit back a sharp retort and tried to answer with a neutral comment. She patted the braid that she'd wound about her head and anchored with a diamond clip. "I have no lady's maid to dress my hair, so I'm afraid a simple style is all I can manage."

He snorted. "When you're my wife, you'll have your own personal maid. You won't have to lift a finger to dress yourself or style your hair."

"I find I quite enjoy my independence. I can get along with just Silvie to help me. I don't care if my hair isn't styled in the height of fashion."

"Your hair will be most fashionable when you're my bride. My wife must be an example for all the other officers' wives to model. One day, when I'm elected to public office, women will look to you to set the standard of what's in vogue. You'll have to dress for teas, dinners, and political events."

"Captain Asher—"

"Quentin. You agreed to call me Quentin."

"Very well. Quentin."

He smiled at her, a melting smile that lit his handsome square features. "My name on your lips is music to my ears."

"Quentin, I must remind you that we agreed to take some time to consider a marriage between us before we came to any decision," she said in a mellow tone, not wanting to sound uncaring. "The truth is, I'm not sure I'll make you a proper wife. I have my doubts that a marriage between us will work."

With his hands on her shoulders, he turned her to face him. "I told you I love you enough for both of us. One day, you'll return my love—I'm sure of it."

"Still, you must give me the time I need. Marriage is an important decision."

He drew her hand through the crook of his elbow and towed her alongside him. "Let's take a stroll through the yard."

They descended the veranda steps and rambled toward the pole corral on the other side of the yard. The horse barn adjacent to the corral cast a long shadow.

At the paddock, they halted. Thirty of the Morgans that they had trailed across the plains had been penned in the corral for Major Sloan's inspection. The remainder of the herd, mares to be used for breeding stock, had been left on the prairie to graze.

With a booted foot propped on the lowest rail and his arms crossed on top of the fence, Captain Asher swept the ranch complex with a contemplative stare. A protective adobe wall encircled the compound. In addition to the house, the barn, and the corral, a bunkhouse and blacksmith shop near the barn completed the ranch facilities. A small adobe house between the men's quarters and the Logan home had been built for Emory Dyer.

"Yes, indeed. General Logan has quite a place here."

"Before they married, Aunt Coral was afraid when Uncle Clint told her he wanted to go west. It was one of the reasons she hesitated to marry him. Now that she's here, though, she's settled right in, even if Denver is two days' ride away."

"Mrs. Logan has a lot of grit. I imagine she could do anything she sets her mind to or live any place she has to."

"She's an inspiration to me." Aunt Coral had been an example to her in the five years since the Southern belle had married Uncle Clint. Aunt Coral was the closest thing to a mother Della had ever known. "And she dearly loves Uncle Clint, so she's happy wherever he is."

A pause hung in the clear western air like a cloud about to blot out the sun. Della waited for her suitor to broach the topic he'd brought her outside to discuss.

"Della."

She glanced at him. Asher's face wore an intent expression, his brows drawn together. "Yes?"

"I've made no secret of my feelings for you, and I've obtained permission from your uncle to ask for your hand in marriage. This is the second time I've formally asked you to marry me. What answer will you give me?"

She scrambled to organize her thoughts in a way that would make him understand why she couldn't give him an answer now. "Don't forget your promise to give me time to consider your offer."

"You've had a month since I last saw you to consider my proposal."

"That isn't enough time."

He sighed. "I was sure of my feelings for you the first night I met you. We've spent weeks on the trail together. You should be able to give me an answer by now."

Della glanced toward the barn, where Shane Hunter had been sleeping in a spare stall. Where was he now? What was he doing? She wrenched her thoughts back to the captain's proposal. "Let me claim a lady's fickleness. I simply can't give you an answer today."

"I'd hoped to take your promise back to Fort Bridger with me, but I can see you'll make me wait. Very well. I'll give you until the horses are broken to ride and I return with Major Sloan to get them. When we come back here to take the Morgans to Fort Bridger, I'll demand your answer."

Could she give the captain an answer then? What of Shane Hunter? He wasn't a man she could railroad into marriage. The pressure of Quentin Asher's insistence built in her chest until she thought she might burst. She breathed deeply and nodded, wishing she didn't feel as though she was committing herself to a prison sentence.

* * * * *

After dinner, while the men closeted themselves in Uncle Clint's office, Della strolled outside and across the yard to the barn. The urge to see Shane Hunter compelled her to seek him out.

Scipio met her at the barn's open double doors. His dark face broke into a broad smile. "Evenin', Miss Della."

"Hello, Scipio. It's so good to have you back with our family."

"It's good to be back with y'all, but I'm glad I didn't have to take Captain and your uncle's black stallion across the plains. A train ride suited me just fine."

Once the barn was completed, Scipio had joined them with his two Thoroughbred charges. Zeus had been settled in a roomy box stall, and Captain had been turned into the paddock with the saddle stock.

Della brushed past Scipio into the wide aisle between a double row of box stalls. She paced to the stall where Zeus munched on a feeder full of timothy hay. The stallion lifted his beautiful head and looked at her, his large eyes inquisitive and his ears pricked, before he buried his muzzle in the hay once more. "Uncle Clint is glad to have Zeus back, as well. He loves that horse."

"Zeus carried him safely through the war. That counts for a lot."

"If you don't mind, Miss Della, I'll turn in," Scipio said after a bit of conversation. "Morning comes early."

She nodded. "Good night, Scipio."

He ambled outside toward the bunkhouse.

The scent of newly sawn lumber overlaid the smell of hay and horses. Shadows crouched in the corners. Through the barn's open doors, she viewed the corral and the yard, golden with evening's light. Beyond the enclosure walls, the pale blue Colorado sky stretched to infinity. In the short time she'd lived here, her heart had been captured by the wild, free frontier, with all its beauty, dangers, and hardships.

She heard nothing to alert her, yet she felt Shane's presence. She pivoted slowly. He stood in the doorway of the end stall he'd claimed. Their gazes caught and held across the length of the barn. Her heartbeat kicked up at the sight of him. Without thought, her feet carried her toward him.

The bridle he'd been oiling dangled from one hand. A cleaning rag drooped from the other. When she halted before him, he hung the bridle on a peg and draped the rag over the leathers. He turned to face her, hooking a thumb in his gun belt and regarding her with a solemn expression. The brim of his hat shadowed his face.

In silence, they yearned for each other, though neither moved. The air grew heavy as they stared.

Della wished he would take her in his arms and hold her tight, whisper to her of his love. In the days since he treated her for the snakebite, he'd never repeated his confession of love. She sometimes wondered whether she'd imagined the words.

He gestured toward her evening gown of peacock-blue silk. "You look the part of society lady again."

215

COLLEEN HALL

"I may be gussied up in silk, but I'm still the same girl who wore a split riding skirt and rode astride all the way across the plains."

"You fit the part of the rich rancher's niece. You'll set Denver on its ears when you hit town."

She shrugged away his words. "I've no wish to set Denver on its ears. What I want is right here."

At her words, the skin around his heavy-lidded eyes tightened, and his mouth firmed. "I see your captain has come back," he said, turning the conversation to a different topic.

"He's not my captain, and he rode in with the regional quartermaster, who's in charge of acquiring mounts for the cavalry. Major Sloan is negotiating with Uncle Clint for the purchase of those Morgans in the corral."

"Once the major buys those horses, we'll slap the army brand on them and break them so they'll be ready for the cavalry."

"You'll help with that?"

He nodded. "I promised to help saddle break those horses for your uncle."

Conversation faltered. Shadows creeping into the barn cast a dusky gloom over them. Della peered through the dimness at Shane's features, trying to read his thoughts. His closed expression shut her out. Taking her courage in both hands, she stepped closer. If he wouldn't show her how he felt, she'd beg. "Shane, call me your darling again. Won't you please hold me?"

He didn't respond, except to stare down at her with pain lurking about his eyes. Finally, he reached toward her as if to cup her cheek, but instead of touching her, his hand dropped to his side. "I should never have held you or kissed you. It was much easier for me to accept my unmarried state before I experienced the closest thing to Heaven this earth could offer."

Was he telling her he wouldn't marry her? Panic lanced Della. "Shane, what are you saying? Are you backing out of our agreement?"

"How can I not? What was I thinkin' of to agree to such a thing?"

216

"We agreed to pray about marriage. You can't stop now."
She stepped closer, coming right up to his deerskin-clad chest. She brought up both hands to grip his arms, but he backed away and shook his head, holding one hand, palm out, to ward her off.

"You'd best not touch me. It's hard enough havin' you standing here close to me, lookin' like an angel and smellin' like roses, without you touchin' me."

Della drew in a sharp breath and lifted her clenched hands to her lips. "Shane. . ."

"Go back to the house, Della. Leave me."

His words pierced her heart. Wounded to the quick, she looked into his face, wondering whether she'd heard aright. He stared back, unyielding. He'd meant every word.

She lifted her chin, refusing to let him see the tears of misery that welled in her eyes. Dropping her hands to her sides, she spun. With her spine ramrod straight and her shoulders squared, she marched the length of the aisle to the barn doors without looking at him, feeling his gaze pinned to her back. Would he call out to her, tell her he'd changed his mind?

She reached the barn doors without hearing him speak, then paused for a moment in the opening to give him an opportunity to retract his words. Silence trembled in the air. When he said nothing to prevent her from leaving, she took a breath and stepped into the yard, leaving her heart at the feet of a tall, tawny-haired army scout.

CHAPTER 29

DELLA, DRESSED ONCE MORE IN her split riding skirt and boots, leaned on the corral's top rail, watching while Shane moved among the horses that milled about the enclosure. They shifted away from him, uneasy at his nearness, but with gentle patience, he persisted until they accepted his presence. He ran his palm down the neck of a sorrel gelding, stroking until the horse relaxed. Shane then turned his attention to a bay mare. Holding out a hand, he let her sniff.

"Easy, sweetheart. I won't hurt you. Just trust me."

The mare blew, swiveled her ears, and stepped back a pace.

Della's heart clenched. The tender words, directed at a horse, should have been addressed to her. The past week, during which she and Shane had established a fragile truce, had been the longest of her life. Whenever he happened to encounter her, he treated her as a casual acquaintance. The intimacy they'd established and the secrets they'd shared had evaporated like mist before the sun. Only the strain about his eyes betrayed that he suffered as much as she did.

He'd been mingling in the corral with the Morgans several times a day all week, but this was the first instance Della had come out to watch. Breaking the horses who hadn't already been trained had become Shane's responsibility.

While he communed with each horse, he worked his way toward the corral fence where Della stood. Propping an elbow on the top rail and hooking one booted foot over the lowest bar, he relaxed against the inside of the barricade. For several heartbeats, they eyed each other across the bars, Shane's expression guarded, not inviting intimacies.

Della took the opportunity to restore some of their previous ease. She gestured toward the horses. "Why do you do that—talk to the horses?"

He glanced over his shoulder at the herd, then back at her. "The Cheyenne gentle their horses, not break them. Each warrior spends a lot of time with his war pony, buildin' trust and respect that will help the horse submit to him. They establish a partnership of mutual respect. When the horse is ready to be ridden, they put him in a river and mount. Bucking in water tires out a horse mighty fast, so that speeds up the process."

Della looked into his face, watching each nuance of expression as he spoke. His countenance had softened while he recounted memories of his time with the tribe. "Did you gentle your mustang that way?"

He nodded. "It took me weeks, but now, I have a trail partner whom I trust with my life."

"So, that's what you're doing with those Morgans the army purchased."

"The army is in a hurry for mounts, so I don't have time to gentle those horses the way I'd like. I'm doin' what I can to build their trust, but in the end, I'll have to break them the cowboy way."

Silence descended. At last, Shane looked at her, remorse written on his features. "Della, when these horses are broke, I'm goin' back to scoutin' for the army. I'm leavin' here."

She felt as though he'd stabbed her in the heart. Leaving? She couldn't imagine her life without him. "But why? Why can't you stay here and work for Uncle Clint? What about us?"

"Us? I thought I made myself clear the other night."

"I won't accept it. We had an agreement."

Dropping his foot to the ground, he straightened. "An agreement I never should have made."

"You're wrong, you know. You aren't giving us a chance." She clutched the top rail.

Thumbing back the brim of his hat, he stared at her across the corral bars. Suffering simmered in his eyes before his expression shuttered. "Seein' you here, in your real element, has made me realize how unsuited we are. You have all this." He swept one hand in a wide arc, encompassing everything in the ranch compound. "I own nothin' except my mustang and my rig. A marriage between us would never work. And that doesn't begin to touch what society would do to you once you married me."

Della gritted her teeth. "I refuse to accept what you're telling me. You're a coward, running from us before you give us a chance."

His head jerked as though she'd slapped him, and his face paled. "Be thankful you can claim the protection of your fair sex, or I'd be inclined to take exception to your slanderin' of my character." The cold steel in his low tone told her she'd pushed him beyond the limits of what he'd tolerate.

Della thrust out a hand in entreaty. "Shane, please, accept my sincerest apologies. I didn't really mean what I said just now. I know you're not a coward. It's just that I know you're throwing away our future."

She paused and drew a deep breath, knowing she gambled her entire future on her next words. "I propose another agreement, if you're brave enough to accept it. For the remainder of the time you're here, we will continue to pray about a marriage between us. And you will court me properly, as if you mean it. If, after we've spent time together and prayed, you still believe you shouldn't marry me, when Major Sloan comes to take the horses, I'll let you go without another word."

Shane stared at her for several long moments, frowning. "And what of Captain Asher?"

"I haven't agreed to marry him. He has no claim on my affections."

Shane's mouth formed a grim slash. "You drive a hard bargain, lady."

"Our whole future is at stake. I'll do whatever it takes to secure that future."

The prairie wind, sliding off the mountains to their west, buffeted them. Della's riding skirt snapped against her legs. Spirals of air danced between them and ruffled the curls at Della's temples. The morning sun slanted across her back, while their shadows mingled in the dirt of the corral.

Shane stirred, shifting his weight to one leg. At his movement, their shadows broke apart. He gave a stiff nod. "I reckon I'll accept your agreement. But if I haven't changed my mind when the time comes, you must let me go."

"I agree." Relief surged through Della at this small victory. "I'll let you go."

* * * * *

Excitement rippled through the air. Except for those men out on the range, guarding the broodmares and yearlings, everyone on the ranch lined the fence to see Shane Hunter ride one of the Morgans.

A chestnut gelding had been turned into a smaller corral between the barn and the main paddock. He'd been snubbed to a post in the center of the enclosure and stood with his legs braced, eyes rolling. Shane approached the gelding, his saddle and blanket slung over one shoulder. When he neared the horse, he twisted and lowered the rig to the ground.

Standing at the fence railing beside Aunt Coral and her uncle, Della watched Shane speak to Rusty, who had taken up a stance at the horse's head. The men conferred briefly before Shane moved to the chestnut's side. Crooning in low tones, he rubbed the horse's neck. His long-fingered hand stroked down the gelding's neck, over his withers, and across his topline. He reached down for the saddle blanket, settled it over the Morgan's back, then tossed on the saddle. When he tightened the cinch, the horse humped his back and flicked his tail.

Della held her breath when Shane gathered the reins and stepped into the saddle. She clasped her hands and brought them up to her chin. The coming battle between man and horse was one she knew the man would win. The gelding would fight, trying to unseat the unfamiliar weight on his back, but in the end, Shane would triumph. The horse would learn the man was master.

Everyone along the fence remained silent. No one moved.

Shane settled himself in the saddle and collected the reins. He nodded to Rusty. The cowboy loosened the horse from the snubbing post and scrambled for the fence.

For a moment, the gelding stood unmoving, legs spraddled, head down. Shane raked his spurs across the chestnut's flanks, and the horse exploded. He crouched, gathering himself, then shot upward and twisted in midair, hindquarters lashing out. The gelding landed with a bone-jarring jolt. Shane's head snapped back, and his hat sailed across the corral to flip over and over in the dust.

Della forgot to breathe.

The horse fought, muscles bunching and flexing. He spun in midair, dropping his shoulder, then pivoted and bucked across the corral. Shane swayed but stayed with the horse. The gelding fought until both horse and rider were drenched in foam and sweat. Then, the chestnut gave a half-hearted crowhop and stood with his head hanging, tail drooping.

Shane drew the horse's head up and squeezed his sides. The Morgan circled the corral like a sedate plow horse.

Shane had done it. He'd mastered the gelding in this first round. There would be other battles ahead before the horse was ready to become a cavalry mount, but the horse had learned that man would be the victor.

Shane dismounted and ran a hand down the gelding's sweaty neck, then led him across the corral. Along the way, Shane scooped up his hat and settled it on his head. When he neared the fence, he turned his blue gaze on Della, pinning her with its intensity. The moment spun out.

She smiled at him. "You did it, Shane. You rode that horse."

Uncle Clint grinned. "That was some good riding."

Shane nodded. "He's the first one, rough broke."

Aunt Coral touched Della on the shoulder. "Come walk with me."

After casting a last glance at Shane, Della accompanied her aunt across the yard. When they were out of earshot, Aunt Coral peered at her niece, her hazel eyes curious. "What's going on with you and Mr. Hunter?"

Della halted in mid stride, swinging her attention to her aunt. "We're courting."

Amazement crossed Aunt Coral's face. "How did you rope him in? The last time we discussed the two of you, he wouldn't consider courting you."

Della summarized the bargain she and Shane had struck. "I don't know if he'll agree to a marriage or not. I may still lose him, but it won't be for want of trying."

"So, now, you have two beaux."

"For the present." Della sighed. "When this all ends, I may have no beaux."

"Well, let's do what we can to help you along with Mr. Hunter. Why don't you invite him to dinner tomorrow night?"

"He may be reluctant to come. He much prefers being out of doors."

"If he's seriously considering marriage, then he must become domesticated. He'll have to accustom himself to living in a house."

Della giggled. "If we should marry, I suppose I could sleep out of doors in a bedroll."

"You'll do no such thing. Mr. Hunter will just have to mend his ways."

CHAPTER 30

THE FOLLOWING EVENING, SHANE SHOWED up at the front door at the appointed time. Della answered his knock, swinging the portal wide. He'd combed his hair and donned a clean flannel shirt. A new red neckerchief had been knotted about his neck. Fresh buckskin trousers encased his long legs, and he'd polished his boots. No gun belt hung about his waist. She thought he looked uncomfortable without his six-shooter.

One hand clutched a nosegay of purple prairie vetch.

She smiled up at him. "My, don't you look fine this evening."

He tugged at the bandana, running a finger between the fabric and his neck. "I feel like a turkey all trussed up for Christmas dinner."

Della laughed. "Well, you're the most handsome turkey I've ever seen. Come in, please."

Shane stepped into the foyer, sweeping his cowboy hat from his head.

She closed the door, then took his hat and laid it on the shelf of a mirrored mahogany hall tree beside the door.

When she straightened and turned toward him, he cocked his head and ran an assessing look over her. "You're cuttin' a swell, yourself."

She glanced at her simple apple-green gown. "Thank you." In that instant, she felt an unaccountable shyness. She'd had beaux at her feet ever since she'd come out in society, but she'd never cared for a man's opinion as much as she did Hunter's at that moment. "I hoped you'd like my gown."

For a heartbeat longer, he stared at her, his gaze intent. Della felt he could see right into her soul. "You look like an angel come down to walk among us mortals. How did you work your magic?" He pitched his tone low, speaking sotto voce. "You've stolen my heart. It no longer belongs to me."

"For a man who's never courted, you seem to be a natural at handing out pretty compliments. A compliment I thoroughly appreciate, by the way."

Shane shrugged. "The words come from my heart. My Cheyenne father would say it's like cool water flowing from a spring."

Della laid her hand on his chest. "That makes it all the more special. I've heard too many calculated compliments that mean nothing. They're just empty air."

He looked down at the flowers clenched in his hand, as if wondering what to do with them. "Here. These are for you." He thrust the nosegay toward her. "I thought I should bring you flowers."

She took the wilting blossoms and held them as carefully as if they'd been hothouse roses. "These are lovely. Thank you." She gave him a little shove toward the wide parlor door. "Uncle Clint is waiting in there. Why don't you join him while I put these flowers in a vase?"

When she'd filled a crystal vase with water and set it on the dining-room table, after moving aside a silver candelabra to make room for Hunter's posies, Della returned to the men.

"Are you ready to eat? Aunt Coral told me to bring you to the table."

Aunt Coral met them in the dining room. The fine Chippendale furniture that had graced the Logan mansion in Boston crowded the smaller room of the ranch house, though it lent an atmosphere of refinement. Moss-green velvet drapery pulled back on either side of the two long windows added an elegant flair. Flames danced in crystal candle sconces on the walls, and a lace cloth adorned the table.

"Silvie and I have been busy in the kitchen," Aunt Coral said, "or I would have greeted you at the door."

"No matter. Della has been a gracious hostess." When Shane glanced at Della, the creases about his eyes crinkled and the corners of his mouth tilted up.

His smiling eyes warmed Della clear through, his private smile especially for her. She beamed back at him, forgetting for a moment Uncle Clint's and Aunt Coral's presence. Silvie's entrance with Flossie on her hip interrupted the moment.

"Flossie wants to say good night, General Logan," Silvie said.

Flossie squirmed to the floor and pattered barefoot around the table to her father's side, her night rail swaying. "Papa! Up, up."

Uncle Clint scooped up his curly-haired daughter and held her high, tickling her tummy. Flossie squealed. "What are you doing at our dinner table, sprite? Did you come to tell your papa good night?"

Flossie's giggles quieted. "Eat. Eat."

"Didn't you already eat in the kitchen?"

Flossie shook her head. "I want to eat wif you, Papa." She pointed to his plate.

"Perhaps, you could sit on Papa's knee." Uncle Clint cast a cajoling glance at his wife.

Aunt Coral shook her head and rounded the table. "You're spoiling her, Clint. She needs to go to bed. She'll be cranky tomorrow if she doesn't get her sleep."

Aunt Coral pried her clinging daughter from her father's arms and returned the toddler to Silvie while Flossie wailed. Fat tears spilled down her chubby cheeks.

"Papa will see you in the morning," Aunt Coral said.

Silvie bore the sobbing child from the dining room. Aunt Coral returned to her chair at the hostess's end of the table. She indicated Della's and Shane's places, and everyone sat.

Della had watched Shane during the byplay with Flossie. An unguarded expression of longing passed over his features while he observed Uncle Clint tease his daughter, and in that moment, she realized her love longed for a family. She guessed his desire for children was a hankering he'd recently acquired, along with his contemplation of wedlock. Was that an indication he was softening toward the notion of marriage?

Sadie, a stout, middle-aged woman whom Uncle Clint had hired in Denver to do odd jobs about the house, served antelope steaks and mashed potatoes. Flaky biscuits were mounded on another platter. Tea filled their glasses.

"How long do you think it will take you to rough break those thirty horses?" Uncle Clint asked the scout.

"Six weeks or more, I reckon. I'll move them along faster than I would otherwise, since I know the army is in a hurry for more mounts." Shane split a biscuit and slathered strawberry preserves over one portion.

"Take as much time as you need. I don't want those horses spoiled." The general sipped his tea.

"I won't spoil them, but the army may have to finish them off, if they want them in a hurry."

"Another thing. I don't need all of the men who helped me move the horses out here for regular ranch work, so I'll have to let some of them go. How many men will I need to run my horse-breeding program?"

Shane laid his knife across his plate. His brow furrowed.

Della traced his features with her gaze, loving the deliberation he put into his answer. The conversation between the men flowed over her while dreams of a future with Shane distracted her.

"Toby definitely will stay to cook for the men." Her uncle's words brought her back to the discussion. "And I'll keep on Emory Dyer. He'll be invaluable to me in keeping up with the bookkeeping."

The men deliberated over who could best help with the ranch work. Content to listen, Della observed Shane's responses to her uncle's inquiries. She hoped being consulted on the business side of Uncle Clint's venture would make him feel engaged and would give him another reason to stay.

Cobbler made from canned peaches and topped by cinnamon-laced cream completed the meal.

Afterward, they retired to the parlor.

"Della, would you favor us with some music?" Aunt Coral asked from her seat by the fireplace.

Della flicked a look at Shane, who sat beside her on the medallion-back sofa, to see whether he showed signs of wanting to bolt from the house. "Only if Shane is willing to hear me play."

"I don't mind hearin' another tune or two of your angel music."

His words took her back to the night they met when he told her she played like an angel. The memory hung in the air between them while their gazes caught and held. Finally, her uncle's discreet cough recalled Della to the presence of her family.

"Very well. One or two pieces." She rose and crossed the room, her footfalls muffled by the patterned Turkish carpet. After settling herself on the stool, she rested her hands on the keyboard. She began with a rendition of "Greensleeves," which she knew was one of her uncle's favorites, and followed with a spritely presentation of "Yankee Doodle."

When the last note died away, Della turned to face the room. She stood. "Uncle Clint, Aunt Coral, thank you very much for a delightful dinner, but now, Shane and I will sit on the veranda for a bit."

Outside, Della ignored the wooden rocking chairs positioned side by side to the left of the front door and turned instead to the right, where a cushioned swing hung by sturdy metal chains from the porch ceiling. "Do you mind sitting in the swing? Or would you prefer the rockers?"

Shane looked down at her, laughter in his eyes. "I reckon the swing would be better for a courtin' couple."

They sat, and Shane draped his arm along the back of the swing. Della nestled against his side. He took her hand and laced his fingers through hers. With one booted foot flat on the veranda floor, he pushed the swing into lazy motion.

"I hope you don't mind me suggesting we come out here, but I thought you'd like to get outside."

"Thanks. I was gettin' a little stir crazy in there."

They rocked in silence for a time, watching dusk leach daylight from the sky. Shadows crept into the corners of the yard. Finally, Della stirred, twisting to peer up into his face.

"I want you to know I'm learning to be a good western wife. I make my own bed in the morning, and I can sweep the floor and dust the furniture."

Shane's arm slid onto her shoulder, and he squeezed her. "I love your willingness to dirty your hands. Many society ladies would consider workin' beneath them." He dropped a kiss on her nose. "At this point, darlin', I don't even have a house for you to clean, so your skills may be for naught."

She laid a palm against his cheek. "You'll have a home one day, I'm sure." She dropped her hand into her lap. "You'll think me a hopeless case, but a few months ago, I never would have guessed I'd learn to do such tasks. Domestics did everything for me. I never even knew where the coal came from to light our fires. The housemaid brought the coal every morning in a bucket. I never questioned where she got it."

Shane grinned at her. "You poor little rich girl."

Della wrinkled her nose at him. "Silvie and Sadie and Aunt Coral and I do the housework together. Silvie does most of the cooking." She shook her head and sighed. "I hope you don't expect to eat my cooking, though. That's one skill I don't think I'll ever acquire. We had to throw out the biscuits I made yesterday. They were so hard we couldn't chew them."

Shane's chest quivered against her shoulder, and she glanced up at him with suspicion. He was laughing silently. She poked him in the ribs. "You won't think it's so funny when you're trying to eat one of my burned biscuits."

"We can always eat in the mess hall with the enlisted men." The lines bracketing his mouth deepened.

Della knew he teased her, but at least, he seemed to be considering marrying her and taking her to live with him at the fort instead of walking out of her life. She didn't pursue the topic.

"Shane, what do you think happened to the men who followed us all the way from Kansas City? The rustlers?"

The swing creaked as they rocked.

"They're still out there, somewhere. No doubt, they'll show their hand before long. Your uncle is takin' precautions, though. The mares on the range are well guarded."

Della shivered. "I wish those men had never followed us. It's nerve wracking, not knowing what they plan to do or when they'll do it."

Shane turned her toward him and wrapped both arms about her. He bent his head. "Darlin'," he whispered. "I'd best be gettin' back to the barn, but I'd like a kiss before I go. I've sure been hankerin' for your kisses."

While they'd talked, darkness had fallen. His face was a pale blur above her. "The other night in the barn, when you asked me to kiss you, refusin' you was the hardest thing I've ever done. It was almost as hard as leavin' you will be."

"Don't mention leaving. I don't want to hear it now. Just kiss me."

His mouth found hers. He thrust a hand into her braid, and his fingers clenched her tresses. Della's arms stole about his neck. They kissed with desperate fervor, pouring out their love, mingled with the uncertainty of their future. Della clutched him to her. Her fingers tangled in his hair. His words of leaving struck terror to her heart. What would she do if he left?

After a time, he lifted his head. "I'd best go now." He rose and pulled her to her feet.

Della tried to restore order to her scrambled thoughts and calm her racing heart. "Yes, perhaps you'd better go." She sucked in a deep breath. "Your hat is inside. I'll get it for you."

They strolled across the veranda, with Shane's arm about her waist. She ducked inside and retrieved his black felt hat from the hall tree. Outside again, she offered him the headgear.

He plucked the hat from her hands, settled it on his head, and tilted the brim at a cocky angle. Della accompanied him to the stairs. He took one more kiss before he whispered a good night and clattered down the steps. With his loose, graceful stride, he crossed the yard toward the barn without looking back.

She leaned against the veranda post and watched the darkness swallow him. A tumult of emotions swirled inside, beating against her chest. She laid one palm against her pounding heart. How could she stay here if he left her?

CHAPTER 31

THE WARRIORS APPEARED AROUND THE bluff, riding single file. A wash of fear swept over Della at the sight of a dozen armed tribesmen approaching.

"Shane!" She jerked her mare to a halt. The chestnut tossed her head at the unaccustomed rough handling.

"I see them." His calm voice quieted her heart's wild thrumming.

"What shall we do?" She cut a glance at him, but he didn't look at her. All she could see was his shadowed profile beneath the brim of his cowboy hat.

His eyes narrowed while he watched the advancing horsemen. "We ride to meet them."

"Meet them?"

Heeling his mustang into motion, he nodded. She signaled her mare forward, keeping the Morgan close to Hunter's grulla.

In the two weeks since Hunter agreed to court her, they'd spent every evening together. Most nights, he'd come to dinner. Afterward, they'd sit in the swing and talk. Hunter had initiated a nightly Bible reading and prayer time for the two of them.

Today, he'd taken the afternoon off. He'd invited Della to accompany him across the vast acreage purchased by her uncle. They rode over the sloping plains, keeping below the rim of the bluff and avoiding the skyline.

"These men are from the band my mother and I lived with. That chief leadin' the group is my Cheyenne father."

Della gaped at the hatchet-faced chieftain riding at the head of the horsemen. Shane's words lent a little comfort and alleviated some of her fear of being murdered. She supposed the chief wouldn't kill his adopted son, though in spite of that reassurance, her heart slammed against her ribs.

The two groups of riders drew near each other. Springy turf muffled their horses' hoofbeats. The tawny grasses bent before the wind, rustling.

"The brave ridin' behind my father is my brother," Shane murmured. "When we stop, stay behind me."

Their mounts took a few more strides. He halted his gelding, and Della backed her mare a pace or two to allow him a position between her and the tribesmen. Unable to tear her gaze away, she watched the men approaching. The warriors curbed their horses mere yards from them, drawing abreast in a line that blocked the trail.

Della swept the Cheyenne with a glance. These men were taller than the Sioux she'd seen and lighter skinned. Their features were handsome, though fierce and hawkish. They were dressed much as Shane was, wearing fringed and beaded deerskin shirts and trousers and moccasins. Eagle feathers adorned their hair. Each man rode with a rifle across his knees.

She brought her attention back to the chief. His weathered face, framed by a feathered headdress, betrayed no expression. Moments of silence ticked past. The feathers in the braves' hair danced in the wind, and their horses' manes stirred. Tension, sharp as a blade, rode the currents. Della grew lightheaded, as if all the air had been sucked from the sky.

"*Haaahi.*" The chief followed his greeting with a sharp burst of guttural speech. After a moment, Shane replied in the same language. Following another exchange, Hunter nudged his grulla toward his father's mount, halting only when the two men were alongside each other. As if by some unseen signal, they reached out and gripped hands in a tight, brief clasp.

Della couldn't help but notice the affection the two men displayed. That Shane loved his Cheyenne father was evident. The old chief guarded his feelings, though his greeting betrayed his love for his adopted son. Years spent apart in disparate cultures hadn't diminished the bond that had developed in a previous lifetime between the boy and the warrior.

Shane spoke again in the strange language, and the chief replied.

Feeling watched, Della shifted her attention from Shane and his father to the other horsemen. Her gaze snagged on the warrior mounted on a black-and-white piebald gelding beside the chief. She recognized Hunter's brother, who stared at her with unblinking intensity that made her uneasy.

Shane's brother couldn't deny their mother's heritage. The younger warrior's skin was a lighter bronze than the other Cheyenne, and his features could have graced Shane's face, so similar were the two. Even his eyes, surprisingly blue, resembled Shane's.

When he kneed his mount forward and rode alongside Della's mare, panic squeezed her chest. She tasted the metallic tang of fear.

Shane's brother halted his piebald beside her, so close his knee bumped hers. His gaze, fierce and bold, perused her. One hand stretched out and touched her cheek.

Della quaked, though she refused to draw back. She lifted her chin and met his stare with courage dredged from the depths of her terrified heart.

He flung a question over his shoulder at Shane in the language the chief had used.

Shane wheeled his mustang, and the grulla plunged between Della's mare and his brother's gelding, shouldering the piebald aside. "You'll not touch her!" His tone was as cold as the wind that howled off the mountains in the winter.

Displeasure darkened his brother's face. He spoke again in the Cheyenne language, though Della knew he could speak English.

"She's the niece of the great chief General Logan," Shane said in English. "Chief General Logan protects what is his. Do not anger him. It will not go well for your people if you should anger General Logan by trifling with his niece. General Logan fears no man. He is a brave warrior."

The brothers faced off; then, the younger sibling shrugged, turned his mount, and rode back to the line of horsemen.

The old chief spoke to his son, and Shane rattled off a comment. The chief nodded and urged his mount forward. The other warriors followed, filing past Shane and Della in silence. Shane's brother fell into line behind the last rider. As he rode by, his bold stare pierced Della. She refused to quail beneath his look, though when he'd passed, she wilted into her saddle. Fine tremors shook her insides.

The Cheyenne left behind them a stillness broken by the pulsing wind and the call of a meadowlark.

"Are you all right?"

Shane's voice pulled her thoughts from her confrontation with his brother. She glanced at him. Concern drew his brows together, and he'd narrowed his eyes.

"Yes. Your brother frightened me, is all." She took a deep breath and tried to control her trembling.

Shane's mouth firmed in a hard line. "My brother rides the wild side. I don't like the way he looked at you."

"What did he say?"

For a moment, Shane refused to reply.

"I know you protected me, but I'd like to know from what."

"Let's ride. We shouldn't stay here."

He turned his mustang in the direction they'd been going before they encountered the warriors. Della followed, spurring her horse into a trot to catch up. When she drew abreast of him, she slanted a glance at him.

"I want to know what he said."

"He asked me if you were my woman."

Feeling a bit deflated that Shane hadn't claimed her but had instead told his brother of her relationship with Uncle Clint, Della didn't reply. In spite of the time they'd spent together in the past two weeks and despite the prayers they'd shared, couldn't he admit they belonged together?

"Della, look at me."

She turned her head toward him, hoping he couldn't divine her thoughts.

His intent gaze slid over her countenance, touching her features one by one. Della felt as if he'd run his fingers over her face in a featherlight caress.

"I know what you're thinking, but I couldn't admit that we're courtin'. My brother envies anything that belongs to me. He's already shown an interest in you. Once he learned of our relationship, you would have been at risk. I thought it best to let him know you live under your uncle's protection."

"Oh. I didn't guess. . ."

Their horses walked on through the rippling buffalo grass. Della swayed with her mare's rhythmic strides. While her curiosity grew, Shane seemed content to let the silence spin out. Finally, she grew weary of waiting for him to discuss his family.

"Tell me. I want to know about you and your brother."

He sighed. "Ever since he was old enough to understand I was the adopted son, he resented my position in the tribe."

"I'm so sorry."

"Things were especially difficult after we'd been rescued and returned to the fort. Even though I tried to protect him from the slurs of society and help him adapt to the white lifestyle, he resisted me at every turn. His relationship with my real father was volatile, to say the least. That was one of the things which made my father's reconciliation with my mother so hard. It was a relief when my brother ran away to rejoin the tribe."

Della didn't know what to say. Shane had shared only a portion of his life. She guessed he'd hidden many hurtful things from her.

The splendor of the high plains edged by the Rockies caught her attention. "Oh, Shane, this is beautiful. Thank you for bringing me here."

"Your uncle owns much of this land."

He swung down from the saddle and ducked around his mustang's head to her side. "Let's rest for a bit." He reached up, and his hands spanned her waist; then, he lifted her from her mare's back. After dropping their horses' reins, Shane curved an arm about her and drew her close. The butt of his six-shooter poked her side. He adjusted his longer stride to match hers, their legs bumping. Several yards from their mounts, he brought them to a standstill.

"Let's sit."

They settled themselves in the tawny grass, with Della seated between Shane's drawn-up knees. She pulled off her hat, laid it on the grass beside her, and leaned against his chest. His arms encircled her, and he rested his chin on her hair. They sat without speaking, enjoying the beauty of the day and each other's company. After a bit, Della twisted to look into his face. The westering sun touched his features with gold, illuminating the creases around his eyes and the brackets around his mouth. He squinted against the glare.

"Shane, tell me about your Cheyenne family. I want to know everything."

He looked at her, studying her countenance as if to determine how much to tell her, before he stared beyond her over the rangeland to the distant mountains. Della pivoted and leaned against him once more. She tucked her head into the dip where his shoulder met his neck.

"What was your Cheyenne father's name?"

"In English, he's known as Yellow Wolf." His voice, with its soft western drawl, sounded in her ear.

"Yellow Wolf. What is that in the Cheyenne language?"

"*Ocunnowhurst.*"

Della tried to imitate his speech, then chuckled when she failed. "I'll never master the Cheyenne language."

"I don't see why you need to."

She rested her hands on his forearms that circled her middle and squeezed. "And what was your name?"

"Little Wolf."

Della tried to imagine the years Shane lived in the Cheyenne culture with the name Little Wolf. "How did it feel, having a Cheyenne name instead of an English one?" She felt him shrug against her back.

"I was young and didn't think much about it, once I got over the shock of the attack and had settled into life with the tribe."

"What about your mother?"

"Yellow Wolf named her *Waynoka,* Sweet Water."

"Sweet Water. That's lovely."

"And very apt. My mother is a lovely woman, inside and out. In his way, Yellow Wolf loved her very much. He never remarried after we were rescued by the army, and he mourned her as though she were dead after we were taken from the village. He loves her still."

"And how do you know that?"

"I returned to the tribe after I left school in Philadelphia and spent several months with my Cheyenne father. I visit him still when I can."

They settled into a silence broken by the tearing sound of their horses cropping grass. One of the horses blew through its nostrils. After a bit, Della stirred. "Didn't you tell me you have a sister?"

"Blue Flower, but no one calls her that now. Her English name is Emma. She's a lovely young woman now, living with my mother and my birth father. I haven't seen her since my parents moved to California, but my mother writes to me and tells me the family news."

"And your brother? What's his name?"

"Wild Wind. *Minninnewah.* The name suits him. He's wild as the wind durin' a summer thunderstorm. He's joined the Dog Soldiers."

Della frowned. "What's a Dog Soldier?"

"Dog Soldiers are warriors made up of many Cheyenne tribes, mostly young men, who have decided that the only way to have peace is to drive out the white man." Shane paused.

Della waited for him to continue, knowing she couldn't hurry him.

"My father, understandin' the strength of the army and realizin' that the white settlers will overrun the land, has tried to walk a middle line and keep his men from engagin' in a war they can't win." He spoke, in a low, ragged voice. "The young warriors are gettin' restless. It won't be long before they stop listenin' to the tribal elders. There'll be bloodshed."

Della shivered.

"I told Yellow Wolf that your uncle is an honorable man who will allow his warriors to hunt on his land, if the braves don't kill his men or steal his horses. I don't think my brother listened, though. He's spoilin' for a fight."

"What will you do then? If the army goes after the Dog Soldiers?"

Shane didn't reply. She twisted, coming up on her knees to face him. A brooding expression pulled at his mouth. His gaze swung back to her, and his eyes warmed, signaling his intent before he lifted his hand to stroke the side of her face. The rough pads of his fingers trailed along her jawline. She trembled at his touch. He dipped his head and kissed the sweet spot at the hollow of her throat.

"Della, darlin', my heart burns for you as the flames of a campfire on a cold winter's day. I crave your love, your presence in my life through the good times and the bad. I want us to have a family together. You give me hope for a better life than what I ever thought possible before I met you."

He spoke with such tenderness that tears gathered in the corners of her eyes.

He brushed his thumb across her lips. "If I have to give you up, my heart will be as the land in winter, dead and frozen, but I love you too much to marry you if it will bring you pain."

Bittersweet joy pierced Della. She'd never thought to be gifted with such a sacrificial love, a love willing to give up the joys of a life spent together if that relationship would bring harm to the loved one. She curled her hand around the back of his neck. His smooth skin warmed her palm. "You won't hurt me, Shane. Our love will make us strong."

Somehow, she must convince him of that truth.

CHAPTER 32

A WOLF HOWLED, ITS MOURNFUL lament trailing off into silence. Della sat up in bed, catching her breath and listening. Quietude filled the night. The wolf didn't repeat its cry.

Wide awake now, Della pushed back the covers and swung her feet to the floor. Silver banners of light from a full moon spilled through her windows, so she had no need to light the lamp. She reached for the wrapper lying across the foot of her bed, stuffed her arms into the sleeves, and tied the sash about her waist. After thrusting her feet into her slippers, she left her room and crept downstairs. The foyer door opened without a squeak. She crossed the porch to the swing and sat, drawing up her knees and wrapping her arms about her legs.

She shivered. The September night hinted at the arrival of autumn. Looking across the ranch compound, lit by the moon's cold light, she wondered where she'd be come the winter.

Would she and Shane be married by then? Or would he be gone from her life forever?

Thinking back to his indirect declaration of love that afternoon, Della smiled. His Cheyenne upbringing colored his speech in ways none of her sophisticated beaux could imitate, yet she wouldn't trade Shane's simple avowal for the most poetic claims of devotion she'd received from former suitors. His love words came from his heart, not from a glib tongue skilled in flattery.

After all the time they'd spent together, he must realize how well suited they were, that together, they could face down society. If he decided otherwise and left her, how could she stay here? Her gaze ranged across the yard once more. Everywhere she looked, memories of Shane abounded. His presence filled the ranch. Her heart would be desolate without him.

Returning to Boston and living with her grandparents held no appeal. Instead, could she agree to Captain Asher's suit and marry him, knowing her affections belonged to another man? And did the captain possess the kind of Christian devotion she wanted in a husband?

People married for many reasons other than love. For her, a marriage between herself and Quentin Asher would be based on practicality. She shrank from committing herself to such a union. She'd hoped for a marriage full of love on both sides, such as the relationship between Uncle Clint and Aunt Coral.

The wolf howled again, lonely and plaintive. Its wail echoed her bleak thoughts.

*****

One morning two weeks later, a smudge of smoke to the west lifted into the Colorado sky, black and ragged like a dirty cloth. Della and Aunt Coral stood on the veranda, watching the wind shred the rising cloud. The men who stayed at the ranch compound had gathered in the yard to watch the smoke, as well.

Shane was working with one of the Morgans in the corral, but now, he dismounted, strode to the gate, and let himself out. In the center of the yard, he came to a standstill, turning to look into the sky. After a moment, he spun.

"There's a fire out there on the prairie, and it's headin' our way. We've got to take precautions, in case we have to leave." He barked orders at the men, who scrambled to do his bidding. He strode toward the house, halted at the porch steps, and looked up at the women.

"Ladies, you should pack a few things to take with you in case the fire gets too close. If we must leave, one of the men will tack up your horses for you."

Aunt Coral glanced toward the smoke. Her husband was out there on the prairie, out with the men who guarded their mares on the plain. "Do you think it's close to our horse herd?"

Before Shane could reply, Emory Dyer galloped through the gate of the adobe wall that circled the ranch compound. He pulled his lathered mount to a sliding halt. "There's a fire out there heading this way. General Logan sent me to get every man you can spare to help us fight the fire."

Hunter nodded and pivoted, ready to bark orders.

"Is Rusty here?" Emory Dyer said before he could speak.

Shane glanced at the lieutenant. "Rusty? No, he's not here. I thought he was with the herd."

"He's supposed to be, but no one has seen him all morning."

"He'll turn up." Hunter wheeled back to the men and issued orders even as he jogged across the yard. While some of the cowboys grabbed shovels, rakes, and gunnysacks and tossed them into the back of a buckboard, Toby harnessed the team to the wagon. Others filled barrels of water from the stream that ran along the inside of one compound wall. Straining and heaving, the men loaded the butts into the buckboard. Within minutes, the mounted cavalcade stormed out of the gate, leaving only two men who'd be needed to turn the horses loose from the corral and help the women escape, should the fire range too close.

Della descended the veranda steps and met Scipio in the yard. Together, they watched the distant smoke haze and billow.

"I'd best get ready to take Zeus out of the barn," Scipio said.

Della nodded. Scipio would place the stallion's safety above his own. "I hope the men can stop the fire before it reaches us." She glanced up when the sunlight dimmed. "It looks like it might rain. Clouds are building up."

Scipio tipped back his head to look at the sky. "We could use a good rain right now."

Upstairs in her room, Della gathered a few things that would fit into her saddlebags. Since they'd be escaping on horseback, she wouldn't be able to take any luggage. When she finished that task, she wandered across the hall to the room Uncle Clint and Aunt Coral shared. The door stood open, so she peeked around the edge.

"Aunt Coral? May I come in?"

Aunt Coral had been laying out some of Flossie's things on the bed. She straightened and turned, tucking a stray lock of hair behind her ear. "This reminds me of the night my mother and I stood on the veranda at Elmwood the night Sherman's men burned Columbia. We didn't know if we'd still have a roof over our heads in the morning."

"Yes, I can see this is much the same. We'll just have to wait and see what happens." Della eyed the clothing strewn across the counterpane. "You're packing for you and Flossie and Uncle Clint, too, I imagine."

Aunt Coral nodded without pausing in her task of sorting through the clothing on the bed. "I'm trying to decide what we absolutely must take and what we can leave."

"I'm not taking much, so I'm ready if we need to leave. I think I'll go down to the barn and tack up our horses. If we leave, we won't have much time."

Aunt Coral glanced up at her niece. "That's a good idea. We should prepare as if the fire will reach the ranch."

"I'm off to the barn, then. I'll tack up three horses, one for you and Flossie, one for Silvie, and one for me."

Della crossed the room and paused in the doorway to look about her. "We haven't lived here very long, but I love this home already. I hope the fire doesn't destroy it." She stepped into the hall and clattered down the stairs.

At the horse barn, Scipio and the two men left behind were occupied with preparation for possible evacuation, so she didn't interrupt them. Within minutes, she tacked up her mare and two other horses, then led them outside to the hitching rail beside the corral.

When she stepped outside into the overcast morning, Rusty's dun cow pony was tied to the hitching rail, standing three legged with its head down. Dried sweat roughened its coat.

What is Rusty doing at the ranch? Shouldn't he be with the other men fighting the fire?

Della looped the reins of her three horses over the rail beside Rusty's mount, then pivoted and surveyed the ranch yard, hoping to catch sight of the red-haired cowboy. She didn't see him. After a moment longer, she shrugged and hurried toward the house.

She'd nearly reached the veranda when a muffled thud sounded from inside Emory Dyer's home. She stopped, cocked her head, and listened, her gaze on the lieutenant's house. With the ranch practically deserted, no one should be inside.

Another thump sounded. Suspicious, Della eased toward the building and halted with her back against the outside wall near the door. Should she open the door and check inside, or should she leave without confronting a possible intruder? Tamping down her misgivings, Della flung open the door and burst into the house.

She halted just inside the threshold. Emory Dyer used the front room, which stretched across the width of the building, as the ranch office. A massive oak desk faced the door. Behind the desk in one corner squatted a square metal safe, where the payroll and other monies for conducting ranch business were secured. The safe door had been opened, and Rusty knelt beside it, stuffing small pouches of coins and stacks of bills into his saddlebags.

At her entrance, he leaped up, drawing his six-shooter. Before she could react, he rounded the desk and bounded to her side. He kicked the door shut and flung one forearm around her throat, then pinned her against him with her back to his chest. He pressed the barrel of his revolver against her temple. Della thrashed, struggling to get free, but his hold tightened until she could hardly catch her breath.

"I'm sorry you had to see this, Miss Della. Real sorry."

"What are you doing?" She gasped against the pressure on her larynx. Her brain refused to process what her eyes saw.

"What am I doing? I'm relievin' your uncle of all the cash he left lying around."

"How did you get into the safe?"

"I've cracked a safe or two in my time."

"But—"

"No more talkin'. I'll gather up my loot and we'll skedaddle." Keeping his forearm pressed against her throat, Rusty dragged her with him to the safe. With his free hand, he scooped up the saddlebags, laden with money, and slung them over one shoulder. He hauled her back to the door. "Now, Miss Della, we're goin' outside and mount up. I can't leave you here to tell your uncle who cleaned out his safe."

Della struggled again, trying to pry his arm from her throat and kicking backward at his shin. Her heel struck his leather cowboy boot without doing any damage to his leg. Rusty shook her until she ceased to struggle.

"I'm putting my six-shooter away. We're goin' to walk side by side to our horses. You will do nothing to call attention to us or try to escape. We wouldn't want anything to happen to your nice aunt or that sweet little girl of hers, would we?"

Della managed to twist her head and glare at him. Anger that he should threaten her family overrode her fear. "You'd better not hurt them!"

Rusty chuckled. "Then, behave yourself. Now, when I open the door, we're goin' outside. If anyone sees us, I'll just say that your uncle sent me and I'm to take you to him. If you do anything that I don't like, you'll have someone's death on your conscience." He grasped her braid and jerked her head back against his shoulder. "Do you understand?"

His demeanor had seemed so honest, so open. How could he have deceived them all concerning his true character? When she didn't reply, his eyes hardened.

He yanked on her hair again. "Do you understand?"

Tears from the pain stung her eyes, though she refused to flinch. "Yes," she muttered through gritted teeth.

"Good. Now, here we go. Stay close to me. My hand is on my six-shooter, and I can use it before you take two steps."

Rusty dropped his arm from Della's neck, and they eased through the door and into the yard. He kept close to her side, his palm on the butt of his sidearm. They strolled to the hitching post. To anyone observing them, they appeared to be two companions in an amiable conversation.

"Very good, Miss Della. Now, you just stand right here beside my cow pony while I tie on these saddlebags." Within moments, he secured the leather bags behind the cantle with the saddle strings, while she waited beside him.

Her heart pounded against her ribs with a frenzied rhythm, and her palms sweated. What would Rusty do if Flossie should come running out of the house? Or Aunt Coral? Fortunately, at this late-morning hour, Flossie should be ensconced in her high chair, eating an early lunch, and Della hoped Aunt Coral was still packing. Fear, more for their safety than her own, made her mouth dry and prevented her from attempting to escape.

Rusty grabbed her arm and hauled her around his pony's rump to her waiting mount. He tossed her onto her mare's back.

"Up you go." For a moment, he tipped his head back to look into her face. His arms caged her with one hand on the chestnut's shoulder and the other just behind the saddle. Regret crossed his face. "You really should have let me teach you to ride astride instead of allowing that scout to teach you."

In response, Della lashed out at him with a booted foot, aiming for his chest. Her attempt to hurt him failed when he grabbed her ankle.

Instead of becoming angry, he grinned. "That's no way for a lady to treat a gentleman."

"You're no gentleman."

He shrugged, then fitted her foot into the stirrup and untied her mare's reins. Still holding the leathers, he mounted his cow pony and walked the horses out of the compound without anyone catching sight of them. Once on the range, Rusty urged their mounts into a lope to put distance between them and the ranch headquarters.

When they'd ridden far enough so they were safe from discovery, Rusty halted the horses and looked at Della. He pulled on her reins, and her mare stepped closer to his cow pony.

Della glowered at him, furious that he'd deceived everyone on the wagon train—her family, Shane, the cavalrymen, and the drovers. He'd taken advantage of everyone's trust and betrayed them by his theft. "Uncle Clint trusted you! How could you betray him by stealing from him?"

Rusty shrugged, appearing unruffled.

Fury washed over her. "I liked you! I danced with you and rode with you on the trail! How dare you deceive me!" Della launched herself at him, her fists pounding his chest and face, anyplace she could land blows.

Rusty grasped both of her flailing fists and twisted her arms behind her, clasping her wrists at the small of her back. She lay, half in her saddle and half over his lap, panting. She glared at him. "You're a thief! A low-down thief!"

"Now, there's no call for you to feel that way. I like you, Miss Della. So much so, that I'll take real good care of you until I figure out what to do with you."

Della struggled again, trying to wrench free. Rusty tightened his grip on her wrists. His freckled face, so deceptively boyish, leaned over her.

"But you do realize I can't let you go? I'll have to keep you with me until we're far enough away so you won't be able to run blabbing to your uncle. Or to that army scout, either." He paused, a thoughtful expression crossing his face. "There are a lot of mining camps between here and California. I can drop you off at one of those camps."

"Shane will hunt you down. You won't get away with this."

Rusty chuckled. "Mr. Hunter—and all the other good men working for your uncle—are a bit busy right now. That prairie fire is taking up all of their attention."

Something in his tone alerted Della. Her head jerked up. "*You* set the fire?"

"Well, I might have had somethin' to do with it." He set her back in her saddle. "Now, it pains me mightily to do this to your pretty wrists, but I have to make sure you don't try to run off." He pulled a length of rope from his saddlebag and leaned toward her.

Della clapped her heels into her mare's sides. The chestnut leaped forward, but Rusty still held the reins. He pulled her horse to a whirling stop.

A flush of anger tinted his cheeks. He bent toward her again. "Don't fight me, Miss Della. You do what you're told, and we'll get along just fine. Now, put both hands on the saddle horn."

Quivering inside, her palms clammy, Della obeyed. Rusty wound the rope around her wrists, securing her hands to the saddle horn. He tied the rope in a tight knot. With her reins in a secure grasp, he turned his dun and headed across the plains.

The prairie spread out before them, broken by low hills and swells. The seared late-summer grasses rustled in the wind. Miles away off to their right, a thick column of black smoke smeared the sky.

They rode without speaking. They'd been riding for some time when they crested a rise and loped down the other side.

At the bottom, more than a dozen mares were being hazed by four men. As she and Rusty pulled their mounts to a halt near the group, she glanced at the strangers. They appeared to be down-at-the-heels saddle bums, scruffy and unkempt. When she looked at their faces, a shiver crawled down her spine. No trace of compassion or human decency softened their expressions.

CHAPTER 33

DELLA SHOT A GLANCE AT Rusty. Fear and suspicion filled her. "Who are these men? What are you doing with them? And what are they doing with Uncle Clint's horses?"

"I reckon you can figure that out."

She turned her attention again to the other riders. They slouched in their saddles. Beneath their hats, they stared at her with cold disdain. At last, the details clicked. "Rustlers? These are the rustlers who've been following us?"

Rusty nodded.

"But why are you with them?"

He stared at her, his face soft with pity. "I'm the leader of this bunch."

Della's mouth dropped open. "You?"

"I'm afraid so."

"But. . . but you worked for Uncle Clint. He trusted you."

He gave a careless shrug. "And I respect your uncle. He's a fine man. Once I got to know him, I might've been tempted to forget my plans to steal cayuses from him, but my pals here, they wouldn't be so willing to let our plan go. And they're not the type of men I want to rile. So, we planned and waited, but with that army scout around, we had to lay low."

Rusty slouched in his saddle, both hands on the horn. "My pals set the fire. When the horses scattered, we cut out fifteen or so of the mares and headed them this away. No one was the wiser. Everyone was too busy fighting the flames. It will be a long while before we're missed. And while my pals guarded the horses, I paid a visit to the ranch. The rest you know."

Della gaped at him, still having difficulty reconciling this stranger with the amiable cowboy who'd danced with her and captivated everyone with his harmonica.

"Let's get these cayuses moving. We've lost enough time already."

With shrill whistles and slaps of their lariats against their legs, the men spread out and urged the horses into motion.

Helpless, her mare being ponied along beside Rusty's cow horse, Della tried not to panic at her dire situation. She was at the mercy of a gang of ruthless rustlers, and no one knew what had happened. Each step the horses took put more distance between her and the ranch. Still, she refused to despair. The Lord was with her, and Shane would track her down. She had to believe that.

* * * * *

Rusty's gang of horse thieves kept the herd moving at a steady trot. They covered miles of grassland, leaving the ranch and safety far behind. A bank of clouds obscured the afternoon sun, though sweat still dripped off Della's nose. She thought longingly of the canteen in her saddlebags, yet she refused to beg for relief. Quenching her thirst could wait.

With her wrists lashed to the saddle horn, she couldn't change position. Her arms and shoulders burned. She rolled her shoulders and wriggled her back to lessen the pain.

Noticing her squirm, Rusty turned a thoughtful look on her. Della pretended not to see, and he didn't offer to give her a drink or loosen the ropes.

During the middle of the afternoon, they entered an area of sandy ridges and coulees interspersed among the grasses. Without warning, a dozen horsemen erupted over the far edge of a ridge and swarmed toward them. Hair-raising yips split the air, and the men brandished rifles over their heads. The horsemen pounding toward them were Cheyenne warriors dressed for battle. They wore only breechcloths and moccasins. War paint streaked their faces and splashed across their chests.

Even as Della watched, stunned and barely comprehending what she saw, they lowered their weapons to their shoulders and began firing.

The rustlers veered off, turning the herd and rousing the mares to a gallop in an attempt to escape the Cheyenne. The horse thieves shot over their shoulders at the pursuing tribesmen. Gunfire ripped the air.

Rusty dropped her mount's reins and pulled his rifle from its scabbard. He lifted the butt to his shoulder, sighted, and squeezed the trigger.

Horror such as Della had never known consumed her. A silent scream tore at her throat. Terrified that at any moment a bullet would end her life, she couldn't think of what to do. For several strides, her mare galloped with the other horses, loose reins flapping. The Morgan leaped through the bunchgrass, following the herd and keeping pace with the rustlers' mounts.

A wild cacophony beat against Della's ears. The thunder of hoofbeats, the savage yells of the warriors, and the crack of rifle fire blended into a chorus of battle. The acrid scent of burnt gunpowder stung her nose.

When the rustler on her left took a bullet and pitched headlong to the ground, her frozen mind began to function. Unwilling to be a helpless passenger on her bolting mount yet unable to grab the dangling reins with her hands tied to the horn, Della kneed her mare to the left. For several strides, the chestnut resisted and continued to gallop with the bolting horses. Della thumped her leg against her mount's side and increased the pressure against the Morgan's ribs. The chestnut plunged and bucked, flattening her ears in protest at being urged to leave the herd. Della clung to the saddle and continued to press her mare to the left, frantic that the attacking braves would overtake her. After several bucks, the mare leaped forward at an angle away from the others. She bolted over a rise and dove down the other side.

The gunfire faded as Della's panicked mount fled across the prairie. The wind whooshed past her ears and lashed tears from her eyes. Just as Della thought she might have escaped unnoticed, hoofbeats behind her filled her with fresh dread. She kicked her mare, and the horse responded with a valiant burst of speed, though she'd been ridden hard that day.

Della flung a glance over her shoulder. One of the braves on a piebald mustang pursued her. Della again urged her mare onward, and the plucky horse responded with another surge. Foam flecked the horse's neck and ran down her legs, but still, the Morgan sped across the plain.

The thudding hoofbeats drew closer. The pursuing warrior closed the gap and drew alongside Della's mare. He reached down, grabbed the trailing reins, and brought both horses to a pitching halt, hooves digging into the turf.

Della struggled to wrench her hands free of the saddle horn, but Rusty had tied the knot so tightly she couldn't pull her wrists through the rope. When her efforts failed, Della squared her shoulders and lifted her head.

Shane had once told her that the tribesmen respected courage, even admiring the brave death of an enemy. If she were to die this day, she'd do so with her head high, her spirit undefeated, though tremors of terror quaked through her. She raised her chin and met the gaze of the warrior who had run her down. Blue eyes glittered at her from a savage face. With a jolt, she recognized Shane's brother, Wild Wind.

Black pigment smeared the upper part of his face and his nose. Red paint covered the lower half of his features, with yellow lines running down his cheeks. Hand symbols and geometric designs decorated his chest and stomach in red and yellow. His piebald warhorse sported similar markings.

Della brought her attention back to Wild Wind's face. She stared at him in defiance, undeterred by her bonds, and waited for him to speak.

After several tense moments, Shane's brother gave her a wolfish smile. "You have fallen into my hands like ripe fruit," he said in English. "This saves me the trouble of taking you from your uncle's home. I meant to have you when I first saw you."

Della willed her voice not to shake. "My uncle, the general, will wage war to get me back. You'll bring much trouble to your village."

Wild Wind shrugged. "He must find you first."

"Shane will find me."

Wild Wind's lip curled. "Little Wolf has grown soft, living with our mother's people. I am a warrior of many battles. I am a Dog Soldier. What I claim, I keep."

If his brother didn't realize the extent of Shane's prowess, Della thought it prudent not to acquaint him of it. Perhaps he'd become careless and leave some sign, making it easier for Shane to find her. She remained silent, while relief that she wouldn't be slaughtered made her lightheaded.

Wild Wind nudged his mount alongside hers. He leaned toward her, curled his fingers about the back of her neck, and tugged her closer. "I will court you in the Cheyenne way," he said when their faces were inches apart. "We will be married before the next moon. You have the spirit of the eagle and will give me many brave sons."

Della stared into his eyes, eyes so like Shane's yet so different. The prospect of being married to a Cheyenne warrior made her breath stop. Her heart slammed against her ribs. What had Shane's mother felt when faced with the prospect of marriage to Yellow Wolf? How had she reconciled herself to that reality? Now, she herself faced the choice of ending her life, if she chose that way, or submitting to marriage with Wild Wind, if she wasn't rescued.

Della wondered how long it would take Shane to find her. She wouldn't allow herself to doubt that he'd track her down, though she hoped for rescue before Wild Wind forced her to marry him.

"Shane will come for me." She refused to flinch under her captor's fierce stare.

Something flickered in Wild Wind's eyes, and his fingers tightened on her neck. "What I have, I hold. Neither Little Wolf nor your uncle the general will take you from me."

Wyoming Territory
October 1870

CHAPTER 34

DELLA SWAYED IN HER SADDLE from exhaustion. If she hadn't been tied on, she would have pitched from her mare to the ground. Wild Wind, with his Dog Soldier companions, had ridden hard for three days, pushing the Morgan horses they'd acquired from the rustlers ahead of them.

She refused to allow her mind to drift back to the moment when she and Shane's brother had ridden to the scene of the warriors' skirmish with the rustlers. To think of what she'd seen when they joined the other braves made her stomach roil. The bodies of the horse thieves had been strewn on the bunchgrass, stripped, mutilated, and plundered. When she saw them, she leaned over her mare's shoulder and retched until her stomach emptied itself of everything she'd eaten that day.

Wild Wind had shown her no quarter. "This is what your uncle the general will face if he tries to take you. I will show him no mercy."

Della straightened in her saddle and faced her captor, wishing she could wipe her mouth. "And Shane? What will you do if Shane comes for me?"

Wild Wind stared at her without expression, while beneath him, his piebald stamped at a fly. "My brother will not take you from me."

Della refused to show fear, though inwardly, she quailed. Wild Wind seemed so adamant that no one could free her, she almost believed him. She tried to peer past the war paint to see his face, but the designs both intimidated her and hid any expression he might betray. Could anyone free her in the face of such ferocious determination?

Whenever they made brief stops to rest during the trek to the Cheyenne encampment, Wild Wind loosened her bonds from the saddle horn but kept the other end of her rope tied to his wrist. At each stop, she collapsed to the grass, drank the water Shane's brother offered her from a leather pouch, and ate a few mouthfuls of pemmican before blessed oblivion claimed her. Now, she roused when the warriors raised their rifles overhead and pushed the horses into a gallop down a slope to the bottomland along a shallow river. Buffalo-hide tepees dotted the level sandy ground along the water's edge. The braves announced their presence with fierce cries.

Della clung to the saddle horn, nearly too wearied to remain upright. Her mare plunged down the hill beside Wild Wind's mount.

The village dogs and a tangle of dark-haired children ran to greet them. Men and women spilled from the lodges or came running from the riverbank behind the village and surrounded the victorious warriors. The dogs' yapping and a babble of voices beat against Della's ears.

Wild Wind flung himself from his warhorse and came around to Della's side. He pulled a knife with a wicked blade from its sheath at his waist, then sliced the rope binding her wrists. He jerked her from the saddle. She almost fell when her feet hit the dirt. Fatigued beyond the limits of her endurance and stiff from hours in the saddle, she swayed and grasped her mare's neck.

"You are weary. Come. My father's sister will care for you." With surprising gentleness, Wild Wind scooped her up in his arms and shouldered his way through the throng.

Startled and discomposed by his action, Della resisted. She put both palms on his shoulders and pushed away.

Wild Wind held her tight, tucking her head beneath his chin, and Della subsided against his chest. The villagers' stares, some curious and some hostile, flustered her. Closing her eyes, she shut them out. Still, she heard the whispers. She swayed with the motion of her captor's strides. Della knew only that, for this moment, at least, she felt somehow protected.

For a brief moment, she lifted her head from his shoulder and peered about. A slender young woman stood nearby at the edge of the crowd, watching the handsome warrior carry her across the encampment. An expression of mingled jealousy and wistfulness flitted across the girl's face. Too exhausted to wonder at the girl's behavior, Della dropped her head again on her captor's shoulder and let her eyelids drift closed.

Too soon, Wild Wind set her on her feet. She opened her eyes. They stood at the opening of a tepee. Wild Wind called out to someone inside, and a moment later, the flap covering the opening was thrust aside. A stocky woman with graying hair ducked out and joined them.

Della and the woman eyed each other. The woman wore a fringed deerskin dress and beaded moccasins. Leather thongs wrapped about two braids hanging over the front of her dress. Squint lines fanned out from her shrewd eyes.

Wild Wind spoke, his words coming in staccato bursts.

The woman listened, surveying Della with an impassive gaze. At last, she nodded and replied.

Wild Wind crossed his muscled arms. "This is Neha, my father's widowed sister. She will care for you. Do what she tells you. I will come for you later."

He pivoted without a backward glance and strode back through the crowd to where his warhorse and Della's mare waited. Since her capture, Shane's brother had stood between her and the other warriors, protecting her from defilement. Now, without his presence, a sensation of abandonment filled her.

Neha spoke in a sharp tone and gestured toward the tepee's entrance. Della turned her back on the curious villagers, stooped, and stepped inside.

The lodge's interior seemed dim after the sunshine outdoors. Della had a vague impression of a conical space with a buffalo-hide floor and a small cooking fire encircled by stones in the center. Off to one side lay a pile of buffalo robes. A smoky scent drifted in the air.

Neha gestured to the robes. "Sleep."

Too exhausted to argue, Della approached the pile of robes and collapsed onto the dark fur without even removing her shoes. Neha tossed one of the robes over her.

Della looked up into her face. The older woman's dark eyes stared at her, unblinking and expressionless. "Thank you." She wondered how much English Neha understood.

Neha nodded and retreated to the other side of the tepee.

Della closed her eyes, grateful for the opportunity to sleep. Before the dark mists of slumber overtook her, the verse she'd claimed floated through her mind. "I will never leave thee, nor forsake thee." Comforted by the knowledge of the Lord's presence, even in this remote Cheyenne village, Della slept.

* * * * *

A hand shook her shoulder. Della groaned and rolled to her back, prying open her eyelids. Neha crouched beside her. When the woman saw Della had awakened, she motioned for her to get up.

Della shoved the buffalo hides aside and rolled to her knees. Every muscle in her body screamed in protest. Gritting her teeth, she climbed to her feet.

Neha spoke and pointed to the fire. A trencher piled with roasted meat rested on the floor just to one side of the ring of stones that contained the cooking fire. Della tottered across the tepee and dropped to the floor beside the wooden plate. Neha pantomimed eating and indicated the trencher again.

Della picked up the platter. Using her fingers, she devoured the meal. When she swallowed the last bite and laid down the trencher, Neha barked another command.

Scrambling to her feet, Della wondered what Wild Wind's aunt planned for her next. She watched while Neha gathered a leather pouch, a colorful blanket, and a pile of clothes.

Neha motioned to her, turned toward the tepee's opening, and ducked outside. Della contemplated defying the older woman, but after a moment's indecision, she decided resistance against Neha would result only in Wild Wind forcing her to obey his aunt's commands. She had no wish to anger Neha. Deciding she should comply, she followed Neha outside, squinting when she stepped into the sunshine. The sun rode low over the encircling hills. She must have slept the afternoon away.

Wild Wind's aunt led her through the village and down to the stream. They walked along the bank away from the lodges to where a stand of cottonwoods and jack pines hid the village from view. While they walked, they collected a gaggle of women and children, who talked about her behind their hands until Della felt like the bearded lady at the circus.

Sheltered from the camp by brush and trees, they halted at the water's edge. Neha indicated that Della should bathe in the frigid stream. After dropping her clothes onto the ground, Della waded into the water. Neha accompanied her. From the pouch, Wild Wind's aunt poured a viscous liquid into Della's cupped palms, then pantomimed washing. Following Neha's instructions, Della scrubbed all over and washed her hair. Her teeth chattered and goosebumps popped out on her skin as the cool air and colder water flowed over her. She tried to ignore the audience gathered on the riverbank and thought longingly of her porcelain hip tub and the warm water used for bathing at home.

Her bath finished, Della sloshed to the bank. Water streamed down her limbs. Neha handed her the blanket, which Della used to towel herself dry. Once dry, she donned the clothing provided by Wild Wind's aunt.

The heavy yet comfortable deerskin dress flowed over her limbs. The hem reached down around her calves. Fringe hung from the bottom of the dress and the edges of the long sleeves. A starburst pattern of blue, red, and yellow beadwork decorated the front of the bodice. Soft leather boots, embellished with intricate colored beadwork across the top and along the sides, encased her feet.

Neha stooped and bundled Della's blouse and split riding skirt. Tucking the clothing under her arm, she began the trek back to the village. Della hurried along beside her, not wanting to be left behind.

Once more within the shelter of the tepee, Neha motioned for Della to sit. Della complied, dropping cross legged to the hide floor. The older woman knelt behind her. Using a bone comb, Neha separated Della's curling tresses into two sections, then ran the teeth through the strands until she removed all the tangles. Then, after working a lotion that smelled of animal fat and flowers through Della's locks, Neha plaited the younger woman's mane into two thick braids. She completed the coiffure by winding leather strips about the strands.

When she finished, Neha nodded and motioned for Della to stand. Della scrambled to her feet, glancing down at her costume. The Cheyenne clothing and hairstyle made her feel displaced, detached from the person she'd always known herself to be. Her life as it had been before Wild Wind snatched her from the rustlers had acquired a dreamlike quality, something merely imagined and not real. She tried to bring her memories into focus, to feel some sense of the person she'd been, but the images slipped away.

Neha moved to the tepee's opening and gestured for Della to follow. Outside in the crisp dusk, Wild Wind stood tall and resplendent in a fringed buckskin shirt and leggings, eagle feathers twined in his flowing hair. He'd scrubbed off the war paint, and now, she saw the strong lines of his face. In spite of herself, Della couldn't help but be impressed. Still, the image of the mutilated rustlers reminded her that this man was a warrior who fought her people.

He smiled when he saw her and uncrossed his arms, surveying her with a sweeping glance. "Now, you look like one of the People."

"The People?"

Wild Wind tapped his chest. "We are the People."

They stood in the midst of the village, conical tepees painted with colored symbols scattered about them. Dogs ran in packs between the lodges. Several families sat on the ground outside their homes, watching the warrior talk with the captive girl. Della tried to ignore them.

"What do your people call you?" Shane's brother asked.

"Della. My name is Della."

"Della." Wild Wind turned the word over on his tongue. "I shall call you Lona, for you have much beauty. You are no longer Della. You are Lona."

Lona. In addition to wearing Cheyenne clothing and a Cheyenne hairstyle, she now had a Cheyenne name. Another facet of her white identity had just been swept away. Della put a hand to her forehead. Dizziness passed over her when an understanding of the absolute changes in her life burst through her.

Wild Wind held out an imperative hand. "Come. My father waits for us."

At the mention of the stern warrior Shane called his Cheyenne father, a tremor of uneasiness shivered down Della's spine. "Why does he want to meet me?"

"You are to be my wife, a member of the family." Wild Wind threaded his fingers between hers and turned her toward the other side of the encampment.

Della allowed Wild Wind to tow her along. Men and women of the tribe stared as she hurried along beside her suitor. One family group, with a slender young woman in their midst, glowered at her when she walked past. Della recognized her as the girl who ogled her earlier.

"Who was the girl who just stared at me?"

Wild Wind glanced over his shoulder. "That was Little Fawn."

"She's beautiful. Why did she glare at me?"

He shrugged as if the other family's displeasure was of no consequence. "Her family and my father have talked of arranging a marriage between Little Fawn and me, but I hadn't agreed to the ceremony. Now, I have you, so they know there will be no wedding for Little Fawn and me."

"I can see why she'd glare at me."

Wild Wind halted before a large tepee decorated with images of buffalo and horses and geometric designs. "This is the lodge of Yellow Wolf, my father. He understands English, so he'll know what you say, but he hasn't spoken the English tongue since my mother, his wife, was taken by the pony soldiers. He will speak only in the Cheyenne tongue. I will tell you what he says."

Della nodded. A fine tremor quivered through her at the prospect of meeting Yellow Wolf.

Wild Wind called out a greeting to his father. A moment later, the gruff voice of the chief bade them enter. Pulling back the flap that covered the entrance, Wild Wind gestured for Della to enter the lodge.

She ducked inside and waited, wondering what she should do next. Across from the doorway and beyond the cooking fire, a regal figure sat cross legged. She recognized the weathered features of Shane's Cheyenne father. To his right lay a pile of saddlery, and to his left, his weapons leaned against the tepee's lining. Behind him, buffalo robes formed his bedding. Any evidence that Shane's mother had ever lived in this lodge had been removed.

Today, he wore only a few eagle feathers in his hair, unlike the first time she'd seen him when she and Shane encountered the Cheyenne hunting party. On that occasion, a full eagle-feather headdress had proclaimed his status as chief.

Behind her, Wild Wind entered the lodge and motioned her forward. "Sit here." He indicated a place before the cooking fire.

Della sat. Wild Wind dropped to the floor beside her in a fluid display of muscle. For long moments, no one spoke. Yellow Wolf stared at Della, his perusal intent and unblinking. When she thought she couldn't sit without fidgeting a second longer, the chief transferred his attention to his son and barked a question.

Wild Wind sent a sidelong glance her way. "My father asks what your name is."

Della met Wild Wind's gaze with a touch of defiance dredged from a well of determination. "Tell him my name is Della."

Displeasure flared in Wild Wind's eyes. Della refused to look away. At last, he turned back to his father and replied in a rapid flow of words. Della heard her name mentioned, followed by *Lona*, the name Shane's brother had given her. When Wild Wind finished speaking, his father nodded.

Wild Wind turned to her. "I told him you were no longer Della, that now, you are Lona. You will never refer to yourself as Della again."

For a moment, Della refused to capitulate. Fierce insistence set Wild Wind's features in an unyielding mask. Recognizing her powerlessness, Della surrendered. The chief's son had the upper hand, and both of them knew it. "Lona. My name is Lona."

He surprised her by stroking her cheek with gentle fingers. "You will forget your old life. I will be a good husband to you, and you will give me brave sons. We will live together many summers until our hair is as the snow upon the ground."

CHAPTER 35

WILD WIND'S WORDS RANG WITH conviction. Della believed him. Her past crumbled beneath his certitude. Her life before this moment vanished like mist before the sun. She *felt* like Lona, the woman who would marry the chief's son.

Yellow Wolf spoke again, bringing her back to the reason they sat in this lodge.

"My father wants to know about your uncle the general," Wild Wind said.

Della thought of Uncle Clint, bringing his image into sharp focus. Remembering him steadied her confusion, freeing her somewhat from the spell Wild Wind seemed to have cast over her. She told of her uncle's dream of raising horses for the cavalry.

Yellow Wolf listened without speaking.

Wild Wind cast her an accusatory glance. "Your uncle the general is providing horses for the pony soldiers to fight against the People. The pony soldiers want to steal away our land."

What could she say? And why did she feel so guilty about Uncle Clint's endeavor? "I don't think he regards it quite like that."

"Our women and children will starve on the reservation. There will be no more buffalo to hunt."

Della had forgotten the fierce warrior Wild Wind had been earlier. She'd seen him as her staunch protector, and since their arrival at his village, he'd beguiled her as her gentle suitor. Now, that warrior fierceness blazed again with blue fire in his eyes. She must never forget that the man beside her had many faces. She held out a conciliatory hand toward him. "I'm truly sorry."

Yellow Wolf spoke again.

"My father wants to know what you were doing with Little Wolf when we met upon the plains."

Recalling Shane's warning that his brother coveted whatever was his, Della deemed it prudent not to betray the love Shane felt for her. She feared that knowing Shane loved her would make Wild Wind even more determined to marry her, so she decided to disclose only part of the truth. "Little Wolf was showing me the land my uncle had purchased."

"The land does not belong to the white man." Wild Wind spoke in a harsh tone. "No one can own Mother Earth. The land has been the hunting grounds of the People for generations."

Yellow Wolf barked a rebuke, and Wild Wind subsided. A few beats of silence passed before the chief asked another question.

"My father asks if you are willing to marry me, the son of Yellow Wolf and Waynoka."

Della caught her breath. How should she reply? Her welfare in the tribe depended upon her answer. To refuse to marry Wild Wind would put her at the mercy of every other man in the village, for only Wild Wind's protection had spared her the fate of most women captives. Yet if she agreed to marry him, her code of honor would demand she fulfill her bargain. She hesitated, conscious of the stares of both men. "If my uncle or Little Wolf does not come for me before the next moon, I will marry Wild Wind."

Apparently satisfied with her answer, Yellow Wolf nodded and made a dismissive gesture.

Wild Wind rose. He grasped Della's hand and lifted her. "Come. My father wishes to be alone."

They stepped out into the night. Darkness had fallen. The flickering orange light of many campfires cast a wavering glow over the village. Wild Wind returned her to Neha's lodge.

Outside the open entrance, he turned her to face him. "My father isn't pleased that I want to take you for my wife."

Della arched a brow at him, shivering in the evening's chill. "I can think of several reasons why he'd disapprove."

"He fears what happened to him with my mother will happen to me. Your uncle will bring the pony soldiers to our village and take you away, perhaps kill many of our people."

"I think that's a possibility. Uncle Clint won't rest until he's done everything he can to find me and take me back."

"Our tribe is far away from your uncle's land. He will not find you."

"Little Wolf will find me."

Wild Wind remained silent for several moments. In the dim light cast by the campfires, Della could almost believe he was Shane, so strong was the likeness between the brothers. She stared into his face, trying to read his expression.

"If we are already married, would Little Wolf then take you back?" Wild Wind asked.

Della hesitated. She considered marriage vows to be binding, no matter the culture. Unlike Shane's mother, she had no husband waiting for her in white society. She had no reason to leave a man she'd married legally in this culture. Though her people might not consider her marriage in the Cheyenne culture either legal or binding, she felt otherwise. "If we marry before Little Wolf comes, I will stay with you."

Wild Wind reached out and once again stroked her cheek. "Lona. Beautiful. You are a woman of courage and honor as well as beauty. I have chosen well."

"If I marry you, you must promise not to wage war on my uncle or his men. You must not steal his horses."

"Horses taken in combat are the victor's prize. They are not stolen."

Della laid a hand on his chest. "Please. Spare my uncle and all that belongs to him."

Wild Wind covered her hand with his. "I give you my warrior's pledge that I will not harm anything that belongs to your uncle, if he doesn't wage war on my village. I will try to persuade the other Dog Soldiers to do the same."

Relief made Della weak. "Thank you."

"Go now. Neha is waiting for you. She will teach you how to be a good Cheyenne wife."

Della turned away and ducked into the tepee. Later, lying awake on her bed of furs, tremors shuddered through her. What had she done? Had she just bartered her future in exchange for the safety of her loved ones? Had she perhaps spared Shane's life?

* * * * *

Following Neha, Della stepped out into the chilly morning air. Since the entrance of each lodge faced east, Della blinked in the dawn. She paused a moment to survey the village. People stirred, rousing from nighttime's slumbers. Dogs rose and stretched. The smoky scent of cooking fires hung in the air. The sun layered a golden blanket over the encampment, embellishing it with romantic atmosphere.

Neha and Della joined a line of women who converged in a shuffling band on their way upstream to collect clean water for cooking and drinking. The other women eyed her askance. Since both Yellow Wolf and Wild Wind sheltered her by their patronage, none of the women dared to show hostility, though no one addressed her.

They reached the stream's edge and waited their turn to dip their buffalo-bladder pitchers into the water. Della looked about her while Neha chatted with her friends. Feeling herself watched, Della turned her head and encountered Little Fawn's stare.

The young woman was beautiful in an exotic way. Della wished she could speak to her, to somehow smooth over the dismay Little Fawn must feel, knowing Wild Wind had rejected her and filled her bridal place with a foreigner. Della stretched out a hand in a gesture of conciliation, but Little Fawn turned away.

The snub cut deep. Della tamped down a flicker of panic at the sensation of aloneness in a strange culture. Wild Wind was her only true ally. Neha accepted her on sufferance because her nephew had requested her to aid his intended bride. Yellow Wolf had accepted her only because his son desired to marry her. A female friend would have lessened her sense of solitude, but Little Fawn could never be the friend whom Della craved.

With their water containers filled, Della and Neha trudged to the lodge. Neha spent the morning acquainting her charge with the furniture and cooking utensils inside the tepee. She gave each item its Cheyenne name. Though Della tried to learn the unfamiliar words, repeating them after Neha, she had trouble forming the sounds.

Yellow Wolf's sister paused and turned toward her protégé. "Soon after the next moon, we will move our camp to our winter place. You will learn how to take down your tepee and put it up again."

Della glanced about Neha's lodge, at the heavy buffalo skins wrapping the long poles holding up the home and the leather laces binding the seams. "The women do that?"

"It is our duty. I will help you, and you will help me. We will do it together."

Della wondered where the men would be while their women did the heavy lifting, but she held her tongue. She still had much to learn about this culture, and the Cheyenne ways weren't the ways of her heritage.

Midway through the morning, when Wild Wind hailed them through the open flap of the entrance, the women left their chores and joined him outside. Relieved to be freed from her domestic lessons, Della greeted him with enthusiasm and pleasure.

Wild Wind was sitting tall astride his favorite piebald mount. "Lona, come see what I have for you."

Curious, Della stepped around the horse's shoulder and stopped at Wild Wind's knee. Draped over the gelding's withers lay an antelope, head hanging off one side and hindquarters over the other. She put a hand to her mouth. In the Plains tribal culture, she supposed the offering of an antelope from a suitor was a coveted gift, and she tried to show the proper gratitude.

"Thank you, Wild Wind. This will help fill the cooking pots tonight."

"Already, I provide for you. You need never fear that hunger will enter our lodge. You and our children will go to bed with full bellies."

The image of children—hers and Wild Wind's—filling a tepee distracted Della for a moment. If Shane didn't rescue her soon, that image could become a reality. She didn't have much time before the next moon. She shook the vision from her mind and focused on a suitable reply. "You will be a good provider."

"It is a pleasure to give gifts to my wife."

Already, Wild Wind had settled on the certainty of their marriage. Della clung to the hope of rescue to keep his confidence from submerging her.

He leaned toward her over his horse's shoulder. "Evening is the time of courtship," he said in a low tone, for her hearing only. "I count the hours until I can return to you."

Neha chose that moment to interrupt his declaration. She stepped forward and made a shooing motion with her hands. "Shoo, shoo! Go away. You cannot be here now."

An unexpected smile crinkled Wild Wind's eyes. "My father's sister is protecting you from me, making sure our courtship is proper. I will come back when the sun hides behind the hills."

He dumped the antelope at Della's feet, wheeled his mount, and cantered away with an exuberant yell. Della watched him disappear through the maze of tepees, then glanced down at the antelope. What was she to do with that?

Neha sidled closer and gestured to Wild Wind's gift. "*Antelope* is *vo'kaa'e.*"

Della repeated the word, frustrated when she couldn't get the proper sound. She shook her head. "I can't say it."

"It will come." Neha nodded and said the word again.

Della tried once more, and this time, she managed a credible imitation of Neha's pronunciation.

Neha smiled at her. "Good. You will learn."

"Did Wild Wind's mother teach you to speak English?"

Neha nodded again. "We teach each other. She teach me her tongue, and I teach her the language of the People."

"Little Wolf told me about his mother."

"My brother Yellow Wolf still loves her very much. And he was a good father to Little Wolf."

271

"And Little Wolf loves his Cheyenne father."

Neha shrugged and stooped to drag the antelope closer to her lodge. "Come. I will show you what to do with this gift. Wild Wind will make you a good husband."

Neha showed Della how to gut the deer and skin it. Della had to turn her head and cover her mouth to keep from gagging when Neha slit the animal's belly. The older woman demonstrated how to roast the meat in a shallow pit lined with hot stones, then covered with coals and hot ashes, with dirt raked on top.

They uncovered the antelope late in the afternoon. The meat was browned and succulent. Bearing choice cuts on platters, Neha and Della took portions of the kill to Yellow Wolf and Wild Wind.

Wild Wind took his share from Della, his expression grave, though his eyes smiled at her. "Thank you, Lona. After I eat, I will come to you for courting."

When the women had eaten, Neha combed Della's hair again. The leather wraps she twined about the plaits had been embellished with yellow, blue, red, and white porcupine quills and beadwork. "You must be beautiful for Wild Wind."

Neha had just finished arranging the last wrap when the breathy notes of a wooden flute rasped through the air. "Wild Wind brought his courting flute." She gave Della's shoulder a little shove. "Go to him. He waits for you."

Della remembered the legend Shane had told her of the cedar courting flute. She'd hoped to one day hear him play the flute for her. Instead, his brother now courted her with flute music.

Glancing down at her fringed deerskin dress, she smoothed her hand over the soft leather and reflected on the bizarre twist her life had taken. When she began this adventure in the West, she never imagined she'd go from being squired in a Boston drawing room to being courted in a Cheyenne village.

The cedar flute continued its music. Lifting her head and squaring her shoulders, Della stepped outside to meet her suitor.

CHAPTER 36

WHEN DELLA STEPPED INTO THE brisk dusk, Wild Wind took the flute from his mouth and smiled at her. He stowed the flute in a thin pouch tied with a rawhide string about his waist and held out one hand with imperative arrogance. The fringe on the long sleeves of his buckskin shirt quivered with the motion.

Della moved toward him and gave him her hand. He gripped her fingers with gentle strength and drew her close. He plucked a colored blanket woven in bright designs from the ground at his feet. With a deft flick of his wrist, he flipped the blanket about them and wrapped Della in his arms. Brought up against his chest, Della wedged her elbows between them. "What are you doing?"

"This is the courtship custom of the People. Look about you. This is proper in the Cheyenne way."

Della peeked around his shoulder. The whole village appeared to be outside on this crisp autumn evening. Family groups gathered in front of their tepees, sitting cross legged on the ground. Children scampered between the lodges, pursued by barking dogs. Other courting couples stood close together, wrapped in blankets before the openings of the girls' families' lodges.

"We do nothing wrong. We stand here where everyone in the village can see us, and we talk. The blanket is a sign that this is my time with you. If another brave desires to court you, he must wait his turn with his blanket."

Still thinking the custom strange, Della nevertheless relaxed and allowed Wild Wind to draw her against him. Her arms crept about his waist. His warmth and the blanket chased the evening's chill from her body.

"Is it permissible for a girl to be courted by more than one brave at a time?" Della asked.

"Yes. She may have many suitors, but she must choose one. She chooses a brave who will be kind to her and who will be a good provider. No wife wants a husband who cannot fill their lodge with food."

"I see."

"No other braves will court you, Lona. I have claimed you for my own, and no one else would dare to come near you. I would fight any man who tries to court you."

"I don't want any other man to court me. Only you."

His arms, with his fists crossed at the small of her back, squeezed her. "That is a good thing. You will not be unhappy in my lodge. One day, I will be chief, and you will be honored among all the other women. You will never go hungry, you will have changes of clothes, and I will be kind to you."

Della nodded. "I think you will be kind." She drew a breath, wondering whether she dared to speak her next thought. "But I would wish that you not fight my people. It would make me happy for the killing to cease."

Wild Wind's body tensed beneath her hands. He frowned. "You sound like my father. He no longer wants to fight. He says the white man will come and not stop and the pony soldiers will drive us away from our hunting grounds. He thinks there is nothing we can do to stop them." Harshness lent an edge to his voice. "I say we must fight."

"But the white men are my people. And the people of your mother."

"They are not my people."

"Their blood runs in your veins. Would you kill the people of your own blood? And the blood of our children, should we marry." Della eyed him, not knowing him well enough to guess whether she'd pushed him too far. Though his eyes blazed, he didn't flare into an impassioned defense of his views.

"I refuse to let our time be filled with talk of war," he vowed. "Already, the sun is hiding behind the hills, and soon, I must leave you. Let us talk of other things. What did Neha teach you today?"

"She taught me how to keep the lodge, and she showed me how to cook the antelope. She tried to teach me your words, but I can't say them."

"You will learn them. One day, we will be speaking as the People speak."

Della had her doubts, and she hoped she'd be back at Uncle Clint's ranch before she learned the Cheyenne language, but she held her tongue. It was easy enough to be drawn into Wild Wind's world without learning his language. "Your mother learned to speak as the People do."

He nodded. "Neha and my father taught her. She learned our speech to please him. She was a dutiful wife."

"Yet she taught you English."

"She taught Blue Flower and me her tongue. And she taught us about her God."

"I know about her God. I worship Him."

"We also have a god. The People worship the Wise One Above. Perhaps he is like your God."

"My God is all wise and all powerful and all loving. I will tell you about Him one day."

While they'd talked, dusk had thickened into darkness. Campfires cast their glow. Wild Wind bent his head close to hers and reached up to caress her cheek. "You have brought the sunshine to my heart. My heart was like the ice in winter, frozen and cold, but like the sun, you have melted the ice and brought summer to my heart."

His words warmed her. The savage warrior in him should terrify her, but in spite of his battle prowess, she recognized a kind and tender facet of his character. That and other qualities drew her to him. "I thank you, Wild Wind. And I thank you for sparing my life and protecting me from the other braves."

"You are my sun, shining upon me. I could not destroy that which I knew would be my life's mate. My heart beats as one with yours."

So fierce was his possessiveness, Della feared he wouldn't let her go, even if Shane should find her. "What if my uncle sends Little Wolf here to take me back? Will you let me go if he comes before we marry?"

"Will you take the sunshine from my life?"

She laid both palms on his chest, torn. "My family loves me. They're worried about me. They want me to come home."

He hesitated for several moments. "If I take you to your uncle's ranch and let you visit, will you come back to me?"

Della understood what this concession cost him. "I gave you my word, on my honor, that if I married you, I wouldn't leave you. I will come back to you."

Beneath her hands, his tense muscles relaxed. He nodded.

Neha had been sitting in the doorway of her lodge. Now, she rose and approached them through the darkness. "Wild Wind, the courting time is over. You must leave."

Wild Wind squeezed Della again. "Neha has spoken. Now, I must go." He unwrapped the blanket and stepped away.

Della shivered from the chill that flowed over her when she lost his warmth. She crossed her arms over her stomach and clutched her elbows. "Good night, Wild Wind."

Neha herded her into the tepee.

Moments later, ensconced on her back in her warm buffalo robes, Della stared up through the night's blackness. She couldn't sleep. She felt caught between two cultures and two men, with her former way of life fading to memories.

Forcing herself to recall the faces of her loved ones, she tried to keep them close. Shane's visage floated before her eyes, dear and beloved. Would he arrive in time to prevent her marriage to his brother? Or would he be too late?

She repeated her verse, feeling its truths quieting her anxious thoughts. Praying for wisdom and guidance, she finally fell asleep.

The next morning, Neha instructed Della in the art of drying meat. The women sliced the antelope into thin strips and smoked them over a fire in front of Neha's lodge. The sudden clatter of hooves brought Della's head up from the meat she was cutting.

Wild Wind approached, ponying along five splendid horses of various colors. Della laid down the knife and rinsed her hands in a kettle of water just outside the tepee's opening. She rose. Her suitor brought his piebald to a halt in front of her and dismounted. He ducked around his mount's head and stopped before her, holding the reins in one hand.

"Greetings, my wife."

"We aren't married yet," Della said.

He tapped his chest. "Here, in my heart, you are already mine."

Unable to think of a suitable reply, she gestured toward the horses. "What are these?"

Wild Wind laced his fingers through hers and drew her toward the horses linked on a lead line beside his mount. "These are my bride gift to you."

"These horses are for me?"

"A suitor may give horses to his intended's family as a bride-price. Since you have no family here, I give the horses to you. And I want you to have standing in the village among the people as a woman of property, apart from me."

Touched at his care of her, Della turned toward him. "Thank you, Wild Wind. These horses are beautiful. I appreciate your thoughtfulness." She stroked the neck of a bay mare while her connoisseur's eye appraised the horses. He'd given her mounts of excellent quality.

"My gift to you is a token of our life together."

Della turned away and rubbed the horse's neck again, conscious that Wild Wind still held her other hand. What would he do should Shane rescue her before the wedding? She feared what Wild Wind's reaction would be to losing her.

The days flowed past, one into the other. The time of the next moon drew near. Her wedding day approached. Wild Wind courted her each evening, and Della went to bed at the end of every day knowing the time for her rescue grew shorter.

One morning, Neha and Della walked upstream to gather berries along the riverbank.

"We will pound the berries to a powder and mix them into the pemmican we make."

Neha talked with the other women as they gathered berries. The village women smiled at Della and tried to include her in their conversation, often repeating words for her to say. She appreciated their overtures of friendship and tried to communicate with words and gestures. Often, the women laughed at her efforts to speak their language, but their humor held no malice.

They filled their pouches with the berries and strolled back to the village. An air of anticipation about the lodges caught Della's attention. Dogs barked and ran about. Women who hadn't gone to gather berries stood outside their tepees, looking toward the hills. The men hurried away from the encampment toward a lone rider who eased his grulla mount down the hill facing the village and approached the lodges.

Della stopped, nearly dropping her container of berries. She knew that rider, sitting easy in the saddle. Shane. Shane had come for her.

CHAPTER 37

A WAVE OF RELIEF, FOLLOWED by an immediate sensation of panic, flooded Della. Her breath caught in her throat. Her heart thumped against her ribs, and a film of perspiration sheened her body. What would Wild Wind do when Shane demanded her release?

Shane and the village's men converged on the level ground before the encampment, with the men engulfing horse and rider. Still, Shane rode undeterred toward the village, coming closer to Della. She stood transfixed beside a motionless Neha, watching her love draw near. The group of men and the rider advanced and drew abreast of the women. Shane rode past without acknowledging Della by so much as a glance. His snub smote her.

Neha clutched her elbow and dragged her away, not giving her time to dwell upon Shane's action. "Come. We must get away from here." She hustled Della back to the lodge they shared.

Inside, Della laid down her pouch of berries and faced Neha. "Little Wolf has come for me."

"It is just as my brother feared. Your uncle has sent Little Wolf to take you back to the white man. Wild Wind will lose you, as my brother lost Waynoka to the pony soldiers."

"Yes. Little Wolf has come for me, but I told Wild Wind if we were already married, I would stay with him. I have no husband waiting for me in the white man's world."

"It is good you should say that. We will wait and see what word Yellow Wolf speaks."

The minutes dragged on. Della fidgeted about the lodge, while Neha sat without moving. How long would the discussion continue? Would Wild Wind convince his father to move forward with their wedding? She wondered what Shane had felt when Yellow Wolf told him of her forthcoming marriage to Wild Wind.

Della paced, her thoughts and emotions a wild jumble, until Wild Wind hailed them from outside the lodge. Della looked to Neha for guidance.

"Go to him. Yellow Wolf has spoken. What he says will be. He is chief."

Della pushed back the flap over the door and ducked through the opening. When she straightened and looked at Wild Wind's face, she knew his father had ruled against his plea. She caught her breath. A mask of anger and denial set his features in bitter lines. His eyes glittered with terrible savagery.

"Yellow Wolf has decreed that you must go back to your people. We are not to marry."

Della stretched out a hand to him, her own emotions tumbling about almost without control. Her heart fluttered against her ribs like a bird struggling to fly free. Should she say she was sorry? Was she sorry? Had Shane's mother felt such a contradiction of feelings when the soldiers tore her from her Cheyenne husband and her life in this village and thrust her back into life with her white husband, a man she hadn't seen in almost ten years? Tears of confusion, of relief mingled with sorrow, burned behind her eyes.

Wild Wind took her hand and pressed her palm against his buckskin-clad chest. "Winter has returned to my heart. Your sunshine has been taken from me."

"I am sorry, Wild Wind. What will you do?"

He shrugged, a very white gesture Della guessed he'd adopted during his time at the army fort. "We must go. Little Wolf waits to take you back to your uncle the general."

With their fingers linked, Wild Wind towed her through the encampment to his father's lodge. For once, a quiet pall hung over the village. Even the dogs had ceased their barking. Men and women stood before their tepees, tracking their progress with solemn expressions. Outside Yellow Wolf's lodge, Wild Wind pulled her to a stop and looked down at her with scorching eyes.

"My lodge will remain empty. There will be no sunshine, no laughter, no children, without you."

Della lifted her free hand and touched his cheek. "May you someday find happiness with another."

Wild Wind didn't reply. His gaze smoldered over her face as if committing her features to memory. Then, tugging her behind him, he entered the chief's lodge.

An odd sensation of déjà vu washed over Della. Everything seemed much the same as it had the first time she entered this lodge. Once again, Yellow Wolf sat behind the cook fire, facing the door, his saddlery on one side and his weapons on the other. This time, Shane Hunter sat where Wild Wind had previously sat, and his brother now stood by her side.

Wild Wind spoke in low, rough tones. Della had learned enough of the language to catch a few words, enough to understand he made one last appeal for their marriage.

Shane didn't glance at her. For all the reaction he betrayed, she might not have even entered the lodge. When Wild Wind lapsed into silence, Shane didn't move or speak.

Several moments of tense expectation hung in the air. None of them seemed to breathe. At last, Yellow Wolf spoke. When he finished, Wild Wind freed her hand from his. He spun, slapped aside the privacy flap, and flung himself out of the lodge.

Shane said something to his Cheyenne father, who nodded once. With fluid grace, Shane pushed to his feet and grasped Della's arm. "Come. We must leave. Now."

Outside, their horses waited in the autumn sunshine. Someone had caught up Della's Morgan mare and prepared her for riding. The horse waited beside Shane's gelding. A young boy held the reins of both mounts.

Della glanced about, at the lodges and the people whom she'd come to know. She saw no sign of Wild Wind or of Neha. With his fingers still wrapped about her arm, Shane hustled her toward her horse. Della dug in her heels.

"Wait. I want to say goodbye to Neha."

"We don't have time. We must leave. Now." Without giving her an opportunity to argue, he tossed her onto her chestnut. He ducked around his grulla's head and stepped into the saddle.

Yellow Wolf had followed them outside and now stood at the doorway to his lodge, watching. Some unspoken communication passed between the two men before Shane reined his gelding about and set out at an easy walk.

With a last look about her, Della followed. Her time here in this village had changed her. She'd never be the same woman she'd been before Wild Wind brought her here. She left a part of her with these people.

They cleared the top of the ridge. Della twisted in the saddle for a final glimpse of the encampment below. The tepees stretched along the riverbank, smoke curling from the vents in the tops of the lodges. From this distance, men and women appeared as toy figures. The camp disappeared when Della's mare followed Shane's mount down the other side.

They reached the bottom and level terrain. Shane reined in his gelding and looked at Della for the first time when her mare halted beside him. His blue stare bored into her, intense and probing. "Perhaps this is difficult for you to talk about, but have you been. . . Are you all right?"

Della reassured him with a tentative smile. "Yes. The Lord protected me the same way He protected your mother. Wild Wind claimed me for his wife and shielded me from the other warriors. Neha was a most vigilant chaperone."

He blew out a breath and nodded. "Thank God. Now, we make tracks. Right now, I'm more concerned about puttin' distance between us and the village than hidin' our trail."

"Do you think Wild Wind will follow us?"

"I've never seen him like he was today. I didn't dare let him guess our involvement. It would have made him worse had he known. I think him capable of anything to get you back."

"What did you tell Yellow Wolf to make him turn me over to you?"

Shante looked at her with steady regard. "I told him you were more trouble than you were worth and he would be wise to give you up."

As she remembered all the trouble she'd caused in the past because of her impulsiveness, his words hit their mark. Della closed her eyes and bowed her head. Then, she lifted her head and met Shane's gaze. "I know I'm a lot of trouble," she said in a small voice. "Uncle Clint has told me that over and over."

Shane nodded but didn't comment.

"What else did you tell Yellow Wolf?"

"I told him that your uncle had called in the army and would raid his village if I didn't bring you back."

"He believed you."

"He remembers how he lost my mother and didn't want military action against his people."

A beat of silence followed, while Della recalled the reason for her being taken. "The rustlers set the fire. Did you put it out?"

"It took us two days, but we saved the ranch house."

"I was beginning to think I'd have to marry Wild Wind before you could rescue me."

"We men didn't even miss the stolen horses—or you—until after the second day when we returned to the ranch. Coral was frantic because you were missing. She'd found the empty safe, so she knew the ranch had been robbed. We figured whoever had robbed the safe had taken you, as well, since your horse was gone, too. By then, it was too late for me to start trackin' you until the next mornin'." Shane twisted in his saddle and scanned the range behind them, then faced forward again to sweep the grasslands with a searching look before he turned his attention once again to Della. "It took me all this time to find you. The trail was old. Much of it was lost, but I found a couple of places where clear hoof marks had been left. I recognized your mare's hoof tracks along with Rusty's cow pony's tracks. When I trailed the rustlers to where Wild Wind's Dog Soldiers attacked them, it was easy enough to see what had happened. I recognized your mare's tracks with the other horses, so I knew you'd been taken by the raiding party."

"Rusty was the leader of the rustlers. I couldn't believe it."

"He sure had us all buffaloed."

Della recalled the money Rusty had stolen from the safe. "The loss of all that money will be a blow to Uncle Clint. He'll never be able to replace it."

A smile creased Shane's cheeks. "Indians have no use for gold or money, so the Dog Soldiers left it. They dumped out the contents of Rusty's saddlebags when they were searching for loot. When they saw it was only money, they left it right there with the dead rustlers."

Della smiled back. "Then, you have the money with you. Uncle Clint will be doubly pleased when we get back to the ranch."

Shane nodded. "Now, let's ride."

Della stretched out a beseeching hand. "Shane, I must tell you something first. You should know this if we're going to have a future."

A wary expression crossed his face, and he thumbed back his hat, shifting in the saddle. "Somethin' tells me I'm not going to like what you're about to say."

Della took a breath, wanting to make her confession and lay the whole truth before him. "I gave my word to Wild Wind that if we married before you rescued me, I would stay with him. I wouldn't go back with you."

"You would have done that?"

She nodded. "He was kind to me and charming in his way. I think he truly loves me, and he remembers too well what happened to his mother. I would have honored my wedding vows to him."

"That explains a lot." Shane glanced away, out over the billowing prairie. He stacked both hands on the saddle horn.

Eying him with apprehension, Della waited for a response. At last, he looked at her again, and his tortured expression frightened her.

"I reckon the question I should be askin' is, do you want me to take you back to the village? Do you want to marry Wild

Wind? I think your uncle would call off the army if he knew you stayed of your own choice."

Their gazes caught and held. The prairie wind stirred the grasses and played about Della's braids. The two of them, alone on the vast sea of the plains, seemed to be the only creatures in all the universe.

Della shook her head. "I want to marry you. I could have made a good life with Wild Wind if you hadn't come for me, but that's behind me now. You're the man who holds my heart."

The lines of Shane's face relaxed. His eyes warmed. "For a minute there, I thought my brother had stolen you away from me."

Della smiled. Relief swept over her.

Shane cued his mount into motion. "We'd better put miles between us and the village. I don't want to fight my brother over you."

They rode hard, with Shane checking their trail. Eating lunch in the saddle, they shared bits of jerky and the canteen. About midafternoon, they came to a meandering stream with shallow banks.

Shane called a halt. "Let's rest a bit here. I'm going to try to lose our trail in the water." He swung down from the saddle and came around to help Della dismount.

She leaned down and placed her hands on his shoulders. He lifted her from her horse and closed both arms around her. She snuggled against his chest and wrapped her arms about him. His heart thudded with a steady rhythm beneath her ear. "Hold me tight, Shane. Just hold me."

They stood in a close embrace for several moments, not speaking. Shane rested his cheek against the top of her head, enclosing her in a desperate clasp, one hand pressing her head into the hollow of his shoulder. At last, she leaned against the band of his arms to look into his face.

"I don't know who I am anymore. I've lost myself. Help me, Shane. How did you find yourself when you went back to the fort?"

His sympathetic gaze roved over her face. "You make peace with yourself, one day at a time. You learn to fit in, even if inside yourself, you feel like you don't belong."

His words brought a measure of comfort. "It must have been very hard for your mother. And for your father, to take her back and for both of them to work at rebuilding their marriage."

"It was a difficult time for the family."

"Your mother was gone so much longer than me. I don't know how she made the adjustment."

Shane squeezed her. "The Lord gave her grace for that as He did during her time with Yellow Wolf. He will guide you, too."

"At least, now, I understand you so much better."

Before they remounted, Shane filled their canteens and let the horses drink their fill. Once again astride, Della followed Shane's gelding into the water. Instead of crossing the brook, he led them upstream for several miles. Finally, at a place where a rocky ledge would hide their mounts' hoofprints, he turned his grulla toward the opposite bank. Della's mare scrambled up behind him. The ledge continued for several hundred yards before a sandy section covered the stone. Once they crossed the sand, Shane dismounted and wiped out their tracks.

"Do you think Wild Wind will find us?" Della asked when he finished his task.

"This will slow him down some, but I don't have time to hide our trail as I'd like."

They rode until dusk cloaked the earth. When they reached an escarpment where the steep, rocky wall would protect their backs and a hillock shielded them in the front, Shane called a halt. They made camp and ate a cold meal, with the horses picketed nearby.

"No fire tonight. We'll leave before dawn."

Della snuggled into her bedroll. After having slept in buffalo robes on the ground, the bedroll no longer felt strange or uncomfortable.

Shane sat beside her, his back to the rocky escarpment, his rifle cradled across his lap.

The silence of the night enshrouded them. Della pitched into oblivion.

CHAPTER 38

THEY LEFT THE PROTECTION OF the escarpment when a rim of gray smudged the horizon. Shane kept a steady pace, and they rode with caution.

Just before noon, as they rounded the shoulder of a slope, the thunder of hooves sounded behind them, and shots rang out. Shane's gelding leaped into a gallop, with Della's mare keeping pace. They plunged down into a hollow. Shane headed toward a hillock surrounded by a jumble of boulders. Their horses arrowed into the cleft between two boulders and came to a sliding halt in a rocky cul-de-sac.

Shane flung himself from the saddle before his grulla came to a stop, pulled his rifle from the scabbard, and leaped toward a marble slab atop one of the large rocks. Della scrambled from her mount and followed him. She leaned against the boulder, her arm brushing his.

"Is it Wild Wind?"

"I don't know. We could have run across a party of Arapaho or Lakota, but I thought I saw his painted war pony back there. If it's him, he's brought some of his Dog Soldiers with him."

Della knew what that meant, having seen what the Dog Soldiers had done to the rustlers. Fear gripped her at the thought of Shane's mutilated body lying lifeless on the ground. She laid a trembling hand on his shoulder. "I'm sorry I brought this trouble on you. Perhaps, I should just let him take me back."

Shane sliced a furious glance at her. "You'll do nothing of the sort."

"Will he actually shoot at you, his brother?"

Shane shrugged. "I wouldn't have thought so, but I've never seen him like he was when Yellow Wolf told him he had to give you up." He peered around the edge of the slab, and a rifle barked. A bullet splatted against the rock inches from his face. "That answers that question."

He pulled his spare six-shooter from its holster and handed it to Della, butt first. "Here. Use this. Make your shots count. They've got us pinned down, so we can't waste ammunition."

The Colt felt heavy in her hand, but she knew how to use the weapon. Shane scooted around her and ducked to the boulder on the opposite side of the opening. A rifle roared, and another bullet cracked against the rock. Shane fitted the Winchester's stock to his shoulder, sighted, and squeezed. The weapon boomed. The sound echoed off the rocky walls of the cul-de-sac.

Answering gunfire ripped apart the morning. Della leaned around the edge of the slab, the muzzle of Shane's six-shooter resting against the marble. She fired off a shot, then another, and spun back against the rock. Leaning against the stone buttress, she breathed heavily. After a moment, she peered around the rock slab again and snapped off another shot. Pressing her back against the boulder once more, she closed her eyes, wondering how she could fire upon the man whom even yesterday morning, she'd thought to marry, a man she'd learned to know and, in his own culture, admire. How much more conflicted must Shane feel, to shoot at his brother?

Silence descended. The acrid scent of gunpowder stung Della's nose. Trickles of perspiration ran down the side of her face, and she swiped the drops away with the back of her hand. The cul-de-sac threw back the sun's heat with the intensity of an oven.

"Lona! You would shoot at me, your intended husband?"

Shane and Della exchanged a look. Now, they knew they fought Wild Wind and his Dog Soldiers, not Arapaho or Lakota warriors. When Della raised a questioning eyebrow, Shane shook his head, so she didn't reply.

The long moments of silence dragged on. Shane ducked back to her side. "I'm going out there. They have us pinned down, and they know it. And I won't kill my brother."

"Shane—"

He silenced her by bringing his mouth down on hers. When he lifted his head, he made a slow, loving perusal of her features. He stroked her hair, sifting one of her braids through his fingers. "Your hair is beautiful. You are beautiful."

His attention returned to her face. "If I live through this, we'll marry as soon as we can. One thing I've learned is that I can't live without you, whatever happens in the future." With both large hands framing her face, he kissed her again.

Della felt the promise, love, and hope in his desperate kiss. He broke away. "I love you, Shane. With all my heart, I love you."

He seared her with another gaze. "You are my life." Then, stepping to the entrance between the boulders, he gripped his rifle with both hands, one on the stock and one on the barrel, and raised the weapon high over his head. He stalked two paces out onto the prairie.

Della's heart hammered against her ribs, and her palms grew moist. She held her breath, expecting at any moment to see him cut down in a fusillade of gunfire.

"Wild Wind! I will not kill my brother! Let us talk." Shane's voice rang out, clear and strong.

Above them, the blue dome of the sky arced in a vivid wash of color. Silence engulfed the plain. Only the sound of Shane's gelding blowing through his nostrils broke the quiet.

Della's pulse raced while the stillness grew, pressing on the earth. At last, a man wearing buckskin stepped around a grassy knoll some distance away and walked with an arrogant stride toward them, his head erect.

Wild Wind. Della would have known him anywhere. She tried to slow her breathing while she waited for him to speak.

He came to a standstill a dozen feet from Shane and addressed him in the Cheyenne language. Shane lowered his rifle and replied. A rapid exchange followed. When the conversation concluded, Wild Wind raised one hand and motioned. Half a dozen Dog Soldiers rose from behind rocks and hillocks and converged on Wild Wind.

Shane pivoted and strode toward Della. She met him at the cleft between the two boulders at the entrance of the cul-de-sac. He brushed past her without a word. She followed him to his gelding's flank, where he rummaged in one of his saddlebags.

"What are you doing? What are you and Wild Wind up to?" she demanded, fists propped on her hips.

"Wild Wind has challenged me to a fight."

She caught her breath. She raised one hand and clenched his bicep. "What kind of fight?"

"Knife."

"A knife fight! Why?"

"The winner gets you."

Fear and fury boiled in a wild tumult. "The winner gets me! I'm not a prize that you men can fight over. Don't I have a say in this? I won't let you fight your own brother for me!"

Shane pulled his moccasins from his saddlebag and faced Della. She glared at him. He stared back at her, resolute and silent.

"I'll talk to Wild Wind, then. If you won't stop it, I'll see that he does." She spun and took one stride toward the exit before Shane grabbed her arm and whirled her back. She collided with his chest. He held her in an unyielding grip and dipped his head to bring his eyes level with hers.

"Stay out of it. Don't shame him before his men."

Della stared back with a determination that matched his and tried to jerk her arm free. Shane didn't loosen his hold.

"You can't stop this, Della. This is bigger than you."

"What do you mean? Can't you tell him that you won't fight him?"

"In the Cheyenne culture, I'd never be able to hold up my head in the tribe again should I decline his challenge. I'd be branded a coward. I'd have to live with that humiliation for the rest of my life. Not only would I dishonor myself; I'd shame Yellow Wolf, my father. I won't do that, Della, not even for you."

Della had no words to tell Shane what she felt. She couldn't even describe her emotions. With sudden gentleness, he loosened his hold on her arm and brushed past her. Sitting on a rock near the back of the cul-de-sac, he removed his boots and shoved his feet into his moccasins.

While Della watched him prepare for the duel, tremors shook her.

Shane stood and moved to her side, so close she felt his body heat. "If it makes you feel better, we've agreed not to fight to the death. Only to disarm or incapacitate." His expression closed, shutting her out as he turned his focus inward, readying himself for combat. Then, he strode out of the cul-de-sac, leaving Della to follow or not, as she chose.

Not wanting to see two men whom she cared about engage in combat yet unable to resist watching, Della drifted from the protection of the cul-de-sac. She thought her knees would buckle. Somehow, she stayed erect.

Shane and Wild Wind faced each other across a grassy expanse of ten feet. Shane unbuckled his gun belt and dropped his weapons. His hat followed. He tugged his deerskin shirt from his pants and pulled it over his head, then tossed the garment to the earth beside his six-shooters.

Wild Wind had already prepared himself for the coming conflict and stood waiting for the signal to begin. Though the men claimed she was the reason for their fight, neither one acknowledged her presence. Their attention centered on each other.

Della scanned the scene before her. With her Boston drawing-room background, she'd never seen anything so raw and primitive as the spectacle before her. A scream clawed up the back of her throat and threatened to erupt. She clamped her hands over her mouth to stifle the sound.

The Dog Soldiers fanned out behind Wild Wind, their faces flat and stoic. Shane stood alone with the cul-de-sac at his back.

Della eyed the combatants. The brothers were evenly matched. Both were men in their prime, equal in height and weight. They'd stripped down to their buckskin trousers and moccasins. Now, supple muscle rippled beneath smooth, gleaming skin.

One of the Dog Soldiers stepped forward and threw two knives down between the rivals. The lethal blades sank deep into

the soil. The brave retreated to give the fighters room to maneuver.
Wild Wind and Shane crouched, gazes fixed on each other's faces,
oblivious to everything around them.

Tension weighted the air and heightened Della's senses.
Her own breathing sounded harsh in the stillness. The sere grasses
rustled in the breeze, and above them, a hawk screamed. The scent
of sun-warmed earth teased her nostrils.

When the Dog Soldier gave the signal to begin, both men
swooped toward the weapons and jerked the knives from the
ground. Crouching, they circled, looking for an opening to attack.
Wild Wind leaped forward, his knife hand flashing out. Shane spun
away. Wild Wind's blade left a thin red line across his chest.

Della gasped and closed her eyes. When she opened them
again, the men were circling, intent on the next move. Time hung
suspended, each second seeming an eon.

Wild Wind lunged again. Shane twisted aside, his own
blade finding its target when his brother rushed past. His knife
slashed a shallow furrow along Wild Wind's shoulder.

Della stumbled back and bumped against a boulder, and her
knees gave way. She thumped down hard on the rock, horrid
fascination keeping her attention on the combat unfolding before
her eyes. She couldn't look. She couldn't not look.

The combatants faced each other again, crouching and
circling. Wild Wind rushed his brother, his knife hand stabbing
toward flesh. This time, Shane reached out and deflected the hand
holding the weapon. He moved in close, his fingers squeezing his
brother's wrist. The two men strained, grappling, their grimacing
faces inches apart, their stares locked. Sweaty muscles bulged. The
tendons on each side of their necks stood out. Their panting grated
in the air.

With slow, inexorable pressure, Shane forced his brother's
knife hand down. With a sudden motion, he twined the fingers of
his free hand in Wild Wind's long hair and jerked. Pulled off
balance, Wild Wind grabbed at his brother's arm, but his feet
slipped from beneath him, and he fell onto his back. Shane
followed him down and pinned his opponent's knife hand to the
earth with a knee. Shane pressed his forearm across Wild Wind's

throat and braced his arm against his windpipe. Motionless, the brothers stared at each other. Wild Wind bucked once in an attempt to throw Shane off, but the effort proved futile. Shane didn't budge.

Thundering hooves pounding toward them caught Della's attention. Yellow Wolf, accompanied by several of his warriors, approached at a gallop. They drove before them the horses stolen by the rustlers and taken to their village by Wild Wind's Dog Soldiers. The band came to a milling halt near the Dog Soldiers grouped about the brothers.

Della pushed off the boulder and stood, her attention now on Yellow Wolf. The chief wore his feathered headdress, the symbol of his position and authority. Beneath the headdress, his craggy face showed no emotion. From atop his mount, he stared down at his sons.

Neither Shane nor Wild Wind acknowledge the newcomers. They glared at each other, their expressions fierce. Wild Wind's lips pulled back in a snarl. Shane muttered something. For long moments, Wild Wind refused to give way. Shane pressed harder against his brother's throat. At last, Wild Wind nodded. Hunter got to his feet in a swift, fluid motion and kicked the knife from his brother's hand. Wild Wind rolled to his side and stood. Seconds ticked past while the two men faced each other, panting, before the younger spun and stalked toward his warhorse.

Wild Wind's Dog Soldiers followed. They leaped onto their mounts and galloped back in the direction they'd come. Within moments, the prairie's rolling vastness swallowed them.

Della looked at the spot where Wild Wind had vanished. Though grateful Shane had won the combat, Wild Wind took a bit of her heart with him, and she'd never forget him. She sighed, remembering to breathe.

Shane rolled his shoulders and passed a hand over his chest, where his brother's blade had sliced. His palm came away bloody. After swiping the blood on the grass, he straightened and approached Yellow Wolf. He came to a halt and greeted his father.

The chief spoke, and Shane nodded. He turned and beckoned for Della to come near. Hurried steps took her to his side. She glanced at him in questioning silence.

"Yellow Wolf is returning your uncle's horses to him in an act of good faith that your uncle won't molest Yellow Wolf's village. He's offering his protection by escorting us to the ranch."

Della looked up at the old chief, fierce and proud even in his acknowledgment of the army's strength. What could she say to this man, who had seen his way of life change and would see more changes in the future? She took a breath. "Thank you, Yellow Wolf, for your kindness. I promise that my uncle, General Clint Logan, will honor your kindness and will not wage war on your village. I also promise that he will allow your men to hunt on his land, land that we all share, if you do not take his horses or fight his men."

Yellow Wolf stared down at her, his expression inscrutable, his eyes flat. Had she said something to offend him? At last, he shifted his gaze to Shane and replied in the Cheyenne tongue.

Shane turned to her. "My father says you have spoken well. You have much wisdom. He can see why both of his sons love you." The corners of his eyes crinkled in a smile.

Della gaped at him. "He knows about us?"

"He sees much, and he saw my heart back at the village. I may have told him of your uncle's warning, but he saw into my heart. That is why he let you go."

Della glanced up at the chief and smiled. She thought he smiled back.

CHAPTER 39

SHANE AND DELLA RODE THROUGH the gate of the ranch late in the afternoon of the next day. Yellow Wolf's warriors had returned the stolen Morgans to the herd and headed back to their village, while Shane and Della continued on to the ranch compound.

They halted their horses before the veranda stairs. Shane stepped down from the saddle and, as had become his habit, came around to help her dismount. He held her tightly for a moment before he let her go, and she gave him a weary smile of thanks.

The front door banged open, and Aunt Coral rushed out with Uncle Clint at her shoulder. Aunt Coral skimmed down the steps before Della could move and enveloped her in an enthusiastic hug. Closing her eyes, Della returned her aunt's embrace. A moment later, Uncle Clint had jogged down the steps and enfolded both wife and niece in his arms.

"You gave us such a fright!" Aunt Coral said when she'd pushed back a little to see her niece's face.

"I'm so sorry. I never intended for any of this to happen. I can promise you I've had enough adventure to last my whole life."

Uncle Clint squeezed her shoulders. "I knew Shane would find you, if anyone could. Are you. . . are you all right?"

Understanding the unspoken inquiry behind his question, Della nodded. "I was treated with great respect because the chief's son wanted to marry me."

That brought a moment of silence before Aunt Coral rested both hands on Della's shoulders and held her at arm's length. "Let's get a look at you." Aunt Coral's hazel gaze appraised her. "My, I almost wouldn't have recognized you. You're as brown as can be, and wearing that outfit, you certainly don't look like a Boston young lady."

"I can assure you, I'm no longer a Boston young lady."

"A detail of cavalrymen is camped outside the ranch walls," Uncle Clint said. "If Shane hadn't showed up with you in a couple more days, we were going looking for you."

Della glanced at Shane, who stood a few steps from the family reunion. "I knew Shane would find me."

Uncle Clint turned to him and clapped him on the shoulder. "Thank you for rescuing Della. I'm sure no other man could have done so. You have my eternal gratitude."

Shane shrugged away his thanks. "I simply had an advantage that other men didn't have."

Aunt Coral linked arms with Della and turned toward the veranda steps. "Let's get the poor girl inside and cleaned up. Della, you look exhausted."

"I am a bit weary."

They mounted the stairs. The door opened again, and two uniformed cavalrymen stepped from the house. The older one, whom Della guessed must be the commanding officer at Fort Bridger, was a middle-aged man with a worn face, as though he'd seen too much of life. The other proved to be Captain Asher.

Della halted, not sure of what to say. She hadn't thought of the captain since she'd been captured. With a touch of cynicism, she reflected that if her rescue had depended upon Quentin Asher, she'd be married to Wild Wind by now.

The captain stood at military attention, hands clasped behind his back. His gaze swept over her, from her leather-wrapped braids, down the length of her fringed and beaded deerskin dress, to the toes of her moccasins. His lip curled just before he dipped his head in a formal greeting. "I'm very pleased to see you've been returned home safely, Miss Hughes."

Della felt the disapproval radiating from him in waves. She wondered at his formal demeanor, since when they'd last parted, he'd pressed her for an answer to his suit. "Thank you, Captain Asher," she said with equal politeness. "I'm quite well."

COLLEEN HALL

"Excuse us, gentlemen. My niece is weary and needs to rest." Aunt Coral hustled Della inside, pausing only long enough to make a brief introduction to the major.

Upstairs in her bedchamber, Della stopped and looked about. The room, with its elegant furnishings, patterned wallpaper, and silk rug, pressed in on her.

Aunt Coral halted behind her. "I've sent for Sadie to bring up some hot water, and Clint will tote up the copper tub. I suspect you have a hankering for a bath."

Turning to face Aunt Coral, Della spread out her hands. "I've been bathing in the river. Do you know that Cheyenne women make their own soap from the soap plant? They believe in being clean."

Aunt Coral raised her eyebrows at Della's random comment. "No, I didn't know that," she said in a faint voice.

"And I learned to cook antelope in a hole in the ground. Wild Wind brought me an antelope as a courting gift. He provided well for me. He gave me five horses, so I would have wealth and standing in the tribe." Tears gathered, with a touch of hysteria, as well. "He gave me a special name. Lona. I was Lona. No one called me Della."

Della moved to her bed and dropped onto the lace coverlet. Aunt Coral sat beside her and took Della's hands between her own. She made soothing noises meant to comfort.

Della pulled one hand from between Aunt Coral's and flicked her fingers toward the room. "This is too much. All this. . . I don't know if. . ." The tears overflowed and rained down her cheeks. "I didn't know if Shane would rescue me in time, but Wild Wind promised to bring me to visit you after we were married."

Aunt Coral gathered her niece in her arms and rocked her. "Shh. . . It's all right. Everything is all right."

A knock at the door interrupted them. Uncle Clint, carrying the copper tub, peered into the room. Aunt Coral shook her head at him. He glanced at his weeping niece and deposited the tub inside before vanishing down the stairs.

"I have a secret to share with you," Aunt Coral said. "A good secret."

Della's head came up. She swiped the tears from her cheeks. "What is it?"

Aunt Coral's face glowed with a tender smile. "I'm going to have another baby."

Happiness chased away Della's gloom. "A baby! Uncle Clint will be so proud. When?"

"March, I think. An almost-spring baby."

Later, after Della took her bath, changed into her night rail, and sent Aunt Coral downstairs, she stood beside her bed, uncertain of what to do. Fatigue dragged her down, and sleep beckoned, but she didn't want to climb into the bed. The feather mattress and downy pillows would smother her, she felt sure. She pulled back the coverlet and dragged the blankets to the floor. After arranging them as a bedroll, she lay down and fell asleep.

* * * * *

The last glimmer of daylight hovered in the sky. Della leaned against the white veranda railing and looked out on the ranch yard. Quentin Asher stopped beside her, keeping a careful distance.

She waited for him to speak, eager to get the conversation behind them. They'd finished supper and left Uncle Clint, Aunt Coral, and the major inside. Captain Asher had requested a private conversation with her. Della had accepted, wishing to dispense with him and send him on his way. Never could she return to the life he offered, a life bound by rules governing what one said, what one wore, and how one interacted with others of a different social class. A life in the society he craved would suffocate her.

Captain Asher cleared his throat. "Miss Hughes."

Della turned her head to look at him. He'd been displeased with the informal attire she wore to dinner, but she couldn't bring herself to care. After the comfort of her deerskin dress, she couldn't suffer the constriction of a corset and yards of fabric swathing her person. She'd donned a split riding skirt and simple blouse and come downstairs to join the family at the table. Displeasure had flared in the captain's eyes. Now, looking at him through the dusk, she guessed what he would say.

"Miss Hughes," he repeated. "I know I offered for your hand in marriage, but that was before your unfortunate experience with the savages."

Anger bubbled to the surface, though she attempted to remain calm. "Unfortunate? Is that what you'd call me being taken captive by the Dog Soldiers? And don't refer to them as savages."

He appeared flustered. "Perhaps *unfortunate* was a poor choice of words." Pausing, he seemed to struggle with his thoughts.

Della waited, staring once again out over the yard, her fingers curling about the railing.

"You understand that in my future political and diplomatic career, my wife must be a woman of impeccable reputation. There can be no stain attached to her name." He paused, as if waiting for her to speak.

Della felt his stare. She didn't glance at him. Maintaining her silence, she let him take responsibility for backing out of his marriage proposal. She wouldn't make this easy for him.

"After your time with the. . . ah, tribesmen, society will consider you. . . well, not as pure as you should be, shall we say?"

Della whirled to face him. "I know very well what society will think of me, but I don't care. I know the truth. Do you know that I was chaperoned as carefully in the Cheyenne village as I would have been in a Boston drawing room?"

Asher cleared his throat again. "Well, as to that, no one will know or care. Perception is everything in politics. I'm asking you to release me from our courtship."

Della lifted her chin and stared him in the eye until his gaze slid away. She took a deep breath and forced herself to calmness. She shouldn't allow Quentin Asher's so very apparent hypocrisy to overset her. Even though she'd never wanted to marry him, it would have been gratifying had he shown her a little support after her ordeal instead of putting his political career ahead of his professed love for her. "I release you from your offer of marriage. I hope you find a suitable wife who will meet your expectations and be an asset to your political aspirations."

The following evening, Shane and Della sat on the porch swing. His arm draped about her shoulder, and her head nestled beneath his chin. They sat for some moments without speaking, while Shane toed the swing into lazy motion.

"I have a surprise for you," he murmured.

Della sat up and studied his face. "What kind of surprise?"

He grinned. "If I told you, it wouldn't be a surprise." He slid his arm from her shoulder. "Wait here while I get it." He pushed to his feet, clattered down the veranda steps, and jogged across the yard to the barn.

Della watched him. When he disappeared through the open double doors, her mind followed him to his room at the far end. What surprise could he have for her?

Moments later, he reappeared. His long strides carried him back to the house and up the steps. Della tilted her head to look up at him when he halted before her. With a flourish, he whipped a courting flute from behind his back, where he'd stuck it in his belt.

"I told you I'd court you with flute music if I had one."

"Where did you get that?"

"When you weren't lookin', Yellow Wolf gave it to me before he left. He brought it with him from the village."

"He knew you'd want to court me," Della said in wonderment. "How kind of him."

Shane put the instrument to his lips and began to play. The breathy notes poured forth, telling Della of his love.

She closed her eyes while the music caressed her heart. Trying not to remember the times when Wild Wind had played a cedarwood flute to court her, she focused on the message Shane sent her. The music stopped, and she opened her eyes.

Shane laid the flute on the swing beside her and knelt before her. He gathered her hands between his. "I know I'm not the man you could have married—"

Della laid two fingers across his lips. "Don't say that, ever again. You're exactly the man I want, the finest man I know, with the exception of Uncle Clint."

He kissed the fingers that still covered his lips before he pulled her hand away and curled his fist about her smaller one. His warm gaze roamed her face. "I love you, Della. My heart bursts with love for you. I want to care for you for the rest of our days and share a life together. Will you marry me?"

She looked into his eyes, eyes the color of the Colorado sky and gleaming with love for her. "Yes! Yes, of course, I'll marry you. I love you, only you."

His arms enfolded her and pulled her against his heart. He rose, sat on the swing, and settled her in his lap. Leaning against his chest, her head tucked beneath his chin, her arms stole around his neck.

She smiled. "You sure were a stubborn one. I thought I'd never get you to see we could have a good marriage."

A heartbeat of silence passed. "You see now why I hesitated."

"All your concerns about what society would think didn't matter once Wild Wind took me."

He shrugged. "Captain Asher proved my point."

"But Major Smith was very kind. He didn't seem to mind what had happened to me."

"I've done some thinking on this. With more people pouring into the West, attitudes such as what my mother experienced will change. The West is changing."

"And I've said all along, I don't care."

"I have some more news for you."

Della lifted her head and looked into his face, hovering just above her own. "What news?"

"Your uncle has offered to make me a partner in the ranch. He wants to be free to travel to Denver, get involved in politics, and have a hand in the development of the Colorado Territory. Colorado will become a state soon, and he sees opportunity there."

Della sat up. "Shane, that's wonderful!"

"I'd stay here to run the ranch and oversee the horse trainin'. And, of course, Clint won't be in Denver all of the time, so when he's here, we'll work together."

She recalled Shane's love of freedom, of riding the range and sleeping beneath the stars. "Will you mind very much, staying here and living in a house?"

Another beat of silence followed. "It will be an adjustment, but for you, I can do it. For you and our children."

Della laid one hand against the side of his face. "When I was in the Cheyenne village, I remembered the verse your mother had claimed. That verse was true for me then, that the Lord would never leave me. Now, I can see it's been true all along. The Lord has been with me, guiding my steps right to you, to bring us together."

Shane nodded. "He brought us together, when I fought to keep from hurtin' you." He paused. "So, in order to bring us together, when do you want to get married?"

"How does one get married in the West? There aren't many churches out here."

"We can bring in a preacher from Denver and be married here, at the ranch house. Or we could go to the fort, and the army chaplain can marry us there."

Della thought of Quentin Asher at the fort. "A wedding here sounds wonderful. Aunt Coral can help me plan."

"You ladies can plan our wedding as long as you hurry it up. Right now, I want a kiss. A kiss to seal our engagement."

"Yes, a kiss."

"One of many more, I hope." Shane's mouth came down on hers, and Della forgot about wedding plans in the pleasure of their love.

Want more by Colleen Hall?
Keep reading for a look at
HER TRAITOR'S HEART

CHAPTER ONE

AS HER BUCKBOARD TRUNDLED DOWN the street, Coral Leigh stared about with embittered eyes. Gaunt chimneys rose amid charred foundations. Tumbled bricks and scorched beams squatted in haphazard heaps on lots where shops, public buildings, or gracious homes had once stood.

The Yankees did this.

The sight of the ruined town brought Coral back to that terrifying night in February when, from the veranda of their plantation home east of Columbia, she and her mother had watched the lurid glow of flames stain the sky red while the city burned. They'd stood huddled together all night, fearing at any time to see Yankee troops riding up the long drive of Elmwood, intending to torch the mansion about their heads. When at last the sun had banished the darkness from the earth the next morning, no troops had rampaged as far east as Elmwood.

"Those Yankees sure did the work o' the devil when they came through with their torches," Silvie said, her brown face puckered.

Coral nodded in stricken agreement.

A profusion of early June roses in the empty lots where homes had once stood flamed in an explosion of crimson against the blackened ruins. Main Street, down which their mule trudged, languished beneath the vindictive hand of Sherman's troops, laid waste by the soldiers on their march through South Carolina. Not one shop remained.

"Pull the wagon in over there. That's as good a place to wait as any." Coral issued her instructions to the muscular black man who drove the mule as she spied an empty spot along the footway.

When the wagon had rumbled to a stop at the side of the street, Coral clambered down by the front wheel. She reached over the side of the buckboard and lifted a muslin-wrapped parcel from the floor.

Before the war, she wouldn't have ridden into the city in a farm wagon. Instead, she would have arrived in her family's elegant equipage driven by a liveried coachman and drawn by a pair of matched thoroughbreds. Nor would her dress be several seasons old, meticulously mended by Silvie's skillful fingers. Her bonnet would have been a stylish confection in the latest Paris fashion rather than a hat refurbished from bits of other bonnets too tattered to wear.

Tucking her parcel beneath her arm, Coral turned to the titan tying the mule's reins to the wooden hitching rail. "Scipio, please stay here with the wagon. Silvie and I will try to find a shop where I can sell my vase. Then I'll fetch the doctor."

Walking along the footway a moment later with Silvie at her shoulder, Coral observed the few shops already rising from the ashes of Columbia. Business appeared to be picking up.

Perhaps she could find a buyer for her vase, get the medicine her mother needed, and leave the city in time to reach Elmwood before dark, after all.

Coral roused from her inspection of the construction along the street, transferring her attention to the crowds jostling the footways. Women wearing dresses of threadbare homespun and haggard Confederate veterans straggling home afoot mingled with blue-jacketed Federal soldiers. Guards stood watch on every street. Sweeping aside her skirts, Coral averted her face as she passed two troopers patrolling Main Street.

"These soldiers won't cause you any trouble, not while I'm here to take care of you," Silvie muttered.

Despite her distress over the desperate position to which the South had sunk, Coral managed a slight smile. "I doubt any Yankee would dare accost me with you hovering at my shoulder like an avenging angel."

"No Billie Yank is going to lay a finger on my baby Coral," Silvie vowed with staunch ferocity, clenching the handle of the straw basket she carried as though contemplating cracking the hamper over the head of any soldier who might dare speak to her charge.

"I haven't been your 'baby Coral' for over twenty years. I'm a grown woman now, a fact you keep forgetting. Don't take your role of protector too seriously, Silvie. You'd probably get arrested if you so much as looked cross-eyed at a Yankee soldier."

As they hurried along the footway, Coral hoped to find the shop of a merchant whom her family used to patronize. She could make a more profitable sale from someone who knew her. Hoping the mercantile she sought might be open for business, Coral forged ahead, ignoring any Federal troopers she encountered.

Near the end of Main Street, a frame structure had been erected on the lot where once had stood an imposing brick edifice. A white sign with black letters hung above the door, proclaiming the establishment Garner's Emporium.

"We'll try here first." Approaching the shop, Coral shook her head in dismay as she observed the inferior clapboard structure that replaced the original brick building. Both windows flanking the door lacked glass; rough shutters standing open against the wall could be closed at night to provide security. The sign above the door, its crude letters splashed in black paint, must have been painted by someone with more resolution than talent. Coral resented the fact that the shop's owner, Mr. Garner, had suffered such a complete loss of property at the hands of the Yankees when he'd been guilty of nothing more than engaging in commerce. During the long conflict, Mr. Garner had never raised a weapon against any Federal trooper, yet retribution had been meted out to him without such consideration.

Forcing her lips into a smile to conceal the ache in her heart, Coral reached for the doorknob. As she made her way through the shop, its interior dim after the dazzling sunshine outside, Mr. Garner called out a welcome from behind the counter.

"Well, if it isn't Miss Coral Leigh. I haven't seen you in town for months. How did Elmwood fare when Sherman marched through?"

Coral halted before the rough planked counter. "We fared better at Elmwood than you did here, it seems. The troops never reached our plantation. What those Yankees did to the city is criminal! And now they're everywhere like a scourge."

A frown puckered Coral's brow. Her nostrils flared with distaste as she contemplated the presence of the scorned Federal blue bellies. Seeing triumphant Northern troops on sacred Southern soil roused in her an unaccustomed waspish temper.

Mr. Garner removed his spectacles, polishing them on his sleeve as he regarded her through faded blue eyes. "Don't keep fighting them, Miss Leigh. They've defeated us. They're here as victors, so we might as well make whatever adjustments are necessary to live peaceably with them."

"Mr. Garner! Surely you don't mean you've bowed your knee to the Yankee invaders."

The elderly gentleman returned his glasses to his face, hooked them over his ears, then adjusted them on his nose before replying. "I'm an old man, Miss Leigh. I'm tired of conflict, and I have to earn a living. The war's over. We'd all best get about putting our lives back together."

Coral stared at him, not crediting what her ears had just heard. She should live peaceably with the victors?

"I'd like to put my life back together, but I'd prefer to do it without the presence of the Yankees." She clamped her lips shut to refrain from continuing her diatribe and laid her parcel on the counter, peeling back its wrapping with careful hands. As the bleached muslin fell away to reveal an antique Sevres vase, she lifted the ornament out of the protective fabric with reverent hands. The *bleu-de-roi* glaze of the vase, lavishly trimmed in gold, glowed in the shop's dim light. Her fingers caressed the graceful lines of the vessel. "I... I know you can't pay me what this vase is worth, but..." Her voice shook, and she stumbled to a halt, snatching a breath to regain her composure. Parting with the vase grieved her, for the antique had been in her family for over three generations. Coral straightened and squared her shoulders. "How much will you give me for the vase?"

"Why are you parting with this treasure, Miss Leigh?" Mr. Garner touched the vase's curved body with an appreciative finger.

"A treasure sitting on a mantel is worthless to me. My mother is ill and needs medicine."

Mention of her mother brought Coral's anxiety back in a sharp rush. Mrs. Leigh had felt too poorly to accompany her today, so she'd stayed behind at Elmwood.

Mr. Garner lifted the vase from the counter and examined the fragile china piece from every angle, tilting the ornament first this way, then that. The early June sunshine filtering through the open shutters gleamed off the lustrous blue glaze and the gold trim. Setting it gingerly back on the wooden planking of the counter, he shook his head. Sweeping his hand toward the merchandise lining the shelves along three walls, he said, "This vase is worth much more than I can pay you. The rest of my stock is definitely of an inferior quality to your fine antique. Right now, I can't afford to stock expensive items any more than the people of Columbia can afford to buy them. People need necessities, not luxuries like this vase."

"I don't expect to get full value. I just want enough money to buy medicine for my mother. Please! I'll be satisfied with whatever you can give me."

Coral touched the tip of her tongue to her dry lips. She needed the money with a desperate urgency. Her best chance of acquiring the cash she needed lay with Mr. Garner.

The shopkeeper scratched his head, his pink pate gleaming through his thinning white hair as he peered with compassion at the girl on the other side of the counter. "I've never cheated a customer yet, especially a Leigh. If I buy your vase, I'll pay you as much as I can without taking a loss. But before we do business, I must ask if you've taken the loyalty oath. Have you?"

"Loyalty oath?" Color drained from Coral's face. Did the Yankees think forcing Southerners to take a loyalty oath would humble them? Surely the North had already stripped the South of everything except pride and dignity. Did the Yankees intend to wrest those qualities away too?

"Before any of us can transact business, we have to take an oath of allegiance to the United States and to the president."

"Never!" Coral backed away. "I could never swear loyalty to the North!"

Mr. Garner let out a long breath. "If you want to sell this vase," he said with gentle sympathy, "and if you want to buy medicine for your mother, you'll have to take the oath. It's as simple as that. I can't buy your vase until then, nor can any other shopkeeper in Columbia. No doctor can sell medicine to you unless you can prove you've sworn loyalty to the Federal government and to the president."

Feeling treacherous tears of frustration prick the back of her eyes, Coral turned to Silvie. The older woman's thin brown face revealed wisdom and understanding. As Coral struggled with her pride, Silvie nodded in approval. If not for the medicine her mother desperately needed, Coral vowed she'd walk out of Garner's Emporium, returning to Elmwood empty-handed. Instead, necessity forced her to take the despised loyalty oath.

Drawing a deep breath, standing with imperious dignity at her full diminutive height with her shoulders barely clearing the four-foot counter, Coral turned back to Mr. Garner. Despite the outrage tearing at her, she managed to keep her voice steady. "Where would I go to take this oath?"

"The military headquarters is located on the south side of Columbia College campus. An army officer will administer the oath and give you a certificate of allegiance."

"Will you keep my vase here until I return?"

"Your treasure will be safe with me."

Mr. Garner set the antique on a shelf behind the counter as the two women left the shop.

During the walk across town, Coral's gloved hands clenched at the sight of every blue uniform she encountered. Though she simmered at the intrusion of the enemy, she maintained an outward calmness. She kept her attention on the scenery, not allowing her thoughts to dwell on the prospect of taking the despised oath. The oath, taken under duress, certainly couldn't change the loyalty of her heart.

Silvie's low voice beside her pulled Coral's attention from the rubble alongside the footway. "When we get to the campus, you keep your tongue on a leash, Miz Coral. If you say what you want to say instead of what you ought to say, you're going to get yourself in a peck o' trouble."

Coral let out a frustrated huff. "You're right. It will be difficult, but I'll try to be civil. You know I can't abide their arrogance."

"I expect you cain't paint all Yankees with that brush."

"Silvie! Surely you aren't beginning to sympathize with the Northern troops! Look at what they did to Columbia! How could they be anything other than inhuman beasts?"

Silvie shrugged. "They're just men, some good, some bad. You need to learn to get along with them, like it or not. You mind your tongue now an' act like the lady your momma raised you to be."

"I can show these Northern brutes what a real Southern lady is like. Never you mind, I'll be a pattern card of propriety, just to spite them."

At the arched brick entrance of Columbia College, however, Coral hesitated. Once she passed beneath this gateway, she'd step into a territory inhabited by men of the occupying force, soldiers who had cut down thousands of Confederate men in battle. She stiffened her spine and took a deep breath. No matter how much she resented their presence on Southern soil, she wouldn't let them overset her.

Coral forged through the entryway and turned toward a three-story brick building with a portico supported by fluted white pillars. From the number of blue-jacketed officers entering and leaving, she guessed this must be the administrative headquarters of the Union army.

Coming to a standstill before the steps, she looked up at the wide paneled entrance. Her breathing quickened at the prospect of taking the oath, and her stomach knotted. She'd violate every principle her loved ones had fought and died for when she pledged allegiance to the United States and the president.

"May I help you, Miss? You look lost."

A masculine voice, spoken in clipped Northern accents behind her, interrupted Coral's musings. She turned about, bracing for her first verbal encounter with a Union soldier. "I'm looking for the administration building. I've been told that's where the oath of allegiance is taken."

"Yes, ma'am. You're going in the right direction." The soldier inclined his head toward the building before them. "The oath is administered in there. Take the first door on your right as you enter the hallway."

Coral almost forgot to reply while she struggled with her reaction to the soldier. The man standing before her was no ordinary trooper. From his uniform, she saw that he was an officer of high rank. She tipped back her head to accommodate his height. He stood with broad shoulders held erect in precise military bearing, with the blue wool of his uniform molding an athletic frame. The morning sun picked out russet highlights in his dark hair. Austere features graced his lean Yankee face, clean-shaven except for a dark slash of mustache. No callow youth, the officer standing before her embodied the confident strength of a fully mature man. Vivid blue eyes scrutinized her closely.

He held the reins of a black Thoroughbred stallion close up by the bit. The black's superior bloodlines and his impeccable lineage were evident to Coral's knowledgeable perusal. As she studied the horse's proud carriage and intelligent eyes, she knew only a proficient rider with a will as strong as the stallion's could control him.

She returned her reluctant attention to the officer, who scattered all her notions of her former enemy. Admiring a Union soldier seemed disloyal to her Southern heritage, yet she attempted to show civility. "Thank you kindly, sir."

"My pleasure, Miss." The officer smiled at her and swept his high-crowned hat onto his dark hair. "If you'll excuse me, I have an inspection tour to do."

"I won't detain you, then. Thank you again."

Coral watched as he turned to his mount and flipped the reins over the stallion's head. He stepped into the saddle with an easy grace, then acknowledged her with a dip of his head and a two-fingered salute. A touch of his spurs to his mount's sides sent the horse beneath the gateway at a collected trot.

"That wasn't so hard, was it, Miz Coral? You can be polite to Yankees when you set your mind to it." Silvie spoke at Coral's elbow.

"I promised I'd behave with propriety when I took the oath. I can't promise my goodwill can extend beyond that to the next encounter." Coral spun back toward the portico and climbed the shallow granite steps. She crossed the porch to the door. Reaching out a gloved hand, she turned the knob and entered a spacious, high-ceilinged hallway.

Orderlies in blue uniforms bustled about, papers clutched in their hands. She halted just inside the door. Should she wait to be addressed or continue to the office where the oath was administered?

One of the men approached her, so she had no need to make the decision. "Are you here to take the oath?"

Coral nodded.

"Right in there." The orderly motioned to an open portal on her right. "Sergeant Thomas will handle it for you."

"Thank you. I'm most appreciative." Coral stepped into a plain office which held only a wide oak desk, a wooden filing cabinet, and a chair angled before the table.

The youngish, sandy-haired sergeant who sat behind the desk rose to his feet when Coral entered. "Good afternoon, Miss. I presume you want to take the oath of allegiance?"

No, I don't want to take the oath, Coral felt tempted to reply, but she tamped down her rebellion and murmured, "Yes."

"Please be seated. This won't take but a moment."

Sergeant Thomas pulled a paper from the filing cabinet and laid it on the desk. He picked up a pen. "What is your name, Miss?"

"Coral Leigh." Her voice shook.

The sergeant scribbled her name on the proper line, then glanced up. "If you'll repeat after me, that will qualify you as having taken the oath." He paused, looked down at the page, and glanced at her again. "I, Coral Leigh, do solemnly swear, in the presence of Almighty God…"

Now that the moment was upon her, she almost refused. Her pulse raced. Her throat closed, and her mouth grew cottony. She could scarcely form the words.

Sergeant Thomas regarded her with sympathy. "Take your time. I can wait until you're ready."

I'll never be ready, she thought. With scarcely concealed reluctance, she drew a breath and spoke in a low voice. "I, Coral Leigh, do solemnly swear…"

"I will henceforth defend the Constitution of the United States…"

Coral repeated the hated words.

"… and support… all proclamations of the president made during the rebellion…"

The words stuck in her throat. For a moment she balked, remembering that her father, her brother, and her fiancé had spilled their life's blood on the battlefield to defend the Confederacy. How could she betray their deaths by pledging allegiance to the Union? She swallowed hard and forced out the words.

"… so help me God."

"So help me God."

The deed was done. She'd taken the oath. Coral shook with the knowledge.

"Miss Leigh, if you'll sign on the line below the oath, everything will be official." Sergeant Thomas passed her the pen and pushed the paper toward her.

Coral took the pen and leaned over the desk to sign the oath. Her hand poised, motionless, over the document. Her fingers trembled. When at last she signed her name, the pen wobbled so she could barely scrawl her signature on the paper. She wrote the last letter of her name and tossed the pen onto the desk.

Sergeant Thomas recorded her name in a ledger before he passed the official document to her. "This is your copy. Keep it with you whenever you intend to purchase anything."

Coral rolled the page into a small cylinder and tucked it into the fringed reticule dangling from her wrist.

"Good day to you, Miss Leigh. Thank you for coming here this morning."

Coral met his concerned gaze, pierced to the heart by her betrayal. "I had no choice."

She fled the building, Silvie trotting at her side. They hurried away from the Union headquarters, back onto the footway leading to the main street, jostling against men and women who crowded the path.

"Miz Coral…"

"Please, Silvie, not now. Not one word. I can't talk about what I've done."

In silence, they made their way to Garner's Emporium. Mr. Garner gave her more money than she expected for the vase, with the promise of more when the piece sold. With some of the extra money she purchased a length of calico, enough to make dresses for her mother, Silvie, and herself. She also bought a pair of stout leather shoes of a kind she never would have considered putting on her feet before the war.

Now she reminded herself those days had vanished like the morning mist, never to return. From this day forward she'd be content with calico or homespun. Serviceable brogans for her feet would have to satisfy.

After locating the doctor, she acquired a brown bottle of Camphor's Soothing Elixir for her mother, along with Dr. Davis's promise to check on Mrs. Leigh the next day.

#

"Money, Silvie!" Coral shook her beaded reticule which held the greenbacks and gold coins acquired from the sale of her vase. She twisted about on the buckboard's seat in order to address her companion, who sat on a blanket in the wagon bed behind her. "I

315

haven't seen real money for months, but now when we get home, I can pay you and Scipio the back wages I owe you."

Silvie waved a hand in dismissal of Coral's words. "Don't you fret, Miz Coral. Scipio and I know you didn't have the money to pay us. We aren't stayin' around just for the money."

"I know that, and I'm ever so grateful. My mother and I would be in a sad way if either of you left us."

"We won't leave you. You're all the family we've got."

Coral squeezed Silvie's shoulder. "Thank you, Silvie."

Swinging around again to the front, Coral slumped against the back of the buckboard's seat. Beside her, Scipio maintained his silence. Although he was invaluable to her in doing the heavy work about the plantation, he spoke sparingly.

Coral's thoughts returned to her visit in Columbia.

"If I never see another Yankee soldier, it will be too soon." She fanned her heated face with a folded scrap of paper. Curling tendrils of hair escaping from her chignon stuck to her cheeks and neck in the afternoon's heat.

"These Yankee soldiers are here to stay, Miz Coral, so you'd best get used to 'em," Silvie said.

"As long as I stay at Elmwood and don't go to town, I won't have to deal with them."

"You have to go to town for supplies, so you'll have to deal with them. You cain't pucker up like a sour lemon every time you see a Yankee soldier."

"Perhaps I'll send Scipio to town for supplies." *Though it might take him a while.*

Scipio let the reins lie slack on the back of the ancient mule hitched to the traces. The wagon creaked harshly with each ponderous turn of its wheels. Coral thought the mule heaved itself along more slowly than it had on the way to Columbia. In her impatience to get home, she felt she could walk faster than the wagon traveled.

"You'll have to go yourself, Miz Coral, and you know it. You cain't send Scipio. You have to take the certificate of allegiance when you buy anything. It has your name on it."

"I never want to see that dratted certificate again. I feel like the veriest traitor for signing the thing."

"You did what you had to do to get medicine for your momma."

"This morning I pledged my allegiance to the Federal government of the United States, while my father and brother lie cold in the ground. They gave their lives for the Cause, while I just signed away everything they died for." Her voice broke on the words as she recalled her betrayal.

"And would you let your pride keep you from gettin' the tonic to help your momma?"

Sighing, Coral declined to answer Silvie's indisputable logic. She wanted nothing more than to return home to Elmwood, to the peace the plantation offered, where no visible reminders of the Yankee conqueror could disturb her.

Like what you read?
Get your copy at
WWW.ANAIAHPRESS.COM

ABOUT THE AUTHOR

Colleen Hall wrote her first story in third grade and continued writing as a hobby all during her growing-up years. In WOUNDED HEART, she was able to combine her love of writing with her love of history and the West. In her spare time, she enjoys spending time with her husband, horseback riding, reading, and browsing antique stores. She lives in South Carolina with her husband and family, two horses, and two spoiled cats.

You can follow Colleen Hall at colleenhallromance.com.

Made in the USA
Columbia, SC
10 November 2020

24248151R00195